THE PUSH

This book is dedicated to my father, Larry F. Fuller. Your absence is felt every day, every hour, every minute, every second. Thank you for being the best daddy.

ACKNOWLEDGMENTS

I wanted to extend some overdue acknowledgments. Thank you to everyone who has read my work and especially to those that have encouraged me to continue. Your words are written on my heart and I am thankful for them.

I would also like to say a huge THANK YOU to my Beta readers: (Heather Garent, Kathy Tripp, Laurel Sorenson, Jeannie Russell, Stephanie Bryson, Doug Jones, Bob and Jane Hutchison, Wanda Fuller, Jessica Dickinson, Mary Westfall, Roberta Goodboy, Susanna Fuller, Anna Fernandez, Sandra Harvey, and Lisa Lambert) All of you have endured countless rewrites and atrocious un-proofed manuscripts. Thank you for your patience and kindness

THE PUSH

A ROCKFISH ISLAND MYSTERY BOOK II

BY J.C. FULLER

CHAPTER 1

Birds exploded from the trees below, their wings furiously flapping against the damp air. Her feet stuttered to a stop, and she watched as they scattered, startled by the loud noise as much as she. Was someone behind her? Another hiker, perhaps? She heard, more than saw, the swaying of motion further down trail. A heavy movement against the bushes.

There again. Closer. Another crack, a snapping of branches underfoot. She sharply turned her body towards the sound.

"Hello?" she called out, a friendly lilt to her voice.

Adjusting the strap around her neck, she waited for a reply. There was nothing... only the sound of pattering raindrops bouncing off the plastic protecting her camera. She adjusted the strap again and took a halting step forward, straining to see through the shroud of morning mist. Was something there? It was hard to tell.

Fidgeting with her ponytail, she unconsciously leaned forward, her eyes raking across the scenery below. The trees and bushes, as if sensing her full attention upon them, sat motionless in the settled silence. An eerie silence she suddenly thought and then scolded herself for being so dramatic. She was alone.

Relaxing her stance, she took a deep breath, slowly exhaling. It must have been nothing. The wind tossing and creaking the branches of a tree. A chipmunk or squirrel jumping from one limb to another. Nature simply being nature.

Even so, her sense of unease still lingered. Keeping her eyes down trail, she anxiously fumbled her cargo shorts. Feeling a familiar lump, she pulled a can of bear spray from her pocket and curled her thumb over the safety clip.

Rumor was, there had been a bear attack earlier in the year, around springtime. She hadn't seen any bear tracks in the mud. However, this didn't mean they weren't around. Not to mention, there were cougars to be concerned about as well. Yet, here she was, up there all alone with just a can of bear spray. Or was she?

Curtly dismissing the thought, she suddenly felt

silly. She was being paranoid and wasting time. Standing there, peering at nothing, while clutching a can of bear spray, wasn't going to get her to where she needed to go.

Shoving the can roughly into her pocket, she gave the slate gray sky an appraising look before tugging her windbreaker hood further over her forehead and trudging ahead. There was still half a mountain to climb and not a lot of time to do it in.

So far, the morning mist layering the rugged terrain had made it hard to see her footing, and the steady drizzle of rain was making it hard to keep it. Both did little to hamper the young woman's mood. The fact that this was her third morning climbing up The Mole Hill, a local nickname for the 5,372-foot mountain, with no sign of a mountain goat to be had... However, did dampen her mood quite a bit. Especially, since this was to be her last day before heading back home to the grind of the Emerald City.

Instructed to visit Rockfish Island by a local Seattle activist magazine, she had gone in hopes of attaining a few picturesque photos of the goats atop their craggy rock perches. The idea had seemed simple enough. Scramble up the rocky terrain. Find a few large, white-haired, black horned herbivores. Snap a few pictures and then down the mountain, she'd go. But the large goats weren't as plentiful or as easy to spot as she had imagined they'd be. This was in part, she was finding out the hard way because the goats hadn't taken to the island. At least, not as well as they had in more conducive areas.

According to her research, the mountain goat population had been introduced to the Rockfish National Park back in the 1920s. Around the same time as their introduction to the massive Olympic National Park where they flourished. So much so, several decades later, the Olympic National Park was wanting to re-home the goats to their natural habitat in the Cascade Mountains.

The magazine, which had contracted her agent for the photographs, wanted to stop the relocation. With their strongest weapon of opposition being the public, the magazine strategized the need to pull on people's heartstrings. A good picture could do just that.

Janie, as most people called her now, intended to go to the Olympic National Park at first. However, her new agent and the pushy magazine editor suggested Rockfish National Park instead. Stating it was a far better example of how a small community could live in harmony with its wildlife neighbors. They also knew her aunt lived on the island and figured it would save the nonprofit magazine a hotel bill. Begrudgingly agreeing to their plan, Janie now found herself hiking up The Mole Hill once again.

Having kept a steady pace for the last twenty minutes, she broke through the thick tree line and found herself staring up at open skies. At her feet, the ground blanketed under muddy layers of pine needles and crushed pine cones had unexpectedly turned bare and rocky. Boulder-like rocks, iced with lime-green moss, speckled the new landscape. Ahead, freed from the masses, sparse and looming trees boasted their towering height with their tip tops swaying lazily in the breeze. At their stumpy bottoms, feathered ferns sprouted flamboyantly, taking root where they could in the rocky terrain.

Janie walked a few paces to the largest tree and gratefully plunked her knapsack down against its trunk. She needed a breather and leaned up against it, looking up at The Mole Hill's peak with an exhausted sigh.

"I swear this mountain gets taller every day," she declared, flipping the spout on her water bottle. "But the rain has lightened up. So, I've got that going for me."

She started to bring the bottle to her mouth, then suddenly stopped, placing it carefully on the uneven ground. With eager tension, she grabbed the camera dangling from the strap around her neck and brought it up to her right eye. Squinting the other eye closed, she fiddled with the focus rings till she was able to bring a large nanny goat into view.

"I should've brought the other lens," she scolded herself.

Even with the zoom feature at full tilt, she knew

it was not the crisp, clean, up close, and personal perspective the magazine was asking for. She was still too far away.

"At least I finally found them," she said, giving herself a mental pat on the back and lowering the camera to her chest.

Suddenly from behind, an earsplitting snap broke the stillness, echoing up from below and jerking her to attention. It sounded as if several branches were breaking at once. Her first thought was a tree had fallen, but as she twisted to peer into the dense tree line she'd come from, she could almost see it. Something was coming, something big.

In one quick motion, the camera was back to her eye, and she peered through the viewfinder, zeroing in on the thick berry-lined brambles. There was a patch of black. It appeared through the swaying bush and then disappeared. Janie held her position, and when she saw it again, her index finger automatically pressed down. The camera made a long shuttering noise capturing repetitive shots in succession. She lifted her finger and fretted her bottom lip. Was that a black bear?

Unsure of what she saw, Janie tried to think of options as she pulled the bear spray from her shorts pocket once more and scanned her immediate area. There was the looming tree behind her. Maybe she could climb that? No good. Bears could climb trees extremely better than she. Quickly she gauged the distance to the large uphill boulders. She might be able to hide behind one of those? She immediately nixed the idea. Bears were scary fast, it would be a short chase. Fighting down her panic Janie shot a fleeting look at the can of bear spray in her hand and made up her mind.

Gripping the camera and spray awkwardly, she peered through the viewfinder catching another brief glimpse of black. Letting the camera heavily drop to her chest she braced herself before squeezing her eyes shut and letting out a large throat-wrenching yell. It wasn't a panicked scream, but a throat burning bellow.

"GO AWAY!"

Janie waved her hands in the air and began to jump up and down, whooping and hollering as loudly as she could.

"GOOOOO AAAWWWWAAAAY!"

She knew she was bringing attention to herself, but that was the whole point. She wanted the bear to know she was there, and hopefully, all the noise and racket she was making would force it to head in a different direction.

Down trail, the swaying of the bushes abruptly stopped. Janie dropped her arms and brought the camera up. She was breathing heavily now, adrenaline vigorously coursing through her veins, the camera trembling in her hands.

"Go away... go away.... go away... please go away," she chanted to herself.

Another flash of black appeared. Keeping her eye to the viewfinder, she watched intently as the brush suddenly parted. She let out a surprised, "OH!" as she found herself looking at a man. He was wearing a black jacket and baseball cap with a black knapsack on his back. He was also looking up at her with great concern. The new arrival, having seen her yelling and waving at them like a crazy person, called up to her.

"You okay? Do you need help?"

Janie dropped the camera with relief and let out a nervous laugh. She began to shake her head no, then realized the hiker might not be able to make the motion out very well.

"I'm okay! Thought you were a bear!" she hollered down in an apology.

The fellow hiker waved as if he couldn't hear Janie and started to make his way towards her.

Feeling greatly relieved and more than a little foolish, Janie quickly gathered up her water bottle, stuffing it into her knapsack. She hoisted the bag onto her back and took a quick glance downhill. The hiker was making excellent progress. By the time she had gotten herself situated she could make him out clearly.

"Uh, Hey!" Janie said, her heart skipping at the moment of recognition. "I didn't realize it was you." She dropped her head back in relief, letting her hand drop from her heart. "Hi!"

"You okay?" he asked, a warm smile on his face.

"Yeah," she laughed. "I'm fine. Thought you might be a bear. I was trying to scare it off."

"Well, you sure succeeded in scaring ME!"

"I suppose I probably did!" Janie laughed again, more relaxed. "Sorry about that, Brent. How... how have you been?"

"I've been good. Heard you were in town visiting your aunt. Whatcha doing all the way up here?" Brent removed his knapsack, unclasping the dangling water bottle from the side. "Just out taking pictures?" He nodded towards her camera before taking a drink.

"Sort of. I've got a piece to do on the mountain goats," Janie explained, shaking her head no as he offered her his water.

"Any luck?"

"Spotted them for the first time today. They're elusive little buggers. All my yelling probably scared them off. I had just spotted a nanny when I heard you."

"Have you been coming up this trail the whole time?"

"Well, yeah. It's the easiest way up."

"That's your problem. You need to cut over more east. It's way rockier, and the climb is harder. But you'll find more goats."

"Yeah. I'd rather—"

"I can show you. I know another trail. We'll have to watch our step, especially with this drizzle. But you're a good climber, right? You can handle it." Brent gave her a confident smile, lightly patting her on the shoulder. Janie paused at the offer and looked at Brent warily. He was a very good mountain climber. She was so-so.

"Uh, okay. Sure."

"Great! This will be nice. Gives us a chance to catch up while we walk." Brent clipped the water bottle back onto his pack. "By the way, you can put away the bear spray. Pretty sure you've scared every bear off the mountain."

Janie looked down at the can of spray still clutched in her hand and blushed prettily.

"Yea, guess so." She stuffed it back in her pocket and stepped aside to let him lead the way.

CHAPTER 2

"Careful here. You don't want to roll an ankle!" Brent called over his shoulder, barely out of breath.

"I know!" she yelled in return, her foot slipping on the loose rock as soon as the words left her lips.

Dark grey scales of shale slid continuously, tumbling down the steep slope taking her with them. Brent started to turn, and Janie wobblily regained her footing in time, snapping "I'm fine!" before he could utter a word.

The two had been hiking for half an hour, making polite chit chat as they crossed the mountain sideways and upwards towards the crest. Janie was guessing it was probably late morning by the sporadic growls of protest coming from her persistent stomach. The grumblings reminding her, she had started the climb without eating breakfast.

"Can we stop for a break soon?" she asked over the rumbling of her tummy.

"Sure. We just need to get over this small ridge here. Not much farther."

They both worked their way through the shale, finally coming to a heavy rock, which then turned into a smoother stone surface. Here the moss covered a good portion of the footing with ferns growing in between the tiny cracks and crevices.

The pair stepped up onto the top of the smooth ridge and looked down. There was a sheer drop off, and Janie took a tentative step back, sucking in a startled breath.

"Wow! We're really high!"

"High as the mountain goats. Look over there."

Janie's eyes roamed to the rock ledge across the way, spotting several white mountain goats speckled against the dark wall of jagged rock. Up to her right, a few big boulders away stood more goats, who were waiting their turn to hop across the crevice. Even without the camera zoom, she could see them clearly as they slowly picked their way along the rocky ledge.

A few small kids, frolicking around their ever-patient mothers, were shadowed by two billy goats. The two elder goats, their black horns menacingly stark against their white-furred faces, plodded a little closer. If in warning or curiosity, it was hard to tell. Janie instinctively brought her camera up to her eye and started to move to her right, searching for a good angle on the nannies and their kids.

"Careful! Don't get so close to the edge! That's a six-hundred-foot drop!" Brent lightly grabbed her upper arm, pulling her back towards safer ground.

"Thanks," she said dismissively, and then in earnest, "I mean it. Thank you, Brent. This is great."

"Glad I could help." Brent stepped back from the cliff's edge and turned towards the two large goats standing uphill, tracking them closely. "Don't forget to keep an eye on these two. They're a bit close." He looked at Janie, trying to catch her eye as she walked past him towards the goats. "Mountain goats have been known to be aggressive. Even attack climbers. They're nothing to mess with," he said, a little louder. Janie, clearly not paying attention to his advice, moved even closer. He tried again. "They like the salt off your skin, you know. So, don't let them—"

"Uh-huh. I know. Read all about it!" Janie hollered back, cutting him off impatiently. She was still trying to find a good angle. And though she was grateful for his help, he was quickly becoming a bothersome distraction. "Don't mother me, Brent. I'm not a little girl," she scolded, scrunching down on her haunches and snapping a few shots of the grown goats before turning her back on them, heading back in his direction. "I'll be just fine." She gave him a smart smile as she walked past him.

Brent, frowning at her cavalier attitude, glanced back at the billy goats. They, in return, watched him with bland interest and continued to stand their ground. Giving his head a shake of frustration, Brent let his backpack plunk down heavily onto the ledge. Apparently, he'd have to be the one to keep a wary eye out. Janie was paying them, and him, no further attention.

Engrossed in her shoot, Janie crawled atop one of the large boulders angling for a better shot. Finding a good spot, she juggled her camera as she sat herself down, her legs tucked beneath her. Satisfactorily arranged, the only sound for several minutes was the mechanics of the camera shutter.

Quickly growing bored and satisfied the two billy goats were finally losing interest, Brent decided to follow her lead and, carefully, sat himself down on the edge of the ledge. With his long legs dangling over the side, he watched Janie, amused by her intensity.

"You hungry?" Brent asked, hearing Janie's stomach growl. He was hoping it was why she seemed so easily irritated.

"Starving! There are a few granola bars in my backpack and some beef jerky. Help yourself if you want," Janie offered, her camera making additional clicking noises as she took another burst of photos.

"I'll take a couple of granola bars."

Brent got up and walked over to Janie's knapsack, unzipping it to peer inside.

"So, how long will you be on the island? You staying over for Labor Day weekend?" he asked, his voice hopeful.

"Leaving today."

Brent frowned his disappointment but didn't say anything. Not seeing the granola bars sitting on top, Brent opened the backpack wider, pulling out an old red sweatshirt, a red water bottle, and then a worn and bent photo. The photo was of Janie and another girl, one who looked enough like her, it wasn't hard to guess they were sisters.

"I've never seen this picture of you and Danie before," Brent said quietly.

Janie lowered the camera from her eye and looked over. He held the picture up for her to see.

"It was taken the day she...," Janie's voice went quiet. "I take it with me wherever I go," she finished.

"It's a good picture of you two." He put the picture back into the backpack carefully and pulled out the granola bars. "Should I toss these up to you?"

"No, no. I'll come down." Janie shook her head with a small smile and started to scoot bottom down first, off the boulder. She walked over and took the offered bars before moving to the cliff's edge to sit down.

"You know, I think about Danie a lot," Brent ventured, taking a seat next to her.

"Me too."

"It'll be a year—"

She cut him off

"Tomorrow."

Brent grunted in agreement along with a curt nod of his head.

"I want you to know... Gabe and I. We tried... " Brent turned to Janie earnestly. "We tried our hardest. We just... we just weren't quick enough. I'm so sor—"

Janie cut him off again.

"Don't say it, Brent. You don't have to say it."

"I think I do, Janie." He took a deep breath and shifted his weight towards her. "Since you've left the island, you haven't taken my phone calls. You don't respond to my text messages or emails. I've been to your place in Seattle, more than a couple of times to see you, and each time, even though your car is there, you never come to the door." Brent shook his head musingly. "You didn't even let me know you were coming back to the island." He locked eyes with her, his voice husky with emotion. "I feel like you blame me."

Janie's eyes closed at the accusation and she suddenly could smell the salt water, see the glittering sun bouncing off the waves of the ocean, and feel the comfort of holding Brent's hand.

Their friend Amy and her sister were laughing

at a dumb joke he had just told. Gabe and Kevin were busying themselves with making a bonfire for later that night and Lucas was still struggling with his camping gear. She was smiling and happy... and Janie had been in love.

It was Lucas, with his big smile and bright eyes, who had asked for her help to put up his tent. She had said yes instead of going down to the water with her sister, who had mischievously said something about wanting to go for a swim. She remembered how hot the late August day had been. It would have been normal to want to go swimming. But she had wanted to stay with Lucas, laughing at him and his collapsing tent.

Fighting the tent poles, they'd just started again when someone yelled for her, shouting she needed to come quick. Danie was in trouble. Danie was drowning. There was a brief moment of confusion. The notion Danie was drowning? She remembered dropping the tent pegs and running as fast as she could in her flip-flops to Shallow Point. When she got there, Gabe was already chest deep in the ocean water, wading out to the floating body.

Running to the scene, Brent had launched himself from the point, diving straight into the shallow waves, only to come up with a sharp shake of his head. He started plowing through the tide towards her sister. She watched as Brent reached her body, turning her limp form face up before wrapping his arm around her neck and grasping her shoulder. He was trying to keep her head above water while pulling her back to shore.

Gabe had finally reached him and the two lifted her out of the water, desperately maneuvering through the sharp and slippery rocks so they could hoist her up to Lucas and Kevin, who were waiting on dry land.

Kevin had dragged her half a foot from the edge before roughly dropping her lifeless body down onto the pebbled beach and immediately starting CPR. She vaguely remembered Amy holding her back. Keeping her from running to her sister's side while she screamed for her to open her eyes.

She had opened her eyes... on the first punch to her chest. Bubbling water had flowed from her mouth. They could even hear the cracking of ribs with each compression as Kevin bounced back and forth from pinching her nose and trying to breathe life into her lungs.

And there they all were, gathered around her. Brent, pacing back and forth. Amy, yelling pointless questions. Lucas, standing mouth agape, and Gabe hurriedly pushing Kevin aside, telling him to go get help. Then Kevin racing to his truck, tearing away from camp, surprisingly coming back a few short minutes later with a forest ranger in tow.

They'd all watched as Gabe labored to save her. Gabe, faithful Gabe. Refusing to give up, even as the ranger had attempted to take over, in an effort to give him a break. Ever persistent, not one to take no for an answer…and she, crying helplessly as her little sister lay there unresponsive, eyes wide open, staring at the sky unblinking.

Her mind had been racing as she took in the scene before her, watching everyone watching Danie, and suddenly realizing what had happened. Quickly accepting the fact things were never going to be the same for her. She'd forever be haunted with the nightmare of watching her sister die and knowing a part of her died with her.

"Janie? Do you blam—"

At the sound of Brent's voice, Janie fitfully shook her memories away. She looked into his eyes, then abruptly turned away, sealing off her emotions. She slowly took a bite of her granola bar… stalling.

"I've been busy with the new job," she finally said a minute later, the smell of salt water still in her nostrils.

"Bull."

"It's not bull, Brent. My new agent has been on my cas—"

"Why can't you just be honest with me?"

Janie sighed heavily. "Let's not do this, Brent. We've had a really nice visit today, okay?" Janie lifted up her camera from her chest. "Thank you so much for helping me get here. If I get the right shot, it'll go a long way with my new agent." She gave him a pleasant, but distant smile. "It was good to see you."

Brent's shoulders sagged in disappointment. Knowing she was dismissing him from her company. The conversation was over. They were done.

Nodding his head in resignation, he got up from the ledge carefully, inadvertently knocking rocks loose in the process. A very large pebble rolled over the side and Janie watched it tumble down with fascination.

"Well, I'll let you get back at it then." He paused, waiting to see if she'd stop him. She didn't. "Good seeing you again, Janie." Brent roughly grabbed his knapsack and started his way back down their self-made trail.

"Bye, Brent," Janie called to him lightly, almost regretfully. She could tell by the color of his neck and the tense muscles in his back, he was angry and hurt. She hadn't wanted to hurt him... ever.

She watched him till he was out of sight and then faced forward towards the ledge, returning to the beautiful view. She felt conflicted. Brent had tried to be there for her afterwards, offering his shoulder and his hand. It hadn't mattered. Though he tried to save her baby sister... He hadn't been quick enough. It really was a shame because Janie loved him... had loved him.

She wondered how long she had been sitting

there reminiscing when she started to slowly stand up, hearing footsteps behind her. Apparently, he'd decided to come back, and knowing Brent, he probably had a few more things to say. She was worried this might happen.

"Did you forget something?" Janie asked, starting to turn around. "Because if you came back to..." The question caught in her throat. "What are you doing—." She was cut off.

"I figured it out and I need to tell you something."

"What did you figure out?" The intense glare of malice frightened her. She no longer felt safe. "What... what do you need to tell me?" she asked cautiously, eying the distance between them.

"I made a mistake and I'm sorry."

"It was an accidental drowning. We all KNOW it was an accident. There's nothing to be sorry about." She shifted her weight, taking a quick peek behind her shoulder. "Danie's death was purely accidental," her voice shook as she took a tiny step back, her heels teetering on the edge. She slowly reached for the bear spray in her pocket.

"No. I'm not sorry about that. I'm sorry about THIS..."

The shove to her chest was so hard and shocking, her teeth clattered together as she flew backward. Her arms shot out, fingers grasping at nothing but wind. A rushing sound of air flooded her senses as it buffeted against her windbreaker and rushed past her ears like thunder. There was nothing but gray sky and wisps of her hair flying back and forth within her vision. Then suddenly, a face... looking down at her from the ledge.

CHAPTER 3

Sheriff Lane looked at her desk phone in exasperation as it rudely interrupted her concentration.

"Caleb?" she called out into the front section of the sheriff's office. She was answered by silence and then another ring of the phone. "Deputy Pickens?" she called a little louder, leaning over the side of her desk for a better view of the front office.

It was vacant and no one appeared to be standing at the greeting counter or the coffee pot stand. Frowning, she glanced at the clock hanging above the entrance of the island's small sheriff's office and noted the time.

Deputy Caleb Pickens was twenty minutes late coming back from lunch and lately, had been making it a habit. There was a good chance he was still over at Hattie's General chatting it up with the pretty new cashier, Amy Holmes. Lane decided she was going to have a word with her new deputy about punctuality. That is, whenever he got back.

The phone persistently rang again.

Noticing the call was coming through the non-emergency line, she half-debated on letting it go to voicemail. It was most likely a traffic violation complaint or a graffiti tagging grievance. If Caleb was around, she was sure it would be something he could handle. But since he wasn't... She sighed heavily, frowning down at her paperwork.

The report, which she was eager to finish, detailed a dispute at the bowling alley the night before. A fistfight, which consisted of two black eyes, one broken nose, and a very large bump on the head. Not to mention, a warped and bent bowling trophy.

The bowling debacle also happened to be the first bit of action she'd seen in the last six months. When she had arrived last spring, with the sheriff's office still under construction, she'd found herself immediately embroiled in a murder investigation.

Obviously new to the island, she'd been at a disadvantage, unfamiliar with the close-knit community. With help from an unexpected partner, she'd discovered the murderer and managed to barely escape becoming a victim herself.

Months later, not much had materialized in the

way of action... which she knew shouldn't be some-thing to complain about. After all, her job was to keep the peace. But...

The phone shrilled again.

With a huff, she snatched the phone off its cradle.

"Rockfish Island Sheriff's Department. How can I help you?" she answered, trying to leave all annoy-ance out of her tone.

"Yes. I'd like, ahh... I want to report a missing person... woman, please," a male's voice came over the phone, hesitant and uncertain. Lane could hear a female in the background, a high-pitched voice telling him what he should say next. He continued, "Okay, okay. I'll tell them. Just a second! Hello? Is there someone I can talk to?"

"This is Sheriff Lane. I can help you. Who is missing, how old are they, and for how long?" She hunched her shoulder, holding the phone to her ear as she opened the bottom drawer of her desk and ri-fled through her files for a missing person form.

"Janielle Engles. Uh, twenty-three years old. Missing for seven days?" The man's voice suddenly sounded muffled as he conferred with the person of-fline. "Yes. Seven days."

"And why do you think she's missing, sir?" Lane's eyes were drawn to the front door as it opened and Deputy Pickens walked through with a whistled tune on his lips.

At her withering glare, he stopped short, his lips still puckered, and winced. He then took a sheepish glance at his wristwatch and quickly headed straight to his desk.

"She hasn't called into work for the last two days. She was supposed to deliver some photos on Tuesday over here in Seattle after the Labor Day holiday. She never showed up. I mean... I didn't think much of it at the time. Thought she decided to take an extra day off, but when she missed our meeting today. I, WE went to her apartment. I thought maybe she was home with the flu or something. She didn't come to the door and her neighbors say they haven't seen her."

"Maybe she's still out of town and traveling?" Lane suggested. "A lot of people travel on Labor Day weekend. Have you called the hospitals? In case there was a car accident?"

"We did, and if I thought she was just on the road, believe me, I wouldn't be giving you a call." He let out an exasperated sigh. "You're not understanding. I was the one who gave her a ride to the ferry, so she could get to the island. Her car is still parked at her apartment. This isn't like her." The man's voice had grown desperate and impatient.

"So, this missing person, Janielle Engles? Why was she coming to visit Rockfish Island?"

"She goes by Janie. She went to the island for a

job assignment and to visit her aunt. A Mrs. Carter?"

Lane figured the caller was speaking of Sue Carter, the owner of the island's Antique shop and the town's flirtatious rich widow. Lane knew Sue herself had just gotten back from a trip abroad yesterday. She wondered if the young woman, given the opportunity to go on one of Sue's European treasure hunts, had played hooky from work. Possibly Sue's niece was with her? Lane scribbled something on a yellow post-it, and then loudly knocked on her office window. Caleb popped his head up and looked behind him. Lane held up the bright post-it.

It read: Call Sue Carter. Find out if her niece Janie is with her.

Caleb rapidly shook his head "NO." Knowing his hesitation, Lane sighed heavily.

Cougar Carter, as the town had dubbed Sue because of her age and unquenchable man-eating ways, had most likely accosted the young deputy once or twice already. Ten to one, the young man had no interest in being propositioned again.

Lane swiftly scribbled on the post-it and slammed it back up against the window with a determined look on her face. NOW!!! had been added to the bottom of the post-it.

Caleb, giving a look of surrender, turned back around obediently, begrudgingly picking up the phone to make the requested call.

"What is your name, sir?" Lane brought her full attention back to the phone conversation.

"Jim Evans. I'm her agent. I helped arrange the assignment on the island. She's a photographer." Jim cleared his throat. "She was supposed to get a few pictures of the island's mountain goats and then come back to Seattle the Thursday before Labor Day weekend."

"So, what day did you drop her off at the ferry?"

"Monday, August 27th. Late afternoon, around four. We'd planned to pick her up at the ferry dock on this side, but she never came off the ferry. I'd assumed she'd come home early and took a cab or decided to stay longer with her aunt."

"Today is September 4th. No one has talked to her since last Monday?"

"No, and her cell phone goes straight to voice-mail," Jim said hurriedly and then added, "I probably should have called sooner."

Caleb, his cheeks a high color of red, knocked on her window partition and said through the glass.

"Coug... um, Mrs. Carter says she got into town last night. Hasn't seen her niece since she left for her trip last week. The niece was staying at her house while Mrs. Carter was gone. She's curious as to why you want to know and would like you to give her a call."

Lane frowned and gave her deputy a brief nod. She addressed her next question to the current caller.

"Mr. Evans, was Janie planning on staying with her aunt the whole visit?"

"That was the plan."

"Mr. Evans, I'm going to need a description of Janie."

"Sure. She's around five-six. Athletic. Brown hair, about to her shoulders. Brown, no... blue eyes. I guess, about a hundred and twenty-five pounds? Very attractive."

"Ethnicity?"

"Caucasian."

"Last seen wearing?"

"Blue jeans, red hoodie, and flip-flops. Had her camera case with her and a stuffed yellow backpack."

"Any birthmarks, scars, tattoos?"

"Her tongue is pierced. Couldn't say about tattoos. Nothing visible, at least."

"Thank you, Mr. Evans. Let me get your number, and I'll make some phone calls. Get in touch with Mrs. Carter and hopefully have some good news for you." Lane jotted down his contact information and hung up the phone. She quickly picked it up again and dialed the number for the antique shop. She had a brief and to-the-point conversation with Sue, promising very much the same thing she had to Mr. Evans.

When she hung up the phone this time, Lane's face was pensive and thoughtful. There was a light knock on her open door.

"Sorry about being late from lunch." Caleb walked around the glass partition and into her office, his stocky figure filling the doorway. His dark hair, which he wore longer than she liked, was swept to the side across his forehead. "I was over at Hattie's and just lost track of time. Amy was telling me about this funny—"

"We'll talk about it later, Caleb." Lane didn't spare him a hard glare. "Deputy, I want you to run down to the fire station and then check the docks. Don't dawdle and stop at Hattie's. I want you to scrounge up as many volunteers as you can for a search party. Then all of you meet me at the park's ranger station in forty minutes."

Expecting her orders to be followed without question, Lane picked up her desk phone and dialed the District Thirteen Coast Guard.

Confirming the coast guard hadn't found a dead body floating in the ocean recently. She requested their SAFE vessels take a cruise around the island to double-check. She then snatched up her cell phone and punched in a code. This sent a text to each volunteer of the small island's search & rescue, instructing them to meet at the park. That task completed, she placed another call, but there was no answer. She tried again and deduced they were out of the office. Lastly, she punched in a well-known number, waiting for the line to pick up.

"Hi!"

"Hi. You busy?"

"Not at the moment and certainly never too busy for you, Sheriff."

Lane smiled briefly at the flirtatious tone.

"Can you meet me at the park ranger's office in forty minutes? I've got a missing person to find, and I need all the able-bodies I can get."

"See you in forty," Jerry Holmes, the town veterinarian and Amy's father, answered with all seriousness and hung up the phone. Lane grabbed her patrol truck keys and headed for the door.

CHAPTER 4

"We need to fix the gate on Naches trail," Kody said, sailing into the park ranger's office. "Stupid thing won't swing all the way open. I thought about ramming it with the truck..."

"Don't you do anything to MY truck!" Philip looked up from his book, giving the young park ranger a warning scowl. "I haven't even had the dang rig for a year yet!" He pulled his readers down to the tip of his nose, leveling Kody with a stony stare. "Not another scratch, Kody. I mean it!"

Kody smiled shamelessly and put his hands up in the air.

"I said, I thought about it. Didn't actually do it. Trust me, I know better."

"Damn straight, kid." Philip gave a curt nod before returning to his book. "Everything else look okay?" He licked the tip of his index finger before idly turning the next page.

"Yeah, I guess," Kody's voice had lost its enthusiasm. "With Labor Day weekend over, the park is far too quiet again." The young ranger couldn't help but sound a little disappointed. Being outgoing and active, he enjoyed the hustle and bustle of the crowds.

"Not quite quiet enough for me. When you going back to college?" Philip peered over the top of the paperback, making sure to hide his smile.

Kody frowned, plopping down behind his desk and tossing his feet up with a loud clunk, despite knowing Philip disapproved of such slouching.

"For the hundredth time, Phil. I'm not going back till spring quarter." Kody reached over to the mini-fridge and yanked the little door open, pulling out an energy drink. "You're stuck with me for a while longer. Besides, you need me around here."

"Only when there's something I don't want to do." Philip took his readers off and added, "By the way, I fixed the gate on Rainier path. The one you DID hit with my truck last week? Just got back into the office."

"Oh, that was hardly a dent. A little ding like that should buff right out!" Kody said defensively, waving him off.

"Just like the rock chips in the windshield? Those

gonna buff right out? You drive too fast, kid," Philip reprimanded, half-joking and half-serious. "Slow it down out there. I don't need you taking out any more gates."

Kody's reply was mostly a gesture, which Philip chose to ignore.

As much as he gave the kid a hard time, Philip had to admit he liked having Kody around. Especially after last spring. It had been six months since he had stumbled across a dead body during his morning rounds. And having reported his find to the mainland, the authorities had sent out their new sheriff.

Faced with an unknown murderer on the island, it hadn't taken Sheriff Lane long to realize she was going to need someone's help. Someone with an insight into the community. Someone who was homegrown and trusted. Someone like Philip. He'd gratefully joined along, curious to discover the body's identity, feeling obligated in finding the killer. The decision had been a good one, yet ended in devastating heartache. And like anyone who has lived through nightmarish moments, he had a tendency to not want to be alone with his thoughts.

The sound of tires crunching over gravel outside of the ranger's office came to his ears, and Philip lowered his book with a frown.

"We expecting visitors?" He peeked through the window blinds as a patrol truck rolled to a stop at the station door.

"Don't think so. Anyone we know?" Kody leaned back in his chair, stretching his neck to see for himself.

"Afraid so," Philip said, watching four additional trucks pull up behind the first. He recognized the sheriff's rig in the lead, then Jerry Holmes's quad cab pickup, followed by the fire station's emergency vehicle. The rest of the rigs he noted belonged to fire department volunteers and various locals.

Philip hurriedly tossed his book and glasses down on the desk and barely beat Kody to the door. By the time he had gotten it open, three more vehicles had shown up. The last one, pulling a horse trailer.

"We got a fire?" Philip practically yelled, addressing the semi-small group of twelve people, eyeing the driver of the fire station pickup.

"No! No fire!" Calvin Morton, one of the town's two full-time firefighters called over his shoulder, pulling a paramedic case from the front cab.

"What's going on then?" This time Philip addressed his question directly to Sheriff Lane. "Afternoon, Sheriff."

The Rockfish Island sheriff and deputy were walking towards him and Kody as the rest of the group seemed to be pulling out backpacks and other gear, quickly getting organized.

"Hello, Ranger Russell. Ranger Kody." Lane smiled warmly, though Philip could tell she was there in her professional capacity. "We've got a missing person. A female by the name of Janielle Engles."

"Janie?" Kody took a step closer out of concern.

Philip put a restraining hand on his shoulder, looking just as worried.

"Kid, go get our climbing gear. Last I talked to her, she was heading up the easy trail on The Mole Hill." Kody nodded curtly, sending his blonde curls bouncing, and hurriedly took off towards the office.

"You've talked to her recently?" Lane asked, nodding for Deputy Pickens to assist the young ranger.

"Not super recently. Talked to her last..." Philip scrunched up his face in recollection. "Last Wednesday. She was on her way up The Mole Hill, to get a few shots of the mountain goats. She asked which was the best way to get there, and I sent her up Indian Flat trail. It's an easy enough climb."

"Do you remember what she was wearing?" Lane had taken out her trustworthy leather notepad.

"Red baseball cap and a red windbreaker tied around her waist. A white tank top, black cargo shorts, brown hiking boots with red laces, and a yellow backpack. She had a fancy camera with her too." Philip noticed another car pull up, the occupants being Pastor Jonas Adams and the girl's aunt, Sue Carter. He watched as the pastor hopped out of the driver's side before rushing over to open Sue's door, taking her hand as she climbed out. She looked concerned and worried as she clung to his arm.

"The group says they're ready, Sheriff." Jerry had come up behind Lane and gave Philip a friendly smile, joining their conversation. "When was the last time she was seen?" Jerry asked, dropping his pack on the ground and stuffing into it a light jacket.

"She stopped here at our office Wednesday and asked for directions, so to speak."

"And her work says she's not been seen or heard from since before Labor Day weekend." Lane motioned for the crowd to gather together as Kody and Caleb came back with the climbing gear and a backpack for Philip.

Philip took the pack handed to him, checking the contents to make sure everything he needed was still inside. They always kept a couple bags ready for such emergencies.

"Listen up, folks!" Lane's voice surprisingly boomed from her small petite frame as she stood with her legs slightly apart and her hands on her hips. Her tone was serious, professional, and chock full of authority. "We are looking for a Janielle Engles. It's my understanding some of you may know her as Janie, Sue Carter's niece. She spent a majority of her summer vacations as a kid staying here on the island." Lane held her hand up to quiet the crowd as rumblings of recognition sounded. "Janielle is approximately five foot six, with brown hair and blue eyes. Twenty-three years of age. She was last seen wearing a red windbreaker, white tank top, and black cargo shorts. I've been told..." Lane nodded towards Sue. "She is an accomplished climber. The last known sighting was Wednesday of last week, here in the park. She reported she planned on making her way up The Mole Hill and may've taken Indian Flat trail. I need for us to split up and cover as much ground as possible. We have no idea if she wandered off to other areas of the park but may have, as she's a photographer. I want to make sure we've hit all the key areas as fast as we can."

Philip leaned over to Kody and whispered for him to grab the two-way radios. Kody took off in a full sprint, and Philip gave Lane a polite and apologetic nod for the interruption.

"I need two volunteers to check the waterfront on the east and south side of the island and another two on the west and north side. Jerry and Calvin, I want you to search the campgrounds and lower level hiking trails. Caleb and Kody..." Kody managed to come to a screeching halt by her side in a cloud of dust and gravel, holding an armful of portable radios. "I want you two to take a rig and search the jeep trails. Shayla and Angie, if you'll cover the horse trails? Ranger Russell and I will hike up Indian Flat trail and..." She stopped, her eyes searching the group. "Who's a good climber?"

Scanning the small group of volunteers, Lane saw two hands poke up from the back.

"You two," she addressed Gabe Garent and Lucas Wilson, both avid climbers, and summertime fire department volunteers. "You make your way up…" She turned to Philip. "What's the second trail's name? The difficult one?"

"Snakehead." Philip recognized the two young men and knew they were more than capable of making the climb.

The young men had begun to lower their arms when Deputy Pickens started to make his way over with a climbing backpack. Philip put a hand on his chest, arresting his progress. He already knew Gabe and Lucas had better gear than the ranger's office, and most likely already in their truck.

"Now, we have no way of knowing what kind of condition Janielle will be in. She could be hurt, unconscious, dehydrated, hungry. Keep your eyes peeled and your ears open. Radio if you see or hear anything." Lane paused, looking each person in the eye before continuing, "And keep an eye on your partner. I don't want this turning into a search party for any of you. I want everyone to check in every hour on the dot."

Philip cleared his throat, eyeing Lane for permission to speak. She nodded and took a step back, letting him have the crowd.

"Everyone! I want you to be aware of your surroundings at all times. Especially when searching outside of the campgrounds and away from people. Remember, this is a wildlife preserve. Keep an eye out for bears and cougars. If you have any questions on how to handle an animal confrontation, come see me before heading out."

The crowd mumbled their understanding and restlessly started to mill around as Kody continued to distribute two-way radios.

"Sheriff, mind if we ask Pastor Jonas to say a quick prayer?" Calvin Morton asked, nodding towards the Baptist pastor.

Without waiting for an answer, all heads immediately bowed, and Pastor Jonas stepped into the circle of volunteers. His voice was strong and carried well.

"Heavenly Father, we ask for guidance as we search for Janie. We pray she is found alive and well and for your protective hand to keep us safe in our search. In Jesus' name, amen." Pastor Jonas raised his head, and Sheriff Lane nodded her thanks before addressing the group again.

"Okay, people! Let's go!"

CHAPTER 5

"So, just out of curiosity, why did you send her up this trail?" Lane asked, pulling a handkerchief from her back pocket.

It was now mid-day, and even though the late summer heat had dissipated somewhat with the early whispers of fall, Lane had a light sheen of sweat beading her brow. In front of her, she could see a patch of damp forming between Philip's shoulder blades as they headed up The Mole Hill.

"Well, I didn't suggest this trail at first. Originally, I told her she'd have better luck on either Shale Rock or Snakehead. The trails are harder, though quicker routes to the summit, and both would have led her straight to the mountain goats," Philip answered, pausing for breath. "I was pretty surprised when she asked for the easiest way up instead."

"Why is that?" Lane had stopped, her weight resting on her back leg, her front leg stretched out in front of her. Philip frowned in contemplation.

"I always thought her to be a good climber and assumed she'd want the shortest instead of the longest route." Philip shrugged his shoulders and started to head up trail again.

"Sue mentioned her nieces come to the island every summer?" Lane tucked the handkerchief away and hoisted her backpack higher up on her shoulders.

"Yup. Parents died in a car accident when they were seven. The girls lived with an aunt back east, and during the summer, they'd come stay with Sue and Henry. Kept up the tradition, even after Henry died, and they graduated from high school." Philip stopped and looked down at Lane, who was making her way carefully up the trail behind him.

She had changed into climbing shorts before they had set off and somewhere along the way, had stripped down to a white tank top, tying her uniform shirt around her waist. Her sheriff's badge, now pinned to the tank top's shoulder strap, glittered in the sun.

At this high angle, Philip had a bird's eye view of Lane's cleavage and quickly averted his eyes. Used to seeing Lane in her unflattering sheriff's uniform, it always seemed to unnerve him to notice she was a shapely woman. Lane, happening to glance up as

Philip was glancing down, smiled at his reaction and politely hauled up on the front of her tank top. A small effort to be modest.

"Speaking of staying over the summer. Any luck finding a new place to live?" Philip shyly brought his eyes down and cautioned a glance at Lane before heading up the trail again

"None," Lane's voice sounded sour. "And I've been told most of the residents plan on opening up their private property to hunters. I have a sinking suspicion Harry would like me gone before hunting season starts rolling."

Lane's tiny apartment, located above Hattie's General, was meant to be a short-term living arrangement from the beginning. It had practically no kitchen to speak of, was unfurnished, except for a twin-sized bed and chair, and had a minuscule-sized bathroom with a broom closet for storage. Lane, having lived there for the last six months, longed for a place of her own where she could take her things out of moving boxes and have more than a few square feet of living space.

However, the island being the size and population it was, she wasn't having any luck in finding a new place. Her deputy had been able to rent the Jensen's house after Lane made arrangements with the elderly couple, who had decided to stay permanently in Arizona. There was also the Esten's cabin, though Lane had no desire to live there.

Then there was her landlord, Harry. Hoping to have the small apartment freed up so he could rent it to the island's fall visiting hunters, at a much more profitable fee. Harry had been eagerly suggesting new places as they became available. None much more desirable than the small apartment she was already calling home.

"Well, I might be able to help you." Philip sighed with relief. They had finally broken through the tree line. "Let's take a break," he suggested, making for a large cedar.

"Really? How?" Lane asked warily. It had been Philip who suggested she take the small apartment in the first place.

"My Uncle Chuck. He's decided to move over to the mainland to be closer to my cousin Julie. He's got a cottage down by the shore, not far from the main point. Nice place. It's not terribly large, but it's a heck of lot roomier than your dinky upstairs apartment."

"How much?" Lane asked, waiting for the expensive answer. She took a tentative look behind them, down trail. She was surprised to see how far they had hiked in the short hour, having made better time than she thought.

"Not as much as he could be asking." Philip smiled.

Lane looked from the trail, back up at Philip.

"How MUCH?" she asked again, highly suspicious

it was a bigger number than she had already estimated.

"Only five hundred a month," Philip announced cheerfully, grabbing his water bottle.

"It must be a dump," Lane surmised, disappointment heavy in her voice. Nothing on the island, for the exception of her matchbox apartment, was anything under a thousand dollars a month.

"Not at all!" Philip looked offended. "It's actually quite... lovely." He frowned at the last word. "It's a nice place. My uncle is loaded and doesn't really need the extra money. He just wants someone to take care of the cottage and the few belongings he's left behind. I told him you would. That is if you're interested?"

"You bet I am! As long as it's not a dump," she teased, wiping the back of her hand against her forehead and smiling up at Philip. "Thanks for thinking of me."

Philip shrugged.

"You're a good answer to my uncle's problem, and you need a place. I'll take you over to see the cottage tomorrow if you've got time." He picked up his backpack and nodded his head towards the trail, signaling for them to start moving.

"Can't tomorrow night. Jerry is taking me to a movie," Lane said, tightening the shirt around her waist.

"That's still going on?" Philip seemed surprised.

"What's that supposed to mean? We're good friends."

"Yeah, that's my point. Friends. You're stringing the poor guy along, Lane." Philip's eyes carefully scanned the area ahead of them. The footing would be cautious from here on out.

"Just because I'm not looking for..."

"All right. Forget I even said anything." Philip held up his hands in mock surrender and then suddenly stopped short, causing Lane to run into him. "Whoa, look over there." He pointed at what appeared to him to be boot-sized indentions in the loose rock heading east.

"What am I looking at?" Lane stepped up beside him, squinting in the direction of his finger.

Ignoring her question, he walked over and bent down, pulling from the loose rock a small book.

"What is it?" Lane hadn't moved, eager to keep going up trail.

"It's a mini trail guidebook. Janie was using one like this. I remember looking at it with her." Philip searched the area focusing on the set of boot prints he could just make out. He surmised they were heading in the direction of Shale Rock trail. "I think she might've crossed this way. Decided to cut over and take the quicker path up to the summit."

"Why do that? Why ask for the easy path, which will take you double the time, then suddenly change your mind and take the harder trail?" Lane approached Philip, taking the trail guidebook from his hand.

"For that very reason. Because it was taking too long." Philip proceeded forward, hunched over, and looking down at the ground. "Looks like she wasn't alone, or someone else came this way as well."

"Should we follow or keep going up Indian flat?" Lane, usually the decision-maker, decided to defer to his tracking abilities and knowledge of the trails.

"My guess is she got tired and decided to cut through here. It's loose rock, and it's sharp, easy to roll an ankle. Follow my steps if you can," Philip directed, and without waiting for confirmation, started to head east towards Shale Rock trail.

Within twenty minutes, the two found themselves standing in front of a small ridge.

"It would make sense if she came this way. Just over this formation, you should start to see some goats. There's a big ledge they like to leap off of, so they can get to the cliff walls. It's a nice viewpoint for climbers, as well. Come on." Philip jumped onto the ridge boulder and held his hand down to Lane, offering to help her up and over the hump.

Looking at his offered palm with a mixture of annoyance and chagrin, Lane sternly shook her head in the negative before jumping up unassisted, giving him a bright smile.

"I'm a big girl, Ranger." She patted Philip solidly on the chest, walking past him, then called over her shoulder, "Even wore my big girl panties today!"

Ever amazed at how independent and stubborn she could be, Philip rolled his eyes and started to follow. He'd only taken a few steps to catch up with her when he heard a gasp of child-like wonder. She'd spotted the mountain goats.

Never having seen one before, except for pictures in magazines like the National Geographic, Lane was surprised at how huge, yet majestic, and nimble the goats were for their lumbering size.

"They're beautiful!" she exclaimed.

"They are," Philip agreed. "To be honest, though, they don't belong here. This isn't their natural habitat. There's no salt in these rocks." He moved up beside her. "They belong in the Cascade Mountains."

"No salt?" Lane looked perplexed. "Why do they need salt?"

"They don't necessarily need it, but they do really like it. They'll lick rocks with urine or sweat on them. Sometimes deciding to skip the rocks and go straight for the hiker." He started to wander towards the ledge. "Olympic Park had a fatality by mountain goat not long ago. They don't know, for sure, if the animal was simply trying to get salt off the hiker or was just being hostile in general. People forget because they're goats, they can be aggressive animals." He nodded towards the closest billy goat. "Using those shiny black horns for more than butting each other."

"You weren't worried about sending the girl up here by herself to find them?" Lane asked, not accusingly but curious. Philip shrugged.

"She had a fancy camera. I figured she'd just zoom in. Besides, I told her to throw rocks at them if they got close and start heading in the opposite direction."

Lane looked at the goats with a bit less wonder and more caution than she had a minute before.

"Hey, Lane! Over here!" Philip's tone changed as he ran to a yellow knapsack. It was unzipped and opened. A sweatshirt and water bottle were lying beside it.

"There's a couple of granola wrappers here," Lane said, looking towards the ledge, watching her step as she climbed down. "I wonder if she's still up here?' Might have sprained an ankle and couldn't get back dow—," Lane started but was interrupted by the sound of Philip's two-way radio.

"Ranger Russell? ...You there? Over." A male voice crackled through the static of the speakers. They were almost out of range.

"I'm here. Gabe? That you? Find anything?" Philip asked, his ear cocked towards the portable radio.

Hearing an echo, Lane realized it was coming from the direction of the ledge.

"Yeah, we found her," Gabe's voice transmitted through the two-way a few seconds after it echoed up from below. Lane wandered closer to the edge of the cliff, and Philip followed, the two-way held against his chest. "She's deceased," Gabe's voice carried upon the wind.

Inching onto the ledge, they peered down together, spying the two young men standing beside the sprawled and lifeless body of Janie Engles.

"She fell," Lane said solemnly, forcing herself to lean over the cliff's edge to get a better look at the body.

Lucas, hearing Lane's voice from above, looked up and waved, indicating he saw them. His other hand was holding his t-shirt over his nose and mouth.

Lane could only imagine the smell. The body, having laid out in the hot August/September heat for days. She started turning green at the mere thought.

"That's one hell of a fall." Philip marveled at the distance.

"Think she slipped?" Lane shook her head and considered the goats, who had wandered closer, attracted to the sound of the portable radio.

"Maybe a goat attacked her? Butted her right off the edge?"

Philip immediately shook his head in the negative.

"Butted her off the edge? You and your imagination, Lane."

Lane opened her mouth to give her next suggestion.

"And don't try to tell me she threw herself off the ledge because a goat was coming at her either." Philip recalled the last time Lane had suspected suicide in an apparent animal attack.

Lane let out a loud huff and gave Philip an annoyed frown.

"That's not what I was going to say."

"Sure, it wasn't." Philip shook his head, mildly amused at her denial, then quickly spoke into the two-way radio. "Gabe, we'll start heading down. Don't approach the body, okay? Best to stay a few feet back. Over and out."

Gabe waved his understanding from below, then ushered Lucas away from the scene, heading back into the surrounding woods.

Philip watched them until they disappeared, absently scratching his head. "I'm more apt to think she slipped and fell," he said, taking a cautious step away from the edge and facing Lane.

Lane frowned at the two granola wrappers by her feet and then over the edge, down on Janie's distorted body.

"Or she was pushed."

CHAPTER 6

Philip, once again using his personal cell phone to document a possible murder scene, took a quick inventory of the area before the two started their way down to the body. Lane, who always kept a few evidence bags on her person out of habit, had quickly scooped up the granola bar wrappers and then directed Philip to put the water bottle and sweatshirt back into the knapsack to carry down with them.

"How did we beat them all the way up here?" Lane asked out of breath, jogging down the trail once again following Philip's lead.

"My guess is they were careful and took their time while we sort of took a shortcut. A good portion of our hike was off-trail." He took a sharp right and then cut across another path, suddenly calling out, "Lucas? Gabe? You close by?"

"Over here, Ranger Russell!" Gabe called in return, and Philip kept heading straight.

As they grew closer, Lane could smell the hint of something foul upon the air. She grabbed her handkerchief and tied it around her head, covering her mouth and nose. It smelled of mild BO, but it would nevertheless smell better than what they were walking into.

Philip, glancing back at her, took note of her bandana mask and asked, "You got another one of those?"

"Sorry." Lane's eyes were sympathetic.

Philip grunted his disappointment.

The two turned slightly left and began to follow the sound of murmuring voices. A few steps more, and Lane could make out a conversation.

"Poor Janie."

"Did you know she was back on the island?"

"No. Maybe Amy or Angie did?"

"Think Brent knew?"

"Hold up... I hear them." Lane guessed it was Lucas speaking. "HEY! We're across the creek!"

"I see you!" Philip yelled in response, stepping around a large cedar.

Sitting on an old stump was Gabe, his head bowed, hastily wiping at his face. He looked up as they approached, his eyes red and cheeks ruddy. Lucas stood beside him with his hand on Gabe's shoulder, comforting his friend.

Philip waved a greeting and splashed through the small creek separating them while Lane nimbly stepped on the large stones avoiding the cold water.

"You fellas, okay?" Philip reached Lucas first, giving him a manly pat on the back.

In response, Lucas nodded his head and pounded Philip's in return.

"We've known Janie since we were kids." Gabe stood up.

"We were hoping to find her alive."

"We all were, Gabe," Lane said kindly. "Why don't you two head on back to the ranger station? We've radioed the volunteers, and I've asked Calvin Morton to take count, make sure everyone made it back okay. I don't want him thinking he's missing you two."

"What about the... um... Janie?" Gabe picked up his pack, staring over to where the body laid, several feet away.

"Got the coast guard bringing in a helicopter to lift her out. We'll take good care of her," Lane promised.

"See you back at the station then," Lucas said, grabbing Gabe's arm and leading him towards the creek.

"Thanks for your help, guys," Philip said over his shoulder, already starting to head in the direction of Janie's body.

Lane, following a short distance behind, gauged the cliff they'd been peering down from. Marveling at the height, she guesstimated it was at least a five-hundred-foot drop... maybe even six? She'd have to ask Philip.

Drawing closer, the two could hear the buzzing of flies, the sound disturbingly loud. They proceeded forward and slowly approached the body.

Philip had to wave his arms several times to disperse the black mass, the stench of decomposition wavering thick in the air.

Together, they watched as the flies settled, finding plenty of space on the legs and abdomen to land. Lane's stomach rolled, and she bit down on the inside of her cheeks, willing herself to inch closer.

"We'll have to hurry. Chopper should be here in a few minutes," Lane urged through clenched teeth, unsure if she could trust her stomach.

Philip nodded and took his cell phone out, once again, sending a black cloud up into the air.

Steeling herself, Lane bent over the body, looking down at the dead girl with pity in her eyes. She noted the body was bloated, straining against the clothing, a sure sign she'd been dead for a few days.

The young woman had fallen flat on her back with one leg tucked under and the other sprawled to the side. The back of her head crushed in, her eyes still open, staring blankly up into the September sun, glassy and glazed.

Taking a deep breath and instantly regretting it, Lane began to look around the blood-soaked rock.

Philip, busy taking photos, held the end of his neck-tie to his mouth and nose, doing his best to stay out of her way.

"Shouldn't there be a camera?" Lane questioned, now standing at the foot of the rock.

"Yeah, a big fancy one. Long lens. She had it dangling from a strap around her neck."

"It's not there now." Lane walked away from the corpse, searching the area.

"Think she was holding it when she fell? It wasn't in her backpack, was it?"

Philip roughly shook his head, "No." He was trying to avoid talking, the smell being so overwhelming.

"Maybe she had the camera in hand and flung it when she fell?" Lane muttered, speaking more to herself than Philip. She made her way over to the neighboring shrubs, parting the branches to look through them.

Philip stopped taking photos and gazed upwards towards the ledge with a calculating eye.

"If she did, it could be quite a few feet away. Might be upstream."

"I'll go check it out," Lane volunteered. The sound of a helicopter hovering in the far distance catching her attention. "Don't have much time."

Philip nodded his agreement and continued to take pictures.

Needing to get closer, he hopped onto the large

rock and leaned over the body, holding his breath. His heart fluttered as he looked into Janie's eyes, remembering the last time they had talked. She'd been smiling, warm, and friendly. His two-way radio squawked.

"This is Coast Guard District 13, Jayhawk 6083. ETA two minutes. Over."

"Roger. We'll be waiting for you. Over and out." Philip could clearly see the bright orange and white helicopter on the horizon flying over the ocean. "Lane, ...Coast guard will be here in less than two minutes!" Philip yelled, putting the portable radio in his backpack. He didn't hear anything in return. "Lane?" he called again. "Lane!"

"Yeah... I heard you!" Lane hollered, pulling down on her bandana mask.

Impatient to answer, her full attention had been concentrated on following the small creek, her eyes glued to the ground. Not finding anything, she continued on, wondering if she needed to double back. Unsure, she paused and held her hand to her forehead, blocking the sun to watch the helicopter come in.

Sitting at its highest point, the sun shone brilliant, and she squinted against it. She blinked a few times, trying her best to peer further upstream. A bright glare on the water caught her attention, and her heart sped up. She eagerly ran down into the creek, water splashing up her leg with each hurried step.

There, crushed against the rocks in the middle of the streambed, was a camera covered in plastic. She bent to swipe it up but stopped short.

There was blood soaked into the neck strap.

"That's odd," Lane said to herself, pulling a pair of latex gloves from her pocket, picking up the broken camera by its strap.

A fine mist suddenly lifted from the creek, blowing cold against her skin. Startled, Lane tucked the camera under her arm for protection, the coast guard helicopter unexpectedly looming above her. She shielded her eyes, squinting against the gale forces, the trees and shrubbery around her violently being tossed back and forth by the fast-moving blades.

The sound was deafening this close, and she could easily see the pilot as the helicopter continued to maneuver downstream and then stop, hovering in place. Doing her best to shield her eyes, she watched as an orange stretcher was slowly lowered to the ground, followed by two men in harnesses.

Dropping her hand from her brow, she started to head for Philip and the new arrivals. As she walked, she examined her find. Careful to remove the torn plastic rain sleeve which held the zoom lens in place, she noticed the lens itself had a long fracture running down the side. The rest of the camera, waterlogged despite the cover, showed clear signs of damage. Cracks and chips easily visible.

Flipping the camera over, she stopped in her tracks. The little hinged door which kept the memory card enclosed was open with no memory card inside. Wondering if she had accidentally left it behind, she returned to where she'd found the camera and started searching for the missing card.

She'd been at it for only a few minutes when she felt the wind shift and looked up to see the chopper flying overhead going the opposite direction. It was heading out to sea where a Coast Guard Cutter was waiting in choppy waters to take Janie's body the rest of the way to the mainland.

"They've got her," Philip called, approaching Lane, carrying their gear. "I see you found the camera. Looks pretty banged up."

"Yeah, and it's missing its memory card."

"Could've fallen out. I'm sure the camera probably bounced a few times when it hit the ground from that height."

"Possibly. But something else is off."

"What's that?"

"If the girl had the camera in hand and it was lost in the fall, landing all the way in the stream... Why is there blood soaked into the neck strap?"

CHAPTER 7

Philip opened his mouth to caution a guess when they heard heavy footsteps coming their way. Distinctly, the sound of someone running and running fast, crashing through the bushes towards them. Both turned in the direction of the incoming noise. Both curious as to what the runner might be running from.

Expecting danger, Philip purposely stepped in front of Lane, stretching his arm out in front of her in a protective manner. At the same time, trained to protect, Lane purposely went to step in front of Philip. The two collided, with Philip outweighing Lane by more than seventy pounds, tripping a step ahead of her.

It was Lucas who came bursting through the bushes and, upon seeing them, stopped short, bending over at the waist with his hands on his knees. Swallowing air, he held up a finger, signaling he'd speak as soon as he caught his breath.

"Glad... I... found you...," Lucas panted. He then stood up, placing his hands on his hips. "Sorry... ran all... the way here."

"Everything, okay?" Lane gave Philip an annoyed look, swatting his protective arm out of her path as she walked towards the young man, offering her water bottle.

Lucas, still gulping in air, nodded his head in the affirmative and accepted the bottle, taking a long pull.

"Yeah. Sorry... I just wanted to let you know... We got you a ride." He was finally catching his breath. "Gabe remembered we weren't far... from a jeep trail... and figured we'd head back that way. We spotted Ranger Kody... and waved him down. If Sheriff Lane doesn't mind sitting on someone's lap... we can all ride back together."

"Excuse me?" Lane asked, appalled at the suggestion.

Philip, just as startled at the thought of Lane sitting on anyone's lap as much as she, quickly volunteered to walk back. Grabbing Lucas's arm, Philip pointed him in the direction of the jeep road, hoping to save the young man from a tongue lashing.

"Why did you run all the way back to find us? Why didn't you use the radio?" Philip asked as they started to walk back together.

Lane, a few steps behind, was muttering to herself about how sheriffs don't sit on people's laps, and what kind of suggestion was that? And whose lap did he suppose she should sit on?

"We did. You never answered. Figured your battery had gone dead," Lucas said, keeping pace with Philip and a wary eye on Lane.

"Ah. Must have been the squawking I heard. Forgot I put it in my backpack." Philip grimaced an apology. "Thanks for coming back for us."

"Yeah, no problem."

Falling in step with the two men, Lane motioned for her water bottle back.

"Lucas, you knew Janie... Can you tell me about her?"

"Sure." Lucas handed the bottle over, his smile gone. His good-natured mood dropping at the thought of Janie. "She was a lot of fun. Always up for a laugh. The kind of girl who would pick dare over truth, ya know?"

Lane smiled, completely relating. She'd been the same type of girl growing up. But then again, she had to be with four brothers.

"She loved the outdoors. She seemed almost tomboyish, except there wasn't anything "tom" about her,... if you know what I mean."

"No, I don't know what you mean." Lane was

amused at his description.

Philip chuckled.

"He means she could hang with the boys but still be a lady."

"Yeah, what Ranger Russell said. She was tough but soft."

"Just like a tootsie roll lolli—" Philip was stopped short by Lane's elbow in the stomach.

He'd once described her the same way when they had first met, pointing out she had a tough exterior but a chewy center, much like a tootsie roll lollipop.

"Complete opposite of her sister." Lucas smiled at the exchange, understanding he'd stumbled across a private joke.

"Sue Carter mentioned the girls come out each summer. What is her sister's name?" Lane turned her attention back to Lucas.

"Danielle. But like Janie, everyone called her Danie."

"They sure were quite the pair." Philip smiled himself, thinking of the girls.

"Hmmm. Being opposite, do they get along?" Lane asked.

Philip shook his head, his smile disappearing.

"Danie WAS the opposite of Janie. She died last summer."

"How?" Lane asked, completely shocked by the statement.

"Accidental drowning here in the park."

"Pretty sad to lose both of them," Lucas said somberly. Philip nodded his head in silent agreement.

"When was this?" Lane was still shocked at the revelation.

Lucas looked at Philip and then straight forward, ignoring Lane's question. "I'm gonna run ahead. Make sure they're still waiting for us."

"Sure, Lucas. Appreciate it." Philip clapped the young man on the shoulder and then watched as he took off in a light jog.

"What was that all about?" Lane whispered. Lucas was still in earshot.

"Danie died a year ago this month," Philip whispered back. "Lucas was sweet on her."

"Geez." Lane's heart broke a little for the young man. "That is so tragic." She shook her head slowly. "Strange to lose both sisters."

"Weird, huh? What are the odds?" Philip asked the question more as a statement than an actual query.

Lane took his question seriously and asked herself just that. What were the odds two sisters would die a year apart in the same park and both by apparent accidents? Lane put her hand on Philip's arm, stopping his forward progress.

"Was it really an accidental drowning?"

Philip looked down at Lane, seeing if she was earnest in her question.

"That's what the coroner reported." Philip looked

perplexed. "Why?"

"Did YOU think it was accidental?" Lane pressed him.

Philip thought about it for a second.

"Never had any reason to think otherwise." He looked back down at her. "As strange as it seems, co-incidences do happen, Lane."

Lane lifted up Janie's camera as they heard a jeep horn blare two impatient honks.

"I agree. But this might not be one of those times."

CHAPTER 8

Kody promised he would return once he'd dropped Sheriff Lane and the others off. Philip told him that was fine, and there was no need to rush. He didn't mind walking the rest of the way to the station. Truth was, he wanted the time to think. Lane had posed him with a question, and like most of his interactions with her, she was forcing him to think outside the box.

Was Janie and Danie dying a year apart just a coincidence? Most likely. Some families were doomed to sorrow and heartbreak. With their parents dying when the girls were little, maybe fate had simply stepped in. That wasn't the kind of answer he could give Lane, though. She would never accept... "because sometimes bad things happen to good people" as an answer.

Instead, Philip began trying to remember everything he could from that September day. He knew Lane would grill him on it, so he might as well be prepared. She was a smart cookie and, if there was anything odd to be found, she most likely would find it.

The first thing Philip recalled was Kevin Givens driving like a bat out of hell towards him. He'd been heading down the park's graveled dirt road at a reckless speed, blaring his horn all the way. Philip, parked on the side of the road, had flashed his caution lights, and Kevin had hurriedly wrenched his vehicle to the side of the road in a cloud of dust and flying gravel. The kid had barely shifted into park before he'd hopped out, yelling to Philip his friend was in need of medical attention.

Philip knew the young man, recalling him and his friends from earlier in the day. They'd wanted to light a bonfire on the beach, and he had told them no, reminding them fires were not permitted this time of year. Convinced they'd decided to ignore his answer, Philip had stayed in the area, determined to check up on the small group later on in the evening when it got dark.

Instructing Kevin to lead the way, Philip had flipped on his siren and emergency lights and radioed for an ambulance. He had then followed Kevin the short mile and half to Shallow Point.

Screeching to a halt, he had hopped out of his forest truck and ran towards the small crowd. Kevin, hot on his heels and panting, was explaining it was Danie Engles who had been found face down, floating in the water.

Reaching the small group, Philip had worked his way through the circle of friends, using his shoulders. Pushing Lucas and Amy aside, so he could see what was going on.

In the center of the small gathering, he had found Gabe bent over a young girl dressed in a yellow bikini top and matching cotton shorts. A sun-yellow flip-flop still on her right foot.

Assessing the situation, Philip had quickly gone down to his knees next to Gabe, hearing the young man talking to himself as he counted compressions. Philip had watched as his pace slowed slightly after each return from mouth to mouth and surmised Gabe had already been at it for quite a while by the blue color of the girl's lips. The kid had been clearly exhausted.

Unable to find a pulse, Philip had put his hand on Gabe's arm, telling him to move over so he could do the compressions. But Gabe had shrugged him off, refusing to budge. Philip had tried again, telling Gabe the ambulance was on its way, and he needed to let him take over. The young man had simply shaken his head no while continuing to count.

Having known Gabe was enrolled in the medical program at UW, Philip had felt confident Gabe knew what he was doing. He had also quickly realized the young man was close to losing his cool. The girl was not coming around, and Gabe was refusing to accept it.

Watching Gabe closely, Philip had reached over and taken Danie's wrist again. There was still no pulse, not even a hint of one. Saddened, he had started to tell Gabe, when it had suddenly dawned on him... Gabe was fully aware it was too late. Which had made sense with his medical background. Gabe would have fully known, once you started performing CPR on someone, you legally had to continue until paramedics arrived. The determined young man would have stayed with it until it was no longer legally necessary. The kid had been a trooper.

Fire engine sirens had suddenly blared in the distance, and Philip knew they'd be on the scene within minutes. Pushing up from the ground, he had walked over to Brent, who was pacing back and forth at the girl's feet, biting his thumbnail, his eyes glued to her face.

"Brent, what happened here?" Philip had taken a spot next to him, trying to view the small group all at once.

Huddled together, Amy Holmes had her arms wrapped around Janie, who was weakly struggling against them. Lucas, still standing in the same spot Philip had shoved him, had his mouth hanging open. Clearly having a hard time coping with what was happening. While Kevin had stationed himself like a brick wall on the other side of Janie, helping Amy to keep her restrained.

At the sound of Philip's voice, Brent had looked up surprised, as if just noticing Philip had joined the group. He had shaken his head and shrugged his shoulders as if he had no words, but had answered all the same. His voice had been pitched low, almost in reverence.

"I don't know, really. Was gathering wood for the bonfire when someone yelled Danie was drowning in the shallows. I dropped everything and ran here. Saw her floating and jumped in. We pulled her out, and Gabe started CPR. That's all I know."

Philip had noticed a trickle of watery blood trailing down the back of Brent's ear and neck. He had lifted the young man's hand to the top of his head, assuming he must have hit it on a rock when he dove in.

"Here, Brent. Sit down. You may have a concussion. Keep your hand there and apply pressure." Philip had then led him over to a fallen log, sitting the young man down, Brent's eyes never leaving Danie.

Philip had tried to ask Brent who had found her first, but his voice was drowned in a sea of sirens. Help had arrived. Calvin Morton and Ethan Richardson, the island's fire department, had reached them.

Running from the truck, Calvin had roughly pulled Gabe away from Danie's body as Ethan had checked for her vitals. Philip could tell by the look on Ethan's face, there was nothing further to be done, and the call had been made. Danie was officially pronounced dead.

Philip stopped walking, his feet still on the jeep road, his memory jolted. Was there something about the look on Ethan's face? Or was it the look on someone else's? Philip closed his eyes, and he suddenly saw her... Of course, it was Janie. He had quickly glanced at her after having seen Ethan's expression and noticed how queer she looked. Instead of being hysterical, as she'd been a moment before, she was calm. No, not calm. Calm wasn't the right word for her wide eyes. Panicked? Scared? Was that the impression he had at the time? And why shouldn't she be? She was virtually alone in the world now. Why should that have perplexed him?

A loud honk blared behind Philip, jarring him out of his memories, causing him to jerk. He opened his eyes and found a jeep quickly approaching, followed by a huge cloud of dust in its wake. Kody was most definitely behind the wheel. Philip frowned, forgetting what he'd been thinking of. He was going to have to lecture his young ranger once again about jeep trail etiquette and driving safely.

CHAPTER 9

Back with the search team at the forest station, Lane borrowed Philip's office to break the news to Sue Carter with the help of the pastor. Next, she had an impromptu news conference with the media, letting them know the hiker had been found deceased and the next of kin already notified. They could expect an official statement to be released within the next couple of days. She then disbanded the volunteers, making sure to thank every single one of them for their time and efforts.

Watching the dust-coated jeep pull up with Kody behind the wheel and Philip holding on for dear life, Lane waved, indicating she needed to have a word with the elder ranger. Guessing what was coming, Philip promised to be at her office bright and early the next day with his cell phone, which contained the scene photos. Almost peeved he'd read her mind, she cautioned him not to share them with anyone else... which meant Kody... or with the media. Philip, knowing better, let her have her say, swearing he wouldn't.

Commandeering Philip's office, she then sat herself down behind his cluttered desk and placed a call to the coroner's office. They immediately placed her on hold. Impatient and feeling antsy from the day's search, she began to straighten his desk in an effort to pass the time. Busily she picked up pens, scooped up loose paperclips, and unstuck his stapler. Then she folded his reading glasses and placed his coffee mug on a pad of post-it notes using them as a coaster. Next, she grabbed the paperback he'd left open, the spine being split in two, lying flat on the desk. She looked around for a bookmark and not finding one, tore a sheet of paper from her own leather notepad, placing it in the novel, and closing it shut.

Glancing at the cover, Lane's eyebrow arched in surprise. She was stunned to find it was a romance novel... a smutty one at that. She'd been expecting a spy thriller or a non-fiction biography. Instead, she was staring at a cover which revealed a damsel in apparent distress. Her blouse falling off her shoulders, revealing a curvy bosom. Long, curly blonde hair blowing in the wind, her eyes looking lost, yet lusting at the same time and set upon the man standing behind her. A handsome, dark-haired, and muscle-bound hero, who held her roughly against his bare chest, his eyes fixed on the far horizon.

"Sort of looks like him," Lane said to herself, snorting at the same time in amusement, oblivious to her own resemblance portrayed on the cover.

Just then, she heard a honk and peeked through the window blinds. The fire engine and ambulance were leaving. She took a quick inventory, wondering who was left, and noticed Gabe and Lucas talking to Brent Allister. It appeared they were having a serious discussion of some sort. Intrigued, she spread her fingers wider, opening the gap between the blinds as much as she could.

Still talking to his friends, Brent suddenly broke away and started to make his way towards Deputy Pickens. Lucas grabbed his arm to arrest his progress, all the while shaking his head in the negative. On his other side, Gabe was busy nodding his head yes and pushing him towards the sheriff's deputy. Lane stood up, curiously leaning into the window for a better look, the phone still held to her ear waiting on hold.

Not to be sidelined, Brent pushed both men away and started stalking towards Caleb, intent on speaking with the deputy. Just inside her line of vision Lane noticed a silver Mercedes-Benz pull up. She watched as Mike Allister, the town's semi-retired lawyer, got out of his car and ordered Brent to get in.

She frowned at this and then recalled the lawyer was his grandfather.

Obviously frustrated, Brent gave a fleeting look towards Deputy Pickens, who was helping load the horses into their trailer. Mr. Allister seemed to say something profound, which caused Brent to break his determination and head towards the Mercedes-Benz. Climbing in, his grandfather turned the vehicle around and then drove off. In turn, Lucas and Gabe continued to have an animated conversation as they themselves climbed into Lucas's truck and followed Mr. Allister out of the park.

Lane let the blinds smack together with a loud clatter as the receptionist came back on the line. She quickly scheduled a meeting for the next day at 1:00 p.m. and hung up the phone, grabbing her leather notepad off of Philip's desk. With her deputy in tow, she then headed back to her own office, intent on tackling the pile of paperwork she knew was waiting for them.

Caleb, who was not as eager to get the paperwork out of the way as Lane, put on a fresh pot of coffee and volunteered to finish up the bowling alley report. Lane begrudgingly agreed, and a short fifteen minutes later, Deputy Pickens was calling it a night.

"Not so fast!" Lane called out, just as Caleb hit the door. "Where do you think you're going?"

Caleb said something indistinguishable through

a wide-open yawn, but Lane had caught the gist.

"Deputy, tomorrow is going to be even longer. Best to get this paperwork out of the way now." Lane gave him a beady-eyed stare until he took his hand off the doorknob. "Unless you have somewhere more important to be?"

Caleb shrugged his shoulders, not really answering her question.

Instead, he said, "Why don't I just come in early tomorrow?"

"You want to come in early?" Lane asked, dumbfounded.

Deputy Pickens not only had a bad habit of returning from lunch late, he also had a terrible habit of coming late into work. Sometimes Lane wondered why the young man had requested the assignment to the island.

"I was hoping to meet up with Amy at Piper's Place."

"The dive bar next to the bowling alley?"

"You mean, the only bar on the island? Yeah, that's it."

"Caleb, you realize Amy is dating Kody?"

"Dating. Not married." Caleb smiled slyly, putting his hand on the doorknob again.

Lane gave out a disapproving huff and eyed her young deputy. She sometimes forgot how young he was, having only turned twenty-four last month.

"Alright. If you're going to skip out on the paperwork, I have a little assignment for you." Lane decided she'd get more work done with him gone anyway.

"What is it?" Caleb sounded less than enthused.

"Nothing difficult. Just, when you are out and about tonight, I want you to keep your ears open about Janie Engles. Emphasis on listening. Information in, not information out."

"What exactly am I listening for?" Caleb perked up, entertained with the idea.

"Anything, really. Who may've seen her last? What people thought of her? Who knew her best or who she used to date?"

"Ohhhhh... I get it! See what kind of dirt I can dig up on her? Try to scrape up anything scandalous? Sure. But why?"

Lane paused before answering. Caleb hadn't quite grasped what she'd meant.

"Because I asked you to. See you tomorrow, Caleb."

"See ya!" He gave her a parting smile and locked the door behind him, leaving Lane all alone with the reports and a fresh pot of coffee.

CHAPTER 10

Smiling at the sound of the golden bell chiming above the door of Hattie's General, Lane greeted Harry Vickers with a wave as she breezed into the island's one-stop-shop grocery store.

"Morning, Sheriff!" Harry gave the pretty blonde a warm welcome in return as he refilled the pepperoni sticks by the register.

"Morning, Harry!" she said in passing, giving a nod towards the old-timers sitting at the picnic table stationed in front of the store's window.

The picnic table, always for sale, had become the island's prime gossip and coffee circle through the years and typically was occupied by at least one or two locals throughout the day. Currently in possession of the table were the fore mentioned old-timers, Dub and Glen. The two bickering back and forth over their coffee. This time, apparently, about the benefits of an electric chain saw vs. gas chainsaw.

Sitting next to the picnic table was an old empty rocking chair, a small sign hanging on its back stating "Hattie's Chair" and in smaller print below, "Not for sale."

Lane made her way over to the refrigerated wall and grabbed a small carton of creamer and a six-pack of Coke. She debated on grabbing an energy drink for Caleb and then decided on two, remembering Kody liked them as well. She'd have Philip bring one back for him after their meeting.

With her hands full, she started to make her way towards the front. Spotting an end cap of Oreo cookies, she snatched up a carton and added it to the pile.

"How's the morning going so far, Harry?" She carefully laid her items on the small counter.

"Oh, no complaints."

"Miss Hattie feeling okay today?" Lane looked towards the rocking chair, slightly concerned it was still sitting vacant.

Hattie, who would be turning one hundred and three in a month, normally was found rocking in her chair happily chatting with customers in the mornings.

"Doing just fine. Finishing up her cocoa and the last fifteen minutes of the Price is Right before she heads out front." Harry started to bag up Lane's groceries.

"And... how's the nose feeling?" Lane asked carefully, noticing Harry's two black eyes were a darker shade of purple than the other night. Harry had been one of the main participants in the bowling alley brawl, and his nose still looked red and swollen.

"Tender. But you should see the other guy." Harry winced, gently touching the side of his nose.

"I have. By the way, he's dropping the charges. Now that he's sobered up."

"Dropping the charges? He's the one who started it! I should be the one bringing charges against him, not the other way around!"

"Harry, ...you clobbered him over the head with your bowling trophy!"

"And his thick skull bent it!" Harry stuffed the carton of cookies into the bag roughly. "I've already told the trophy store to fix it and send him the bill."

"Please tell me you didn't." Lane shook her head, trying to sound disapproving behind her smile.

"Oh, you bet I did!"

"Do me a favor, Harry. Call them back. Be the bigger man and let it go."

"Bigger man?" Harry stopped bagging her items. "Sheriff, that's what started the fight in the first place!" He put his hand to his heart as if wounded. "I'd won the final frame, fair and square. Went over like a good winner should. Extended my hand in friendship, and the loser sucker punched me!" He musingly shook his head in disbelief. "All I was trying to do was be a good sport."

"Witnesses say you'd been running your mouth at him all night, Harry. By the time the game was over, he was as hot as a pistol. Some say you went over to rub his nose in it."

"Ahhh... Phil knows how I get when I play." Harry waved his hand in the air, dismissing the accusation. "I've always been real competitive. He knows that." Harry folded the top of the paper bag nicely, avoiding Lane's judging stare.

"That's why he's dropping the charges." She tried to catch Harry's eye and smiled. "You two are best friends. This is a silly way to break up a friendship."

"It's not broken," Harry said sharply. "It's just on hold till he fixes my trophy."

Lane rolled her eyes, taking the bag. Starting to leave, she paused in thought.

"Harry, did you know Sue Carter's nieces?"

"Oh, sure! Everybody did! They were a summer staple around here." His smile faltered. "I was sure sad to hear about Janie. Hell of a thing."

Lane nodded her head, agreeing, and started again towards the door with her purchases in hand.

"Saw her on Tuesday. Full of life, pretty smile as always. Just sad." Harry had turned to walk around the corner of the counter as Lane turned back to face him.

"You said you saw her Tuesday?"

"Sure did. She visited with Hattie for a few minutes, got a couple of things, and then headed out to the park." Harry turned towards Lane, standing behind his cash register again.

Lane put the paper bag on the counter and pulled out her leather notepad.

"What did she and Miss Hattie talk about?"

"Oh, just niceties, really. Asked how Hattie was feeling. Talked about how hot the weather has been lately. Chatted about Hattie's upcoming birthday party in a month."

"So, she was a friendly girl?"

"Both girls were. Everyone kind of looked at them as their little kid sisters. Well, except for the boys their age."

"What did she end up buying?" Lane had been taking notes and flipped to the next page. Harry shrugged his shoulders and thought.

"Not much. A box of granola bars, a few bags of beef jerky, a small bag of nuts... a couple of Gatorades. Normal hiking food."

Lane nodded her head as she wrote the items down, agreeing with Harry it was a pretty normal list.

"You said, two Gatorades?" she asked for clarification.

"Yup. Oh, and one of those trail books for the park." Harry pointed towards a metal tower filled with small booklets and road maps standing by the door. "I thought that was a little odd."

"Odd? Why say, odd?" She walked over to the metal tower giving it an idle twirl. She then picked out a book matching the one found on the trail and turned towards Harry, showing it to him. "Was this the one she bought?"

"That's the one."

Lane brought the book over to the counter, indicating for Harry to ring it up. The other one was in an evidence bag.

"Janie had been all over that mountain. I just didn't think she needed one."

"Did you ask her why she bought it?"

"No." Harry paused for a second, unfolding the top of Lane's grocery bag to slip the book inside. "If I think about it though, she volunteered she wanted the book because she'd always been with someone who knew the way. Figured she'd better get it since she'd be hiking by herself this time." Harry shrugged his shoulders, dismissing the thought and the conversation.

Lane closed her notepad and stuck it in her back pocket, once again grabbing the brown paper bag from the counter. She suddenly remembered she had something to tell him.

"OH! Phil says he's got an uncle who will let me rent his place. Looks like I may be out of the upstairs apartment soon."

Even with two black eyes and a broken nose, Lane couldn't miss the look of utter relief on Harry's face.

"His Uncle Chuck's place?"

"Yeah, that's it."

Harry chuckled fondly.

"Uncle Chuck, crazy coot. Heck of a nice guy, though." Harry laughed again, pointing at Lane. "You? You're going to be the one living at Uncle Chuck's place? That's great news!" Harry pounded on his counter. "Just great news!" He was suddenly abashed at his own enthusiasm, noticing Lane's hurt expression. "Not that we haven't enjoyed having you upstairs, Sheriff. It's just... we could use the extra money. What with the damage to the store last spring and losing a night cashier for well over a month? And well, Hattie doesn't feel right asking for more rent money from YOU. But the hunters? They'll pay a good deal more if..."

Lane held up her hand, arresting Harry's explanations.

"I understand, Harry, and to be honest, I need more room. I think this will work out best for everybody. Phil said he'd show me the place this week. In fact, he's probably at my office right now, waiting on me. I better get going." Lane regarded Harry carefully. "Should I tell Phil you say hi?"

"No." Harry frowned, crossing his arms over his chest. "But you can tell him he owes me thirty bucks."

CHAPTER 11

"Sorry, I'm late. I was getting a few things before work," Lane apologized to Philip, who was leaning up against the front door of the sheriff's office waiting on her. "I was hoping Caleb had beat me here."

"Haven't seen hide nor hair of him." Philip grabbed the grocery bag from Lane, freeing her hands to unlock the door.

"Why doesn't that surprise me?" Lane mumbled to herself, swinging the door open.

"How's Harry's nose looking?" Philip asked, walking in behind her and placing the grocery bag down on Caleb's empty desk.

"Large, swollen, and still broken," Lane said over her shoulder before flipping on the lights and making her way over to the little coffee station.

"He still sore at me?" "He says you owe him thirty bucks for the trophy."

"Thirty bucks!"

"Yup, thirty."

"For that lousy piece of plastic junk?" Philip shook his head musingly. "Did you tell him I dropped the charges?"

"Sure did. Didn't seem to help." Lane busied herself, pouring fresh water into the Keurig's tank. "I think it's his pride that's hurt more than anything. You really should apologize."

"Me, apologize? He's the one who hit me over the head with his dumb trophy!" Philip absently rubbed the back of his head.

"After you punched him!" Lane couldn't help but chuckle.

"Well, that was because he was popping off his mouth."

"You still shouldn't have hit him, Phil." Lane leveled him with a disciplinary frown. "And you both shouldn't have had so much to drink."

"Neither of us was driving," Philip deflected instead of agreeing. He looked inside the grocery bag, pulling out a carton of creamer. He smiled up at her, her back facing him now, as she fiddled with the coffee machine. Lane knew he didn't drink his coffee black.

"Suit yourself. He's only your best friend in the

world." Lane looked over her shoulder at Philip, who was emptying out the rest of the grocery bag. "One of those energy drinks is for Kody, by the way. And don't eat the cookies," Lane directed, removing the filled coffee mug, placing an empty one in its place.

"Thanks. Just what the kid needs. More energy. He's already bouncing off the walls half the time as is." Philip put the tall energy drinks to the side and pulled out the small trail booklet, holding it up to look at it.

"That's the same one Janie had, right?" Lane brought the filled coffee mugs over and indicated with her shoulder for Philip to follow her into the glass-paned office.

"Same one." Philip quickly flipped through the pages, using his thumb to bend the book back, causing the little pages to flip rapidly.

"Harry seemed surprised she bought it."

"I was surprised she had it!" Philip agreed, grabbing the creamer and other coffee supplements, following her into the office.

"Apparently, Janie told Harry she wanted it since she'd be climbing up The Mole Hill all by herself. Who did she normally go climbing with?" Lane blew on her coffee while punching in her log-in passcode one-handed into the computer.

"Usual suspects?" Philip poured creamer generously into his hot beverage, followed by four sugar packets. "That would be Gabe Garent, Lucas Wilson, Kevin Givens, and Brent Allister."

"All boys?"

"She was a tomboy."

"She didn't have female friends?"

"Sure, she did. There was her sister and Amy... Jerry's daughter, and Angie Bennett, Kevin's girl-friend." Philip gave his coffee a good stir with a plastic stir stick. "Wait! You know Angie! She was out there with her horses helping in the search."

"I do. So, four boys and four girls? Were they all paired up or just a group of friends?" Lane had pulled her notepad out, busily writing down the names.

"That's tough to say. When they were younger, I would have said a group of friends. After the teen years, I think things started to change." Philip tapped his stir stick on the rim of his mug before chucking it into the trash can. "Might want to ask Sue about their dynamic. I only saw them when they were in the park, and they all looked pretty friendly."

"Tell me about Danie's drowning." Lane had her pen ready, hovering over her notepad.

Philip wondered why she didn't type every-thing into the computer instead of taking it down by shorthand. Then again, he knew she studied her notes at the end of each day and probably fell asleep, analyzing everything to death.

He took a hasty sip of his coffee, nodding as he

swallowed.

"It was last year around the end of August. The group had gone camping together, staking close to the coast by the water and pebbled beach. I'd spoken with them earlier in the day and was still in the area when Kevin Givens tore up in his pickup truck. I followed him back to Shallow Point and—"

"Shallow Point?" Lane looked up and grabbed the little booklet, flipping towards the end where there was a map of the whole island.

"It's a nice viewpoint, lots of pointy rocks at the bottom. Some people like to jump or dive from it as there's a sliver of a spot where there are no rocks. We've got "No Diving, No Swimming" signs posted as most people aren't that lucky. Kids ignore them most of the time." Lane put the book down, frowning.

"It's not roped or fenced off?"

Philip shook his head no.

"Would ruin the view."

Lane could tell by the tone of his voice he didn't agree with the logic.

"What happened next?"

"Well, I followed Kevin to the shallows and found the group of young people gathered around Danie. Gabe was performing CPR. By the time I got there, there was nothing else to be done. Tore the kid up pretty good. He'd been attending UW's medical school. Ended up taking this year off and has been working for Doctor Hadley instead. I hope he'll be ready to return next quarter and finish up his degree. Doctor Hadley is retiring here soon, and Gabe's got a good chance of taking over his practice."

"How did everyone else react?" Lane asked, more interested in the past than the present.

"Like they would with any accident." Philip put his coffee mug down and sat back in his seat. "Shock, sadness, tears."

"So, had she jumped from the point? Anybody see her dive off?"

"No. Apparently, no one had been around to actually see her get in the water."

"Where was the rest of the group then?"

"Janie had gone off with Lucas to help put up a tent. Brent said he was wandering around looking for wood for a bonfire they'd planned that night. Kevin and Amy had decided to grab some lunch and were making sandwiches for everybody. Gabe said he was in his tent, trying to take a nap."

"What about Angie?"

"I don't remember her being there." Philip shook his head, trying to recall. "Pretty sure I didn't see her."

"So, Danie decided to jump off Shallow Point with warning signs posted all over and all of her friends doing something else?" Lane tilted her head back, staring up at the ceiling. "Not very smart."

"Actually, the coroner didn't think she took a dive.

What with how she was dressed and the condition of her injuries. He thought she might have been leaning over the edge too far, lost her balance, and fell in, landing on the jagged rocks below."

"What was she wearing?" Lane sat up, her full attention on Philip.

"Shorts, bikini top, flip-flops."

"You said she had injuries? I thought she drowned?"

"She did, but she got bunged up pretty good by the rocks below. Cracked her head open."

"The back of the skull? Front of the skull?" Lane's head turned at the sound of the front door opening, Deputy Pickens having sauntered in. "You're late!" she called out and then muttered under her breath, "Like usual."

Caleb waved her off, apparently nursing a hangover.

Philip, curious to how late Caleb was, glanced at his own watch.

"Speaking of being late. I gotta run."

"But we're not done!" She stood up with him, slightly peeved.

"Here." Philip dug out his cell phone from his front pocket and handed it over. "Download the pictures and then pick me up before noon at the ranger station."

"But I'm heading over to the mainland at noon

to meet the coroner," Lane complained, tossing the phone onto her desk.

Philip, already half-way to the door, swiped one of the cans off of Caleb's desk to his protest.

"I know. That's why you're picking me up before noon so we can make the ferry on time, and after we see the coroner, you can take me to lunch." He gave her a playful smile and a parting wave.

CHAPTER 12

Lane downloaded the pictures from Philip's phone and began to scrutinize them on her computer screen, her stomach squirming with each scroll of the mouse. A few photos in and already her pallor was turning a greenish-white, her face slowly scrunching up into a permanent 'Ewwww' expression as a purely imagined stench seemed to fill her office. She took a deep breath and forced herself to click on the next picture, thankful she had decided to skip breakfast.

Caleb, entering with a half-eaten sandwich in hand, gave the door jamb a brief rap on his way in before standing behind her. He had started to ask her what she was working on and stopped mid-chew. Through the reflection in the window, Lane could tell he'd just lost his appetite.

"You probably don't want to see these," Lane warned a bit late, scrolling to the next picture.

"I've seen a dead body before," Caleb said nonchalantly, though his face said something else. Lane doubted he'd seen one in this condition before.

"Hot sun, a couple days of exposure, insect activity. It's not pretty, is it?"

"She was, though. At least, that's what people were saying about her last night." Caleb threw the remains of his sandwich in the small trash can beside Lane's desk.

"They say anything else?" She scrolled to another picture. This one was a close-up of Janie's bloated face. Caleb sat himself down in the chair by Lane's desk, facing away from the computer monitor, looking slightly nauseous.

"Well, she hadn't been back to the island since her sister died last year. Even Cougar Carter didn't know she was coming till she showed up on her doorstep."

Lane shook her head musingly.

"I wonder why she didn't tell anyone she was coming to the island? Granted, she was on a work assignment, but she'd planned on being around for a few days. She was bound to run into someone she knew. The island being the size it is. Why not let them know she was coming for a visit, work or not?" Lane clicked on the next picture and paused, waiting for Caleb to provide an answer.

"Beats me." Caleb shrugged his shoulders, not having a clue and not particularly caring.

Lane leaned in, her finger hovering over the roller. "What is that?"

Caleb twisted around, angling his neck so he could see the screen.

"High up on the wrist? Hard to tell." He sat back, looking up at the ceiling, trying to forget the image.

Lane leaned in further, squinting at the screen. She could barely make it out.

"It looks like prayer beads." She leaned back. "Maybe a beaded bracelet?"

Caleb took another quick peek, his eyes not lingering on the photo.

"A rosary? It's hard to tell with it tucked under her sleeve."

"I think it's a bracelet. Look, it's got a D carved into one of the beads."

Caleb decided to take her word for it and stared at his shoes instead, waiting for the roll of nausea to pass. He was about to lose what little lunch he had.

"Can I ask a question?" Caleb stood up, deciding he'd rather be sitting at his desk than looking at photos of a dead corpse.

"Sure."

"Why are you looking at these?"

"What do you mean?" Lane looked up at her deputy confused.

"Well, it was a climbing accident, right?"

"It would appear so," she answered, not sounding quite convinced.

"You think it's not?" Caleb looked down at her, mild surprise in his eyes. He'd caught the doubt in her voice.

Lane shrugged her shoulders.

"Just making sure." She gave him an innocent smile.

"Guess that's why you're the boss." Caleb started to walk out. But remembering why he came into her office to begin with, abruptly turned in the doorway. "By the way, just finished cataloging and bagging everything in her backpack."

"What was in it?" Lane looked over at her deputy, nodding for him to sit back down. He did, slouching down into the seat.

"Like, you want to know everything?" he asked, his tone sullen. Lane said nothing in return and glowered at him till he sat up straight. "Fine." Caleb abruptly crossed his arms and heaved his shoulders in annoyance before looking up in recollection and reciting.

"One bag of beef jerky, three granola bars, a bottle of Gatorade, a used wrapper which once contained mixed nuts. One red hoodie in size medium, one red water bottle filled with water. In the front pocket, I found a cell phone, small wallet, and a set of keys. I'm guessing her car and house keys." Caleb leaned forward, preemptively answering Lane's next question. "And yes, the phone was password protected. It's gonna have to go to the mainland." He leaned back and continued, "The wallet held her driver's license, three credit cards, and a total of five bucks in one-dollar bills. Coin purse on the side held three quarters, two dimes, and four pennies."

"That all seems pretty normal," Lane noted, disappointed at his findings.

"Yup. Normal and boring." Caleb stood up and slapped the door jamb on his way out. Heading back to his desk, he sat down and brought up a tv streaming service on his phone. It appeared to be another episode of "Cops".

Lane returned to the photos, clicking on the next one. It was a shot of Janie's arms, each laying palm up, straight by her side. The beaded bracelet was a little easier to see, though something didn't look right. Lane sat back in her seat, her head tilted to the side, contemplating the photo.

Is that how a body would land? She tried to envision falling backwards and imagined herself trying to grab at the cliff's edge. But what if her hands were full? Clutching something? Like a camera to her chest? Lane looked at the girl's palms. They were pale blue, bloated, and clean. Lane's thoughts went back to the camera she'd found upstream and the bloodied neck strap. Where had the blood come from? If there was no blood on her palms, it would mean she wasn't holding the camera by the strap. Lane quickly clicked back a few pictures, finding a side shot of the body. The picture clearly showed where blood had seeped down and stained the rock under Janie's head and neck.

Lane had no doubts.

"She had to be wearing it."

CHAPTER 13

"Lane, what are you doing?" Philip asked sternly, holding the door open to the ferry's observation deck.

"Whatever do you mean?" Lane opened the opposite door, walking through it instead.

"You're trying to make this into a murder case." Philip let the door swing shut behind him, following close on her heels.

"There's no trying about it, Phil. It IS a murder case."

"You don't know that for sure. You haven't even heard what the coroner has to say yet." Lane tossed her head side to side and amended, "Potential murder investigation, then.

He eyed her for a minute, debating on whether or not he should say what was on his mind. After the close call they shared together last spring, Philip and

Lane had become close, but he still had to choose his words wisely. She could be very touchy when it came to her job.

"Go ahead. Spit it out." Lane could tell he was mulling his words over.

"I think you're bored."

"What?"

Philip smiled apologetically.

"I... think you're bored. You're looking for something to do."

"That's ridiculous!" Lane walked over to the ferry's green railing, turning her back on him and thus avoiding his eye contact.

"I don't think so. It's been six months since anything has happened on the island and what did happen was pretty dang exciting... if not incredibly scary." Philip paused again, debating if he should continue. "Take last Tuesday at the bowling alley. You should have seen your face when they called you out to the fight. You were like a pyromaniac who was handed a match." Philip followed her over and leaned up against the railing, trying to catch her eye.

"Gee, you say the nicest things." She gave him a frustrated scowl and then added, "Alright. I admit it." She paused, taking in the ocean view before turning her gaze to him. "It's not been very exciting lately. But I'm not creating a murder out of nothing. There are indicators, Phil."

Philip thought the comment over. She had him wondering again. She did that to him.

"I have a theory then." Philip pulled down his baseball cap, trying to block the brisk wind and ocean spray blowing against his face.

"Let's hear it." Lane herself closed her eyes and took in a deep cleansing breath of sea air, enjoying the feel of the cold mist against her skin.

"She may have committed suicide." Philip held up his hand, arresting Lane's wide-eyed protest. "You made a good point about the way the body was found. Her hands posed palm up, her arms stretched straight out to her sides. What if she simply turned her back to the cliff and let herself fall backwards? After all, it's the anniversary of the death of her sister. She tried to not let anyone know she was coming to the island. Not even Sue, right? Maybe she was overcome with memories and emotions and took a backward leap."

"Did she seem suicidal when you saw her? Give you any indication she was?" Lane looked at Philip, an almost annoyed tone in her voice.

"Admittedly, no."

"And why stay at Sue's house? Why not stay in the park and camp?"

"Maybe she wanted to say good-bye? Maybe she wanted to talk to somebody?" Philip cocked his head to the side. "Maybe she was looking for a reason not to jump?"

Lane shook her head stubbornly.

"Suicide also wouldn't explain someone taking the camera from around her neck."

"Well, that depends. Could have been someone who came upon her and thought the camera might tell them what happened."

"So, they smash it against the rocks and steal the storage card?" Lane, putting her elbows on the top rung, leaned her back against the green railing so she could face Philip.

"Our killer..."

"If there is one," Philip amended.

Lane ignored him and continued on, "Throws or pushes Janie off the cliff. Possibly taking her by surprise. Then runs down to her body, grabs the camera, smashes it against the rocks, and steals the storage card. They wouldn't take the camera with them. Way too bulky to hold with the bloody neck strap removed."

"IF you're right, it most likely was someone she knew," Philip raised his voice, the ferry suddenly blasting its horn, signaling their arrival.

"Why do you say that?"

"The way they posed the body. They couldn't cross her arms across her chest. Would have been an obvious clue to someone messing with her corpse. So, they did the next best thing. Put her in a peaceful position, palms up."

Lane chewed on the theory, then offered one of her own.

"I think she was clutching the camera. They had to move her arms out of the way so they could grab it, and that's how they fell to her side."

Walking towards the doors, Philip grunted, liking her idea better.

"Still think I'm imagining a murder?" Lane, not waiting for his answer, opened the door for Philip and let him walk through first.

CHAPTER 14

C oroner Ralph Ames was interrupted by a loud, repetitive noise. Tearing his eyes from his papers with great annoyance, the coroner glanced up to find before him an outstretched arm holding a tray of Oreo cookies. Instantly his eyes brightened, and a smile touched his stern face, even before looking up to discover he knew the bearer.

"Sheriff Lane!" Coroner Ames stood up, happily taking the offered cookie tray and pointing his guests to the chairs sitting in front of his desk. He'd already peeled back the plastic covering before they had sat down, a cookie in hand. "Hello, Phil! Is it one o'clock already?"

"Actually, it's a few minutes after. Sorry, we're late," Lane said, giving a glare of warning in Philip's direction. They had argued on the way over, debating on which shortcut to take to avoid traffic. Lane had made the wrong choice, and Philip was still being smug about it.

"Oh, that's alright." He popped a whole Oreo into his mouth and sat down. "I was just reviewing my preliminary notes on your climber." He picked up his papers and gave Lane an expectant look. "I suppose you'd like to take notes? Ready?"

"Ready." Lane had her faithful leather notepad and pen posed.

The thin coroner nodded and began to read.

"Time of death, by my best guess, was Thursday morning between nine and eleven. No weapon wounds to speak of. Little to no abrasions or deep bruising on her hands and face. In all honesty, there's not much to glean from the body. Now, if this was indeed an accidental fall..."

"Is that what it looks like to you?" Philip leaned in, grabbing an Oreo from the plastic carton.

"On the surface, I'd say yes. Falls are hard to determine as a general rule. It's difficult to tell if a tumble was on purpose or accidental. And it's extremely hard to determine if someone was actually pushed."

"So, no chance she was a jumper?" Philip separated the cookie in two and licked the white icing. Lane gave him a disapproving stare. He wasn't quite sure if it was from the jumper suggestion or the way he was eating the cookie. Probably both.

"It's not likely. The damage to her body was in the upper half. Her head, spine, rib cage. If she'd jumped off the cliff feet first, she'd have had extensive damage to her lower extremities. On the other hand, her fingernails were unbroken, so no evidence of her grabbing at the cliff wall or terrain on her way down." The coroner tilted his head towards Philip. "Which could be taken into consideration as support towards a jump." The coroner held his handwritten notes upright in front of him, giving them a good smack on the desk, before handing them to Lane. "But then again, she died of a heart attack before she'd even hit the ground."

"Did she have a heart condition?" Lane asked, surprised, browsing the coroner's notes.

"Heart was healthy. It's common in high fall victims to experience cardiac or aortic ruptures on the way down."

"Considering it was almost a six-hundred-foot drop. I guess that's not surprising," Philip ventured.

"And a blessing. Upon impact, her ribs shattered, piercing her lungs, along with breaking her spine and fracturing her skull. She would have suffered and bled out otherwise."

"So, nothing to indicate she was pushed versus simply falling from the cliff?" Lane handed the notes over to Philip to review.

"There was no alcohol in her system, and the toxicology test came back clean. She wasn't under the influence of anything which might have caused her to lose balance. Of course, that could be a point in either camp." He popped another cookie in his mouth and continued, "I was hoping that's where you two could help me. I heard both of you were there when she was found? Find any evidence leading to a possible suggestion of homicide?"

"We discovered two granola bars at the top of the cliff along with her belongings. Seems to indicate she wasn't alone." Philip looked up, placing the preliminary notes on the corner of the coroner's desk.

"But we also know she bought a box of granola bars, so she may have eaten both. We're having them tested for DNA." Lane smiled, apologetically as Philip looked at her in surprise.

"We also found multiple sets of footprints on the trail up, which also indicates she might have been followed." Philip turned back to the coroner.

"However, this was right before Labor Day weekend, I'm sure there were a lot of other climbers who might have simply been on the same trail for a while," Lane countered.

Philip's forehead wrinkled, and he shook his head, disagreeing.

"Not necessarily. Most Labor Day visitors are day campers or water bugs, as I call them. They're there for kayaking, whale watching, day fishing. That type of thing. Weekend climbers usually take the trails on the west side of The Mole Hill. More scenic views of the harbor and an easier, safer climb. The only real reason someone would take the east trail is if they wanted to see the mountain goats, and most people aren't really aware we even have them. It's not something we've advertised heavily for various reasons."

"Did you find any footprints on top of the cliff? Signs of a struggle?" The coroner managed to squeeze his question in before Lane could launch a counter comment.

"No. It's solid rock up there."

"And don't forget, you said the trampled ferns and moss you found could easily be explained away by mountain goats grazing," Lane tried to add casually, avoiding Philip's eyes.

Coroner Ames watched the two curiously.

"So, nothing that would prevent me from ruling this as an accidental death?" Coroner Ames directed his question to Lane. He sensed she was holding something back. He became sure of the fact when Philip bumped her arm, encouraging her to speak.

"She was a photographer...," Lane started.

Coroner Ames held up his hand and asked a question, "Could she have been taking a selfie and fallen?"

"We don't think so," Philip answered for her. The thin coroner shook his head slowly.

"Happened in Yosemite. Silly way to die." He made

some notes, quickly jotting down the new suggestion.

Lane continued, warning Philip to stay quiet until she finished talking.

"I found her camera a few feet away from the point of impact in the middle of a running creek."

"She dropped the camera?" the coroner asked, his eyes still on his paper, his other hand reaching for an Oreo.

"I don't believe—" her next words were interrupted by Philip's hurried explanation.

"Originally, we thought it had been flung from her hands, landing several feet away," Philip added stubbornly. Stumped as to why Lane was suddenly taking the accidental route. Lane spoke up, giving Philip a light elbow to the ribs.

"However, the camera was missing the memory card and there was blood on the neck strap."

"Interesting. The blood on the neck strap." The coroner looked up at her. "Go on, tell me. What you are thinking?"

Lane pursed her lips together and took a deep breath.

"I believe someone removed the camera from her dead body and took the memory card. They then took the camera away with them when they left the scene and ditched it."

"Why?" the coroner asked, not looking up from his new notes.

"Maybe she'd taken a picture of them?" Lane looked over at Philip. He nodded his head in encouragement, furrowing his brow for her to continue. "Trying to destroy any photos providing evidence of her not being alone?"

"No, why take the camera with them? Why not take only the memory card? Leave the camera with the body." The coroner looked up.

"Oh, well. Possibly they were concerned it had an internal memory, or they were having second thoughts about taking the camera. So, they decided to smash it against the rocks and leave it in the running water. Probably hoping it'd stay lost or be damaged beyond repair. Either way, it lends to the suggestion she wasn't alone."

"You think she was pushed?" The coroner leaned in, locking eyes with Lane and placing his arms on the desk over his notes.

"I do, sir," Lane answered honestly.

"I see." The coroner suddenly leaned back and stacked his notes again on the desk, taking a deep breath while looking at the two of them. "Well... Homicide it is then."

CHAPTER 15

"Eating on the ferry isn't exactly what I had in mind when I suggested you take me to lunch." Philip looked down at his meal of clam chowder and saltines with lackluster desire.

"I know, but I'm in a hurry to get back to my office." Lane gave an apologetic smile. "You'll like their chowder. It's better than you think."

Philip nodded he'd try and dipped his spoon into the thick soup giving it a speculative stir.

"So, now that you've got your murder investigation..." Philip gave her a small smile and then dropped it, remembering someone had to be murdered to make it so. "What are you going to do?"

"Well, for starters. We're going to have to find out as much about the victim as we can. Make appointments to interview her agent and the magazine who employed her. Then we'll head over to her apartment. Speak with her landlord and neighbors. See if we can get a feel for her life and if she knew she was in any kind of danger. We will even—"

"We?" Philip gave her a flat smile.

"Yes, we. What's wrong with—" Lane stopped, perplexed. Philip was moving his head in a slow negative shake.

"I'd love to help. But frankly, I can't. Today was an exception. I don't have the freedom to come and go to the mainland like you do. My job is on the island. IN the park. Not to mention I've already used all my vacation time I had stocked up with…with getting over what happened last time, and Kody, I can't leave him alone..."

"Phil..."

"I appreciate you wanting my help, and you don't have to say it. I know you could really use my insight here."

"Yes, but Phil..."

"Here's a thought!" Philip perked up, an idea suddenly popping into his head. "Maybe we could do the mainland interviews on my days off? Yeah! Think that would work? Then I don't have to worry about—"

"PHIL!" Lane gave him a wan smile. "When I said 'we'... meant, Deputy Pickens and I."

"Oh, yeah. Of course, you did." He chuckled, embarrassed. "That's why you have a deputy now, isn't it?" Philip said, feeling more disappointed than he could have imagined.

"It is," Lane said, with the same amount of disappointment Philip felt. She had a sinking feeling he would have been more help than Caleb on this investigation. "However, there is something you can assist me with. If you're still interested?" Lane cheered up, remembering she did need Philip's help on something. She suddenly gave him a wide, Cheshire Cat smile.

"Sure! I'll help where I can," Philip said earnestly.

"You mean that?" Lane looked at him seriously, her blue eyes skeptical.

"Yes!" Philip straightened his back. He wanted in on the investigation more than he had realized. Maybe he needed it? Maybe Lane wasn't the only person guilty of being bored?

"Good." Lane smiled again and then said in a hurried rush, "Because I need you to come with me to interview Sue Carter tomorrow morning."

"OH, no!" Philip started shaking his head, chuckling. "That's definitely a job for your deputy!"

"Please, Phil. I can't get Caleb anywhere near the woman, and let's be honest, he'd just be a distraction to her. Plus, she likes you! I mean, she likes you as in she likes you. Not as in she LIKES you... Though I know, she does LIKE you. She likes you like she likes everyone, on top of just plain liking you." Lane sighed looking exasperated. "Please. You're the only one who seems to be able to handle her without getting all flustered." She leaned towards Philip, her hands lying flat on the table in a pleading gesture. "I could really use your help, and I'm sure Sue would appreciate having you around when we talk about Janie." Lane suddenly smiled, tilting her head playfully and batting her eyelashes. "I just know she'd appreciate your big, buff shoulder to cry on."

Philip exhaled heavily, "What time?"

"I already told her we'd be there at eight tomorrow morning." Lane smiled coyly behind her spoon of chowder before taking a bite.

"Of course, you did." Philip's mouth quirked with predictable annoyance, signaling for her to hand over her soup crackers with a waving gesture.

Pleasantly pleased, she happily passed the pile of saltines.

CHAPTER 16

Kody, meeting them at the dock, gave Philip a ride back to the park, while Lane headed straight to the sheriff's office. She had a million and one things on her mental to-do list, the first being a heart-to-heart conversation with her young deputy.

Pulling into her parking spot, Lane admired the new building. The front door was dark glass, the hours listed clearly in white print with a sheriff's star etched at the base. Two benches lined the sidewalk on each side of the door, along with four large flower pots to add color. The building itself had the look of a cabin with stained pine paneling and dark green trim, a bright yellow sheriff star painted above the sign stating Rockfish Island Sheriff's Office. It fit well with the rest of the downtown motif, inviting and neighborhood friendly.

Stepping out of her truck, she was surprised to see Deputy Pickens at the front door to greet her.

"I'm glad you're back. There are some people here wanting to speak with you," he said in a low whisper and opened the door, ushering her in. Before Lane could ask, exactly, who he was referring to, Caleb quickly added, "They've been waiting for an hour."

As they walked into the entryway, Mr. Allister and his grandson Brent both stood up.

"Sheriff, may we have a moment of your time?" Mr. Allister asked politely, without much of a smile.

"Of course. Afternoon, Mr. Allister." Lane offered her hand to the lawyer and then to Brent, offering him a smile along with an "Afternoon." She then opened the waist-high swing door built into the front counter and walked through, indicating for them to follow. "Deputy Pickens, would you be so kind as to bring us some coffee and a soda or two?" Lane smiled at her guests and then led them past her office, heading towards the back of the building.

"We're not going to your office?" Mr. Allister asked, following Lane past her door to a small conference room further down the hall.

"More room in here," she said with a smile but mentally answered, "And this room has a security camera." She hadn't forgotten the scene in front of the ranger's station between Brent and his friends.

She couldn't help but wonder if Brent had come to confess something. "The chairs are more comfortable, as well," she added out loud and nodded for them to take a seat.

"Thank you. I know you weren't expecting us. We appreciate your time," Mr. Allister said diplomatically, pulling out a chair and indicating to his grandson to sit beside him. "We are hoping to be of some assistance to you and are here of our own volition."

Caleb entered with two sodas, three mugs, and the small carafe of coffee they kept upfront for visitors, placing them on the table. Brent leaned forward to grab a soda, only to be stopped short by his grandfather, who put a gentle hand on his arm and shook his head no. Lane arched an eyebrow at the exchange and then asked Caleb to shut the door. Her deputy complied, taking a seat with a curious, but serious expression. She smiled at that. Deputy Pickens had his game face on.

Lane followed suit and pulled her leather notepad out, placing it on the table.

"So, what would you like to tell me?" she started, her smile genuine as she clicked her pen and flipped open the notepad.

"Against my advice..." Mr. Allister gave his grandson a sour smile. "My client would like to inform you he may have been—"

"I WAS the last person to see Janie alive," Brent

blurted out, cutting off his grandfather mid-sentence. "She needed help getting up the mountain, up to the goats. She was so focused on taking pictures and not watching where she was stepping..." Brent's face turned red, visibly choking back emotions. Lane immediately sat up straighter, pulling her notepad closer.

"Are you saying you saw her fall?"

"Not at all!" Mr. Allister's voice boomed through the room at the same time as Brent started to say, "I did—"

Mr. Allister cleared his throat and continued on, giving his grandson a stern look.

"My client is simply trying to convey he believes he was the last person to see her alive. He has no direct knowledge as to what happened to Miss Engles or what exactly caused her demise. His assumption is she became distracted and lost her footing. When he left the young woman's presence, she was alive and well." Mr. Allister eyed his grandson and then leaned over to whisper in his ear, "Let me do the talking here, Brent."

"Is this true, Brent? You didn't actually see Janie fall?" Lane watched the young man, looking for signs of deception.

Brent looked at his grandfather before answering.

"No, ma'am. I didn't see her fall. When I left, she was sitting on the edge of the cliff taking pictures with her camera."

"What day was this?"

"Thursday morning," Mr. Allister answered for him.

"How did you come to be with Janie? Had you plans to meet?" Lane grabbed one of the sodas and cracked it opened, taking a sip. She decided it might be more profitable to create a laid back, non-interview vibe. She wanted the young man to be comfortable and the lawyer to lighten up.

"They did not have any prior plans," Mr. Allister answered again. "It was pure coincidence bumping into each other."

"What were you doing out in the park?" Lane kept her eyes on Brent, politely ignoring Mr. Allister.

"It's a public place," Mr. Allister said tartly. Lane gave him an even look and re-worded her question.

"Out of all the public places one can go on the island, what made you decide to go to the park?"

"Research," Brent answered quickly before his grandfather could reply.

"Research?" Lane repeated his answer in a dubious tone.

"Yes, Sheriff. Research. Brent has endeavored to start a climbing business. Guiding and tutoring beginner mountain climbers. He goes out almost every day to scout various routes up the mountain in an effort to discover new trails." Mr. Allister reached over and grabbed one of the coffee mugs, tilting the carafe to fill it. "He was beginning his morning climb when he became reacquainted with Miss Engles."

"Alright. And how did it come about that you ended up going with her on the trail to the goats?"

Brent looked to his grandfather, who motioned he could answer before he brought the coffee mug to his mouth.

"She said she was having a hard time finding them, and I pointed out she was on the wrong trail. She needed to be more east. I offered to take her."

"What trail was she on when you saw her?"

"Indian Flat. We cut over and headed for Shale Rock."

Lane nodded her head, recognizing the route Philip and she had followed the day before.

"What kind of mood was she in? Was she happy? Stressed? Depressed? Anxious?" Lane rattled off the various emotions.

"More frustrated than anything," Brent answered. "She was under a bit of a time crunch and was eager to get the photos to impress her new agent.

"New agent?" Lane emphasized the word "new."

Brent shrugged. "That's what she said. I don't know what happened to her old one."

"What else did you talk about?"

"Several things," Brent said, somewhat evasively.

"Such as?" Caleb broke in, asking the question in a surprisingly forceful manner.

Everyone in the room blinked and looked at the young deputy sitting by the door, his chair tilted back against the wall. They'd forgotten he was even in the room.

"Just catching up on old times," Brent said casually, looking over to his grandfather, avoiding Lane's eyes.

"Brent, I find it a little hard to believe on the anniversary of her sister's death, the two of you only made polite chit-chat the whole time." Lane tapped her fingers on the table. "Did her sister Danie happen to come up in your conversation?"

"Uh, sure."

"Who brought her up?"

"I did, I guess."

"How?"

Mr. Allister leaned forward, his elbows on the table eyeballing Lane.

"I assume, you're asking these questions simply to assess the mindset of the victim?" Mr. Allister leaned back into his chair heavily and folded his arms across his chest.

"Just so." Lane smiled, looking at Brent, expectant of an answer.

"She'd asked me to grab a couple of granola bars from her backpack. They'd fallen to the bottom. While I was digging around, I found a picture of her and Danie. I asked her about it." Lane perked up at his answer. They hadn't found a photograph in

Janie's backpack. She shot Caleb a quick questioning glance, and he nodded in the affirmative. He'd understood the unasked question.

"What happened next?" Lane asked lightly, not wanting to let on he'd given them something.

"I gave her my condolences again." Brent shrugged his shoulders, unconsciously signaling their conversation had ended.

"Did you remember to give the photo back?" Caleb asked, his voice not matching Lane's light tone.

"Well, yeah. I put it back in her bag. I wouldn't have taken it!" Brent's face flushed, almost embarrassed at the suggestion.

"And why didn't you climb down with her?" Lane looked at her deputy, warning him to let her do the talking.

"The conversation had died down, and she was busy taking pictures. I still had to get down the mountain, so I wouldn't be late for work."

"At what time would you say you met Janie on the trail to when you left her?"

"Um, I'd say, I bumped into her around seven in the morning. Started back down around ten? Maybe ten-thirty?" Brent shrugged his shoulders again. "That's just a guess, though. I made it to work on time. A little before one-thirty."

"And where do you work, Brent?" Lane asked, noting down the times.

"He works for me part-time at my law firm as a courier. Just till he gets his own business underway." Mr. Allister took another sip of coffee and smiled at his grandson.

"Brent, did you see anyone else on your way up or down The Mole Hill?" Lane offered him the un-opened soda can with a smile.

"He's not thirsty," Mr. Allister affirmed and leaned in towards the sheriff. "And if you want his DNA, you should just ask him nicely."

"So suspicious, Counselor." Lane gave the older man a slight smile. "But since you brought the subject up. How about it? Willing to give a DNA sample?"

"Not at this time," Mr. Allister said with a wolf-ish grin.

"That's what I thought you'd say," Lane said wryly and turned her attention back to Brent. "Back to my question. Did you see anyone?"

"You don't have to answer, Brent. If you don't want to," Mr. Allister advised his grandson. "We've already told them what you felt they should know."

Lane thought the lawyer's advice odd. Why shouldn't the young man want to answer that particular question? Had he seen someone else on The Mole Hill? A friend? A stranger? Or had he thought he was all alone, and now he was worried answering might call forward a witness to his deed?

"Brent, if you saw someone, you should tell us. It

could be crucial to our investigation." Lane gave him a serious frown, hoping to express the importance of his answer.

Brent looked down at his hands, mulling the question over. His grandfather put a supporting arm around his shoulders.

"Take your time, Brent."

Lane didn't like the hesitation. It didn't make sense. If he saw someone, why not tell them? Maybe the young man didn't understand how serious this was? In fact, why did he make it known he was with her? Unless he was trying to confirm their suspicions, reporting it as an accident? Or he knew his DNA was on the granola bar wrappers, and he needed to establish why he was there?

Lane smiled sweetly and tried again, changing tactics.

"So, no one saw you who could possibly confirm your alibi or backup your timeline for heading up or down the mountain?"

"Alibi?" Mr. Allister's face instantly turned serious. "Did you say, alibi?"

"Yes, Mr. Allister. I met with the coroner's office earlier today, and he's declared Janie's fall a homicide." Lane looked directly at Brent. "We are now investigating a murder."

Brent flinched at her words. Confusion, fear, guilt, and something else she couldn't quite put her

THE PUSH · A ROCKFISH ISLAND MYSTERY : II

finger on flickered across his face. Anger?

"On what basis did the coroner decide this was a homicide instead of an accident?" Mr. Allister asked, genuine curiosity lacing his voice.

"I can't disclose that information at this time," Lane said, honestly.

"I find that completely unacceptable!" Mr. Allister blustered. "We came here in good faith. You could at least extend to us the same courtesy."

"I'm sorry. I'm just not at liberty to do so at this time." Lane smiled smartly. "Besides, I had planned on speaking with Brent later today. So, this was actually quite fortuitous." She turned her eyes back to Brent. "I happened to notice an exchange between you and your friends, Lucas and Gabe? At the ranger's station yesterday?" Lane glanced back over to his grandfather.

"Brent seemed to want to have a word with Deputy Pickens here. However, he was greatly discouraged by your presence." She flipped over a page on her notepad. "You weren't wanting to confess to anything, were you, Brent?"

"Brent, don't answer that." Mr. Allister pushed the coffee mug back and faced his grandson. "This is exactly why I didn't want you to say anything. See how they are already twisting things?"

"Mr. Allister, with all due respect, it's a simple question."

"No, Sheriff. It's not simply a question. It's an allegation!" Mr. Allister fired back. Lane could see he was used to theatrics in the courtroom.

"If he doesn't want to answer, I have to ask myself, why? Is it because Brent didn't want anyone to see him?" Lane turned up the heat.

"We came here in hopes of helping you—," Mr. Allister started, his face reddening.

"It's an easy question." Lane leaned towards him, her face grave and her palms flat on the table. "Brent! Did anyone see you going up or down The Mole Hill?" Lane asked sternly, her eyes intent on his and giving the table a slam. She could do theatrics too.

"Don't answer that question!" Brent looked between the sheriff and his grandfather, trying to decide on what to say... or not to say. He shook his head, making up his mind.

"Yes, ma'am. I did."

"Damn it, boy!" Mr. Allister stood up. "What good am I to you, if you won't listen to me?"

"Sorry, Gramps." Brent looked to his grandfather, his face flushed with embarrassment and confusion. "I just want to be honest."

"Not saying anything isn't being dishonest, Brent. It's your right to not self-incriminate," Mr. Allister said sharply, shooting a hard look at Lane as he sat back down. "You don't know how things can get turned around and how quickly it can happen."

"No one is trying to entrap anybody here, Mr. Allister. We're only looking for an honest answer as to what happened to Janie. Isn't that what we all want? To find out what happened to Janie?" Lane decided to play on Brent's heartstrings. He appeared to be racked with guilt of some kind. One could assume it was the guilty conscious of a killer. On the other hand, it could just as easily be guilt from having been the last person to see Janie alive.

Brent stared at his hands, thinking the answer over, biting down on his lower lip in concentration. "I saw a couple of people."

"Who?" Lane was ready with her notepad.

"The first was Gabe Garent. But he'd never hurt her."

"Which way did he see you?" Deputy Pickens suddenly asked, dropping his chair back to the floor with a clunk. Everyone looked at the deputy mildly surprised.

"What?" Brent asked, not understanding the question.

"Which way did he see you? Going up or going down?" Caleb clarified, an official tone in his voice, his face a blank mask. Lane had to admit it was impressive.

"Up."

"And he was going which way?" Caleb asked, putting his hand up to halt anyone from interrupting.

"Down. He was going downhill. On his way out of the park."

"What time was this?" Lane asked, nodding to her deputy. He'd asked a good question.

"At the beginning of my climb. I'd say six-thirty a.m. Way before I saw Janie."

"Did you talk with Gabe?"

"For a minute or two, shooting the breeze."

"What was he doing out there?"

"Huckleberry picking."

"Huckleberry picking?" Lane raised an eyebrow of doubt.

"Sure! You can find them higher up this time of year and less likely to be eaten by the bears on The Mole Hill. He collects them for his grandma Betty. She makes jams and preserves with the berries. The town goes nuts for them at the farmer's market on Sundays," Brent explained with a smile.

"Do you think Janie saw Gabe?" Lane suddenly wondered.

"If she did, she didn't say anything."

"And was Janie happy to see you?" Caleb asked, seeming to know something Lane didn't.

Brent looked at Caleb, who was waiting for his answer, his face red.

"Listen, I never would have hurt her. I can tell that's what you're thinking. That I pushed her off the cliff?"

Caleb shrugged his shoulders, not admitting it

was exactly what he thought.

"And Gabe wouldn't either." Brent shook his head, turning back to Lane. "I don't know who would have. Honest."

"Who was the other person you saw?" Lane asked, waiting for the lawyer to advise Brent to stay quiet.

"Angie Bennett. She was on horseback. I don't think she saw me, though." Brent licked his lips, staring at the pop can again. Lane pushed it towards him only to have his grandfather push it back.

"Anyone else?" she asked, frowning at the lawyer before returning her eyes to Brent.

"Um... I don't know if this counts, but I saw Lucas Wilson's truck."

"Doesn't he drive a blue Chevy?" Caleb asked. "With the funny bumper sticker in the back window?"

"What does it say?" Lane asked curiously, looking over at Caleb.

"I stop for hot chicks and Big Foot."

Lane cracked a smile, then turned back to Brent. "You didn't actually see Lucas, correct?"

"Correct."

"What time was this?"

"When I pulled in, six in the morning. He was still parked there when I left to go to work."

"Any idea what he was doing in the park?"

Brent shook his head no. "He might have been with Gabe. I didn't think to ask when I saw him."

"Speaking of Gabe and Lucas. Can I ask why I didn't see you when we were searching for Janie? The other two were there." Lane flipped her notepad closed, indicating this was an off-the-record question.

"I was on the mainland running errands for the office. Gramps called me when he heard and let me know Janie was missing, so I rushed back. They'd already found her by the time I got to the park," Brent's voice was thick with emotion again.

"I understand you and Janie spent your summers together as kids, and I heard you were there when her sister Danie drowned. Could you tell me—," Lane was interrupted.

"Sheriff, I think we've taken enough of your time today." Mr. Allister gave a frosty smile while standing up, grabbing Brent's elbow, and pulling his grandson up with him.

"Well, I'd like to ask a few more questions if I may," Lane ventured, startled by the abrupt closing of the conversation.

"I'm sure you would, but we have to be going." Mr. Allister made for the door, waving Caleb out of his way.

"Well, then." Lane stood up herself. She knew the interview was over no matter how nicely she asked or rudely complained. "I appreciate you coming forward, Brent. This gives us a timeline to start with. And... I need to advise you to please not leave the island. We'd like you to be readily available for any questions which might arise." Lane offered her hand to Brent.

"We will take your request into consideration. Please give my client the courtesy of calling my office first before reaching out to him directly," Mr. Allister said formally, taking Lane's outstretched hand before Brent could. "Good day, Sheriff."

CHAPTER 17

"Are you doing okay?" Jerry Holmes reached over and took Lane's hand as she poked at her food with her fork. Lane looked up from her dinner plate, surprised at his touch.

"Oh, yeah. I'm fine." She smiled and squeezed his hand lightly before taking it back and placing it in her lap.

"You sure? You seem a little distracted." Jerry picked up his napkin, dabbing carefully at his curled mustaches.

"Yeah, I just have a lot on my mind," she said truthfully, her conversation with the Allisters still bouncing around in her head.

"I can imagine," he said warmly, his eyes sad. "I think we're all still thinking about Janie's death. Amy is especially taking it hard." Jerry started picking at the wrinkled label on his beer bottle. "As a dad, I hate seeing her in pain."

"She was good friends with Janie?" Lane knew the answer but was curious about Jerry's take on the friendship.

"Amy was much closer to Danie than she was Janie. But yes, she considered her a good friend."

"Did she get to see Janie at all before...?" She let the question hang in the air between them.

"No. That's partially what's bugging her. It's the shock of it all. Amy didn't even know Janie was back on the island." Jerry took a swig from his beer. "In fact, it was Harry who told her. I guess Janie stopped by Hattie's to buy a few things."

"Why do you think Janie didn't tell her?"

"Slipped her mind? Busy? Who knows?"

"You don't think they had a falling out?" Lane asked, pondering the question herself.

"I wouldn't have thought so..." Jerry's phone buzzed on the table, and he glanced at the caller ID before hitting the silent button. Lane noticed it read the name Heather. "But then, Amy can be difficult at times. I'm more apt to think Janie didn't realize or know Amy was living back on the island." He slipped the phone into his shirt pocket. "I believe the last time they talked was when Amy was still living in Seattle."

Lane knew Jerry's daughter had been somewhat estranged from him as he and her mother had gone through a messy divorce the year before. Amy had left the island to live with her mother in Seattle, but after starting to date Kody decided to move back. Now she was living with Jerry and working at Hattie's General until she could afford her own place.

"Janie lived in Seattle as well, though. They never got together for coffee or shopping?"

"Hmm... You'd have to ask Amy."

"Has..." Lane had to raise her voice over the loud chatter from the table behind them. "Has Amy ever talked to you about Danie's drowning?" She pushed her plate back and pulled her drink closer. "Expressed any doubts about what happened? Being she was there and all?"

"Doubts? No. But then, we weren't exactly on talking terms at the time. Things between my ex-wife and I were broken, and Amy and my line of communication kind of broke down with it. Why do you ask?" Jerry picked up the menu stuffed between the salt and pepper shakers. "Feel like a dessert? We've still got time before the movie."

Lane shrugged her shoulders to both questions. "Just curious. If you asked her now, do you think she'd—?"

"Why would I ask her?" Jerry continued to peruse the menu. "It was an accidental drowning. There's nothing to doubt."

"Well..." Lane leaned in so the table behind them

141

couldn't hear. "I'd heard talk it might not have been an accident." Lane knew that to be a lie, but she was fishing for a varying opinion. She was curious about what people really had been saying.

Jerry's head popped up from the menu in surprise.

"What?" His face darkened with a perplexed expression.

"Oh, it's only talk, Jerry. I'm sure there's nothing in it," Lane said dismissively, casually browsing the back of the menu. "How about splitting a banana split?"

"Uh, sure." Jerry waved at their waitress and then turned back to his dinner date. "People said that? Not an accident? That's strange. I don't know what would make someone say that."

Lane shrugged her shoulders as if to say, "Me either," and then added, "Jerry... Lane looked over her shoulder briefly before whispering, "The coroner ruled Janie's death a homicide today."

"Based off of what?" Jerry practically scoffed. "Gossip?"

"No. Mostly my recommendation," Lane admitted, suddenly feeling defensive. "I found a few odd things about her fall."

"Such as?" Jerry asked, his voice lowered to a strong hush, his eyes darting over Lane's shoulder to the table behind them.

"Well, her camera was—," Lane started and then stopped short, startled. "Are you okay?" She had watched Jerry cram the menu back between the salt and pepper shakers with more effort than necessary.

"I'm fine." He waved her on. "What about her camera?" Jerry prodded.

"No. You're not fine. What's the matter?" Lane shooed away the waitress approaching their table.

"I think you're making a whole something out of nothing," Jerry said through clenched teeth, giving the dismissed waitress an apologetic smile.

"How so?" She was surprised at his comment and more than a little offended.

"You've heard a rumor about Danie's death, and then, all of sudden you've decided Janie's been murdered! You've jumped to a terrible conclusion. I'm surprised at you."

"Surprised at me?" Lane's eyebrows arched as she leaned in and whispered, "Jerry, I haven't jumped to any conclusions. There are several indications..." She stopped at the incredulous look on his face and leaned back heavily in her chair, giving him a hard look. "I'm amazed you think I'm swayed that easily."

"I'm sorry, I didn't mean... Look, I just don't see how Danie's drowning has anything to do with Janie falling off a cliff," Jerry said firmly.

"I didn't say they did, Jerry." Lane looked at him, her eyes slit. "I didn't say they had anything to do with each other at all."

"Well, it was implied," Jerry said stubbornly.

"And it's all hearsay. That's what gets my goat."

"Who says it's all hearsay? Maybe, it's not?"

"You've got proof then?"

"Proof of what being done to who?" Lane pounced, curious to which death he was going to question.

"To Janie's fall," Jerry clarified, frustration in his voice. "What proof do you have it was not an accidental fall? You started to say something about a camera. Tell me."

"I... I can't," Lane lied stubbornly. She didn't feel like telling him anything anymore. "I can't share what proof I have. It's an open investigation, and I'm not at liberty to say yet. I'm sorry I even mentioned it." Jerry stared at Lane for a long minute, and then his stern face crumbled into a patient smile, somewhat obscured by his mustaches.

"No. I'm sorry." He busily straightened the napkin in his lap. "I shouldn't have asked. Especially if there is an open investigation."

"No. It's my fault," Lane said stiffly. "I never should have brought up the subject of Danie."

"No, no. I'm the one who got touchy about it." Jerry extended his hand across the table, palm up. He left it there until Lane placed her small hand in his. He held on and leaned in, asking gently, "Still want to split a banana split?"

CHAPTER 18

Philip scanned the sparse parking spots in front of Hattie's General and noticed Harry's brown beast of a pickup truck was conveniently absent. Secretly relieved, he decided this was as good a time as any to get his grocery shopping done. He had already put it off prior to the fight with Harry at the bowling alley, and now a few days later, he was down to a couple cans of soup and a packet of top ramen. But, most importantly, he was out of beer.

As he pulled open the door to Hattie's, the golden bell atop gave a welcoming chime. Philip briskly walked in, giving Amy the new cashier standing behind the counter a warm smile and a nod, before grabbing one of the small shopping baskets by the end of the front counter. He had started to head towards the beer case when he spotted Miss Hattie sleeping in her rocking chair. Philip slowed down, cautiously taking a look around. If Miss Hattie was still there, Harry was most likely as well.

"Harry in the back?" Philip whispered, doing his best not to wake the dozing Hattie.

Amy smiled and shook her head no, then whispered in return, "He had to run a short errand before heading home. I told him I'd keep an eye on her, so she wouldn't have to wait out in the truck in this heat."

Philip nodded his approval, giving her a grateful smile, then pointed towards the aisles. "I'm gonna do some quick shopping before Harry gets back."

"Better hurry. He left like five minutes ago," Amy said lightly, picking up the magazine she'd put down when he walked in.

After a quick trip up and down the various shopping aisles, Philip returned to the register, placing his overfilled basket on top of the counter, along with a full case of beer.

"Find everything, alright?" Amy asked, ringing him up while trying to keep an eye on the door.

"Think so." Philip pulled out his wallet. "How's your dad, Amy?" He leafed through his bills, pulling out two fifties. "Saw him the other day but didn't get a chance to actually visit."

"He's doing good. Spending a lot of time with the sheriff," Amy said, punching keys on the register. "She seems nice..."

"That is nice," Philip said distractedly, not really paying attention to her response. He'd noticed Hattie had woken up and was rubbing her eyes, looking around seemingly confused as to where she was. Philip nodded in Hattie's direction and said to Amy, "I'll be right back." He then laid some money on the counter for his purchases and walked over to the rocking chair.

"Evening, Miss Hattie." Philip stooped over the elderly lady, lightly putting his hand on her shoulder, giving it a gentle squeeze.

Hattie blinked up at him, hearing his voice above her. With some effort, she focused on his face and gave him a big smile.

"Phil!" She reached up and patted his hand. "Good to see you. Sit a spell and take a load off." She waved him towards the picnic table, inviting him to sit. Philip obeyed, cautiously glancing at the front door before taking the seat.

"How are you, Miss Hattie?"

"Well... I'm upright and on the right side of the dirt," Hattie said with a denture smile. She then leaned towards him and asked in a low hush, "How's your noggin'?"

"Sore, but thick as ever," Philip winced, a little embarrassed. "How's Harry?"

"Oh, he's fine. Other than he looks like a raccoon." She leaned back into her chair with a bemused smile. "Looks mighty funny."

"I'm sorry, Miss Hattie."

"You should be. Picking on my grandson like that." She shook her head. "Though I've been told, Harry had it comin'." Philip smiled, mentally agreeing. "Harry says our lady sheriff is moving out to your Uncle Chuck's cottage." Hattie rocked in her chair, sleepily closing her eyes. "She like the place?"

"She hasn't seen it yet. Probably will show it to her tomorrow."

"Oh! Think she'll like living there?"

"I don't see why not."

"Have you told her about..." Hattie leaned forward, her eyes blinking open.

"No. It's not come up yet."

"You should tell her." Hattie leaned back with a smile and closed her eyes sleepily again. "Some people might be opposed—"

"Don't worry, I will. She's got to decide if she likes the place first. No point telling her if she's not going to stay there," Philip said stiffly.

"Fine, fine." Hattie opened her eyes and gave Philip a wink. She rocked her chair a few more times and then said, "I heard about the fall in the park." She stopped rocking. "The girl should have known better."

"Should have known better?" Philip asked, confused by her statement.

"Sure. Silly to put herself in that kind of danger."

Hattie shook her head in annoyance and started rocking again. Philip realized she'd meant the mountain goats.

"Oh, I don't think she was in any real danger. The goats up there will usually leave you alone if you discourage them with a few thrown rocks," Philip said lightly and then looked over at Amy, who signaled she'd put his change in the grocery bag. He waved his thanks. "She was safe enough. That reminds me though, I heard Janie visited with you here the other day."

"No... no, I don't think so." Hattie pulled a tissue from under her wristwatch band and dabbed her runny blue eyes.

"When she came in to buy some groceries? Right before Labor Day weekend?" Philip prompted, trying to joggle the old woman's memory.

"Danie visited the week before Labor Day," Hattie said firmly, shaking her head, her white brows knitted together.

Philip smiled affectionately at Hattie, lightly shaking his head.

"Miss Hattie, you've got the girls confused. You were visiting with Janie. Danie died last year. She drowned, remember?" Philip took a fleeting glance towards the door and the empty parking spaces upfront. He decided he better get a move on. Hattie's cherub face scrunched up into an annoyed grimace and she tucked her tissue back under her wristband.

"Danie... Janie... same girl." Philip sighed heavily and decided not to correct her. With Hattie turning a hundred and three in a month, she was bound to be muddled in her memory, and the girls were easy to confuse.

"Well..." Philip lightly slapped his thighs as he stood up from the picnic table and walked over, giving Hattie a light peck on her rosy wrinkled cheek. "I better get going. You have a nice night, Miss Hattie."

Hattie's brow cleared. and she beamed up at him, nodding her head good-bye.

"I'll tell Harry you asked about him."

CHAPTER 19

"How close to the coast is your uncle's place again?" Lane was watching the sea and shore through the trees as Philip drove them to Sue Carter's house. They'd taken his truck this time after he complained she always did all the driving.

"It's close to North Point," Philip answered, slowing down to let a hurried killdeer cross the road on its little stilted legs.

"Oooooo... on the fancy part of the island." Lane smiled, tilting her head side to side in a la-di-da fashion.

"Well, as fancy as we get. Sue lives just down the road from his place." Philip sped up. "We've got time to stop and see the cottage before our meeting or we can see Sue first, and then the place, if you want?"

"Cottage first," Lane said, with no hesitation. "Will your uncle be there?"

"No. He's already moved out."

"No one is watching the cottage?" Lane looked away from the window and over at Philip.

"People tend to steer clear of the place." Philip cleared his throat. Lane frowned at his words and what she took to be a nervous gesture.

"Why?" she asked curiously, twisting in her seat.

Instead of answering, Philip turned down a nicely paved road leading up a steady incline, which quickly turned into a lane.

"So, what do you think?" Philip nodded towards the windshield.

At the end of the lane, against a beautiful backdrop of ocean and a miniature Seattle in the distance, stood a white cottage surrounded by trees and tall grasses bordering a well-manicured lawn. It had a red metal roof that stood out bright against its white exterior and ivy-covered windows.

"It's... it's..." Lane was a little lost for words. "It's adorable!" She quickly looked over at him. "What's the catch?"

"There's no catch." Philip stopped the truck a few feet away from the back door.

"Oh, yes, there is. You're acting funny. This place is gorgeous AND dirt cheap." Lane gave him an analyzing stare. "What are you hiding?"

Philip opened his door and started to climb out.

"Would you like to look around, or should we just skip it?" Lane pursed her lips together and opened her door, jumping out as well.

Together they walked to the backdoor, where Philip grabbed a blue hatted gnome from the flower garden next to the stairs and picked up the house key lying underneath it.

"Top notch security, I see," Lane teased, reaching down to straighten the toppled gnome he'd sloppily put back.

"Small town honesty," Philip countered. "Plus, a built-in security system."

Turning the deadbolt, he opened the top section of the white dutch door and leaned in, punching a code into a small box mounted inside by the door jamb. There was a loud beep and Philip pushed the bottom part of the door inward gesturing for Lane to go in first. They walked into a warm and cozy, yet modernized kitchen.

"It's been recently updated with all new appliances," Philip pointed out, as Lane made a straight bee-line to the huge stainless-steel refrigerator, taking a quick peek inside. "Keep going. There's more." He shut the refrigerator door on her and prompted her forward. "It's also partially furnished. What you don't like, he'll put in storage."

"Wow," Lane said, more to herself than Philip,

stepping into the small dining room.

A round table, adorned with a pretty lace tablecloth, was placed in the middle of the room. Shadowed by a large hutch, standing up against the wall. Lane absent-mindedly straightened the chairs around the table as Philip headed through the archway into the living room.

"I told you it was nice." Philip smiled, pointing to a large stone fireplace set between two large windows. Lane, coming up behind him, pulled a white sheet off the chair facing the fireplace and sat herself down.

"This place is more than nice, Phil." She put her booted foot up on the sheet-covered ottoman and snuggled back into the leather chair. "Where is the bedroom?"

"There's one downstairs and a guest room upstairs."

"There's an upstairs?" She sat up, springing from the chair.

"Yeah, and what they call a sunroom. Here, I'll show you."

Lane quickly followed, noticing there was a small entryway leading to the windowed front door and screened porch with the upstairs directly behind them. At the base of the front door was a small doggy door. She guessed Philip's uncle must have had a cat or small dog, and she suddenly warmed to the idea herself.

It might be nice to have a cat. One that could

come and go as it pleased. Then she wouldn't have to worry about feeling guilty if she worked late at night, yet, would have a little company when she was home.

Lane walked past the door and popped her head into the open room at the base of the stairs finding a stark bedroom. Its windows were covered with ivory lace drapings, so the view was only lightly obscured. Light and airy, it had a decent closet. Not a walk in... but she couldn't have everything. All in all, it was a heck of a lot bigger than the broom closet she'd been living with.

"Up here." Philip was already halfway up the stairs and had stopped, waiting for Lane to join him. She grabbed the wooden banister, running her hand along the polished wood, slowly making her way up. She stumbled on her way up, daydreaming of possible names for her maybe future cat.

Reaching the top, there was a low-ceiling bedroom on the right side of the stairwell. On the left side, taking up the rest of the floor, was the sunroom.

"This is my favorite part of the house." Philip walked into the room and took a deep breath. "Look at this view." The sunroom, aptly named because the walls were all windows, provided them with a glorious view of the island and the sea ahead.

"Your uncle only wants five hundred a month for this place? He could get ten times that for this cottage... and that..." She pointed out the window... "That view."

"Already told you. He doesn't need the money. He's loaded."

"Why don't you take it then?" Lane's smile widened, watching a ferry trek across the waves of the sound. She looked back at him. "You know? I've never even been to your house." Philip shrugged his shoulders.

"I like my place, and you need one. I'm fine where I'm at."

"What's the catch?"

Philip looked down at her with a confused and guilty smile.

"What?"

"Don't you WHAT me, Ranger. There's a catch. What's wrong with this place?"

"Absolutely nothing." Philip turned around and headed for the stairs.

"It's haunted," Lane said firmly and then added, "Is it haunted? Please tell me it's not haunted." Philip laughed, turning around with a large smile.

"Don't tell me you believe in ghosts!"

"I didn't say that! I just... Is it haunted?"

"Lane, if you don't like the place, my uncle can find someone else." Philip started down the stairs, hiding his amusement.

"No! I'll take it! Just tell me it's not haunted."

Lane quickly followed after him, taking another quick look at the view before following him down.

"It's not haunted." Philip shook his head, chuckling as he ran his hand down the banister.

"I don't think you're telling me everything."

"You're paranoid."

Lane stopped mid-way down the stairs.

"Phil, would your uncle be okay if I got a cat?"

Reaching the bottom of the steps he turned and gave Lane a pleased smile.

"You thinking about getting a cat now?"

"Thinking about it. Do you think he'd allow it?"

Philip's smile got even wider but he didn't seem to hear her question. Instead, he said, "You can move in as soon as you like."

"I'll do it this weekend. Wanna help me move?" Lane gave him a hopeful smile.

"What time is it?" Philip dodged the question.

She glanced at her watch. "Five til eight."

"Let's get going then." He tossed her the house key and smiled. "You told Sue eight sharp, remember?"

CHAPTER 20

"Here, Sheriff. Why don't you sit here?" Sue led them through an elegant hallway into a vast living room, motioning for Lane to take the wingback chair facing the Chesterfield leather couch. Her little Pekinese, Sweetums, followed closely behind, continuously barking at their heels.

"Thank you, Mrs. Carter," Lane said, taking her appointed chair and giving the little dog, a light pat on the head, once seated. "I appreciate you talking with me today. I'd like to once again extend my condolences."

"That's kind of you, Sheriff," Sue said over her shoulder, walking to a side table. "Thank you." She picked up a large antique silver platter, it overloaded with an abundance of morning pastries and dainty teacups.

It was easy to see Sue was in the habit of keeping all the good pieces from her antique shop for herself. As the house was decoratively filled with beautiful furniture, rich artwork, and expensive trinkets.

Setting the silver platter down on the coffee table next to a beautiful teapot, Sue glanced at Philip, who had stationed himself by the fireplace admiring the large painting hanging above it.

"Phil, come have some tea." Sue sat down on the leather couch and smiled welcomingly. "I saved you a seat."

Philip, turning from the painting, found Sue tenderly patting the cushion next to her.

"Are those cream cheese danishes?" Philip spotted the silver platter and eagerly made his way over, taking the reserved seat by their hostess.

"How are you holding up, Mrs. Carter?" Lane took the offered cup and saucer, making sure to set them down carefully on the table so as not to spill over the edge.

"Sheriff, please," Sue tsked, handing Lane a napkin before passing a small plate topped with a miniature poppy seed muffin. "You can call me Sue. Everyone does."

"Thank you, Sue." Lane's smile warmed, gently placing the small plate beside the teacup. "You seem to be doing well?"

"Ohhh, depends on the time of day." Sue smiled

weakly, taking a delicate sip from her own tiny cup. "One moment I'm fine, the next, I'm a wreck." She put the cup down and looped her arm through Philip's. "It's so hard going through something like this alone." She looked up at him, sighing heavily, leaning up against his arm. "Makes me miss my Henry so much." Philip politely patted her hand, which was tightly wrapped around his bi-cep, and went back to eating his danish.

"I can imagine," Lane hesitated, feeling guilty. "I don't mean to add to your sorrow, Sue. However, ...I need to inform you that the sheriff's office is investigating Janie's death as a homicide." She paused, waiting for Sue to finish picking up her cup before looking the older woman in the eye. "We don't think it was an accidental fall after all. We believe she was pushed."

Sue's cup clattered shakily against the saucer as she lowered it back down to the coffee table.

"She... she was pushed?"

"Yes. There's no indication she jumped or slipped off the cliff."

"But that's... that's terrible. Pushed? Why would...," Sue's voice trailed off as she fought her emotions, blinking back tears. Philip quickly licked sticky danish off his fingers and put a reassuring arm around Sue's shoulder, pulling her close to his side in a hug.

"I know it must be a shock." Lane leaned forward, awkwardly patting Sue's knee in an offer of comfort, and rushed to ask her next question, "Can you think of anyone who would want to harm Janie?" Sue looked up at Philip, giving him a polite smile and a light tap on the knee, silently asking him to release her.

"No. I mean, occasionally mad at her? Sure. Didn't like her? A few people. Hated her enough to kill? I can't think of a soul." Sue shook her head in disbelief.

"I always thought both girls were very popular?" Philip asked conversationally, picking up another pastry from the platter. Sue's Pekinese promptly settled himself by his feet, hopeful for a crumb or two to fall.

"Oh, they were! It was mostly petty jealousies. It's sort of a family curse." Sue attempted to look bashful and continued, "The girls were very pretty... and Janie, well... she was a lot like me. More comfortable amongst the men than the women." Sue picked up her teacup, the shock having passed. "The local girls were always gossiping, saying Janie was trying to take their boyfriends, and in all fairness, she may have once or twice. But when she went home in the fall, the couples would always get back together. It was just harmless flirting."

"Do you know who may still have held a grudge?" Lane didn't think a small summertime fling was serious enough to toss someone over a cliff, but she needed to follow every lead.

"Stacy Jensen and her were rivals each summer."

162

Sue shook her head sadly. "But well, Stacy couldn't have done it." She took another quick sip and then frowned in consideration. "Last year she and Angie Bennett bumped heads a bit over Kevin Givens. Though I know for a fact, Janie wasn't interested in Kevin. She was always serious about Brent Allister."

"Wait, Janie and Brent dated?" Lane asked surprised, taking out her notepad in a hurry. That was important information Brent, possibly at the advice of his grandfather, had failed to mention. "How long were they together?" Lane started scribbling on the paper, idly trying to get her pen to work.

"Oh, I'd say the last two or three years? Once Janie turned twenty-one, they'd matured into a couple and found themselves in a long-distance relationship. Up till last summer, she was bouncing back and forth from Pennsylvania and here. In fact, he's why she took an apartment over in Seattle, so she'd have a place to stay when she came to visit."

"Seattle? Why didn't she stay with you on the island?" Lane asked, now furiously trying to get her pen to work.

"Really, Sheriff." Sue gave Lane a condescending look. "I'm sure they wanted to be... alone."

"Oh. Well, then how did Janie afford an apartment and the airline tickets to come back and forth?"

Philip reached over and took a pen out of his shirt pocket, lightly tossing it to Lane. She was still

163

struggling to get hers to write.

"Both girls had a trust fund and came into their money at the age of twenty-one. Their parents were well off, not to mention, my Henry left them a nice sum when he passed. Bless his heart. They were my nieces, not his. But we never had children, and we always felt like the girls were ours." Sue looked over at a picture frame sitting on the fireplace mantle. It held a photo of a handsome, silver-haired man, who Lane surmised was Henry. Sue's eyes watered again, and she quickly blinked them dry, giving Philip's knee a squeeze.

"But Janie still had a job? She was a freelance photographer, correct?" Lane took a sip from the delicate antique cup, her hand lightly shaking as she returned it to its dainty saucer. For all she knew, it was a few hundred years old, and valued at ten times more than her annual salary.

"It was a hobby, really. That's not to say she wasn't good at it or didn't take it seriously. She was a very talented young lady. Enjoyed all the travel and activity of it. Excellent eye."

"Deputy Pickens said you were surprised when Janie showed up on your door?"

"Yes!" Sue's smile turned practically carnivorous. "By the way, how is dark and handsome Deputy Pickens? He wasn't able to come today?"

"He's quite well and very, very busy." Lane hurried on, "So, you weren't expecting her?"

"No! Not at all! There was a knock on my front door, and there she was! Asked if she could stay with me till Friday at the latest. I, of course, told her yes, but that I was flying to Europe the next day."

"Sue, we found a backpack with Janie, but it didn't hold her daily clothes. Like underwear, socks, toiletries. Things she would need if she was going to stay a few days. Did she leave any bags behind?"

"No. When I got home, there was a load of her clothes still in the dryer. I folded them and put them in the guestroom for her next visit. As far as cosmetics, she didn't need to wear make-up. Natural beauty. And for hygiene, I keep plenty of extra toothbrushes and such in the guest bathroom. I so enjoy having guests spend the night."

Philip cracked a goofy smile and raised his eyebrows up and down at Lane, taking a big bite of danish.

Ignoring his antics, Lane made a quick mark across her notepad, scratching the question off her list.

"Was Janie upset when you told her you were leaving?" Lane asked, decidedly changing the subject.

"Disappointed, but not upset. Still, we had a very nice dinner at The Royal Fork and then said our good-bye's in the morning. When I came home, everything was in its place, and the house key in the hiding spot like it should be. I'd thought she'd gone back to Seattle..." Sue's voice dwindled into a sniffle.

"I'm sorry." She grabbed a tissue from the box on the table, clutching it in her hand.

"When you went to dinner, did anyone stop at your table? Did Janie see anyone she knew?" Lane leaned forward, pen at the ready.

Sue dabbed at her eyes and tilted her head to the side in thought. "It was pretty slow for a Wednesday night, and it was an early dinner. Pretty much had the whole place to ourselves. There was our waitress, Lacey. Oh, and she did have a short conversation with Kevin Givens. He's a cook in the back... and then, Doctor Hadley and his wife were at the table next to us. That's all I can remember."

"How did Janie get around town? Did she borrow your car?" Lane suddenly wondered, a sinking feeling of regret hitting her stomach. Maybe she should have put a call into Rowles's Towing company already? She hated making the same mistake twice. "I told her she could, though my car was parked in the garage when I came home." Sue turned to Philip and offered, "Another danish?"

"Did she mention if she was getting a ride to the park?"

"No. Not that I can remember. We were trying to fit a whole year of visiting into one dinner. I had to take the five o'clock ferry to be at the airport by seven in the morning, so we called it an early night after dinner."

"Do you know why Janie was being so secretive about her visit?" Lane noted Philip had loaded his plate up with two more danishes. Sue's Pekinese watching his every move.

"Secretive? I wouldn't use that word, Sheriff. I think it was just a last-minute assignment. I'm sure she visited with her friends the next day," Sue admonished lightly.

"And who do you think she called?"

"Well, Brent. Though they'd had a bit of a falling out after... and um," Sue hurried on, starting to tear up again. "She most likely would have reached out to Amy Holmes or Gabe Garent. Possibly Lucas Wilson."

"Why, possibly, Lucas?" Lane was intrigued by the slight separation.

"Well, Danie and Lucas were dating when she drowned." Sue added in a confidential tone, "Though, I don't think it would have ultimately worked between them." She took a dainty sip of tea. "And it might have been difficult for Lucas to see Janie. You know, looking so much like her sister." Sue sighed, shaking her head. "I can't believe both of them are gone."

"Did Danie also have an apartment over in Seattle?" Lane was suddenly curious. "Or did the two share an apartment?"

"No." Sue shook her head. "Danie loved living in Pennsylvania. In fact, she was planning on going to

167

the University of Pennsylvania that fall. She wanted to major in fine arts."

"So, the girls were sort of going their separate ways? Did they still seem close?" Lane asked, picking at the top of her breakfast muffin.

"As two peas in a pod." Sue smiled fondly. "Here, I'll show you." She patted Philip on the leg before getting up and making her way to a large antique credenza. She came back holding three thick photo albums, placing them on the coffee table. Philip reached over and moved the silver platter out of the way.

Settling back onto the couch, she flopped the top one open on her lap. "That's not to say they didn't bump heads from time to time. I mean, who doesn't fight with their sister? But overall, they were very tight. Even for being so different."

"Different, how?" Lane scooted to the edge of her chair, trying to see the photo album on Sue's lap as she flipped the pages, apparently looking for a particular photo.

"Oh, well. They were complete opposites. Janie was athletic, Danie was studious. Janie was outgoing, Danie was shy. Janie would rather hang with the boys and Danie... you get the idea." Sue stopped flipping pages and angled the album towards Lane, so she could see the page. Philip leaned over Sue's shoulder so he could see as well. "Just to give you an idea, here is a picture of Janie as a little girl. She had won her first swim meet. She was an excellent swimmer." She turned to Philip, her face close to his. "My sister used to send me pictures of them while they were in school over in Pennsylvania. She had Janie in swimming classes and Danie in tennis." Sue lightly patted the picture. "Danie was afraid of the water as a little girl."

Lane peered down at the album, spotting among the photos a polaroid of a dripping wet little girl in a red swimsuit. She was holding a gold medal, a big smile on her face. By the missing two front teeth, Lane guessed the girl was roughly seven years of age. Sue flipped two more pages and pointed at another picture of Janie, now in her late teens. She had a shapely figure, wearing a school blue swimsuit and a red swimming cap. Her smile was just as wide as she held her gold medal.

"How did she get into photography?" Lane smiled and nodded as Sue turned more pages.

"That was Danie's influence." Sue stopped and wiggled her fingers towards the large painting above the fireplace. "That painting was originally a photo Janie took. Danie painted an exact replica." She looked at the picture proudly. "Danie used to ask Janie to take a few pictures while hiking, so she'd have some views to reference when doing her paintings. Janie instead started dragging Danie with her on her hikes, and they'd take photos together. Danie would then in turn, drag Janie into the studio, teaching her art techniques. Janie decided to make a career of it. They were a good team."

"How did Janie deal with Danie's death?" Lane stood up, walking across to the fireplace for a closer look at the painting, resting her hand on the large mantle.

"Oh, she took it incredibly hard. Completely cut herself off from everyone, including myself. I'd offered to go back with her to Pennsylvania to clear out Danie's apartment, but she declined my offer. Poor thing did it all by herself." Sue inched over to make room for Sweetums on the couch. "And while she was back east, my youngest sister, her adopted mother, sadly lost her battle with cancer. I saw Janie at the funeral, of course. I had wondered if she was going to stay in Pennsylvania, but then a month later, she called to say she was back in Seattle. I like to think she came back to Washington to stay close to me."

"I'm sorry to hear about your sister," Lane said sincerely and walked back to her chair. "I can imagine losing both so close together was beyond heartbreaking."

"Now, I've lost Janie too." Sue suddenly looked tiny and very frail.

"Sue... It sounds as if the girls really enjoyed their time here on the island." Lane tapped the photo album, still sitting on Sue's lap, hoping to lighten the mood with better memories.

"Oh, they did! Henry and I looked forward to it every year as much as they did. We tried our best to make their summer vacations fun."

"I'm sure you did. So, who was the oldest?" Lane watched as Sue started flipping album pages again.

"Danie, I believe. But not by much." She suddenly let out a squeal, "OH! This was a good day!" Sue moved the scrapbook closer to Philip, pointing down at the photo. "Do you remember this?"

Philip tilted his head and chuckled. "They sure were covered head to toe in mud. The dog looks happy, though!"

"Excuse me. What do you mean, not by much?" Lane asked, straining to see the photo, wanting to be included.

Sue looked up at Lane with a vacant smile before returning to the album.

"Oh... by like, five minutes?"

"Five minutes? Are you saying the girls were twins?" Lane asked flabbergasted, bouncing back and forth between Sue and Philip, both looking at her in return with confused smiles.

"I thought you knew that?" Philip said, somewhat surprised, looking back down at the photo album, turning a page himself.

"No! Nobody mentioned it," Lane said in shocked annoyance.

"I'm sorry, Sheriff. I thought you knew." Sue tore back the cellophane cover and pulled a photo off the sticky surface of the page handing it over to Lane. "They were identical twins."

CHAPTER 21

"I don't see why you're mad at me," Philip complained as they climbed back into his truck, having said their good-byes to Sue.

"You don't?" Lane slammed the truck door and held up the photo Sue had leant her. It showed two twenty-something girls, arms wrapped around each other's shoulders, both smiling prettily for the camera. The only difference between them was one was wearing a yellow top and the other a red one. "How could you forget to tell me they were identical twins?" Lane asked with a huff, slapping the photo down on the dash to clip on her seat belt.

"To my defense, it's common knowledge."

"Common knowledge to who, Phil? To anyone whose lived their whole life on Rockfish Island?" Lane shook her head and rolled down the window, muttering something about small-town logic.

"Sorry-ee. If I'd known you didn't know, I would have told you. It's not like it was a capital secret." Philip maneuvered the truck down the hedged driveway. "What does it even matter?"

Lane bit her tongue, shooting Philip an annoyed look, grabbing the photo off the dash.

"They were very pretty girls," she said instead, in an attempt to cool her temper. "I noticed in the other photos Sue shared, one of them always seems to be wearing something red and the other yellow. Were those their favorite colors?"

Philip shrugged his shoulders. "I guess so." Reaching the end of the driveway, he looked both ways before pulling out onto the road. "Janie always wore red and Danie yellow. It was how you could tell them apart from a distance."

"Was it the only way?" Lane asked suddenly, bringing the photo up closer.

"Pretty much. From what I recall."

Lane gave him a skeptical frown, her blue eyes doubtful.

"So, same laugh? Same walk? Same gestures?" Lane prompted, slipping the photo carefully into her notepad.

"Yeah, I suppose. I never really paid any attention." Philip looked over at Lane. "What?"

"Identical twins are not THAT hard to tell apart...

typically. There's got to be some kind of attribute separating their identities. I mean, I went to school with twins. It was easy to tell them apart after you got to know them."

"Yeah. But you have to keep in mind, we only saw these girls a couple of months and a whole year in between. Each year they came back looking a little different. A little taller, different haircut, wearing make-up. They grew up between visits."

"Sure. I guess that makes sense."

"I personally only saw them off and on during the summer. Didn't spend any actual quality time with them. Was friendly with them, though. You know, kept an eye on them when they were in the park. Bumped into them downtown occasionally. Saw them at a few picnics and barbecues. They were nice girls. Polite, friendly, but they were playing with their friends. Enjoying their summer vacation."

"As they got older though..." Lane paused, trying to form her question. "You didn't notice more of a distinction between the two physically?"

"Well, um. They were both built... um..." Philip cleared his throat, "the same. Not that I ever looked at them in a sexual manner. They were just kids. But there was a point, where you couldn't help but notice the awkward and geeky girls of a few summers ago, had returned to the island looking much more..." Philip cleared his throat again and glanced out his side window, "mature."

Lane smirked at his explanation but understood what he was trying to convey.

Philip continued, "As they got older, Janie seemed more comfortable around the boys in a way Danie didn't. Not..." Philip scrunched up his face. "Not in a bad way. I don't want to give you the impression Janie was... uhh..."

"Loose?" Lane offered.

"I guess that's as good of a word as any," Philip agreed. "It was like Lucas had said. She was always hanging with the boys. Hiking, rock climbing, swimming, riding bikes through town. Where Danie was in the library reading, sitting with the girls over at Gelato Deli, or jumping the ferry to go shopping. That sort of thing."

"Did you think they were close?" Lane asked, giving Philip a questioning eyebrow.

"Very. Sure, I suppose they needed their time apart. But most of the time, they were inseparable."

"I wonder how Danie felt about Janie and Brent getting together?" Lane pondered out loud.

"That you'd have to ask Brent... or maybe, Amy Holmes would know? She and Danie were best friends."

"Pull over, Phil." Lane pointed to the side of the road.

"Something wrong? You not feeling good?" He

maneuvered the truck over and put it into park.

"Just need to stop and think for a second." Lane was still getting used to it only taking a few minutes to get anywhere on the island, and she had a few thoughts she wanted to work out before they got back to her office. She took out her notepad and flipped a few pages. "We need to make a suspect list."

"Oh, is that all." Philip rolled his eyes and turned off the engine. They were going to be there for a while.

"Who would have a motive to kill Janie?" Lane asked, writing down the words 'Suspect List' on the notepad. Before Philip could answer, she said slowly, "Brent... Allister" as she wrote down the name. "He admits to being the last person to see Janie alive, and according to Sue, is the ex-boyfriend. Maybe he wasn't happy about their breakup?" She peered over at Philip, seeing if he had a counterview. He usually did.

Philip made a face and shook his head.

"Brent's a good kid. I can't see him doing anything to hurt anybody."

"Uh-uh. Figured you'd say something like that." Lane wrote another name. "Sue Carter."

"Noooo. Sue?" Philip looked down at the notepad to make sure she'd really written the name. "She wasn't even in the country!"

"Ranger, I've told you before. You have to look at these things objectively. Sue said both girls had money. Now, let's assume, when Danie died, her money went to her sister. So, what happens to all of the money when Janie dies? Who's the next living relative? Could it be Sue? And as for her being out of the country? It could be a murder for hire."

"Wait a second. Sue didn't even know she was coming to the island," Philip said smugly, mentally racking up a point for his side.

"We only have Sue's word for that. She could be lying. Maybe she knew Janie was coming all along. When Janie arrives, Sue gives her a story about an emergency trip and encourages her to stay at the house anyway."

"Smarty pants." Philip mentally erased his point.

"Which leads me to the third suspect, her agent, Jim Evans. He's the one who reported her missing."

"You think he ferried to the island, hiked up the hill, and tossed her over? Then went back to the mainland, waited a few days, and called it in?" Philip was skeptical. But then, it could have been done.

"It's something I need to look into and cross off the list." She wrote his name down, then added, "Now, on to number four."

"Which is who?" Philip turned his head slightly, giving Lane a suspicious look out of the corner of his eye. "You better not say, me or Kody."

"A stranger," Lane said loudly, giving him an irritated look. "Either a random person who saw an opportunity to push someone off the cliff or someone who was hired to kill her. Admittedly, it's more likely to be a hired killer than some psycho. But as I've said before, I'm being—"

"Objective," Philip said it with her. "Next? If there is a next?"

"There is. Angie Bennett."

"Because Janie flirted with Kevin a couple of summers ago? That's a stretch. Kevin and Angie are still together. What's the motive there?"

"Phil, of all people, you should know how unbalanced a jealous woman can sometimes react." Lane gave him a level stare.

Philip grunted in return and looked out his window, silently agreeing.

"There's nothing to say the two weren't having an affair. May have been why she avoided the island?" Lane tapped her notepad and looked over at Philip with a slight grimace. "I've also written down Gabe Garent."

"Whatever in the world for?" He looked at her, truly surprised.

"Because he was in the park, the morning Brent met Janie on the trail."

"You said he was coming down as Brent was going up. Janie was still alive and well."

"According to Brent."

"No. According to the timeline of the coroner."

Lane shook her head. "I'm not disagreeing with the coroner. I'm questioning Brent's timeline. Until I confirm he was in the park during the time he says he was, then Gabe is just as capable of killing Janie as Brent."

"But why would Brent say he was the last person to be with Janie if he wasn't?"

Lane shrugged her shoulders. "How close are Brent and Gabe? Could he be covering for his buddy?" She wrote another name. "Oh, and there's Lucas Wilson."

"And why would Lucas want to hurt Janie?"

"No clue. But he was in the park. So, it puts him at the scene."

"How do you even sleep at night?" Philip asked, wowed by her cynicism.

"Not very well," Lane admitted. "Can you think of anyone else?"

Philip frowned in thought. Lane had already come up with seven suspects, maybe not all optimal, but seven all the same.

"How about someone from the mainland? Could they have followed her to the island?"

"So, a stranger to us, but not to Janie? I like the way you're thinking, Ranger."

Philip smiled, feeling a little proud.

"Anybody else?" she asked, continuing to write.

"Not that I can think of."

Lane flipped a page. "Okay, so now. Who could

have killed Danie?"

Philip shook his head sadly. "Lane, Danie's death was an accident. Not everything has to be a murder."

"Just... humor me, Phil." She gave him a pleading look. "There's Brent."

"He's the one who jumped in the water to save her!"

"But you said he had a head injury. Maybe it was from being scratched or pulled at."

"He hit his head on a rock when he dove into the water."

"That's an assumption."

Philip shook his head stubbornly.

"And then there's Gabe again."

"Gabe was giving her CPR!"

"After the fact. Possibly he had tried to kill her, then seeing she might be rescued, he had to save her. It would have looked odd not to do so."

"But why revive her, only to have her point the finger at him?"

"True." Lane shook her finger at him, nodding her head. "It would have been dangerous for him if he had succeeded." She made a checkmark by Gabe's name. "Angie?"

"I still don't remember her being there."

"Okay, we'll have to find out why she wasn't there or if she was even on the camping trip. Maybe she didn't go because of Janie and Kevin?"

"Brent and Janie seemed to be together by then.

Who's next?"

"Lucas. He has to stay on the list."

"Why?" Philip scoffed. "He was sweet on Danie. He was the last person who would have wanted to hurt her."

"Everyone seemed to be doing something when Danie walks off on her own. What if Danie arranged to meet someone at the point and made the excuse she was going to go for a swim? Maybe that person was Lucas?"

"He was with Janie!"

"So, he says. Janie's not around to confirm it now, is she?"

"I like your theory, don't like your person of theory. It fits, but not for Lucas."

"We'll agree to disagree for now. Then there is Sue. I still think murder for hire is the best solution. She picks off the first sister, waits a year, then picks off the next." Lane flipped her notepad closed and handed Philip back his pen. "We can head out now."

Philip stared at her for a moment in awe before starting the truck and pulling back onto the road.

"You really think Janie and Danie's deaths are connected?" He looked at her with a serious expression.

"I do."

"But their deaths were a year apart."

"By one day. I doubled checked. That's more than coincidence, Phil."

"Might be. Might not be." He pulled up to the sheriff's office, taking up three parking spots sideways.

"I know." Lane rolled up the window before grabbing the door handle and sliding over to climb out. She then paused, looking back towards Philip. "Phil…"

"Yeah?" Philip was grinning into the rearview mirror, checking for poppy seeds between his teeth.

"I have a project for you." Lane smiled, inching closer.

"What's that?" He studied Lane cautiously, suspicious of her sudden forgiving nature.

"Do you think you could find a way to talk to all of Danie and Janie's friends? Find out what they remember about the girl's relationships? Focusing on the day of Danie's drowning?" Lane asked, really curious if he could do it.

"Sure. But why would I do that."

"Because you're going to investigate Danie's death while I investigate Janie's."

Philip opened his mouth to protest.

"I know, it's only a hunch. Call it a sneaking suspicion or a cop's intuition. But it needs looking into."

"Why have me ask—"

"Because people talk to you, Phil. People like you, and frankly, I'll just scare them off. You'll be able to ask questions I couldn't. Not without raising an eyebrow or two." She punched him lightly in the arm. "Besides, I'll be doing the real investigating.

Heading over to the mainland, meeting with Janie's agent, going through her apartment. You're just nosing around a bit."

Philip's face was a mixture of irritation and amusement. He felt like the B squad.

"Might have to skip lunch to do it." Philip shot her a sideways glance.

"That's fine." Lane scooted to the door and grabbed the handle.

"Probably the majority of it after-hours."

"I know you'll find a way." She opened the door.

"Spend my entire day off—"

"You're the best!" Lane hopped out and turned back towards Philip, holding the door open.

"I guess, any real spare time I have..."

Lane sighed heavily.

"I'll pay you in beer. Happy?" She shut the truck door with a bit of a slam, pounding heavily on the side, signaling her goodbye.

Philip quickly rolled down the passenger window and hollered at Lane's retreating back, "I don't accept light beer!"

CHAPTER 22

"Caleb, mind stepping into my office?" Lane requested, walking through the sheriff's office main door to find Caleb watching TV on his phone.

"Sure," Caleb yawned, stretching his arms up in the air, cell phone still in hand. "I've got five more minutes on this episode. Be a few."

"NOW, Caleb!" Lane raised her voice, marching towards her office, not looking to see if he was following behind. By the sound of his chair lurching back and springing up, she knew he was. "Have a seat," she added, opening the door and grabbing her own chair. She spun it around, sat down, and leaned forward-facing Caleb, who seemed more annoyed than wide-eyed with fear as she was hoping. She frowned at him for a solid minute before starting.

"Caleb, I need to know something. Why are you in law enforcement?"

"To better serve and protect the people of Washington State and to uphold the Constitution and laws of the State of Washington and the United States—"

Lane shook her head, interrupting him.

"No, Caleb. Don't recite to me a mission statement. I want to know why YOU wanted to be in law enforcement."

"To stop bad people from doing bad things to good people," Caleb said, oversimplifying his answer this time around.

"You wanted to do some good in this world," Lane shortened it even more. "That's a great reason, Caleb. Why aren't you doing that?"

"What do you mean?" Caleb's brow crinkled in confusion. "I'm here every day and I—"

"That's my point, Caleb. You're just... here. You're not present, here." Lane reached over and lightly tapped him on the side of the head. "Or here." She moved her hand down to his heart. "I want to know how to change that."

Caleb pulled back from Lane's reach and looked down at his feet.

"Sheriff, may I be frank?"

Lane tensed and sat up straight, bracing herself. "Of course, Deputy."

He paused a moment longer, then blurted, "I hate it here."

Lane was almost relieved at his answer. That was something she could work with. An unwilling heart was something else.

"It's hard living on an island, even one so close to the mainland. It's isolated. Everyone knows your business. There's not much variety in our choices of stores, restaurants, ...people."

"I don't mind any of that." Caleb slouched in his chair. "Though it would be nice to have a Starbucks around here." He gave a half-smile.

"You're disappointed," Lane said with realization. "This post isn't what you thought it would be, and you're, what? Bored?"

"Out of my mind!" Caleb leaned back in his chair, throwing his head back in exasperation. "I mean, nobody does anything around here but argue over their stupid parking tickets. I thought..." Caleb shook his head. "I thought there would be more discord on a small island. You know, property wars! Illegal poaching! Maybe some drug smuggling up to Canada? That sort of thing."

"What made you think that?" Lane asked, surprised at his assumptions.

"You're kidding, right? When you got here, you had a murder to investigate right out of the gate!"

"Yeah, but..."

"I mean, it just fell in your lap. You even had a shootout! You were almost killed! That's pretty damn exciting." Caleb threw his hands up in the air as if to make his point. "I thought it would be more of that."

Lane looked down at her hands, suddenly remembering the thrill of the chase as she and Philip did their best to track down a murderer.

"Caleb, to use your words, that murder investigation didn't just fall into my lap. I had to follow the trail. I had to put in the footwork. Ask the hard questions. I had to go out and solve it. It didn't solve itself."

Caleb sighed and tossed his head side to side. "I know."

"Do you? We have a murder investigation needing to be solved sitting in your lap right now, and you don't seem even excited about it."

"That's because I'm stuck manning the office while you do all the investigating. What's there to be excited about?"

"Being part of a team. Caleb, I saw you come alive in the interrogation room. I need that Caleb all the time. I need your eyes open, ears perked, and your feet moving. Your input is invaluable."

Caleb half-smiled, realizing he was being given a pep talk. "Yes, Sheriff."

"You wanna be a part of this?"

"Yes, Sheriff."

"I need you to mean it."

"I mean it, Sheriff." And he did.

"Alright, then. Now, tell me. What's your opinion of Brent Allister?"

"I don't trust him," Caleb said firmly.

"Why is that?" Lane asked, curious to his answer.

"He was being evasive. Even though he was there about Janie, you could tell he didn't want to talk about her." Caleb grabbed the chair's arms, lifting himself into a better sitting position. "And why didn't he want to tell us who he saw on The Mole Hill? Or give us his DNA?"

"Caleb, you asked him an interesting question. If Janie had wanted to see him? What made you ask that?" Lane was seeing a spark, and she wanted to flame it.

"Amy mentioned Brent had complained to her about Janie avoiding him. Said he'd gone over to Seattle to see her a few times, and Janie refused to come to the door. Got me thinking, maybe he's sort of a stalker?" Caleb looked up at Lane and seeing an approving smile continued, "Maybe he was stalking her on the mountain, and when she got to the cliff, she had nowhere to go, and he pushed her. Would explain the guidebook being left behind on the trail?"

"That's a theory. But remember, I found a couple of granola bar wrappers."

Caleb shrugged his shoulders. "Maybe he was

hungry afterwards."

Lane smiled. Her deputy had a bulldog attitude. Which would be helpful if put on the right scent.

"Deputy, you and I are heading over to the mainland tomorrow."

"We are?" Caleb scooted to the edge of his chair, an eager tone in his voice, "What for?"

"We've got some people to interview and an apartment to catalog. So, don't be late, or you will be left behind manning the desk."

CHAPTER 23

"Mr. Evans?" Lane approached the middle-aged man sitting in a patio chair outside of Starbucks. He was wearing a Seattle Seahawks jersey, shorts, and sandals with socks. Exactly, what he said he'd be wearing over the phone.

"Yes. Hello, Sheriff Lane." Jim Evans stood up and nervously waved at Deputy Pickens, who walked past him, heading into the shop to order coffee. "Hello."

"May I?" Lane pulled out a chair from his table.

"Please." He extended his hand towards the opposite seat and sat himself down. "I hope you don't mind meeting here. I don't have what you would technically call an office. I work from home."

"This is fine." Lane smiled and gave Jim Evans a brief evaluating glance. He seemed nervous. His smile was slightly crooked, and he kept looking over at Caleb in a somewhat jittery manner. "Mr. Evans, I appreciate you taking the time to talk with me. I'm hoping you can give us some insight on Janie."

"I wish I'd reported her missing sooner," Jim bowed his head, his voice sounding sincere.

"It wouldn't have made a difference, Mr. Evans. Janie was killed on Thursday morning. Even if you'd called as soon as she didn't show up at the ferry dock Thursday evening, she was already deceased," she said the words in an effort to comfort his guilt. His expression seemed to say it only made him feel worse.

"It's my fault she even went to the island. I should have let her go to the Olympic National Park like she asked." He grabbed his coffee, but quickly put the cup down, standing up from his chair as Caleb returned to the table with two iced lattes.

"Janie didn't want to come to the Rockfish Island National Park?" Lane nodded her thanks and took the iced beverage handed to her, pushing a chair out with her foot for Caleb.

"Not really. It made more sense for her to go to the Olympic National Park. Especially since those are the goats they're removing. Of course, you know journalism. The reader doesn't know those goats aren't from the Olympic National Park unless you tell them." He gave a nervous chuckle and then stopped, seeing Caleb's stoic stare. "Anyway, the magazine is a non-profit and barely standing on its own two legs. They couldn't really afford hotel and rental car fees, so I mentioned Janie's aunt lived on the island. It's what got her the shoot. Her costs were way below the other photographers who were being considered."

"So, Janie didn't automatically have the job?" Lane took out her leather notepad and flipped it open.

"Well... Um, not exactly. See, I'm new at this whole agent thing." Jim fumbled his shorts pockets and pulled out a bent business card. "Janie was my first... um... person to represent."

"How did you meet Janie?" Caleb swished his iced coffee, rattling the ice cubes against the plastic cup before taking a sip.

"She was a referral." He smiled at Caleb and then looked back at Lane. "Actually, it was her old agent who referred her, Albert Gutierrez."

"Why were they parting ways?" Lane's pen hovered over the notepad, anxious for an answer. "Did they have a falling out?"

"Oh, no. Nothing like that." Jim shook his head. "Al is a good guy. He said Janie had experienced a great loss in the family and seemed to have lost her interest in the work. At least, the work he was offering."

"And what kind of work was that?"

"He offered her an assignment covering the Jackson Hole mountain guides for the Grand Tetons. It seemed right up her alley, according to Al. He said she turned it down flat. Then he got her a gig in Yosemite Park for El Capitan, covering the free climbers. She didn't want that one either. Al assumed she was still in mourning. She had recently lost a sister and then an aunt back east to cancer."

"So, Albert then hands her over to you?" Lane slipped his business card into her notepad.

"Just till she was ready to get back in the saddle. She was basically on loan. Al knew I was getting started as an agent. I've been in the magazine world for eons, and I have a lot of connections. I was a writer for several of those years and... well, the wife and I have three kids, and writing from home seems almost impossible at times. Decided I'd give this a try and do the occasional writing gig on the side."

"How did Janie feel about the switch?" Caleb shook his cup again, swooshing the coffee and ice together before taking a sip.

"Fine! She and I met once a month. She'd let me know she was still looking for low-key assignments. Stuff close to home, here in Seattle." Jim smiled nervously, watching as Caleb took a long pull off his drink. "I was able to find a few local assignments for her. She seemed happy."

"Except, she balked at the mountain goat assignment?" Lane shot Caleb an annoyed look as he shook his cup again, the ice rattling noisily against the half-empty cup.

"Not at the assignment itself. Just going to the island. She really wanted to go to the Olympic National Park." He took a quick sip of his coffee and managed an anxious smile. "Couldn't really blame her for arguing with me. The place is gorgeous, but I convinced her." Jim looked between the sheriff and deputy, waiting for the next question.

"How?" Caleb asked, seeing the man blanche at the simple question. "How did you convince her exactly?"

"Um... I told a little white lie. Said it would be a good angle for the magazine. Small community living with their loving animal neighbors." Jim looked over at Lane, hoping to find a sympathetic listener. "I knew the magazine wasn't going to go in that direction, but she didn't." Not even remotely finding a sympathetic glint in Lane's blue eyes, he looked back over at Caleb. "The girl needed to get back on the horse. She was losing her confidence." Still not finding it, he turned back to Lane, almost pleading, "I felt like a momma bird trying to push her baby bird out of the nest..." Jim's eyes grew to the size of quarters. "That didn't sound right. I didn't mean push! Not in the sense you might have thought I meant..."

"It's alright, Mr. Evans. We understood your meaning," Lane reassured, finally realizing why he seemed so skittish. He truly blamed himself for Janie's death and thought they might as well.

Something suddenly occurred to Lane.

"Mr. Evans, did you give Janie the impression if she didn't do this assignment, she might lose you as an agent?"

Jim's neck turned red, and he immediately looked down at his hands.

"I may have, but I thought it was for her own good."

"I see." Lane wondered if maybe Mr. Evans was paid to get Janie onto the island. That is, if he was part of a murder for hire plot. She quickly wrote the theory down.

Caleb took a long and noisy draw off his straw, shaking the cup again before setting it down on the table to give the nervous man a glare.

"For her own good, huh?" Caleb said dubiously, lightly shaking his head side to side.

"I feel terrible about it now," Jim added, dropping his chin to his chest and giving Caleb a sideways glance.

"Mr. Evans, when you realized Janie was missing..." Lane reached over and grabbed Caleb's cup before he could pick it up and shake it again. It was obvious to her, behind Caleb's stern poker face, her deputy was nervous. She moved the cup out of his reach. "Exactly what had you thought happened to her?"

"Um, not quite sure. My wife was more worried than I was, to be honest. She was the one who in-

sisted I give your office a call and report her missing. That's not to say I wasn't concerned about Janie.
Well, more annoyed than anything. My client wasn't
very happy to have her miss the deadline."

"So, what did your wife think happened?" Lane
closed her notepad and picked up her own drink.

"She watches a lot of those investigation shows
on that crime channel. She had all sorts of wild the-
ories." Jim started to relax, seeing Lane's notebook
was now closed. "Even thought maybe her crazy ex
had kidnapped her."

"Crazy ex?" Lane flipped open her notepad again
and leaned in. "Who's the crazy ex? Was his name
Brent Allister?"

"Oh! I don't know for sure. At least, I don't know
his name. Just a guy who used to have a crush on
her or dated her for a little while? She'd mentioned
it to my wife once over coffee at our house." He
looked over at Caleb, who had leaned in as well. "I...
uh, I can call my wife if you want me to?"

"We'd appreciate that, Mr. Evans." Lane smiled
and sat back as the man dug his cell phone out of his
shorts pocket.

CHAPTER 24

"Hi, Lacey. How's the baby?" Philip greeted the young waitress while taking a seat at the small table facing the front window.

"Precious as ever!" Lacey said cheerfully, pulling out a baby picture from her order pad. "She turns three months on Friday." She handed the picture to Philip, who made the appropriate oohs and ahhs.

"She sure is a cutie," Philip said warmly, handing her the picture back.

"Thanks." Lacey stared lovingly at the photo, an adoring smile on her lips.

"Sooo, is Kevin working today?" Philip asked casually, perusing the breakfast menu.

"Yeah. You want me to tell him you say, hi?" Lacey offered, tucking the photograph back between the bottom sheets of her order pad.

"Actually, if he's got a break coming up. Could you ask him to join me?" Philip put the menu back between the salt and pepper shakers. "And I think I'll have the Denver Omelette."

"With extra bacon on the side and sourdough toast," Lacey recited knowingly, writing the order down on her pad before Philip could finish. "The usual, then?"

"And a coffee."

"Sure thing. I'll tell Kevin to come out with your plate." Lacey tucked her pencil behind her ear and headed for the kitchen. Philip, sitting back in his chair, folded his hands in his lap and closed his eyes, contented to wait.

The Royal Fork, the town's only sit-down dining restaurant, wasn't extremely busy at the moment. It didn't start to get the mid-day rush until eleven, which is why Philip came in for a late breakfast. If he'd actually come in earlier, there was no way Kevin would have had time to come out and chat. In fact, Lacey was busy wiping down tables and placing the silverware with napkins out in anticipation of the lunchtime rush. It would be a little bit before he'd get his coffee.

It was ten minutes later when Philip looked up to find Kevin Givens standing above him, a plate of food in each hand. Kevin was almost as tall as Philip's six-four, with strawberry red hair and green eyes, a row of freckles running across his nose.

"Hey ya, Phil. Lacey said you wanted to see me?" He placed the large omelette down in front of Philip, with the extra bacon on the side, and a small plate of toast beside it.

"Sure did. Join me?" Philip nodded his head towards the empty chair and gave the young man a friendly smile. He then pushed his plate to the middle and offered Kevin his fork.

"Thanks, man." Kevin sat down and took the handed fork loosely, not sure what to do with it. "I'm not hungry."

"Shame. You're a great cook." Philip grabbed his spoon, using it to cut into his omelette. "You like working here?"

"It's alright. Why? You offering me a job?" Kevin chuckled and then looked over his shoulder to make sure Lacey wasn't eavesdropping. "Because I'd be interested."

Philip lowered his voice, taking Kevin's cue. "I hate to poach you from the restaurant and especially while you're working." Philip looked both ways and leaned in. "But we might have an opening come spring. Kody is going back to college after the winter quarter."

"Amy has mentioned it a few times. She's worried they're going to break up or some kind of nonsense, like that. At least, that's what Angie says. I don't listen half the time," Kevin said, honestly.

"With the spot opening up, I thought of you. But didn't know if you'd be interested after what happened last summer."

"Last summer? Oh, you mean with Danie." Kevin bowed his head. "Yeah, that was a rough day."

"You seemed to keep your head, though." Philip reached over and grabbed a slice of toast. "That's hard to do in a situation like that." He took a bite, chewing slowly, as he said, "I can't remember. Were you the one who found her?"

"Was I the one who... what?" Kevin leaned in, unable to understand Philip, who was talking with his mouth full.

Philip swallowed. "Found her floating."

"Oh. No, man. I heard someone yelling Danie was drowning."

"Who was yelling?" Philip picked up a piece of bacon.

"You know, I don't remember. Might have been Gabe?" Kevin shook his head, looking down at the checkered floor, trying to recall. "Yeah, I can't remember for sure."

"A lot happened that day. I'm sure it was a shock for you all. So, was it you who jumped into the water to save her?" Philip took another bite of toast.

"By the time I'd gotten there, Gabe was wading his way out, and Brent was racing from the woods, full board. The guy dove into the water with absolutely no hesitation. Hell, I hadn't even gotten my toes wet by the time he'd reached her."

"Good swimmer, huh?"

"Yeah, Brent's good at everything," Kevin admitted sourly and then perked up. "I was the one to give her CPR, though." His face fell a little as he continued, "Until Gabe got to shore, and then I took off looking for help and found you."

"Kid tried his hardest," Philip said sadly. "You all did."

Silence fell over the small table as Philip chewed on the last piece of toast.

"You know…" Philip scrunched up his face, trying to appear as if he was thinking. "I don't recall Angie being there. Was she with you guys that weekend?"

"Oh yeah, Ang was there." Kevin picked up a napkin he'd knocked off the table with his elbow. "She'd gone for a walk, basically blowing off steam. She and I had gotten into a fight about something dumb. She had heard the emergency sirens and started to make her way back to camp, only to find us tearing down our tents."

Philip decided to change the subject.

"Shame about Janie," Philip said sincerely before taking another bite of omelette.

Kevin, seeing Philip struggling with the spoon, offered his fork back.

"Yeah, heartbreaking, really."

"Did you know she was back on the island for a visit?"

"Saw her on a Monday night when I was getting off shift. She was having dinner with her aunt."

"You go over and say hi?" Philip tried to grab Lacey's attention with no luck. He was really wanting that coffee.

"Sure, of course. Hadn't seen her in almost a year. Told her Brent and I were getting together at Piper's Place later that night and invited her to come out."

"Did she?" Philip dropped his hand, his full attention back on Kevin.

"Nah. She politely blew it off. Something about her aunt leaving town and spending time with her before she left. She said she'd give Angie a call the next day and try to arrange lunch or something. She didn't, which hadn't surprised me."

"I always got the impression Angie and Janie didn't like each other," Philip lied. They always seemed to get along fine to him, but he was wondering about what Sue had said the day before.

"They didn't. Heck, they barely tolerated each other," Kevin said, with a grimace.

"Was that because of you?" He gave Kevin a crooked smile.

"Me?" Kevin sat back, surprised. "Ohhhh, because... I see what you're thinking." Kevin rubbed the back of his neck and smiled shyly. "You have to understand. All of us guys had a crush on one or both of the twins at some point." He started to fiddle with the napkin, folding it and then unfolding it. "If you wanted a girl to go do stuff with, like…" He shrugged, trying to think of an example. "Off-road jeeping or fishing off the cliffs. You'd call Janie. If you wanted someone to listen to your problems, be a shoulder to cry on, or watch a movie with, you called Danie. They were both special in their own way and both beautiful. I…" He suddenly looked bashful. "I was going through a Janie phase last summer. She wasn't interested, and I came back to my senses."

"And her and Angie didn't get along because of it?"

"No, that's what I was trying to explain. They didn't like each other because of money problems."

"Money problems?" Philip asked, surprised.

"Yup." Kevin nodded his head up and down. "It was a mess." He started folding and unfolding the napkin again. "You know how Ang is about her horses. Well, there was this horse she wanted to buy from a guy in Scottsdale, Arizona. Someone she knew through competitions was getting rid of his, and he was willing to give her a good deal. Believe me, she went on and on about it all the time. Drove me nuts."

"What kind of horse?"

"Arabian. But she didn't have anywhere near the money to buy it."

"How much was it?"

"Ten grand."

Philip let out a low whistle.

"That was just for the horse! She needed another five for getting the thing up here along with equipment and feed."

"And she asked Janie for a loan?" Philip guessed.

"No!" Kevin leaned in, grinning. "Janie offered to buy it for her!" He suddenly flopped back in his chair, slamming a hand down on the table for emphasis. "About knocked Ang off her saddle!"

"So, Janie just GAVE Angie fifteen grand?"

"It ended up being twenty after all was said and done... and no, she didn't just give it to her." Kevin's smile disappeared. "She'd changed her mind after talking with her trust fund lawyer back in Pennsylvania. Something about taxes? I don't know. Anyway, she'd shown up the next month in Seattle with the money and a form her lawyer wanted Angie to sign. I don't think Angie even read it. Just scribbled her name on the dotted line, grabbed the check, and made a mad dash for the phone to call the seller."

"I take it, this is where things started to go sour?" Philip pushed his empty plate away and noticed a few people coming through the door.

"Oh, did it. The horse ended up having tumors in its small intestine, and Ang was advised by the vet to put it down. Cost her every penny she had in the bank and a few of mine."

"So much so, she couldn't afford to pay Janie back?"

"At first, Janie seemed understanding. Then Angie got another horse. She didn't buy it, and it wasn't an Arabian. But it was something else she was spending money on instead of paying Janie back."

"Janie felt taken advantaged of?" Kevin nodded his head.

"Something like that. She had her lawyer threaten to take Angie to court."

"What did Angie do?" Philip could see Lacey was heading their way and knew he was running out of time.

"Started to sell off her horses to pay back the loan. She hated Janie for that." Kevin shook his head sadly. "She's only got a few horses left. Her last-three favorites." Kevin brightened, scrunching the napkin into a small ball and tossing it onto Philip's empty plate. "Now, she doesn't have to get rid of them or pay the loan back."

"Hey, Phil. Here's your coffee." Lacey placed the steaming mug down, and the rich aroma sang to Philip's senses. "Sorry, Kevin. I've got two tickets up and waiting. Need you behind the grill."

"We'll uh..." Kevin waited for Lacey to walk off. "We'll talk more about the job later?"

"For sure. On your day off, come down, and fill out an application." Philip gave him a brief nod and watched as Kevin returned to the kitchen.

CHAPTER 25

"Which one is Janie's car?" Lane asked, slightly out of breath, following Caleb through the entrance of the underground parking garage. They'd parked five blocks over and paid half an arm and a leg for a parking spot before hiking their way through the streets of Seattle to Janie's high-rise apartment building.

"Suppose to be sitting in spot E, one thirty-four." Caleb jostled the apartment keys and referred to the piece of scratch paper the main office had scribbled the parking lot number on. "Jeep Grand Cherokee Limited. White with black trim."

"We're on the wrong level. Let's take the elevator." Lane pointed to the shiny double doors with a large letter C printed on the outside, indicating their current location.

"Pretty nice building." Caleb stepped into the elevator and held the door for Lane before pushing "E" and leaning against the wall.

"Nice doesn't even begin to describe it," Lane acknowledged, noting she could see her own crystal-clear reflection in the elevator doors. "This place must cost a fortune."

"Twenty-five hundred a month, one bedroom."

"You're kidding me."

"Not one iota. I asked."

"So..." The elevator doors opened and they stepped out. "What did you think of the information Jim Evans told us?" Lane led the way.

"You mean, what his wife said about Janie having a stalker?"

"Sure. We can start there."

"She gave us a name. Not the name I was expecting."

"I'll say. I was all prepared to hear Brent or even, Kevin Givens." Lane slowed down, noticing the numbers were now in the hundreds. "Lucas Wilson was a total surprise."

"He was a friend of hers though, wasn't he?"

"He was. Part of the tight group she hung with." Lane sighed. "He was dating Danie when she died. Possibly Lucas started stalking Janie because she looked so much like her sister. Even Sue Carter mentioned Janie might not seek him out for a visit for that very reason."

"So, there could be something there."

"Could be." Lane stopped in front of space E134 and looked at the brand-new Grand Jeep Cherokee parked between the white lines. "Here it is." She walked over and cupped her face, peering inside the front passenger window. There was nothing suspicious to note, and all windows were intact. She tried the door handle, feeling the resistance of the lock. "Let's head up to the apartment."

"I think Mr. Evans makes a good suspect." Caleb started to lead the way back to the elevator.

"That he does. Though..." Lane paused in front of the doors and punched the button going up. "My gut says he's not our killer." The elevator suddenly chimed, and the doors opened.

"He's got a flimsy alibi." Caleb held the door for an elderly couple exiting, giving them a polite nod as they stepped off.

"Being at home with the wife and kids, who would more than likely lie on his behalf, can be considered flimsy. But..." Lane punched the button for the apartment level they needed. "It's easy enough to check on. Unless he's got his own personal boat to transverse the water, he'd have to take the ferry to get over to the island."

"Let me guess who gets to view hours of ferry footage," Caleb said, a pout heavy on the end of his sentence. The elevator doors opened, and they both stepped out. Lane pointed to their right and started down the hall.

"Gotta earn your stripes, Deputy." She stopped in front of a dark, solid mahogany door with a gold E134 emblem placed neatly in the middle. "I don't think Jim Evans pushed her off the cliff, but he did push her onto the island. You have to wonder if it really was for the innocent reason he gave."

Lane motioned for Caleb to hand her Janie's apartment key and gave the door a polite knock before putting it in the lock. "Let's see if we can find anything which might shed some light on Janie's personal life." She turned the knob and opened the door to a spacious and lavish apartment.

"Fancy schmancy." Caleb gave a low whistle and walked straight to the large window overlooking the city skyline.

At the moment, the heavens were a clear, beautiful blue with nary a cloud to be seen. The typical rain clouds haunting Seattle had apparently decided to wander off and shower over some other part of the state for a short while. It was days like this, Caleb realized, that the view was worth every penny paid. Lane walked up beside him, pulling back the drapes to look down at the street below and the cars parked nose to nose beside the sidewalk. A transit bus drove by, creating a dark plume of exhaust in its wake, leaving the black cloud to linger in the street. Lane's thoughts differed quite a bit from Caleb's.

"Here, you take the living room and I'll take the bedroom." Lane snapped on a pair of latex gloves and tossed an extra pair to Caleb. "Let me know if you find anything interesting. Especially a laptop or computer."

"Will do." Caleb caught the gloves and looked about the tidy apartment, trying to decide where to start. Lane pointed to a small writing desk against the wall, artfully placed in the corner.

"Why don't you start there?" Lane suggested and then headed down the narrow hallway leading to the rest of the apartment. She tried the first door and found a bathroom. Giving it a quick once over, she then walked further down the hall and found the only bedroom.

Opening the door wider, she noticed the bedspread was a golden yellow while the lampshades and the drapes were a deep red. The two colors blending well together and highlighting the beautiful gold and red painting hanging on the wall above the headboard. Scattered across the bedspread and on the floor were various items, mostly hiking or camping related, along with a large camera bag holding a multitude of photography equipment.

Sitting in the middle of the bed was an oversized red backpack left half-filled. It looked to Lane as if

Janie had struggled figuring out what to bring, sur-
mising the young woman had decided to pack light.
Most likely, not relishing the idea of lugging all her
gear up the mountain, on top of, wearing a heavy
camera strung around her neck.

Wandering closer to the bed, Lane took a mental
inventory of what was left behind. In doing so, she
stepped on a pair of yellow shoelaces left unstrung
and lying on the floor next to a very well-worn pair
of hiking boots. Next to the shoes was a pair of red
and yellow socks, a couple of white tank tops, and
a pair of black cargo shorts. Lane suddenly realized why Janie had washed her clothes at Sue's, the
girl simply having taken a limited wardrobe for the
three days.

On each side of the bed was a small nightstand.
Lane opened the little drawers finding nothing of interest besides a few magazines, a nail file, two hair
scrunchies, and a bible.

Standing in the corner of the room, next to the
window for lighting, was an art easel, a large canvas on display. Beside it was a small table with an ar-
ray of colored bottles and several little pots, sprout-
ing various paintbrushes, the jars aimlessly littering
the top. Alongside them, a smothered paint palette
covered in dry blotches of various blues, greens, and
browns had seemingly been tossed down, left for another day.

Lane lightly touched the painting. It didn't feel tacky. No one had been painting recently.

"Wonder if she decided to take up painting and give up photography?" Lane mused to herself, standing back in an effort to decipher the many swipes and daubs of color blended across the canvas. After a minute, Lane shrugged her shoulders and turned her back on the easel. There wasn't enough progress for her to even wonder if Janie would have been successful.

Next, she walked to the double-doored closet, swinging them open, and let out an appreciative sigh. Having basically lived out of a suitcase for the last six months, Lane marveled at the organized wealth of space the apartment closet possessed.

Her eyes scanned the clothes hanging on the wall, noting they were hung in order of the rainbow. Reds, then a small section of orange, followed by a larger section of yellow. This last section, she assumed, were clothes Janie had kept of Danie's. A few items of green and a large section of blue jeans and shorts followed. Lastly, whites and blacks.

Shoes were sectioned off the same way, the majority being either red heels or red sneakers, followed up by a litany of yellow-colored footwear.

Lane wondered what it had been like for Janie to go through Danie's stuff after she had died. Deciding what to keep and what to throw away. What to hold onto, to remember her sister by, and what to let go.

"Sheriff, I think I found something," Caleb's voice floated from the front of the apartment.

"On my way," Lane called back, taking one final longing look at the closet before turning off the light and closing the doors behind her. "Find her computer?"

"Yeah, but that's not it," Caleb's voice sounded excited. Lane picked up her pace.

"Oh? What then?"

"Might be nothing." Caleb held out a thin spiral notebook. "Looks as if someone was practicing writing Janie's signature."

"What?" Lane looked down at the notebook, analyzing it closely.

Written several times across the paper was the name Janielle A. Engles.

"This was laying on top of it." Caleb held a single leaf piece of paper, and Lane tilted her head to read it as he handed it over.

"Looks like a copy of her apartment application." Lane scrutinized the signature and the spiral notebook for comparison. "Yeah, they were trying to match her signature." Lane looked up at her deputy and then towards the desk. "Where did you find this?"

"It was laying on top. Out in the open." Caleb walked over to the desk, indicating where he'd found the items. "Think she was working on her penmanship?"

Lane shook her head, mulling the suggestion over.

"I'm more inclined to think someone gained access to her apartment after her death and was trying their hand at forgery. Possibly to cash checks or something. We need to call her bank and see if any large amounts of money have been withdrawn after she died. Better bag it. Might be able to lift fingerprints off the pages."

"Think it's one of the apartment staff?" Caleb took the plastic evidence bag handed to him. "Should we ask for an employee list?"

Lane frowned as she placed the paper and the notebook into the open bag Caleb held.

"No, I don't think so. They'd most likely would have made off with her TV or laptop... stereo. Stuff like that. Easy to pawn." Lane raised an eyebrow in thought. "But then, if it was the building staff, they weren't very smart to leave it out in the open like this."

"Maybe someone with a key to the place?" Caleb sealed the bag. "Think Brent Allister had a key to his ex-girlfriend's apartment?"

"Possibly. Though, she likely would have asked for it back."

"If she was smart."

"Something seems off. Eventually, this place will have to be packed and moved. Why leave it out to be found?" Lane pulled open a desk drawer revealing extra pens and blank papers. "Unless they planned on being the one to pack the place up?"

"Sue Carter?"

"That's who I'm thinking."

CHAPTER 26

Philip was completely intrigued by what he was seeing. For the last twenty minutes, Brent had been repetitively walking up and down beside the creek bed, his head bowed, scouring the ground at his feet. He had suddenly stopped and was now gazing up into the sky in a reflective manner.

Curious to what the young man was searching for, it had not missed Philip's attention, they were only a few feet away from where Janie's body had been found. Starting to feel a little guilty, Philip decided to make his presence known and walked out from behind the large girthed spruce he'd been hiding behind.

"I thought that was you," Philip said, with a friendly smile, doing his best to be disarming. "You lose something?"

At the sound of Philip's voice, Brent's head jerked down in surprise, and he took a tentative step back, his hands immediately going to his pockets, his face turning red.

Cautiously taking a few steps forward, Philip slowly approached the young man, sensing he was as spooked and flighty as a startled deer.

"Didn't lose your car keys, I hope?" Philip asked lightly, trying to give an easy-going smile with the question.

"No. Nothing like that." Brent, quickly regaining his composure, smiled weakly. Though Philip sensed he was slightly annoyed to have been interrupted. "How are you, Ranger Russell?"

"I'm good, Brent." Philip made his way across the small creek using the larger rocks to keep his boots from getting wet. "Sorry if I startled you. I know it's typically pretty solitary out here." Philip extended his hand out for a handshake.

"Oh, you didn't startle me," Brent fibbed, his face turning redder, taking Philip's hand in a hardy shake.

"What were you looking for?" Philip casually glanced around at the ground by their feet. Brent's smile, not as easygoing as Philip's, tightened.

"I'm not looking for anything. Why would you think that?"

Philip shook his head at the same time as he shrugged his shoulders. "If you don't want to tell me, Brent. You can just say it's none of my business." Brent's bluffed denial, which was nothing compared to his grandfather's grandstanding personality, dwindled.

"Sorry. Yeah, I am looking for something." He ran his hands through his hair, looking up at Philip with uncertainty. "I thought I might be able to find the missing memory card from Janie's camera."

"That so?" Philip's eyebrows shot upwards in surprise. That particular bit of information had not been made public. "How did you know the card was missing?"

"Deputy Pickens told me about it. Well, actually. He told Amy, and Amy told Lucas, who told Gabe, who told me," Brent clarified. "I thought if I could find the memory card, I could still get the pictures over to the magazine. She really wanted to get those shots to her agent."

"That the only reason?" Philip gave Brent a skeptical look while making a mental note to tell Lane about her deputy's loose lips.

"That's the main reason. But..." Brent dodged a bee as it buzzed by his face. "If I did happen to find the memory card, it could also prove Janie was alive when I left her. If the photos are time-stamped..." He lurched to the side, the bee buzzing by again. "My lawyer, you know my Gramps. He says it would be good for my alibi."

"Why do you need an alibi, Brent?" Philip took his hat off, waving away the bee, which seemed attracted to his shiny tie clip and forest ranger badge.

"Careful! Don't tick him off. I'm allergic to anything with a stinger." Brent took a cautious step back from the bee and Philip's waving arm.

"I hate to break it to you, Brent. But the woods might not be the safest place for you then."

"I know." Brent chuckled, patting his cargo pants thigh pocket. "I've always got my EpiPen on me, just in case."

Philip put his hat back on, the bee having buzzed off, and squinted down at Brent.

"So, you were saying?"

"Well, Gramps says it's just a matter of time before they bring charges against me. They've decided Janie's fall was a homicide. And since I was the last person to see her alive, they'll naturally suspect me." Brent swayed his head side to side, disgusted with the notion.

"Hope not." Philip pulled his hat down tighter. "Brent, you don't think she jumped... or was pushed?"

"Jumped on purpose? Of course not! And pushed? No! Nobody would ever want to hurt Janie!" Brent's face grew serious, not liking the question. "She had to have slipped. And if I can find the memory card... Well, then it might put the questions to rest about me or even the whole damn thing."

"Finding that memory card will be a big task, Brent. Not to mention, the card might be damaged from the fall. Might have landed in the creek and has been soaking in water this whole time," Philip cautioned before adding, "Or maybe someone walked away with it? If the sheriff's department is correct about her being pushed off the cliff..." Philip couldn't help himself and looked back behind them, up to where Janie had fallen. "Could you use some help?"

Brent had followed his gaze and then turned to face Philip, surprised. "Really?"

Philip shrugged his shoulders. "Sure."

"Um, yeah. Okay." Brent quickly surveyed the search area. "I've checked this spot right here pretty thoroughly. But the section over there and there." Brent pointed ahead of them, indicating both sides of the creek. "I haven't gotten to yet."

"Well, let's finish this section here, and then we can each take a side." Philip nodded towards their feet and started wandering away from Brent, working his way downstream. "By the way, I'm sorry for your loss. I know you and Janie were..." Philip searched for the right word to describe what Sue had shared about their relationship and settled with, "very close."

Brent nodded, not saying anything in return.

"It's sad to have lost both sisters so close together."

Brent closed his eyes and shook his head, stopping to face Philip. "It's devastating." He took a handkerchief out of his pocket, dropping it on the ground, marking his location before walking over to where Philip stood. "It's the worst of coincidences."

"Do you think it really is a coincidence?" Philip asked bluntly.

"It has to be!" Brent's eyes went wide, seeming to take offense. "Everyone loved those two. Who would want to hurt them?"

Philip shook his head, not having the answer himself.

"Tell me. What do you remember about the day Danie drowned?"

"Why do you want to know?" Brent asked, a tinge of anger creeping into his voice. "Is it because you think I pushed her too? That's what Gramps thinks people will start saying. It's not true. I'd never hurt either one of them."

"Never said you did or would," Philip said calmly. "Just asking you because you were there."

"Still don't see why you're asking," Brent said stubbornly, crossing his arms across his chest.

"Brent, you and I both know Janie didn't jump, and she was too good of a climber to have accidentally fallen off that cliff." Philip put a halting hand up, stopping Brent's hot words. "Now, I don't think you hurt her. Which means somebody else did." Brent's scowl lessened, a slow realization replacing it. "And if the two girls dying a year apart, really isn't a coincidence, then we might want to look at Danie's death a bit closer. Now, what do you remember?"

Brent, the wind of defiance out of his sails, sat himself down by the creek bed. "I guess you've got a point."

"Tell me about last summer." Philip squatted down, keeping his eye line level with Brent's. "Was it a good summer? Everyone getting along?"

"It was a great summer." Brent gave a small smile, meeting Philip's eyes. "Both Janie and Danie had decided to come back."

"Didn't they always come back each summer?" Philip asked surprised, trying to think of a summer without both girls.

"Yeah, but Danie had been hemming and hawing about staying in Pennsylvania. Janie talked her into coming back."

"Do you know why Danie had second thoughts?" This was something he was pretty sure Lane would want to know about.

"No." Brent shrugged his shoulders. "Don't get me wrong. I liked Danie, but Janie was the only one I cared about making the trip." Brent turned his body, facing Philip. "It might have been because their aunt back east was fighting cancer or maybe something to do with getting ready for college? I honestly don't remember."

Philip nodded his head and pondered, "So, when both girls got here, everything was normal with everyone?"

"Oh, yeah! It was like always!" Brent's face lit up. "We spent a good portion of the summer on Lucas' dad's boat, did a ton of hiking, horseback riding, camping, drinking..." Brent looked nervously over at Philip. Not seeing a look of damnation, Brent continued, "In fact, we had a spodie the night before at the campsite."

"Spodie?" Philip asked, not familiar with the term, strictly a beer man himself. "You hollow out a large watermelon, throw a whole bunch of fruit inside with vodka, and let it sit all day, soaking up the alcohol."

"Gotcha."

"Anyways, we were having a blast. Sitting around the campfire, roasting marshmallows, while Kevin played his guitar. All of us laughing and joking around." Brent suddenly laughed out loud. "And Lucas! He was drunk, hamming it up real good. Danie was annoyed at that. Thought he'd gotten a little too friendly."

"How so?" Philip asked, tossing a small pebble into the creek before turning back to Brent. "He didn't overstep his bounds, did he?"

"No. Nothing like that. Besides, if he'd tried, Gabe would have kicked his ass," Brent reassured, his smile growing wider. "The poor guy just had too much liquid courage in him and ended up confusing Janie for Danie. That's all."

"That made Danie mad? I would have thought they'd be confused for each other most of the time?"

"Sort of. If you messed up their names, that didn't bother them. But Lucas..." Brent shook his head, a small chuckle bubbling up with the memory. "He'd gone up and slapped Janie's butt. Gave her a good spanking. Playful, you know. Nothing malicious," Brent clarified. "Ticked Danie off good, though. And embarrassed Lucas terribly." Brent chuckled again. "Made the rest of us laugh our heads off."

"How did Janie feel about it?" Philip smiled with him, picturing the scene in his head.

"Other than a sore bottom?" Brent laughed. "She was a good sport as always. Nothing ever really got under her skin." Brent paused. "Actually, that's not true. I guess it did bother her a little."

"Oh?" Philip encouraged. "Did she say something to Lucas?"

"No. Not to him, to me! I'd smarted off. Saying something about Lucas being as blind as a bat if he couldn't tell the two apart." Brent started picking up pebbles and tossing them as well. "Janie, for some reason, took exception. Told me on my brightest day, I couldn't tell her and Danie apart. Then I snapped something about how any dummy could figure it out." Brent shrugged. "That seemed to upset her."

"Was it the truth? Could you really tell them apart?" Philip smiled, curious to know.

"Physically? No. They were the spitting image of each other and proud of it. Personality-wise, hell yeah. Those two were night and day."

"So, it was an empty boast, so to speak?"

"Completely," Brent said honestly, a sad smile on his face.

"Did Janie call you out on it?" Philip watched as Brent found a smooth flat pebble and tried to skip it across the creek.

"Nah, she let it drop and went off to calm Danie down. The party sort of broke up from there, and we all went to our own tents."

"The next morning, how was everyone's mood?"

"Normal. We'd all had quite a bit to drink, so I don't think any of us got up till around ten, ten-thirty. Poor Lucas. He'd gotten to the campsite super late, hadn't even gotten a chance to put up his tent. Found him sleeping out in the open on his sleeping bag, the tent poles and canvas, a stacked mess from the night before." Brent laughed again.

"Everyone else?" Philip smiled, imagining a drunk Lucas trying to put together a tent in the dark.

"Angie and Kevin, they'd immediately gotten into a fight, which was totally normal for them. Don't even know if they knew what they were fighting about. Angie took off for a walk to cool down and get some space."

"What did Kevin do?" Philip asked, guessing the fight might have been over him ogling Janie.

"He and Gabe started to gather wood close by. We'd decided to build a big bonfire on the beach for our last night."

"Yeah, and I recall telling you guys absolutely no bonfires," Philip said sternly, giving the young man a firm scowl.

"I know. Sorry about that." Brent winced, giving Philip an apologetic smile. "Danie was going to be flying back to Pennsylvania, Gabe was heading back to school, and we all had jobs we were returning to. It was supposed to be our last hurrah for the summer, and I just really wanted the night to be a big deal. Something to remember. Something... special."

Philip wondered if Brent had planned on asking Janie to marry him but decided not to ask, knowing Danie's death had sidetracked any plans Brent might have had for that evening.

"What about Janie and Danie? How were they the next morning?"

"Oh, fine! When we all got up, Janie suggested going down to the beach to look for driftwood for the fire. Danie didn't feel like it. Said she and Amy were thinking about going swimming because it was so hot."

"So, Amy went with Danie to go swimming?"

Philip asked, surprised. He'd always been told Danie was alone.

Brent thought for a second, his brow creased.

"No, no. I guess she didn't. I'd forgotten. She and Kevin, they decided to make everyone sandwiches while the rest of us searched for wood."

"Why didn't her sister go with her?" Philip was starting to get a picture of who was where in the campsite.

"Oh, she'd taken pity on Lucas and decided to help him get his tent set up, so he wouldn't have to sleep outside with the mosquitos for another night." Brent's smile was fondly sad. "And I'd wandered off to find a place to relieve myself and then started picking up wood."

"And Gabe?"

"Fighting a hangover. He'd decided to go back to his tent and take a nap when Kevin bagged off to help Amy make lunch."

"I've noticed you all seemed to be paired off. You and Janie, Kevin and Angie, Lucas and Danie? Were Amy and Gabe a thing?"

"Oh, no! Not even close, and it was Gabe and Danie, not Danie and Lucas."

"But you just said Lucas was sweet on Danie?" Philip frowned, knowing this to be the case as well.

"He was! So was Gabe."

"And Danie chose Gabe?" Philip was still confused. He'd always thought it was Lucas who was with Danie. Even Sue had thought the same.

"Well, not exactly. That's just who I thought she preferred. I don't think she wanted to be tied down to anyone, to be honest, especially since she'd be going to Penn State. That's a hell of a long ways from Rockfish Island. Believe me, Janie and I struggled being apart."

"Then, who was Amy with?"

"No one. Though she was hoping Gabe would take an interest in her after Danie left to go back to Pennsylvania. Don't get me wrong. She and Danie were tight, but I think Gabe sort of became a sore subject between them."

"So, that morning, Danie ended up going swimming all by herself?" Brent lowered his head, his chin resting on his chest. "If I'd been faster." He looked over at Philip, his eyes sorrowful. "I'd heard yelling, but I'd ignored it at first. I don't know what I thought it was. I didn't think it was something to do with us. When I finally realized they were yelling something about Danie, I dropped the firewood and ran back to camp." Brent tilted his head back, gazing up at the sky. "I saw everybody running to Shallow Point and started to follow. As I got closer, the trees were sparse enough, I could see Danie floating face down in the water. Gabe was trying to wade out to her while Kevin and Lucas were still trying to scramble down the rocks to get to the water. I knew none of them would get to her in time, so I just dove off the point."

"That was a dumb thing to do, Brent. You could have broken your neck," Philip admonished, at the same time, impressed with the young man's bravery.

Brent shrugged the rebuke off and continued, "I got to her before Gabe and managed to pull her to shore with his help. Then Gabe started CPR..." Brent took a deep breath. "He gave it everything he had. The guy was a machine."

Philip agreed. Gabe had been exhausted by the time Philip had arrived on the scene.

"Do you remember who spotted Danie in the water first? Who called the alarm?" Philip stood up, his legs getting stiff.

"I think it was Lucas." Brent got up with him, dusting off his pants.

"Lucas? I thought he and Janie were putting up his tent?" Brent shrugged. "Maybe they'd finished, and he went to see what Danie was doing?"

"You've never asked him?"

"It's not a subject I enjoy talking about," Brent said flatly, starting to wander off.

Philip put an arresting hand on Brent's chest.

"One last question. Did you know Janie was back on the island?"

Brent pursed his lips together, chucking another

small pebble into the creek.

"Kevin mentioned he saw her at the restaurant. I was hoping she would contact me the next day or so." He turned to Philip. "She didn't."

"How did it end? You and Janie?"

"She blamed me for Danie." Brent looked up at the cliff, his eyes sad. "She never came out and actually said it, but I could tell. After Danie's funeral, I did everything I could to be there for her. Nothing I did seemed to bring her closer, so I tried giving her some space. Soon the space turned into unreturned phone calls and one-sided text messages." Brent put his hands in his back pockets, turning his gaze down to his boots. "I tried going to her apartment. Was worried she was suicidal... or she'd met somebody else. She didn't even bother to come to the door. I gave up after that."

"Must have been one hell of a surprise finding her on The Mole Hill that morning." Philip's gaze was glued to Brent's face.

Brent's smile was thin and unconvincing. "Complete surprise."

"Was it, Brent? Really?" Philip put his hand on his shoulder. He could see the young man was fighting his emotions.

"I thought... I thought if we spent some time together like we used to... Things would click back into place." Brent lightly shrugged Philip's hand off his shoulder. "I left Janie on that cliff in more than one way," Brent's voice cracked, and he turned his back on Philip. "It's going to be dark soon. Better get back to looking." He halfheartedly wandered over to his dropped handkerchief and picked it up, resuming his search.

Philip watched the young man for a moment before he leapt over to the other side of the creek and started to look himself.

CHAPTER 27

"Hello?" A male's voice, heavy with sleep, came over the phone line, and Lane winced, realizing she hadn't considered the difference in time zones.

"This is Sheriff Lane with the Rockfish Island Sheriff's Department." She thought it best to start off with her title, less chance of getting confused for a telemarketer. She was wrong.

"I've already donated to my local department. Good-bye," the voice answered, sleep still heavy in the East Coast accent.

"Mr. Levens? This isn't a telemarketing call. I'm contacting you in regards to Danielle and Janielle Engles," Lane said loudly, into the mouthpiece, hoping he'd hear her voice before hanging up the phone. "I need to ask you a few questions." Lane could distinctly hear rustling in the background and assumed the man was sitting up in bed.

"Couldn't this wait till morning when I'm at my office?" Gerald Levens, the attorney for the Engles family estate, said testily into the phone.

"I apologize, Mr. Levens. I didn't realize I'd called your home number," Lane lied, never having been one to be patient.

"Well, now that you do. You can call me back tomorrow morning at my office." Mr. Levens went to hang up the phone.

"Mr. Levens! Since I have you on the phone now, this won't take long," Lane said quickly. "You know how things are with an official murder investigation. Time is of the essence." Lane bit her lip, hoping that was a big enough lure to keep the family lawyer on the phone.

"Did you say murder investigation?" Mr. Levens turned the lamp next to his bedside on. His wife, lying beside him, rolled away from the glare.

"Yes, sir. I meant to call you earlier, but today has been hectic. Janielle Engles was found deceased on September 4th. The coroner has declared her death a homicide, by person or persons unknown. We believe she was pushed off a cliff while hiking."

"Oh, Janie." Mr. Levens threw back the sheets and sat on the edge of his bed. "That would explain why Mrs. Carter called and made an appointment,"

The lawyer mumbled to himself and then said into the phone, "What can I do for you, Sheriff?"

"My understanding is Janie had a will?"

"Of course."

"Can you tell me who stands to benefit from it, and do you know if she had any life insurance policies?" Lane had her notepad and pen ready.

"Just a second. Let me switch phones." Mr. Levens shook his wife awake and told her to wait till he picked up the line in the other room. A minute later, Lane heard him say, "Okay, Lori. You can go back to sleep." There was a huff of annoyance and a click. "Sheriff, are you still there?"

"Yes, sir. I apologize for waking your household. But with a murder investigation—"

"I know. You said that already," Mr. Levens interrupted. "I can't tell you every detail of the will, being it's not in front of me. But the majority of Janie's wealth goes to her aunt, Susan Carter." Mr. Levens leaned back in his button-back chair and closed his eyes, trying to stifle a yawn. "A few thousand, here and there, goes to charity and some additional funds to a couple of close friends. Neither sister had a life insurance policy."

"Nothing to her family in Pennsylvania?"

"The will was amended after Danielle's death and the passing of her aunt, Cheryl Martin." Mr. Levens blinked his eyes rapidly, fighting the urge to fall asleep.

"And nothing for her uncle, Mr. Martin?" Lane wondered if maybe she had been shortsighted. Possibly they had a suspect all the way in Pennsylvania?

"Their Uncle, Thomas Martin, died of pneumonia two years ago. Both he and Cheryl were in their mid-forties when they adopted the girls after their parent's car accident and demise. No cousins to speak of."

Lane couldn't help herself and started to doddle the math on her notepad, wondering exactly how old Sue Carter was. If she surmised correctly, Sue must have paid a fortune to her plastic surgeons.

"Anything else, Sheriff?" Mr. Levens broke into her thoughts, the impatience in his voice easy to hear.

"You mentioned additional funds to some of her close friends? Do you recall who and the amount?" Lane scratched out her quick mathematical scribblings.

"Let me think..." Mr. Levens looked down at his desk, trying to recall. "I believe the sum was close to a million each. I don't recall the names. I could fax the information over in the morning when I'm back in my office if you'd be kind enough to send over an official request via email." Mr. Leven's didn't bother to stifle his yawn this time.

"I'd appreciate that. One final question. Do you represent the Carters, as well? Or just the Martins?" Lane found herself yawning along with the lawyer, even though it was only 9:00 p.m. her time.

"Neither... if you are speaking of the husbands. I

represent the Hamilton estate. Cheryl, Susan, and Lisa's family. Lisa Hamilton-Engles was the girl's mother."

"Wait. Sue Carter's wealth didn't come from her husband?" Lane asked astonished, having always been told Henry was the wealthy one.

"Henry was rich in his own right. But no, Sue, as you refer to her... her family is old money," Mr. Leven's East Coast accent was thick with pride. "I'm the fourth generation to proudly service this line of the Hamilton dynasty."

Lane's eyebrows shot up, recognizing the name of mass wealth. No wonder Sue pretended all her money came from Henry's side of the family. If everyone knew her family lineage, half the island would be at her doorstep, begging for a handout. And the other half, accepting her sexual advances, in a hope of a monetary windfall. Lane quickly scratched out Sue's name from the suspect list. Money would not have been a factor... for Sue. "Mr. Levens, when Danie died, how was her wealth distributed?"

"Everything went solely to Janie. Her will was an exact duplicate until Danie's accidental death. Like I mentioned before, it was changed a short while ago."

"A short while ago?" Lane's attention was caught at his last words. "Mr. Levens, what exactly do you mean by a short while ago?"

"A few weeks," Mr. Levens mumbled, jerking his head up, having started to nod off. "Last month, around mid-August, I believe. Definitely before Labor Day. I helped her draft it personally at our office." He yawned again. "Really, Sheriff. I don't see how any further questions you may have can't wait until tomorrow morning."

CHAPTER 28

The parking lot of Piper's Place looked fairly vacant for a Friday night. Though the ambiance of the small dive bar, set by the various neon beer signs and hanging lamps stationed over the pool tables, gave Philip a claustrophobic feeling as soon as he stepped through the door.

Dressed in his favorite plaid shirt and comfortably crumpled Levi jeans, Philip begrudgingly let the door close behind him, and wrinkled his nose at the smell of deep-fried onion rings, stale beer, and clove cigarette smoke drifting in from the smoker's lounge outside.

Five seconds in, and he was already longing for the bright lights of the parking lot and the familiar rumble of the bowling alley next door. He stepped further in and waited for his eyes to adjust to the dim light, scanning the room for a familiar face... or two.

He recognized the man standing by the old juke-box, plunking in quarters, drinking away his sor-rows. Up by the bar, he saw a young couple who vis-ited the park earlier in the morning, though he didn't remember their names. They were happily chatting over their beers and a basket full of pull tabs.

Philip wandered closer to the small tables sur-rounding the minuscule dance floor, where he spot-ted the waitress. She was humming off-key to the jukebox, bouncing from table to table, barely giv-ing the tops a wipe down. Further to his left, a man playing pool by himself raised his hand, indicating he could do with another beer.

"That's not how it happened!" Philip, slightly startled, turned his head to the far right. "You're pull-ing my leg!" the raised voice said loudly, an amused laugh quickly following behind it.

"I swear!" declared Lucas, his hand up in the air as if to take a solemn oath.

In a dark corner, back by the door, sat Lucas and Gabe. Both discussing something with conversational intensity, a half pitcher of beer sitting between them.

"Hey, fellas. Buy you another round?" Philip of-fered heartily as he approached the table and signaled the waitress.

"Hey, Phil! Never seen you here before." Lucas gave him a big smile and waved him over.

Philip, swiping a spare chair from against the wall, scooted up to their table just as the waitress approached.

"What can I get—," she paused, recognizing him. "Phil? What are you doing over here? Don't you normally socialize over at the bowling alley?"

"Hi, Leslie. Can I get another pitcher of beer and an extra glass?" Philip smiled widely, politely ignoring the question.

"Sure thing." She slipped a pen behind her ear and cocked her hip to the side, leaning up against the table. "So, is it because you and Harry are still fighting? Because that would be a real shame." She shook her head side to side to emphasize the shame it would be.

"Yeah, I heard about that!" Gabe leaned across the table, pulling the half-filled pitcher closer. "Heard you punched him out cold."

"I heard Harry practically cracked Phil's head open," Lucas joined in, pushing his empty glass towards Gabe for a refill.

"Well, I heard it's gonna be thirty bucks to fix his nice trophy," Leslie added and then asked with wide eyes, "You ARE going to pay to get his trophy fixed? Aren't you, Phil? I mean, Harry was JUST trying to be a good sport."

"Leslie! Order up!" a voice barked from behind the bar. "While it's hot!"

Rolling her eyes with a huff, Leslie yelled over

her shoulder as she stood up straight, causing the table to rock back and forth.

"Hold your britches, Derrick. I'm coming!" Then to Philip, "Well, you're a good guy. I'm sure you'll do the right thing. You'd be a real creep if you didn't." She then turned on her heels and casually tossed over her shoulder, "I'll be back with your pitcher and a fresh glass in a second."

"Thanks, Leslie," Philip said flatly and grabbed the ketchup-smeared menu pinned down by the napkin dispenser. He gave it a quick once over, his facial expression turning disappointed. "I see the title of "Grill" on the menu of this place is purely for show," Philip sighed. Nothing but deep-fried appetizers were offered. And he'd been craving a cheeseburger and beer all day, having spent the majority of it helping Brent with no luck.

"We got an order of fries coming if you want some." Gabe hitched a thumb in Leslie's direction, who was already making her way back to their table.

Philip watched as she expertly held the pitcher of beer in one hand and balanced the heaping plate of fries in the other. She also had a glass ketchup bottle tucked under one arm and a mustard squeeze bottle tucked under the other. Philip's requested clean glass was securely clutched in her teeth.

Sloppily she placed everything down with a loud clunk, resulting in foam spilling over the pitcher's rim and a majority of the fries toppling off the side. With her hands-free, she happily handed Philip his glass, her lipstick stain clearly visible.

"Just drink from the opposite side," she said in response to his disgusted look and took off her apron. "My shift is over, guys. You can leave my tip on the credit card receipt, okay? Night, fellas!" And with that, she made her way back behind the bar for her purse and headed out the back door.

"Here, Phil. I'll get you a different one." Lucas laughed and got up from the table, taking the lip-marked glass from Philip's hand.

"Thanks, man." Philip watched Lucas head for the bar and let his eyes lazily draw across the room. "So, you guys come here often?" Philip casually drew his eyes back to Gabe and watched as he started to pick up the spare fries off the table.

"Yeah, it's sort of our hangout." Gabe popped a fry into his mouth.

"I wouldn't..." Philip tried to warn, doubting the cleanliness of the table. Failing, he asked genially, "So, how have things been?"

"Alright."

"Just alright?" Philip asked jovially, sliding the ketchup bottle closer to Gabe. "That doesn't sound very exciting."

"It's been a couple of tough days." Gabe shot Philip a hard look. "As you can imagine."

"Sorry." Philip put his hands up in a helpless gesture. "That was a dumb thing for me to say."

"It's alright," Gabe said quietly before taking a deep breath. "So, ..." his voice lightened. "Brent told me how you helped him out today." He gave the bottom of the ketchup bottle a hard smack before taking off the lid. "I invited him out tonight, but he didn't feel up to it."

"Yeah, I guess he was out there all day looking. He's probably pretty tired." Philip cleared his throat. "We... we uh, sure had an interesting conversation while we were searching." Philip nervously drummed his fingers on the table. He was debating on how to move forward. He wasn't as friendly with Gabe as he was with Lucas and didn't quite know how to approach the young man.

"Gabe, what's your opinion of Janie falling off the cliff?" He decided to be direct and just ask the question. He'd already put his foot in his mouth, and it wouldn't be long before Lucas came back with a clean glass. At the moment, the kid was happily chatting it up with the new barmaid on duty.

"I think it's nonsense," Gabe said bluntly, a large splatter of ketchup plopping down on the fry plate. "Brent says she was pretty distracted by the goats, moving around trying to get the right angle or whatnot and must have lost her footing. I don't buy it."

"Why not?" Philip sat up straighter, intent on

Gabe's next words.

"Because Janie was a well-seasoned and traveled photographer. She'd seen mountain goats before. Heck, I was with her the first time she climbed Snakehead trail and spotted them a couple of years ago." Gabe dragged a French fry through the tomato sauce. "Brent's theory just doesn't make sense."

"What theory?" Lucas asked, sitting down and handing Philip a lipstick-free glass.

"That Janie was so wowed by the mountain goats, she wasn't paying attention and lost her footing," Gabe explained, his disgust still apparent even though he was talking through a full mouth of hot fries.

"Oh... well, I don't know. They're pretty cool animals, and people don't get to see them all that often. It's not like seeing a cow or a horse in a field on the side of the road. I'm sure she was still pretty amazed by them." Lucas had grabbed three small plates while fetching the extra glass and passed them one each before piling his own plate full of fries.

"So, if she hadn't been distracted, how do you think she fell?" Philip asked, doing his best to sound casual while pouring himself a glass from the new pitcher.

"She didn't jump if that's what you are thinking," Gabe said quickly, shooting Lucas an unforgiving look. "And she wasn't rappelling down either."

"I only said it was a possibility," Lucas countered. "If someone took the memory card... why is it so farfetched to think they might have taken her climbing gear?"

"Lucas, no one throws somebody off a cliff, just to rob them of a lousy memory card and a few rappelling ropes," Gabe pointed out, frustrated with the suggestion. "Besides, if they were planning on robbing her, I would have thought they'd have taken the camera from her before throwing her off."

Philip was impressed that Lucas and Gabe's friendship could handle such differing opinions and viewpoints about such a defining event. They obviously felt secure enough with themselves and each other to express opposing viewpoints. In a good forty years, future generations might find them sitting at Hattie's picnic table, the modern-day version of Dub and Glen.

"Well, all I know for sure is, Brent wasn't the one to push her off," Lucas said stubbornly, stuffing a fry into his mouth.

Philip glanced over at Gabe, waiting for his agreement, but was surprised to find the young man simply frowning down at his dwindling plate of fries.

"You've got a point there, Lucas," Philip ventured, watching Gabe. "I mean, Brent doesn't strike me as a homicidal murderer. Especially after diving into the water to save Danie last summer."

"Practically suicidal," Gabe grumbled, before taking a drink. "Could have broken his neck."

"Won't argue with you there," Lucas agreed, his eyebrows raised in amazement, shaking his head in wonder. "That reminds me of the time..."

"You know, I still think about that day," Philip spoke over Lucas, sensing the subject was about to be changed and wanting to keep it on Danie. "Brent said you were the one to alert everybody. How'd you spot her in the water?" Philip had directed his question to Lucas, but it was Gabe who responded.

"It wasn't Lucas who saw her. It was Kevin." Philip tried to think back to his conversation with Kevin. If he was remembering right, he was pretty sure Kevin had said Gabe was the one who called everyone's attention to Danie. Strange no one could remember exactly who.

"Really? I always thought it was you," Lucas said with some surprise. "At least, it sounded like you."

Gabe shook his head, his lips pursed together. "Nah, man. I was asleep in my tent." He turned to Philip. "I had a killer headache and decided to lay down. Rest up for the evening bonfire."

"Well, then how was it you were already in the water by the time I got there?" Lucas asked, his forehead scrunched in confused curiosity.

Philip's eyes quickly bounced back and forth between the two young men, suddenly deducing the two friends had never traded stories about that day.

"Lucas... I heard Kevin running outside my tent

and yelling about Danie. He was already at the point when I got there, and I clambered down the rocks. Gave myself some good scratches on my arms and legs." Gabe showed Philip a light scar by his elbow. "Started to wade out to her when Brent came flying into the water."

Philip thought he heard a tone of anger in Gabe's voice. If it was for himself or for Brent, Philip couldn't tell.

"I don't remember it the same way," Lucas said distractedly, frowning in thought. "Janie was helping me put up my tent when I heard who I thought was you, yelling Danie was drowning. We ran like hell, and when I got there, you were already chest-deep in the water, and Kevin was running up behind us."

"No, man! Kevin got there first. But you know how he is about heights. So, I climbed down and started my way out there. You've got it backwards." Gabe gave his friend an annoyed look.

"Gabe, I don't mean to be a jerk, but you're wrong. Trust me. I've thought of Danie's last day a thousand times."

"You don't think I haven't?" Gabe's voice turned fierce. "Don't forget, Lucas. You weren't the one who felt her life slip through your fingers."

Lucas bowed his head in shame, not having anything to counter the comment. He took a quick drink of his beer and then guzzled the rest down with his cheeks red.

To Philip, it was obvious both men still held a torch for the dead girl. Though they had remained friends, he imagined they'd purposely never spoken about it. That is until he'd brought it up.

"Well, you both can agree it was a man's voice yelling about Danie drowning, right?" Philip decided he needed to get them back on even ground. Both nodded their heads it was so. "Did either of you know Janie was back on the island?" Philip pushed his empty plate back having used his last French fry to wipe the plate clean before popping it in his mouth and somewhat changing the subject. Both men shook their heads. This time, answering no.

"I wish I had. Hard to believe I missed her," Gabe said, his tone quite mellow from a moment before. "I guess I was in the park around the time she was there. That is, according to Brent. I never saw her."

"What about you, Lucas? Were you in the park?" Philip emptied his glass with a final swallow.

"No. I was at home, playing video games." Lucas gave Gabe a quick glance before pushing back his chair from the table. "Should we get another pitcher?" he asked, standing up while pouring the last drop of beer from Philip's pitcher into his glass.

"Yeah, think so." Gabe smiled up at his friend. "I believe it's your turn to buy!"

"Count me out, guys." Philip stood up, pushing

in his chair. "I gotta be bright-eyed and bushy-tailed in the morning, and this old man can't hang like he used to." He clapped Gabe on the back. "See you two at the memorial tomorrow?"

Both smiles dropped, and the two young men nodded their heads yes. Philip gave an apologetic smile, having ruined their returning good mood.

"Alright. See you, then. Have a good night."

CHAPTER 29

L ane looked at her "Suspect List" in exasperation. The day before, it had been a clear, con-
cise, and organized list of names. Now names
were scratched out, re-written, and then scratched
out again. She ripped the offending page out and
wrote at the top of the next "Updated Suspect List"
before adding a list of reorganized names below it.

"Who's left?" Philip asked, blowing on his steaming cup of coffee, taking a seat on the end of Lane's
bed. It was his accustomed spot when visiting her
small apartment since there was only the one chair.

He had come over to help her move, which was
apparent by the state of her place. The room, normally clean and tidy, was currently disheveled, packing peanuts on the floor, wadded old newspapers,
and several moving boxes stacked by the door.

Eyeing Lane, Philip covertly grabbed the discarded list off her makeshift dinner tray desk and gave it a once over. The name Sue Carter and Jim Evans had both been scratched out. It reasoned, since money was no longer a factor, the murder for hire theory was dead in the water and if, that was so, then Jim Evans most likely was not paid to get Janie onto the island. However, Lane started speculating. Even with all the money in the world, a business could go bankrupt and find itself in the red. Possibly Sue's business was no longer profitable? She even wondered if Jim Evans, trying to work from home, was still able to pay his bills as a struggling agent. Both names had been dutifully put back on the list.

After a few discrete inquires, Sue was found to be as filthy rich as reported, with her business lavishly in the green. As for Jim, his wife ended up being the breadwinner of the family, which allowed him to do his writing jobs on the side and give the new agent venture a try. Lane, unable to think of any other motive Sue or Jim might have, struck both names from the list once again.

Lucas Wilson's name had two stars by it. One for being a potential stalker, according to Jim Evan's wife. The other, for stating he was at home playing video games the day Janie died when according to Brent, he'd seen Lucas's truck in the park that same morning.

Angie Bennett's name had three stars. One for

being on the camping trip the day Danie died. Lane argued just because she went for a hike didn't mean she really had. She could have snuck back into camp, found Danie at the point, and pushed her off. The second star was for being jealous of Kevin flirting with Janie. The last star, which was three times bigger, was for Angie owing Janie money.

Philip suddenly realized Lane was rating the suspects. The more stars, the stronger the suspect. Brent's name had six stars and, by far, was leading the pack. Philip didn't believe Brent had the psychological make-up to be a murderer, but facts were facts. At his own admission, he had been the last person to see Janie alive. He'd gotten a lawyer, even if it was his own grandfather. He also refused to give his DNA, which was curious since he'd already admitted he was there.

On top of that, he'd neglected to share he and Janie had been romantically involved, which made him all the more suspicious. And there was still the strange scene at the ranger station between Brent and his two pals. What would he have said, to Deputy Pickens, if given the chance? Not to mention, Philip had found him searching for the memory card. Which Lane immediately thought proved a guilty conscience, allowing for a very large star by his name.

This was until Philip said he'd volunteered to help, and Brent had taken him up on the offer. Philip argued, if the boy had anything to hide on the memory card, he probably wouldn't have allowed it or would have made an excuse to leave. Lane countered. She thought, since Brent pointed out where he wanted Philip to look, it was most likely because he knew where the memory card wasn't.

Both Gabe and Kevin had only one star by their names, simply because both had been thought to be the first on the scene of Danie's drowning. Lane thought it odd no one could remember exactly who had called the alarm. She even wondered if Angie might have yelled out in a lowered-toned voice, running back into the woods, where she conveniently stayed until everyone left.

At the very bottom of the list was Amy's name. A question mark and a very tiny star placed beside it.

Philip crumpled the paper into a small ball and tossed it at the wastebasket in the bathroom. He missed and it ricocheted off the door, landing in the open closet.

Lane arched an eyebrow as she flipped her notepad closed.

"I'll get it," Philip said, standing up from the bed and walking over to retrieve it. "Think we're getting anywhere?"

"Well, I think after we speak with Angie and Amy, things might fall into place a little better. Might be a good idea to split up Gabe and Lucas, see how they talk about Danie when the other guy isn't around. Janie too, for that matter. Think you can take one while I take the other at the funeral today?" Lane folded up the small TV tray she used as a makeshift desk and put it against the wall.

"I don't know how I feel about questioning someone at a funeral," Philip said, honestly. "It seems a bit..." He shrugged and gave Lane a grim smile. "Disrespectful."

Lane tossed a small stack of books into the last empty box, shaking her head at Philip's comment. "Funerals are perfect for something like this. People are grieving, their emotions are high, and they have a tendency to want to reminisce. Share things they most likely wouldn't in everyday conversation. Half the time, you don't have to ask any questions, just be a shoulder for them to cry on. You can do that, can't you, Phil?" Lane motioned for Philip to hand her the packing tape sitting on the nightstand.

"If it's just being a shoulder, then yeah. I can feel good about that." He tossed it to her as he sat back down.

"I think you should take Lucas. You seem to have a good rapport with him." Lane stretched the tape over the opening and sealed the box closed.

"I went to high school with his dad. He owns a couple of upscale spas in downtown Seattle. Invites me out onto his yacht every now and then for a cruise. Lucas usually tags along."

"What about Gabe? What does his family do? Must be well off if he's going to UW in the medical field." Lane hefted the box up and added it to the stack piled by the door.

"That the last one?" Philip asked, getting up from the bed.

"Yup." Lane dusted her hands off on her jeans and gave the little apartment one last look to make sure she'd not forgotten anything.

Philip grabbed the two top boxes and started to head out the door.

"He's not, by the way," Philip suddenly said, turning around to face her.

"What?" Lane closed the closet door, having pulled out two jackets and her old yellow rain parka, laying them across her arm.

"Gabe. He's not rich. He was going to school on scholarships and working side jobs. Probably owes a crap ton in student loans."

"Oh," Lane said, grabbing a box herself and starting to follow him down the apartment stairs. "Must be hard having two best friends who have money and being in love with a girl who was a multi-millionaire when you have no money of your own to speak of."

Philip waited till he got to the bottom of the stairs before adding his two cents.

"I think he's okay with it. After all, he was working

his way to a high paying job. He'd be on the same level as them soon enough, and I never got the feeling any-one treated him differently or excluded him. In fact, he lives in the Wilson's guesthouse, rent-free. I think he benefits quite a bit from having rich friends."

"So, money wouldn't be a driving factor for mur-der?" Lane made it safely down the stairs, and the two walked the length of the alley out to the street where their trucks were parked.

"I wouldn't imagine so. Why?"

"I'm still thinking about the forgery sheet Caleb found at Janie's apartment. According to the bank, no huge withdrawals were taken before her death, and no funds have been removed after. I was just wondering, if Gabe was hurting for money, maybe he'd found a way into her apartment and was trying to copy her signature. Obviously, unsuccessfully."

"That's still not a bad theory. It..." Philip noticed Harry's brown beast of a truck parked next to his. "It would be an easy way to pay off some student debt," Philip admitted, putting the moving boxes in his truck bed.

Lane caught the pause and nudged him with her boxes.

"Looks like Harry's working. I need to get a few cleaning supplies for the new place. Want to come in with me?" Lane offered. Philip smiled at her, taking her two boxes.

"Nah. I'll finish loading up the rest. You go shop. I'll meet you at the cottage."

"Oh, come on, Phil. I'll loan you the thirty bucks if it's the money," Lane said, still surprised the two friends were fighting.

"I've got the money!" Philip said defensively.

"Then what's stopping you from going over and making nice?" Lane put her hands on her hip, giving him a demanding glare. "He's your best friend. He's only wanting an apology."

"I already apologized by dropping the charges." Philip lightly brushed past her and started his way down the alley towards the upstairs apartment. "It's now up to him to make nice."

CHAPTER 30

J anie's funeral wasn't so much a funeral as it was
a community potluck. The last will and testa-
ment of Janielle A. Engles dictated for her body
to be buried in Pennsylvania. Sue, still wanting to
give people an opportunity to grieve and show their
respect, opened her home for a brief memorial.

Most of the island residents came, and with
them, food to feed Sue in her grief. It didn't take
long before her authentic 1700s Queen Anne dining
table was cleared, the guests plugging in their crockpots while plunking down various salads and casse-
roles, along with a myriad of desserts. The helpful
neighbors, happily, yet somberly, passing out Sue's
best china and antique silverware.

Enamored with the small island's sense of community, Lane stood over the delectable food offer-

ings feeling slightly guilty, wishing she had brought something... even if it was store-bought. But having to quickly freshen up and change into her uniform after Philip helped her move, she hadn't had enough time to stop and get something. Let alone make anything. With a regretful sigh, she carefully picked up a second cupcake and placed it next to its twin. A dainty cucumber sandwich and a trio of baby carrots already residing on her plate.

"Sheriff?"

Lane, licking excess frosting off her fingers, turned to find Gabe smiling at her with his hand extended for a handshake. She hastily wiped her hands on her trousers and then reached for a napkin.

"Hi Gabe," she quickly said, wiping her hand thoroughly before taking his. "Nice to see you."

"Do you... do you have a moment?" Gabe asked, lowering his voice slightly and looking past her shoulder.

"Uh, sure. We can step over there." Lane's eyes followed where his had lingered a second before. He'd been looking at Brent and Angie, who were talking with their heads bowed together. Lane made a mental note as Angie was one of the people she wanted to speak with at the memorial.

In search of some privacy, Gabe led the way, and Lane followed, finding a small hallway off from the kitchen. There was still foot traffic, with people making their way in and out of Sue's kitchen for plates and glasses, but they would be able to speak freely without being overheard.

"What can I help you with, Gabe?" Lane asked, taking the young man in with a quick once over. He stood about five-ten with a muscular build, deep brown eyes, and dark hair. A good-looking kid with a nice smile, but at the moment, had a very serious face.

"Well, I was curious. If... If someone was to know something about Janie's death. Would they get in trouble for not coming to the police immediately?" He looked over his shoulder and then back at Lane with a weak smile. "I'm asking for a friend."

Lane nodded, understanding the "friend" was most likely Gabe himself.

"Well, Gabe. It's always best to come forward with information immediately. But, I'm understanding, if sometimes people need time to think things through. Sort their thoughts." Lane gave Gabe a probing stare. "What does your friend know?"

"Oh, he doesn't know anything... not for sure. It's more of a feeling and a few odd comments." Gabe frowned, scrunching up his face, trying to find the right words. "He's got a friend who trusts him."

"He's worried about betraying his friend," Lane surmised, finding loyalty admiring, but one of the biggest roadblocks in an investigation.

"Something like that."

"Here." Lane handed him her business card. "Have your friend call me, and we'll talk. Off the record." Lane smiled, encouraging him to take the card.

"Thanks, Sheriff. I'll be sure to ca— er, have him give you a call." Gabe took the card and put it in his pocket.

"I hope he does." Lane gave him a meaningful look before Gabe turned and walked off, leaving her standing in the kitchen hall by herself.

"Cupcakes? I didn't see any cupcakes! Where did you find those?" Philip whined, he and Jerry walking up, plates piled high with food.

"You can have one." Lane offered her plate, and Philip readily swiped up the small dessert, using his teeth to pry the paper off the cupcake. Frowning at his manners, Lane dismissed him with a roll of her eye and turned her attention to Jerry. "You're here!" she greeted warmly, surprised when he put his arm around her shoulder. "I thought you couldn't make it?"

"Amy asked me to come, so I changed my plans." He gave her a squeeze, jostling her plate. "Glad I did. Phil was just telling me how he got you all moved in." He gave her a smile, which didn't quite meet his eyes.

"Yeah, it was only a few boxes." Lane took a small step back, though Jerry kept his arm in place.

"A few!" Philip said, icing crusting the top of his lip. "You make it sound like two or three boxes. Should have rented one of those big U-hauls or an interstate van."

"Stop! You're exaggerating." Lane laughed, pushing lightly on Philip's arm. "Interstate van... Whatever!"

"Well, you should have called me." Jerry nodded at Philip, lightly punching him in the arm with his plate, "Instead of bugging this guy."

"I did!" Lane gave Jerry a surprised look. "You had plans, remember?"

"You could have asked me to reschedule," Jerry countered, shrugging his shoulders.

"Oh, I didn't want to be a bother. Phil was free and—"

"It wouldn't have been a bother!"

Lane's mouth opened a little in surprise. Philip cautiously looked between the two and then excused himself, mumbling something about going back for seconds.

Lane shrugged Jerry's arm off and sighed, "Well, that was embarrassing."

"I'm sorry." Jerry leaned up against the wall. "I didn't mean for that to come out so..."

"Possessive?" Lane finished his sentence.

Jerry frowned back at her. "Rude." He shook his head. "Phil's a good guy. But I think he's got a thing for you."

"No, he doesn't." Lane looked over at Philip, who had indeed headed to the table for seconds. If he wasn't careful, he'd have more than a slight beer belly to worry about.

"You can't tell me you haven't noticed the way he looks at you?" Jerry leaned in closer as Martha Barnes, the town gossip, walked dangerously close.

"Jerry, you're seeing things!" Lane protested, shooting him a severe look. "Stop being jealous."

"So, you're telling me I have nothing to worry about?" Jerry nudged her lightly, giving her a questioning look.

"Listen, Jerry. I think you've got the wrong—" Lane stopped. Angie Bennett had walked into view heading for the kitchen. "I need to talk to her," Lane said quickly and started to follow behind the young woman. Jerry went to tag along, but Lane swiftly shook her head, holding up her palm. "Alone."

Jerry put up his hand in surrender and turned to go back to the dining room and silently mouthed the word, "Okay."

"Angie?" Lane called, lightly touching the young woman on the shoulder. "Hi."

"Oh! Hi, Lane! Or should I address you as Sheriff since you're in uniform?" Angie gave Lane a warm smile. "I was going to come over and say hi, but I saw you talking with Amy's dad, and I didn't want to interrupt," Angie whispered, with an arched eyebrow. "It looked like things were a bit heated?"

Lane smiled at the young girl she had befriended earlier in the summer. "No, no," Lane reassured her, worried word might get back to Amy. "It was nothing." She briskly changed the subject. "How is Tamarack?"

Late last spring, looking for some low-cost therapy and something to do outside of the tiny apartment, Lane had stumbled across a flyer advertising horseback riding lessons. Giving the number a call, she had been introduced to Angie and her Appaloosa horse, Tamarack. A sore bum and a few horse bites later, she had quit with no desire to ever pick up the reins again.

"He's great!" Angie lit up when talking about her horses. "You know, you're always welcome to come out for a ride. In fact, I'm going ridin—"

"Listen, I wanted to tell you how sorry I am," Lane cut her off, knowing Angie could go on and on about her horses if left to do so. "It must be so hard to lose Janie, her being your best friend and all." Lane rubbed the side of Angie's arm, giving her a false facade of sympathy.

"Yes. She was a friend." Angie smiled politely and then added, "And thank you."

"I couldn't believe it when someone said her sister died last year from drowning. How terrible." Lane let her arm drop and picked up her cucumber sandwich.

"Yes. It was... terrible," Angie agreed, her voice sounding more sorrowful than a moment before.

"She was on a camping trip with friends or some church function?" Lane shook her head, acting as if she couldn't remember.

"We'd gone camping. It was a camping trip," Angie said, distracted, pulling open a drawer by the kitchen sink.

"Oh, you were there?" Lane asked, feigning surprise.

"Yeah, I was on the camping trip, but I wasn't there when she drowned." Angie grabbed a large spoon, facing back towards Lane, holding it up high. "For the meatballs," she explained, then turned to leave.

Lane eased her way in front of Angie blocking her path.

"You weren't?"

"Uh, no." Angie gave Lane a funny look and went to move around her. Lane casually switched her weight to her other hip blocking her again.

"Could you tell me a little more?" Lane smiled sweetly. "I hate looking like a gossip, but I'm really curious."

"Sure."

Lane casually waved towards the small kitchen table, and Angie followed, taking the seat across the way.

"There's not much to tell. Danie wasn't a great swimmer, but she wanted to go for a swim. Everyone else was busy doing something else, and I guess she went swimming all by herself. She ended up hitting her head on the rocks and drowning."

"Why didn't anyone want to go with her?" Lane scooted her empty plate onto the table and dabbed her mouth with her napkin. "You didn't want to go swimming, either?"

"Well... it... it just ended up being one of those things. The boys had decided to build a bonfire on the beach, so they'd split up to go look for wood. I overheard Kevin asking Janie if she wanted to go with him, which royally pissed me off. Caused a huge fight between Kevin and me. I ended up wandering off to cool down and went for a walk." She flicked her hair out of her eyes. "I didn't feel like being around anybody, let alone going swimming."

Lane gave Angie a skeptical look.

"A walk? One which lasted half a day and was so far, you didn't hear sirens or screams for help? Where exactly did you walk to?"

Angie suddenly looked nervous.

"Ohhh. Just around the campsite... and..." She bit her lip. "Actually, Lane. That's not true."

"It's not?" Lane leaned in.

"No, it's just what I told Kevin." Angie shook her head, looking down at her hands. "I mean, I did wander off. I headed towards the campsites along the beach and stumbled across this cute guy walking his dog. He was super friendly, and we got to chatting. He offered me lunch, so I... I stayed at his camp." Angie suddenly waved her hands in front of her. "But nothing happened! He was married, and his wife was off hiking. I basically kept him company until she returned."

"But you were hoping Kevin would come looking for you and then see you with this other guy?" Lane gave Angie a sly look. "Maybe, make him jealous?"

"Except he never came looking for me. When the camper's wife finally showed up, I decided to head back to camp." Angie's eyes dropped. "We'd heard sirens, but I never dreamed it had anything to do with our group. If I had, I would have come back right away."

"Angie, don't take this the wrong way, but is there any way this camper or his wife could confirm you were with them?" Lane had pulled out her notepad and flipped it open.

Angie's face hardened, but she nodded her head yes. "Yeah, they own a donut shop in Wenatchee. I don't remember their names, but I remember the bakery because it had a cute name. Holy Donuts." Lane smiled at the double entendre as she wrote it down. "They use to be missionaries before they came back to the states and opened a bakery."

"Did you ever ask Kevin why he didn't come looking for you?"

"No. When we talked about what happened afterwards, he mentioned he and Amy had started to make sandwiches. He'd been annoyed because she'd left to go see what Brent and Danie wanted on theirs and was taking forever. He ended up doing it all alone until he heard the call for help." Angie leaned towards Lane, trying to take a peek at her notepad as Lane scribbled down notes. "Can I ask why you're asking about Danie?"

Lane ignored her question. "After Danie died, did you see much of Janie? Have much interaction with her?" Lane decided it was time to talk about the money loan and the horses.

"Listen, Janie and I were never close. She and I didn't see eye to eye very much, unlike Danie, who was a total sweetheart. She and I would go on rides together, and we'd go out—"

"SHERIFF!"

A woman's piercing scream resounded from the dining room in a sharp report, interrupting Angie and propelling Lane to her feet.

All at once, several people could be heard yelling for somebody to call nine-one-one, their voices severed by the sound of breaking glass and toppled chairs. The sudden grinding noise of heavy furniture moving against the floor was accompanied by a male's commanding voice. Booming over the disjointed commotion, directing people to stand back and make room.

Lane sprinted from the kitchen and jetted down

the short hall into the dining room, where she skidded to a halt. A gathered group was blocking the archway, and she quickly shoved people to the side, sternly directing them to let her through. Reluctant feet shuffled, bodies inched to the side, and Lane busted onto the scene.

Slumped against Gabe for support was Brent, wheezing and struggling for breath, his face red and puffy, his eyes swollen shut. Clasped limply in his hand was an EpiPen, the gray safety cap rolling up against the tip of his shoe.

"Try to take a deep breath, Brent. Nice and easy. The medicine will start working any second now," Gabe's voice rang with authoritative calm.

"I have some liquid Benadryl. Should I get it?" Sue Carter asked, her voice shaking as she headed for the bathroom medicine cabinet without waiting for an answer.

"He's having an anaphylaxis reaction to something." Jerry walked up from behind and whispered in Lane's ear.

"Is he going to be okay?" Her eyes were glued to Brent's heaving chest.

"Should be. Gave himself an injection of Epinephrine." Jerry leaned in closer. "That will help the airways open."

"Has the fire department been called?" As if in answer, sirens suddenly wailed in the distance.

"Listen, I'm going to see if I can help," Jerry said, rolling up his sleeves. Brent's wheezing was getting louder and more desperate.

"I think that's a good idea," Lane said, pushing Jerry ahead, her hand on his back.

Stepping forward, Jerry stopped short, startled as Brent completely collapsed, the EpiPen rolling out of his open hand. Letting Brent drop to the floor, Gabe scrambled over his body, grabbing for the EpiPen, assuming Brent's attempt had not broken the skin. He impulsively thrusted the pen into Brent's opposite thigh, searching his swollen face for any kind of reaction.

"Brent? Can you hear me?" Gabe asked, panic lifting his voice to a yell. "Brent?" Gabe leaned over his friend, putting a hand on his heart. "Brent!" The wheezing abruptly stopped. "No... no, no, no." Gabe put his ear to Brent's mouth. "Damn it! He's not breathing!" Gabe tossed the EpiPen aside and started to do CPR compressions.

The crowd, aghast at Brent's collapse, started to gather around him.

Lane watched as Philip walked to the discarded EpiPen, picking it up. He gave it a curious study before putting it in his pocket, juggling the two plates he held in hand. She fleetingly wondered if the extra plate was Brent's before she started to snap commands at the crowding guests. "Let's get the front door open! Come on, folks. Stand back!" Lane barked, turning to the crowd behind her, blazing sirens blaring outside the front door. She found Angie and Amy inching forward to see and briskly pushed them back using her outstretched arm as a barrier. "You're no help if you block the stretcher!" Lane thundered, jarring people out of their stupefied shock in an effort to get them moving. The stunned guests started to numbly back away as Kevin, standing behind the girls, gently pulled them to the side.

Crashing through the doors, Ethan and Calvin pushed an ambulance gurney through Sue's entryway. While Jerry, who was waiting for them, led them over to Gabe, still hovering over Brent's prone body. Philip stood close by, the plates held in one hand and an arm protectively wrapped around Sue, still clutching her bottle of liquid Benadryl.

Lane began directing most of the guests into the living room, making sure everyone was staying on the outskirts of the situation and out of their way. By the time she'd made it back, the EMT fireman already had Brent strapped to the stretcher and were rapidly walking him out.

"He's had a shot of Epinephrine from the EpiPen already. He's going to need to be airlifted," Gabe was running alongside, briefing them of Brent's condition.

"We'll get a chopper on the way and head straight to the landing pad. Hop in, Gabe," Ethan grunted as he and Kevin hefted the gurney into the ambulance.

Gabe, without hesitation, followed the gurney and Kevin, while Ethan shut the doors behind them. A second later, the ambulance was tearing its way out of Sue's driveway, heading for the small landing pad beside the high school football field.

"Think he'll make it?" Lucas asked, his voice frail. He'd been standing in the archway between the hall and the dining room. He looked shaken, his eyes a little too wide, his lips tinged blue with shock. Lane walked over and gave his arm a reassuring squeeze.

"I think they got him in time." Her eyes fell down to his hands. "Lucas? What's that?" She gently took a worn and crumpled picture from his fingers.

"Uh, it's a picture of Danie and Janie. I found it on the ground after they hoisted Brent onto the stretcher. I think it fell out of his pocket..."

Lucas reached for it, but Lane pulled it back, holding it against her chest.

"I'm going to need to keep this, Lucas."

"Sheriff." Philip walked up and grabbed her gently by the elbow, pulling her to the side. "Excuse us, Lucas." He handed her the EpiPen and whispered, "It's expired."

"By how much? I know you can use them a few months after..." Lane was turning it around in her hand, trying to find the expiration date.

"See the little bit of liquid left? See how discolored it is? It's no good," Philip's voice was grave.

"Expired two years ago," Lane said slowly, her hands dropping to her side. She looked over at Lucas, who was being comforted by Angie, Amy, and Kevin, and then looked back up at Philip. "He's not going to make it, is he?"

CHAPTER 31

Laced sunshine cascaded through the bedroom windows creating a delicate pattern across the bedspread. Stretching her arms up in the air, she let them fall to her side like wings, moving her hands back and forth, relishing the feel of the queen-sized mattress below her. Taking a deep breath, Lane lazily sat herself up and threw her legs over the side of the bed, using her toes to find her fluffy pink slippers. She then casually grabbed the terry cloth robe slung over the chair by the door. Wrapping it around her oversized "Bigfoot. Hide and Seek Champion" t-shirt, she shuffled her way across the foray into the living room.

Giving way to a large yawn, she continued to pass through into the dining room, dodging moving boxes as she headed for the kitchen and the coffee pot. Having found both, she then slowly rummaged the cupboards till she found a tin of coffee and proceeded to make her first pot in the new place.

It was while going through the practiced motions of filling the carafe with water, putting in the paper filter, and carefully scooping the dry coffee grounds into the machine, her thoughts were free to recall the previous night.

Brent's friends had immediately left for the next ferry, intent on getting to the hospital as quickly as they could. While Lane, after a bit of elbow twisting and promises to keep everyone posted on his condition, managed to get Sue's guests to gather up their crockpots and head out to their cars to go home. Philip and Jerry had stayed behind at her request.

"Do we know what caused his allergic reaction?" Lane asked, lifting up the small plate Philip had said was Brent's, looking at it closely. It held a scoop full of macaroni salad, six toothpicks which originally skewed tiny cocktail wieners, three Ritz crackers, some crab dip, and a half-eaten chocolate brownie.

"Lucas said he was allergic to bees and tree nuts. Walnuts, almonds..." Jerry said, popping a black olive in his mouth. "He must have eaten something made or contaminated with nuts."

Lane had walked over and was tearing into the few brownies left on the silver platter on the banquet table.

"I already checked. There's no nuts in the brownies." Philip picked up a brownie and gave it a suspicious look before taking a big bite. "Tastes good." Lane frowned at him and brought the brownie up to her nose.

"I smell almonds." She took a deeper breath. "I think they used almond extract instead of vanilla. Maybe even almond flour." She looked over at Sue. "Do you know who brought the brownies?"

"I have no idea. So many people brought food!" Sue said, her Pekinese wiggling in her arms, freshly freed from the laundry room. "I'm sure whoever did had no idea Brent was allergic to almonds. I mean, everything being gluten-free is so popular now."

Lane nodded her head, agreeing at the same time, her cell phone rang. She answered the phone and took the call in the other room.

"If the kid was allergic to bees and nuts, why do you think he let his EpiPen expire?" Jerry asked, taking Sweetums from Sue, hoping to calm the little dog down.

Philip shrugged, taking another bite of brownie. "How often do you check the batteries in your flashlight? You don't know they've gone bad till you go to use it."

"It's not the same thing, Phil. He should have been more care—" Jerry stopped, seeing the look on Lane's face as she walked back into the room.

"Well? Is he gonna make it?" Philip asked, putting the brownie down.

"He was pronounced DOA on the hospital's helipad."

Lane's coffee machine beeped loudly, announcing it was done brewing, abruptly forcing her thoughts back to the cottage kitchen. She poured a cup, then grabbed her notepad and cell phone before heading out to the screened porch, where she sat in one of the two white rocking chairs adorning it.

Taking a tentative sip and inhaling the rich aroma of liquid bliss, she pushed the number two on her speed dial and waited, confident he'd be up to take her call.

"Hello?"

"Hi, Daddy."

"Morning, Pumpkin! It's good to hear your voice," Retired police chief, Donald Lane said happily into the phone, then added cautiously, "Everything, alright?" With his children working in the line of duty, in either the police force or military, he never knew when bad news was coming.

"Yeah, Dad. Everything is fine. Just calling you from my new place."

"So, you got all moved in, huh?"

"Yup! Still need to unpack my boxes from the apartment, which shouldn't take long, and I plan on moving everything from my two storage units on the mainland next weekend. Fairly settled for now."

"Good. Glad you were able to find a bigger place."

"Me too. How are things for you?" Lane, who knew she should call home more often, sat back in the rocking chair and braced herself, waiting to hear about the slow goings of Montana and her dad's absolute boredom with retirement from the police force.

"Well, to be honest. I'm a bit bored."

Lane sighed. "I know, Dad. You miss the force."

Donald grunted. His daughter had heard his complaints plenty of times before. "You working on anything interesting?"

"I am. If you don't mind, I'd like to run the whole thing past you. Get your thoughts?" Lane smiled, knowing her father would be more than happy to do so.

"Let me freshen up my coffee. Hold on." Lane could hear him banging around in his kitchen before making his way to his favorite chair, putting up his feet. "Ahhhh. Okie dokie, I'm settled. Tell me all about it."

Lane proceeded to relay the circumstances of Janie's fall and the coincidence of her twin's death a year prior in the park. Followed by her suspicions, the two deaths were somehow connected. Reading from her notepad, she laid out what she and Philip had discovered. The variances in everyone's recollection on the day of Danie's death and the whereabouts of those who were in the park the day of Janie's fall. She then told him of Brent's demise and how she felt he was still the most likely suspect in Janie's death since he was admittedly the last person to see her alive. Practically confessing to Philip, he'd stalked Janie up The Mole Hill, and had in fact, kept the picture from Janie's backpack... Lane felt secure in her assumption. However, with his accidental death, there was no way to prove it, and in essence, the case was closed. Which was not sitting well with her.

"I think you're right. Sounds like a dead-end to me. No pun intended," Donald agreed, then asked, "This ranger friend of yours. What does he think?"

"He thinks I'm nuts. Though he agrees Janie's death wasn't accidental. He's not convinced Danie's death was. He thinks the two deaths being a year apart is pure coincidence."

"He could be right, Pumpkin." Donald flipped back and forth between his pages of notes, his leather notepad worn thin through the years. "Anything come back on the granola bar wrappers you found on the cliff?"

"I'll hopefully be able to find out tomorrow," Lane sighed, feeling tired and frustrated.

"And the camera's memory card was never recovered?"

"Nope."

"Well, that's no surprise. That would be like finding a needle in a haystack out in the wilderness like that." Donald took a sip of his warm coffee and sat up a little straighter. "Speaking of cameras. Has your ranger friend checked the trail cameras?"

"Trail cameras?"

"Yeah. I knew a ranger here, working in the Glacier National Park, who caught poachers picking off grizzly bears using trail cameras. Think your ranger might have a few hanging up in his forest? Might have caught something?"

"I don't know. But I'll be sure to ask him." Lane scribbled "trail camera" on her notepad and underlined it three times. "That's a really good idea, Dad. Thanks."

"Well, I'm not senile yet! If I think of anything else, I'll give you a jingle."

"Thanks, Daddy." He was forever her hero.

"Heard anything from your brothers?"

"I plan on having dinner with Kent tonight. Mindy's cooking is getting better, so I don't feel like I'm putting my life in mortal danger every Sunday now." Lane laughed. "I also got a postcard from Jimmy. He's enjoying his conference in Norway. That serial killer lecture sure is taking him on a world tour."

"I got a postcard too. Starting to get a nice right pile." Donald moved in his chair, trying to find a more comfortable position. "Lex is heading home for leave next week."

"Will you give him a big hug for me, please?"

Lane sighed. "And please, tell him he needs to stop calling me kiddo in his emails. He won't listen to me."

Donald chuckled, knowing his sons used the affectionate nickname "kiddo" to get under her skin.

"That reminds me. Clark was hoping you'd be able to make it out to his neck of the woods in the beginning of November. He thinks it would help to have you and your brothers support him on election night. You know, stand behind him as he gives his final speech."

"Oh, I don't know, Dad. Virginia is so far awa —"

"LOIS... He'd really like you there," Donald Lane used his "don't argue with me, young lady" tone, which he'd perfected over the years.

Lane quickly answered, "Yes, sir."

"Good. I'll tell our future Congressman Lane. He'll be happy you'll be in attendance."

"Okay, Dad. Listen, I better get going. These boxes aren't going to unpack themselves." Lane stood up from the rocking chair and started her way back into the house.

"Okay, Pumpkin. Love you, and thanks for calling."

"Love you too, Dad. Bye." Lane hung up the phone and started searching her phone directory as she walked back into the kitchen to refill her coffee mug. She found the number and punched send.

"Hello?" A gravelly voice answered on the fourth ring.

"Morning, Ranger. Thought you'd already be awake."

"Well, I am now." Philip blinked his eyes a few times, pulling the phone back from his ear to squint at the phone screen. "Good grief! It's six in the morning." He put the phone back to his ear.

"Lane, it's my day off, and I'm allowed to sleep in. Call me back in four hours."

"I just have a quick question," Lane said, hurriedly into the phone.

"What?" Philip swiped up an extra pillow from the end of the bed and tossed it behind his head.

"Do you have trail cameras in the park?" Lane put her cell phone on speaker, placing it carefully down on the kitchen table.

"Uhhh... Yeah." Philip sat up. "I use them for keeping an eye on where the wildlife is roaming the most and to catch the occasional poacher."

"Any posted near or on Indian Flat trail?" Lane hefted a cardboard box onto the round table, the word KITCHEN written in black marker on the side.

Philip frowned in concentration. "Yeah? Actually, I think we do."

"Any chance it might have footage from over a week ago?" Lane pulled the packing tape off the top and opened the box, peering inside.

"Depends. It's a motion sensor camera. So, based on how much traffic has come and gone, it may have run out of memory. I usually send Kody out to check them, so I'll have to find out when the last time he did that."

"Would you mind doing that today? I know it's your day off." Lane pulled a pile of dish towels and oven mitts out of the box.

"I suppose so. It's just a matter of pulling the memory cards."

"Thanks, Phil."

"You hoping to find Brent following Janie on camera?" Philip closed his eyes, remembering Brent's swollen face from the night before.

"It would tie up the loose ends. Put my mind at ease."

"Well, if he did kill Janie, then it would mean Danie's death was really an accident."

"Why? His whereabouts were unaccounted for. Everyone admits they didn't see him until he came running out of the woods, and we only have his word, which isn't apparently worth much, that he was wandering around looking for wood. Maybe they fought over Janie? Maybe Danie didn't like that Janie had moved to Washington and wasn't returning back with her to Pennsylvania?" Lane opened a kitchen drawer and started placing the kitchen towels inside. "You know, we never did find out what Danie thought of Brent? We just assumed she was happy for her sister. What if she didn't approve of him? Maybe she and Brent got into an argument? Brent, angry, pushes her down into the jagged rocks below, where she hits her head. When she eventually drowns, he yells for help and runs into the woods. Then, after everyone has arrived on the scene, he makes his gallant effort to save her."

"But you'd have no way of proving it. It's all speculation." Philip, giving up on going back to sleep, flipped his sheets off and sat on the edge of his bed.

"True. But if I can prove Brent was stalking Janie, I could get a warrant for his place. Who knows what I might find then?"

"Alright, I'm getting up. Hold your horses," Philip said through a yawn. "Sheesh, you're grouchy in the morning."

"I'm sorry?" Lane looked at her phone, surprised at his words. "I don't mean to sound that way. If it's that big of a bother, don't worry abo—"

"No, I wasn't talking to..." Philip stopped and stretched. "I'll do it this afternoon, Lane. It's no bother, really."

Lane suddenly wondered if Philip had company, and a surprising jolt of jealousy shot through her. She shook her head, scolding herself. It was none of her business if Philip had someone spend the night.

"Appreciate it, Phil. Listen, I'll even treat you to lunch at my office tomorrow when I get back from the coroner?" Lane offered, still distracted by who might be in his bed. "Unless you've got plans..."

"Nope. Works for me. As long as it's not ferry boat clam chowder. Talk at you later."

CHAPTER 32

Before setting off into the woods as promised, Philip stopped by the ranger station to look over Kody's records. Quickly verifying the camera locations and the last time they were scheduled to be checked, Philip felt a mixture of encouragement and disappointment. Kody's slipshod records showed the young ranger hadn't bothered to check them in over a month. Irritated, Philip had half a mind to send Kody out to retrieve the memory cards himself, while he went back home and actually enjoyed his day off. But being a man of his word, Philip headed out on his own.

Finding the trail cameras was easy enough, and he was pleased to note both cards still had memory space. The chances of actually catching something on them, in Philip's opinion, was pretty dang good.

Trekking himself back out, Philip popped into the ranger station to say good-bye to Kody and put a bug in his ear about doing a thorough job. Unfortunately for Philip, but fortunate for an out-of-town camper, he ended up helping pull an RV out of a ditch with the help of Rowles's towing. All in all, the errand had taken longer than he expected. Resulting in a missed lunch and a half-day of work under his belt.

Still actively avoiding Hattie's General, Philip made for the mini-mart by the docks, suddenly craving a corn dog. Once there, he chatted it up with the owner Mr. Wong for a few minutes, who happily reported business was steadily improving. Pleased to hear it, Philip purchased three corn dogs and scored another two for free, as Mr. Wong was throwing them out anyway.

Saying his good-byes, Philip headed out to his truck, taking a hesitant glance towards Bert's Outdoor Supply Shop and Kayak Rentals... or what use to be. Hung from the store's awning was a brand-new vinyl sign, a corner torn loose, flapping loudly in the breeze. Philip knew as soon as the new owner could afford it, they would replace the old signage with a new permanent logo of their own. For now, the vinyl sign boasted the new name of Ernie's Outdoor Supply Shop and Kayak Rentals. Having bought it from the bank a few months ago, Ernie Reames never dreamed the place would be available for sale.

The faithful store employee, as surprised as anyone the shop had gone into foreclosure, had scraped up every penny he owed and borrowed a few to buy the place. Like most of the island residents, he'd always assumed the store would stay family-owned. Though, by the large group of ferry visitors heading towards the door, the name change hadn't seemed to affect business. The outdoor supply shop, under any name, was still considered the hot spot of the docks.

Next in line at the gas pumps, a 1988 three-series BMW in mint condition pulled up, blocking Philip's meandering path back to his rig, and parked at pump one. Recognizing the driver as Lucas's father, Philip waited for him to climb out of his car as he chomped down on a corn dog.

"Hey, Mitchell." Dropping the corn dog back into the paper sack, Philip hastily wiped his greasy fingers on his Levi's and took the outstretched hand offered to him, giving it a hardy shake.

"Did I about run you over? Sorry about that, Phil." Mitchell smiled, flipping the gas lid open with a finger. "A little distracted today."

"I bet." Philip gathered Mitchell was referring to his son dealing with the loss of his best friend. "How's Lucas doing?"

"He's holding up. Putting on a brave face and all that. It's hard on him, though. Heck, it's been hard on me. I've known Brent since he was born. He was always a good kid." Mitchell had taken out his wallet and pulled out a credit card giving it a quick swipe. "Of course, they're not kids anymore. Shame he won't grow into an old man." Mitchell started to tuck the card back into his wallet, shaking his head. "Anyway, I just got done dropping Lucas off at my brother's place. Thought he needed to get off the island for the day."

"I think that was a good idea." Philip ran his hand across the back of the car, admiring the paint job.

"It's Gabe I'm actually worried about, though. He's been beating himself up something terrible." Philip shifted the paper bag over to his other arm, placing a resting hand on the car.

"I can imagine. Poor guy, he did what he could for Brent. But I don't think the kid had much of a chance. Brent was carrying around an expired EpiPen."

Mitchell nodded his head as he flipped the gas latch and squeezed the handle, the black hose jerking as gas started to pump through the rubber line into the tank.

"Gabe says he's going to quit college. Give up medicine and throw it all way." Mitchell propped up the tiny stand on the handle, keeping the line open, then crossed his arms across his chest, leaning up against the car. "I've spent a good portion of the morning trying to talk him out of it. But after not being able to bring Danie around last summer, and now Brent..."

His voice trailed off as he shrugged in defeat.

"Give him some time. Wait for the shock to pass. Maybe Doctor Hadley can talk to him. I think he's got plans for the boy." Philip peeked into the back window of the car, smiling in happy recollection of the times they'd had in high school trolling the island for girls. "Can't believe you've kept this car all these years. Not a scratch on her!"

Mitchell grinned as the handle popped. "Had some good times, didn't we?" He pulled the nozzle out, making sure to avoid spilling any drops of gas on the paint. "I only take her out on Sundays. Trying to keep the mileage low."

"You don't let Lucas drive her around at all?" Philip lightly buffed his handprint off the trunk with his shirttail.

"You kidding? Ever see how many dents his truck has? I only bought him the damn thing a year ago. Treats it like some kind of Tonka toy!" Mitchell roughly put the nozzle back into the cradle on the pump. "I'll get buried in the damn thing before I let him touch it."

Philip could relate. Kody wasn't much better than Lucas when it came to dents.

"I remember us putting a few dings in your dad's car a time or two," Philip teased, taking a step away from the BMW as Mitchell sat down into the driver seat. "He's a good kid, Mitch."

Mitchell rubbed the car's dash affectionately before looking up at Philip. "Yeah, I know. I just wish he had the drive Gabe does. If he's not outdoors playing, he's indoors wasting away on those damn video games. I actually had to change the wi-fi password in an effort to get him out of the house. Let me tell you, made for one hell of a long Labor Day weekend!" Mitchell shut the car door and rolled down the window. "If you're not busy next weekend, I'm planning on taking the boat out."

"Sounds great!"

"Oh, and tell Harry? He's always good for a laugh."

Philip smiled a tight smile.

"For sure."

CHAPTER 33

Having lived without an oven in the old apartment, Lane was overcome with a sudden desire to bake in her new kitchen. Excited with the prospect, she dug out her never before used Betty Crocker Cook Book, searching for a recipe, and decided on chocolate chip cookies. Reading the ingredients, she did a quick inventory of her fridge and pantry, discovering she needed eggs, butter, sugar, flour, salt, baking soda, and... chocolate chips.

Undeterred, she was on her way to Hattie's when she spotted a bicyclist on the road. Taking a wide berth around, she carefully passed and recognized the rider to be Gabe. Seeing an opportunity, Lane drove a little further before pulling to the side, letting the truck roll to a slow stop. She then hopped out, waving him down, indicating she wanted to have a word.

Bringing the big-wheeled mountain bike to a skidded halt, Gabe planted his feet, leaning against the handlebars, his breath labored.

"Hi, Sheriff. Everything, okay?" Large beads of sweat were pouring down Gabe's face, soaking into his shirt, plastering his hair to his forehead.

"Saw you riding and figured with it being such a hot day you might want a lift? Why don't you toss your bike in the back, and I'll take you the rest of the way into town?" Lane offered, watching Gabe use the bottom of his t-shirt to wipe his face dry.

"Thanks." Gabe got off the bike and walked it over, easily lifting the bicycle onto his shoulder as Lane pulled down the tailgate.

"Looks as if you got a good workout." Lane shut the tailgate and motioned for him to head front to the passenger side of the vehicle.

"Yeah. I needed to get out of the house." Gabe took his backpack off, dumping it on the floor-board. He suddenly looked around him as if he didn't know where he was.

"You went farther than you meant to, huh?" Lane climbed in herself, giving the young man an understanding smile. "I like to drive when I need to think things through. Usually, find myself a good hundred miles or so away from home if I'm upset about something."

Gabe smiled back and nodded, then looked down at his backpack.

"Been thinking about Brent's death?" Lane winced as she turned the key, wishing she had been a little more thoughtful in her choice of words. Gabe stayed quiet, his eyes downcast, focused on the knapsack. "I don't know if they told you, Gabe. His EpiPen was expired. There wasn't anything you could have done."

Gabe's brow furrowed, but he still didn't look up.

"Sorry. You probably don't want to talk about it," Lane apologized, pulling out onto the road. "Just don't want you blaming yourself."

"Appreciate it, ma'am," Gabe said quietly and then hefted the backpack up onto his lap. Lane grimaced at the title of ma'am, feeling all of her thirty-five years. "Sheriff, remember when we talked yesterday, and you gave me your card so my friend could call you?"

Lane nodded yes, slowing the truck down a little, suddenly not in hurry to pull into town. "I do."

"Well, I'm my friend." Gabe gave her a sideways glance, unzipping the backpack.

"I kind of already figured, Gabe." Lane kept her eyes on the road.

"Guess I wasn't being as clever as I thought."

"It's alright. It's hard to know what to do sometimes." Lane gave him a quick look noticing he'd opened his backpack and was rooting around for something. "What was it you wanted to talk to me about?"

"This." Gabe pulled out a memory card. "I thought you might want it."

Lane slammed the brakes and yanked the patrol truck to the side of the road, throwing it into park.

"Is that what I think it is?" She leaned over and popped the glove box, pulling out a plastic evidence bag. "The missing memory card from Janie's camera?"

"It's damaged," Gabe said somberly, dropping the small card into the open evidence bag. It stopped halfway, sticking between the plastic sheets. Lane quickly sealed the bag before bringing it up to her face.

"You're right. Somebody has scratched the living tar out of the metal prongs." She again leaned into the glove box and grabbed a black sharpie, scribbling the time and date on the bag. She then tossed the bag and pen back, banging the little door shut. "Where did you find it, Gabe?"

"I didn't. Lucas did."

"He did? Where? Why didn't he tell me? When did he give it to you?" Lane reached for her back pocket, realizing she'd left her leather notepad on the kitchen table.

"He said he found it the day before yesterday at Brent's house. We'd gone over to play video games.

He said he found it on the floor next to a pair of hiking shorts."

"Did he ask Brent about it?"

"Yeah. Brent said he'd found it where Janie had fallen. Said he was going to give it to you, but he didn't even try to talk to you at the memorial. I started to worry he was lying." Gabe fiddled with his backpack. "I was going to come see you on Monday and give it to you, but since we're here..." Gabe started to zip the backpack up.

"I'm glad you did," Lane said, distracted, several questions racing through her head.

"Lucas didn't want me to tell you. He was scared it would get Brent in trouble." Gabe looked out the passenger window. "I was worried about that too. But... since Brent is gone." Lane gave Gabe a long stare as she waited for him to add more, noticing he was fidgeting and moving his knee up and down in a nervous gesture.

"Gabe, is something else bothering you?" Lane pressed, deciphering his body language. She'd seen this a time or two in an interrogation room. He was holding something back.

Gabe nodded his head, a heavy frown on his face.

"I feel like a jerk for even thinking it." He turned his gaze to Lane.

"Gabe, you shouldn't feel ba—"

"But if he did hurt her," he sighed heavily, interrupting her, "It's not right." He licked his lips. "When I saw Brent Thursday morning in the park, the day they said Janie was pushed? He seemed like he was in a big hurry. Like he didn't really want to stop and talk... and... I've been thinking about that. Made me wonder if he knew Janie was going up The Mole Hill, and he was trying to catch up to her." His words were said in a rush as if scared he'd lose his courage.

Lane nodded her head, knowing it was pretty much what Brent had told Philip.

"And... well, I hate to even think it. It's pretty off the wall."

"Think what, Gabe?"

"I'm starting to wonder if Brent pushed Danie off the point last summer."

Lane felt goosebumps ripple up her arm. "What makes you think that?"

"Janie avoided him like the plague after her sister died. I would think, after something so traumatic, you'd cling to the man you loved. It's just been something in the back of my mind I've not been able to shake."

"But what would be Brent's reason to kill Danie?" Lane was desperately missing her leather notepad.

"Money, lots and lots of money."

Lane nodded her head, understanding Gabe's theory. With Danie's death, her money had automatically gone to Janie. If he and Janie were to get married, he'd have enjoyed the wealth as well. It was an angle she had considered but had dismissed since Brent came from a wealthy family himself. But now faced with the theory again, she realized just because his family was wealthy didn't mean Brent was personally.

"Gabe, you also said something about odd comments. What was said to catch your attention?"

Gabe swallowed hard before answering, thinking his words over. "I'd rather not say. It has nothing to do with Brent."

Lane decided to take a stab in the dark. "Lucas said something you found odd?"

Gabe gave her a hard look, hesitant to say anything more.

"Come on, Gabe. It could be important. Then again, it might be nothing. Let me be the judge. Lucas doesn't have to know we even had this conversation," Lane coaxed, trying to put him at ease.

"You'll keep it between us?"

Lane nodded, avoiding a verbal promise.

"Okay." He started to fidget with the zipper on his backpack. "Lucas told someone he'd been playing video games the day Janie died, and then he told someone else he'd been on his dad's boat. I thought it strange."

"You didn't ask him about it?"

"I did. He just told me I heard wrong."

"Gabe, Janie told a friend Lucas was stalking her.

Know anything about that?"

Gabe looked surprised. "No! How? Janie hasn't been around all year."

"Well, apparently, he'd been driving over to Seattle and stalking her there."

Gabe shook his head, not liking the idea.

"I know he and she were fooling around last summer. I didn't think it had gone to that level."

"What?" Lane's eyebrows shot up. "Lucas and Janie?"

Gabe nodded his head, giving Lane a sheepish look. "Yup."

"Did Danie know? What about Brent? Did he know?"

Gabe shook his head no. "Lucas swore me to secrecy."

"Were they serious?"

"Drunken one-night stand. Nothing more." Gabe looked at Lane, worry in his eyes. "Then again, if Lucas was stalking her. Maybe it was more serious than he told me?"

"Gabe, the day we found Janie's body. The day of the search? At the end, before everyone left, I noticed you and Lucas were having a heated discussion with Brent. He seemed to want to have a word with Deputy Pickens, but the two of you were stopping him? What was going on there?"

Gabe blushed, letting go of the zipper and lightly

kicking his backpack.

"I know what you're talking about. Brent had shown up to help look, and we had to tell him we'd been the ones to find Janie. He wanted to tell the authorities he was the last person to see her. He was convinced she'd taken a misstep off the ledge."

"And you guys thought it was a bad idea?" Lane's voice had an edge.

Gabe's eyes went wide.

"I didn't! It was Lucas who said it was a bad idea. He thought it might look bad for Brent, and I reasoned it would look bad if he didn't come forward."

"Anything else you can think of, Gabe?" Lane's head was whirling.

"No. I'm pretty sure that's it. I mostly wanted you to have the memory card. Hopefully, you'll be able to find something?"

"I doubt it." Lane pulled back onto the road. "Any idea how it got so scrapped up?"

"No. I'm guessing that's how he found it."

"Who, Brent or Lucas?"

"Lucas," Gabe said the name slowly as if an idea had suddenly popped into his head. "Lucas might have..."

"What, Gabe?" Lane frowned as they hit the main street.

"Nothing." Gabe shook his head and then smiled. "You can drop me off here."

"Do you know where I could find Lucas?" Lane pulled in front of Hattie's General. "I'd like to talk to him about the memory card."

"He's over at his uncle's place on Mercer Island. He'll be back tomorrow. Late in the evening, probably on the eight o'clock ferry."

"Thanks. I'll try to catch him at the docks for a quick talk." She had several burning questions for Lucas, and she wouldn't forget her notepad this time.

CHAPTER 34

Philip made a U-turn at the end of the road having driven past the sheriff's office, finding the windows dark and parking spots empty. After leaving the mini-mart he'd headed downtown, curious to see if Lane had decided to work on her day off as well. Seeing she hadn't, he now was heading home in hopes of catching the last half of the Seahawks game.

Coming back up the road, he happened to spot Doctor Hadley stalking out of his office. The elderly doctor was wearing his stethoscope over his white coat and a stern expression. He had taken off his dark-rimmed glasses and was waving them in the air, trying to garner Philip's attention.

"Phil, I need a word!" The white-haired doctor walked out to Philip's pickup, ignoring the fact

Philip was now parked in the middle of the road.

Doctor Hadley, on the verge of retirement, was the island's only medical doctor. Even with Seattle only a ferry ride away, most of the islanders and their children were his patients. And for the most part, though the doctor had a brisk, no-nonsense approach to medicine and was usually short on bedside manner... The white-haired physician was still adored and revered amongst the small population. Especially since he still made house calls, even on football Sundays.

"Hi, Doc! Is everyth—"

"Park the truck and come inside." Doctor Hadley didn't wait for Philip's answer before heading back across the street towards his office.

Surprised at the invitation, but not by the way it was requested, Philip swung the pickup into the first parking spot and hopped out, quickly making his way into the small building.

"Have a seat," Doctor Hadley addressed Philip when he walked through the door, giving him a general wave towards the waiting room. He'd said it casually as if Philip were there for a scheduled check-up.

Obediently sitting down in one of the well-worn waiting room chairs, Philip watched as the elderly doctor made his way over to a wooden coat rack standing in the corner.

"I heard about Brent Allister." The doctor started

to shrug out of his white coat. "You saw it happen?"

Philip nodded his head slowly, his face sullen. "It was terrible to watch."

"He had an expired EpiPen? At least, that's what our local gossipmonger Mrs. Barnes is saying."

"Yes, sir." Philip sat back in the chair with his arms on the armrests. "It's a shame. Expiration was two years past. Liquid was discolored inside."

"Hmmm, that's very interesting." Doctor Hadley hooked the coat onto the wooden rack and added the stethoscope to the next rung before turning around to face Philip with a tired smile.

"What are you doing in your office on a Sunday?" Philip suddenly looked around, noticing there was no one else in the building. "Returning from a house call?"

"Ohhhhh," The elderly doctor sighed heavily, settling himself down painfully next to Philip, his knees stiff. "Checking my records." He took off his glasses, giving them a quick huff before using the end of his tie to buff the lens. "It's habit for me to put the coat and stethoscope on when I'm in the office," he confessed lightly and then suddenly put on a serious face. "Back to this EpiPen business, Phil. If I tell you something, will you pass it along to that pretty little new sheriff?"

"Yes, sir." Philip smiled, knowing Lane would have bristled at the description.

"Brent's EpiPen couldn't have been expired." The doctor tapped Philip's knee hard, punctuating every other word.

"But it was, sir." Philip turned in his chair. "I checked it myself."

"I'm not saying the EpiPen Brent had on his person wasn't expired. I'm saying the EpiPen I prescribed to Brent wasn't." The doctor gave Philip a severe nod.

"How do you know?" Philip felt strange questioning the old doctor.

"I checked." By the blank stare on Philip's face, Doctor Hadley saw his brisk answer wasn't enough and continued, "It's not commonly known. But adults can develop allergies later on in life. Granted most allergies form while in childhood, but now and then... an adult, who wasn't allergic to something, can suddenly become deathly allergic."

"Huh." Philip raised his eyebrows, his bottom lip stuck out, impressed by the little-known fact.

"In Brent's case, he was always allergic to bee stings. It wasn't until he hit his early twenties that I sent him in for an allergy test after complaining about a plant rash. On top of bee stings, we discovered he had become deathly allergic to tree nuts as well." The doctor held his glasses above his head, squinting through the lens, checking for smudges before putting them back on. "I tell you this because I only prescribed Brent the EpiPen eleven months ago."

"Eleven months ago?" Philip's eyebrows almost met in the middle, he frowned so hard. "But if he was always allergic to bee stings?"

"Allergic." Doctor Hadley suddenly held his index finger up as if pointing at the ceiling. "If he ever got stung." He then tapped lightly on Philip's knee. "Bees are pretty easy to avoid unless you go looking for them." The old doctor smiled wisely. "It was just a childhood condition he lived with. It wasn't until the beginning of this gluten-free craze and his daily trips up The Mole Hill that I began to insist he start packing around the EpiPen."

"Makes sense. You didn't like the idea of him being so far away from medical assistance. Especially if he was out in the park." Philip could understand the doctor's worry. Working out there himself, it was always a concern if something were to happen to him or Kody on the job that medical assistance might not make it in time.

"Nope. Not one bit." He gave Philip a grave smile. "So, you can see my concern."

"Maybe he bought it off eBay or something?" Philip shrugged, figuring there was a logical explanation.

"Illegal. It's only available by prescription," the old doctor said gruffly.

"Could the pharmacy have given him an expired one by accident and not have noticed?" Philip thought it unlikely, but stranger things had happened.

"Practically impossible. Those things are double and triple-checked."

"Maybe it accidentally got switched with a friend's or stranger's?"

Philip felt like he was reaching.

"Doubtful. You don't swap them like baseball cards."

"Well..." Philip shook his head, out of ideas. "What do you think happened?"

"Don't know." Doctor Hadley gave a huff of irritation. "Spent the last half hour looking back through my records, making sure the blame didn't fall at my feet. Couldn't live with that."

"But you think it's something the sheriff needs to know about?"

"Best to have all the facts. If she thinks it's something worth looking into, send her to me."

CHAPTER 35

Coroner Ames, wearing a heavily padded winter jacket, was furiously digging through his metal filing cabinets, apparently on the hunt. Bouncing from tower to tower, his fingers dexterously flew through the tabbed manilla folders yanking and pulling at will. Upon finding what he was looking for, he gave a triumphant yelp before tossing the file to the pile sitting on the carpeted floor and progressing to the next drawer.

He was obviously busy. Lane brought her hand up, hesitating to interrupt. He wasn't exactly expecting her.

"Mind if I come in?" Lane asked lightly, knocking on his door. To her surprise, the little coroner didn't bother to look up. He simply waved her in with one hand and yanked another drawer open with the other.

"Glad you're here, Sheriff Lane." He plopped another file on top of the growing stack and kept digging. "Thought about calling you at home yesterday, but then they added Allister to my roster. Figured I'd be seeing you soon enough, and here you are!" He glanced up at the clock hanging on the wall above his door. "A few hours earlier than I expected, though."

"I'm afraid your secretary is learning I don't take no for an answer," Lane admitted, with little to no guilt, walking over to his desk. "What did you find out that deserved a phone call?"

"Fingerprints." The coroner turned to her with a sly smile, his jacket's fur hood circling his gaunt face. "Or rather, a lack of fingerprints."

"I'm not following. On the granola bar wrappers?" Lane questioned, slowly lowering herself into one of the two waiting chairs.

The coroner shook his head, pulling his hood back.

"The spiral notebook you brought in for fingerprinting? The one found in her apartment? It had Janie's fingerprints all over it." He pulled his jacket back from his waist to avoid snagging it on the file drawer. "Alllll over it," he repeated again, more to himself than Lane.

"Naturally. She probably was the one who bought the notebook. After all, it was found on top of her writing desk," Lane said casually, watching him pull

312

another file, then with some difficulty, heave the old metal drawer shut with a loud bang.

"No. What I'm saying is they found ONLY Janie's finger and palm prints. They'd attempted to rule out her prints to focus on anyone else's... but there was only hers." He walked behind his desk and plopped the file down on top.

Lane leaned over and read his handwritten note below the file case number. It read "The Push." Remembering the coroner's habit of labeling his cases with his own thoughts or comments, he'd apparently taken Lane's theory to heart.

"So, they wore gloves when trying to mimic her signature?" Lane sat back, still not seeing what he was excited about. To her, it sounded like another dead end.

"You're still not understanding, Sheriff. The victim was the ONLY person writing on that piece of paper."

Lane frowned, a deep wrinkle set between her brows as she shook her head, trying to make sense of what he was saying. She was still clearly confused.

"You see, the position of the palm matches the signature placement." Coroner Ames pointed to the plate of homemade cookies Lane had put on his desk and gave her a questioning look. "You made these?"

Lane curtly nodded her head, wanting to keep his attention focused. "So, you're telling me that—"

"That only Janie's palm print and fingerprints matched up with the writing." The coroner slowly nodded his head up and down, pleased to see she was following along.

"Are you sure? Because..." Lane stood up, walking over to the file cabinets, pacing her thoughts out. "It doesn't make any sense. Why would she be practicing her own signature and using an apartment application to copy..." Lane quickly returned to the chair, a bright light in her eyes. "Twins share the same DNA, right?"

"Yes. They're split from the same egg," the coroner answered automatically, pulling the plastic cling wrap from the plate of homemade goodies.

"So, basically duplicates of each other. Same eye color, same hair color, same height."

"That's the idea when it comes to identical twins," he said blandly and then smiled brightly. "Are these chocolate chip or raisin?"

"Chocolate chip." Lane waved his question away as if it was a fly. "What about fingerprints?" Lane was mentally searching her mind, feeling as if she'd been taught the answer at some point in time. However, running into murdered twins didn't happen every day, and it most likely was stuffed into the "useless information" file located in the back of her brain.

"Those are NOT identical. Each twin has their own separate fingerprint. In fact, it's little know—"

"Can you pull Danie's file? You took her finger-prints as well, correct?" Lane had pulled out her cell phone and was searching her call history.

"Yes, and of course." The coroner got up from his desk, walking over to the last filing cabinet while Lane made a phone call.

"Hello, is Wanda available? Yes, I'll hold." Lane impatiently tapped her foot, waiting for the line to pick up. "Yes, Wanda? Hi, this is Sheriff Lane. We spoke the other day in regards to the Engles sisters?" Lane paused impatiently. "Yes, I'm fine. Thank you. I was wondering when the girls opened their banking accounts and lockboxes, did you take their finger-prints? Or even just their thumbprint?" Lane nod-ded, receiving the answer. "Great, great. I need you to fax a copy of those records to this number." She put her hand over the phone. "What's your fax number?"

The coroner pointed to an ancient fax machine sitting behind his desk, where someone had labeled the number onto the machine's phone handset. Lane read off the number and thanked her lucky stars Wanda wasn't asking for a warrant before faxing the information over.

"Thank you, Wanda. You've been a great help!" Lane said as the fax machine started to spit out pa-per at a snail's speed. She snatched up the faxed pages, handing them to the coroner. "We need to compare these fingerprints and see if they indeed match the same girl."

The coroner took the papers gingerly, looking at Lane questioning. "What will that prove?"

"That Janie wasn't actually Janie. I think Danie was masquerading as her dead sister, and it was Janie who drowned all along! Can you compare the prints?"

"I'll get an ID tech over here. Hold on." Coroner Ames made a quick phone call, mumbling his request through a mouth full of cookies. "I've got someone on their way," he said, hanging up the phone and sitting back in his chair. "I suppose now you'll want to go through Danie's file while we wait for the ID tech?" He gave a knowing smile before tossing her a new file.

It was titled in his handwriting "Shallow Point Diving Club Member." Lane assumed the girl hadn't been the first one to ignore the "No Diving" signs to their detriment.

"I ruled it an accidental drowning since there was no reason to believe foul play had taken place, and there were witnesses, so to speak. The girl had told her friends she was going swimming, and its common practice to ignore the no swimming signs. However, as you read my notes, you'll see I theorized she didn't actually dive off the point. She still had a flip-flop on one of her feet. I made the assumption she may have dropped something over the edge or saw something which struck her interest. And, in an attempt to reach it or see it better, leaned over too far and lost her balance."

Lane was analyzing the injuries listed, reviewing the drawn outline of a female body. There was a mark at the top of the head and another by the base of the neck.

"So, she had a head injury on top of drowning?" Lane held out the body outline sheet.

The coroner grabbed another cookie before taking the paper from Lane's hand, giving it a once over.

"Yes. She had an open wound on the back of her head and bruises around her neck and upper chest. I deduced the head injury was from hitting a rock when she fell. The bruises around her neck and chest area from when the young men hauled her back to shore and the CPR attempts." He handed the sheet back, and Lane took it, reading his small notes in the margins.

"The wounds on her upper chest and neck. Could those also be consistent with someone maybe... holding her down?" Lane asked cautiously, not wanting to offend.

The coroner, about to take a bite, paused in thought. "Possibly. In light of new findings, I wouldn't disregard it."

"Excuse me? You requested an ID tech?" A young woman stood at the door, a questioning smile on her face.

"Yes, yes! Come on in. Have a seat here," Coroner Ames directed her to his chair. "I want you to compare these prints." He pulled a fingerprint sheet from Janie's file. "With these prints." He handed her the faxed copy of Danie's lockbox application. "I apologize. It's not the best image to work with."

"Can you tell us if they match?" Lane scooted to the edge of her chair, her stomach in knots. The young ID tech took out a small tripoded magnifying glass and laid it over Janie's prints before folding the fax machine copy of Danie's prints and aligning them next to each other. She then bent over the desk and put her eye to the magnifying glass.

"I can. They match perfectly." The ID tech smiled brightly, hoping it was the answer they wanted to hear.

"Can you..." Lane snatched the prints out of Danie's file and then the other faxed page. "Can you see if these two... if they match as well?" She gave the little coroner a quick shrug. "Just double-checking."

The ID tech took the pages and carefully placed the first two sheets aside. "Sure."

"Well?" Lane bit her lip.

"Looks as if these prints match with each other as well. They are distinctly different from the first set you handed me."

The confirmation hit Lane like a ton of bricks, and everything clicked into place. The reason why Janie had avoided the island and kept her distance from friends and family. Why she turned down the photography assignments and had so much yellow in her closet, and why she was wearing a beaded bracelet with a letter D carved in the bead.

"It's never been about Janie." Lane looked up at the coroner, her eyes wide. "It's always been about Danie." She stood up, shaking her head, holding Danie's case file to her chest. "They thought they had killed Danie and Danie knew it. She's been in hiding, posing as her dead sister. It was Danie, not Janie, who was pushed off the cliff."

CHAPTER 36

Lane briskly walked into Hattie's General, looking for Amy Holmes, the golden bell above the door declaring her arrival.

"Sheriff Lane! Come take a look!" Harry's disembodied voice carried from somewhere by the register. Most likely originating from behind the towering, triple-tiered, shiny bowling trophy sitting on the front counter. "Isn't it a beaut?" Harry asked gleefully, having to lean way to the side before she could see him. With an eager wave, he beckoned the sheriff over, giving the golden little bowler on top a quick buff with his cleaning rag. "Well, what do you think?" He stepped back so she could admire it properly.

"Wow. Pretty nice trophy, Harry. Way nicer than the first one." Lane marveled at its height and grandeur.

"Sure, is!" Harry's chest puffed with pride.

"It's so... so tall and so much BIGGER than your last one."

"I know!" Harry turned the trophy so Lane could see all sides. "Trophy store called this morning. Said Phil told them I could have the pick of the litter. Reckoned he'd want me to have the best. Right, Sheriff?" He looked to Lane, eyebrows raised as he nodded his head up and down, seeking approval.

Lane found herself nodding with him, glad to see Philip had finally come through. Apparently, witnessing Gabe failing to save his best friend had prompted him to make the first move of reconciliation with Harry.

"Did you call him to say thank you?" Lane asked, reading the tiny plaque on the front of the trophy.

"I did, but he didn't answer. I left a message. Told him beers were on me tonight over at the bowling alley." Harry's smile widened. "Hey! You should come down! Play the lanes with us!"

"Ohhhh... I'm not much of a bowler." Lane looked around the store, checking the close vicinity for Amy.

"Phil could teach you. He's a real good bowler." Harry nudged Lane's arm, giving her a playful smile. "Maybe the two of you could make a date out of it?"

"What did you just say?" Lane looked at Harry as if he'd sprouted horns and a long tail.

"And then I could ask out the pretty new teller at the bank next door. We could make it a double date!"

"Um, I suppose Amy isn't working, is she?" Lane started to rubberneck the aisles hoping to spot the young cashier.

"Sure, she is. Had to stick the poor thing in the backroom. She's been crying all day." Harry spit on his rag and shined up the plaque a bit more. "She and Kody got into a fight, I guess."

"Do you mind if I visit with Amy back there? I need to talk to her about a few things."

"Not at all!" Harry found another spot needing a shine. "Hey, she's not in trouble, is she?" He stopped buffing. "Because she does a good job around here, and having her cover the mid-afternoon shift to closing has taken a huge weight off my shoulders. Especially with Hattie's birthday party coming up."

The golden bell chimed, this time declaring Dub and Glen, who had come into the store for their afternoon coffee with Hattie.

"Hey, Glen! Dub! Come check out my new trophy! Ain't it something?" Harry welcomed them with open arms, steering them away from the picnic table.

Seeing her opportunity, Lane started making her way down aisle one towards the back of the store. Passing the two-way mirror window, she slowed down as she approached the entrance, stopping in front of the swing doors leading to the storeroom and Harry's office. She hesitated for a moment, tracing a bullet hole in the door with her finger, her heart skipping at the touch. This would be the first time she'd step foot in the storeroom since the incident last spring. And though she wasn't scared or superstitious... it was still a place of traumatic memories.

With a quick inhale, she righted her shoulders and made her way through, standing just inside the doors. Little had changed. There were still piles of unbroken down cardboard boxes and pallets of product here and there. Racks of inventory stocked high to the ceiling with various products and unopened boxes left abandoned in the aisles. She could even see Harry's office, a bright light under his closed door. Of course, there were some changes too. The room was brightly lit, better than it had been before, and Harry had removed the empty bullet-ridden refrigerated cases.

Gazing at the floor, she felt the slight movement of air behind her, the doors softly swinging back and forth, eventually slowing to a complete stop. And there, right at her feet, she could see the concrete. Now a shiny dark black, succeeding in thoroughly covering the large bloodstain left six months before.

"That you, Harry?" A croaking voice came from inside the rows of shelving. It sounded raw and sore from crying. Lane headed in the direction of the call and found Amy sitting on the storeroom floor. Her hair was tied back in a ponytail though most of it was falling out, and she looked extremely tired, her eyes wet and red-rimmed from crying. She was busy pulling out boxes of pasta from a large cardboard box, carefully pricing each one before placing them in a tidy row on the bottom shelf.

"Hi, Amy. Can we talk?" Lane gave her an easy-going smile. "I wanted to discuss something with you." Amy looked surprised to see her and got up from the floor, straightening her work smock.

"I don't know, Sheriff. I've had a really bad day and... Well, don't take this the wrong way, but if you're here wanting advice about my dad... I really don't think I should get involved in his love life." She nervously tugged on the end of her ponytail. "Angie told me you guys were fighting at the memorial."

Lane shook her head quickly. "No. This isn't about your dad, Amy. I wanted to talk to you about Danie."

"You mean, Janie?" Amy lightly tossed the pricing gun into the large cardboard box, scooting it aside with her foot.

"I don't know? Do I?" Lane asked, an edge to her voice.

Amy suddenly looked wary and gave the sheriff a nervous look, fretting her bottom lip.

"Tell me, Amy. When did you guess it was Janie who drowned last summer and not Danie as everyone was led to believe?" Lane had taken a wild guess. Amy, out of all of the friends, had seemed to be the closest to Danie. And though she was on good terms with Caleb... Not to mention, her dad was dating the sheriff, Amy hadn't bothered to ask either one of them about Danie's death or the investigation. Lane thought she knew why. She watched as Amy's shoulders drooped, and her hands came up to cover her face, large sobs suddenly shaking her small frame. Taking the girl's reaction as a positive answer, Lane gave her a moment before continuing, "Did you know it on the day she drowned?"

Amy shook her head no, her hands still covering her face.

"But you figured it out later?"

Amy nodded yes, a large sobbing sigh bursting from her chest.

"Did Danie know you knew she was pretending to be her sister?" Lane asked gently, leaning up against the metal shelving.

Amy dropped her hands, tears freely rolling down her cheeks, her mascara running. "No..." She took a couple of deep breaths, trying to calm herself, and then sniffled. "No, I never let on that I knew." She wiped at her eyes. "I was hoping someday she'd tell me, but I think she was too scared. I know I probably should have said something, but I was so—"

Lane held her hand up, indicating for Amy to hold on, and quickly walked through the shelved aisles. Spotting a stack of Kleenex boxes, she grabbed one, ripping the top open as she walked back.

"Here. I'll pay for it on my way out."

"Thanks." Amy took the box with a grateful smile.

"Let's start at the beginning. Do you know why Janie was pretending to be Danie while you guys were out camping?"

The young girl blew her nose and then pulled two more tissues out of the box. "I do. It started as sort of a practical joke. The night before, Brent had made some smart mouth comment to Lucas. Bragging he could tell the twins apart, and Janie... that is, the real Janie, wanted to see if he really could. Those two, the twins, prided themselves on being exactly alike physically. Except for the whole red and yellow thing." Amy took a deep breath, starting to calm down. "Janie also suspected Brent was going to propose, and I think she wanted to make sure he really did love HER and not a copy." Amy suddenly shrugged. "I don't know how to explain it."

"You're doing fine. Keep going," Lane encouraged.

Amy nodded hurriedly, indicating she would continue, stuffing the used tissues in her smock pocket. "She really had to coax Danie into doing it." Amy rubbed her nose with a new tissue and then chuckled. "Danie didn't want to get stuck in an awkward moment, you know. In case Brent tried to kiss her or put his hands somewhere."

Lane nodded her understanding. That would have been expected considering how everyone described

Danie as being so extremely shy and uncomfortable around men, unlike her sister. The shy twin most likely would have been hesitant.

"She only went along with it because Janie promised they'd switch back before lunch so she wouldn't have to pretend all day. They had swapped identities that night, sleeping in each other's tents instead of their own."

"And do you think Brent figured it out?"

"He was completely clueless."

"Janie must have been disappointed. Did she try to drop any helpful hints for the poor guy?"

Amy nodded her head. "A few. She was acting more flirtatious than Danie would ever have dreamed of being. Hanging on Gabe. Rubbing his back or shoulders, holding his hand, being really cutesy. Oh, and she ate some watermelon. Danie didn't like watermelon. The biggest hint, though, was saying she wanted to go for a swim. Danie was scared of the water. But... then again, it was a super-hot day. I think Brent assumed she was going to dip her toes by the shore."

"Amy, do you remember who found her floating in the ocean?" Lane reached for her pad but kept her eyes on the weeping girl. Amy shook her head. "It was one of the guys. I don't recall which one, though. Maybe, Gabe?"

"So, after she said she was going swimming, what happened next?"

"I thought the swimming comment was code for them to switch back. I assumed they were going to sneak down to the water, quickly swap clothes and flip-flops, and then return back to camp as their normal selves. That's why I decided not to go with her." Amy took a deep breath, trying to fight off the coming tears again. "Sorry, Sheriff. With Brent dying and losing Danie... again... on top of Kody and I getting into a huge fight this morning." Amy started to play with the end of her ponytail. "I'm a bit of an emotional mess. Sorry."

"It's alright. You're allowed to be." Lane gave the young woman another minute to compose herself. When she thought she was settled enough, she asked, "Did Danie love Lucas?"

"Sort of. Both Lucas and Gabe were really into her, but she was planning on going to college back east, so she didn't take either one of them very seriously."

"But she did prefer one over the other, didn't she?" Lane asked, a knowing smile crossing her face.

"She liked Lucas more than she did, Gabe. He made her laugh, and Danie was so shy most of the time. I think it made her feel less self-conscious, you know?" Amy stared down at the floor, a lost look on her face.

"But she did like Gabe too?" Lane asked, wanting to clarify if both boys had the young woman's attention or if it was only one-sided.

Amy simply nodded her head, still staring at the floor.

"What do you think she liked about Gabe?" Lane gently moved a piece of fallen hair from Amy's face, tucking it behind her ear.

"Um, I think she liked the fact he was striving for a future. Going to medical school really impressed her. She told me Gabe had even talked to her about maybe switching his credits to the Perleman School of Medicine at Penn State and getting his medical degree there."

"Did she like the idea?" Lane asked, surprised Gabe would follow her all the way to Pennsylvania.

"I don't really know. Though she probably thought it might be nice to have a friend close by. She only brought it up the once."

"Lucas and Gabe, they both knew they were going after the same girl?"

"Yeah, but it didn't seem to affect their friendship. Besides, Lucas didn't think he had a chance in hell, and Gabe, he's always such a gentleman. I think if Danie had flat out picked Lucas over him, he probably would have stayed silently devoted." Amy's eyes got weepy. "He tried so hard to save her..."

"And why did Lucas think—" Lane tugged on the girl's smock collar, trying to keep her on subject.

"That he didn't have a shot in hell? Oh, that's because Lucas isn't brainy. He'd rather play video games, or go climbing, or boating. Anything else other than stick his nose in a book. Danie was an intellectual. She enjoyed literature, art galleries, documentaries. Stuff like that. She and Gabe had way more in common than she and Lucas in that area."

"Well, they do say opposites attract." Lane gave a small smile, a flickering image of Philip popping into her head. "So, um... you're sure the two never argued over her?"

"No. Don't think so." Amy daubed at her eyes, smearing black mascara across the white tissue.

"What about Brent or Kevin? Could they of had a secret thing for Danie?"

"Mmmmm." Amy's eyes looked doubtful. "All the boys liked one of the twins at some point over the years. But I don't think so."

"What about you? You liked Gabe, didn't you? You weren't jealous of Danie since Gabe had such strong feelings for her?" Amy shrugged her shoulders along with a sniffle.

"Maybe a little, but nothing I couldn't get over," she said, somewhat defensively. "Besides, once Danie left back east, who knows what would have happened."

"Janie... Sorry, who we thought to be Janie, she told someone Lucas was stalking her while she was in Seattle. Know anything about that?"

"Really?" Amy looked honestly surprised. "Lucas never leaves the island. I mean, if he's not climbing, he's plopped in front of his tv playing video games, or down at Piper's Place drinking with the boys. He'll go boating with his dad from time to time, but he stays put for the most part. He's a lounger."

"Let's move onto Angie. Did she get along with Danie?"

"Yeah, really well. They both had a love for horses."

Lane frowned, realizing the loan from "Janie" to Angie, made sense now.

"The loan to buy the Arabian horse. It really came from Danie. But then, that went sour, didn't it?"

"I suppose no one likes feeling they've been taken advantage of... even Danie."

Lane agreed. No one likes being played the fool. She took a deep breath and gave Amy a hard look, wondering if that was exactly what she was being taken for.

"Amy, are you telling me everything? You sure you don't know who wanted to kill Danie?"

"No!" Amy flung her hands to her side helplessly. "We all loved her!" She took another tissue from the box.

"When did you suspect it was Janie who actually drowned?"

Amy looked up at the ceiling as if the answer was floating above, her shoulders heaving in a long sigh. "When Gabe was trying to save her, I was holding on to who I thought was Janie. But when the med-

THE PUSH - A ROCKFISH ISLAND MYSTERY : 11

ics showed up and pronounced Danie dead... the look on her face... it wasn't sorrow. It was fear. She looked absolutely petrified!" Amy shook her head as she continued, "And then at the funeral, I noticed she kept as far away from Brent and the rest of the guys as she could. She even seemed distant to Angie and me, which was really odd," Amy's voice cracked. "And I suddenly had this crazy idea flash through my head. What if they hadn't switched back? What if the sister, who loved to swim and who knew better than to go jumping off Shallow Point, was the one who actually drowned? That's when... that's when I think I realized they hadn't gotten a chance to switch back."

"And you kept Danie's secret? You let her pretend to be her dead sister. To keep her safe?"

Amy slowly nodded, her hands wringing the used tissues.

"Did you tell anyone else your suspicions?" Lane tilted her head, trying to catch her eye.

Amy shook her head no, giving her shoulders a light shrug.

No one? Not even Angie?"

"No... nobody. To be honest, the idea freaked me out. It's why I moved to my mom's after it happened. I didn't know what to think! All I knew was I didn't want to be around my friends anymore... any of them. You know, just in case."

"So, when you left... Did you see Danie or visit

her when you lived in Seattle?"

"No." Amy frowned. "I tried to meet up with her a couple of times. We made plans, but she always blew me off. I reasoned she was either scared I'd realize she wasn't really Janie... or..." Amy shuddered. "Or she was scared of me. Maybe she thought I did it? I don't know."

"Amy, you wandered off that afternoon before she was found. Where did you go?" Lane tried to ask the question gently, knowing it would sting all the same.

Amy's mouth twisted into a sour smile. I know you have to ask. It's okay." She straightened up and pulled down tight on her smock. "I went to find Brent, so I could tell him what the twins were doing. I thought it was a lousy trick to play on him."

"And did you find him?" Lane asked curiously. Possibly Brent had an alibi for Danie's death after all?

"No. I'd called his name a few times but never spotted him. I'd given up and was heading back to camp when I heard the yelling. I just followed everyone to the point."

"I see." Lane believed the girl. "Amy, it's very likely, whoever accidentally killed Janie discovered their mistake, and to rectify it, they pushed Danie off the cliff. You're a smart girl. I'm pretty sure you've already pieced that together?"

Amy looked down at her feet and gave no reply.

"Amy, who killed the twins?"

The young woman closed her eyes as if she was trying to wish away the question.

"I don't know. I don't know which one of them did it."

CHAPTER 37

Philip looked at his cell phone for the fifth time, still finding no response to his text message. Annoyed, he shoved the phone back into his pants pocket and settled into the park bench stationed in front of the sheriff's office.

When he had arrived, there was an 'Out to Lunch' sign hung on the door. And neither patrol vehicle had been parked in front of the building. It looked as if both the sheriff and deputy were gone. Eager to speak with Lane in person, he'd been forced to wait. That had been thirty minutes ago, ...and counting.

Philip sighed, glanced at his watch, then sighed again. He had planned on showing up much earlier in the day, eager to tell her about his conversation with Doctor Hadley the night before. But when he'd strolled into the ranger's office that morning, he was confronted with a distraught Kody.

After not getting much work done and receiving monosyllable responses to his questions, Philip finally asked him what was wrong. The young man, after some persistent coaxing, had finally divulged he and Amy had gotten into a fight.

Apparently, Deputy Pickens had been foolishly trying to poach Kody's girl. Kody was upset she hadn't discouraged his actions more thoroughly, and Amy was convinced he was trying to break up with her. It all boiled down to the fact Kody was going off to college soon, and she was staying behind on the island. Philip did his best to give what advice he could.

Deciding he might as well wait out the full lunch hour, Philip watched the traffic as it slowly meandered down main street. The cars making a steady parade, the occasional honk grabbing his attention as his fellow islanders came and went, all acknowledged with a nod or a wave.

The lunch hour dwindling down, Philip found himself stifling a yawn. The sun hanging high in the sky bore down upon him, and the heat of the day, hotter than usual for this time of year, was making him drowsy. The light buzzing of bees hovering over the large flower pots on each side of the park bench wasn't helping either. Tired of fighting his drooping eyelids, Philip decided to take a bit of a cat nap as he waited on someone to show up.

It was the sound of his own snoring that jarred him awake, his head jerking back and rapping hard against the building wall. Gingerly rubbing the back of his head, Philip rapidly blinked himself awake and wiped a small amount of drool off his chin. Taking in his surroundings, he was surprised to see Deputy Pickens's patrol car parked next to his rig with the 'Out to Lunch' sign still hung upon the door.

Philip gave a fitful yawn as he stood up from the bench and stretched. As he did so, he noticed Lucas was parked across the street, his truck backed into a parking spot in front of Doctor Hadley's office. Figuring he still had some time to waste till either Lane showed or Caleb finished his lunch break, Philip decided he'd go over and say hi.

Looking both ways for traffic, he half-walked, half-jogged across the street.

"Hey, man! You finally woke up!" Lucas teased. "Been watching you for the last ten minutes."

"Yeah, yeah. You waiting for Gabe to get off work?" Philip asked, pounding the truck's hood in a friendly hello.

"Yup. Should be out in a minute. We're heading up to Cougar's Cap. Gonna check out a cool cave we heard about." Lucas gave Philip a bright smile.

Philip frowned. "A cave, huh? Doesn't sound like a good idea to me. Could have a bear or a cougar stored up inside. Who told you about it?"

"Don't remember." Lucas shrugged.

Philip grunted and then added, "Well, make sure you check in with Kody at the ranger station, so if anything happens, we know where to find you. We've had enough accidents to last us for a while," Philip instructed, giving Lucas a fatherly look.

"We will, Phil. I promise. We just need something to take our minds off of... you know."

"Yeah, I get it." Philip shifted his weight, putting his elbow on the hood, giving a casual look around them. "Lucas, since it's only you and me. Can I ask you a personal question?"

"I guess." Lucas gave Philip a lopsided smile, curious about what was coming.

"You and Danie. Why didn't you go with her when she said she was going for a swim? Why did you stay behind with Janie?"

Lucas's light smile dropped, his eyes suddenly glued to the steering wheel, avoiding Philip's gaze. He started to say something and then stopped, pressing his lips together in indecision.

"I don't mean to pry, but I've always been curious. I would have thought you'd ask Danie to help put up your tent. Not Janie," Philip prodded, knowing Gabe might come out and interrupt them. It would be all the excuse Lucas would need to not answer the question.

"Yeah, I see why you're asking." Lucas turned

to Philip, finally meeting his eyes. He nervously drummed his fingers along the curve of the steering wheel for a second longer before saying, "The night before, I'd made a right ass of myself and mistook Janie for Danie. Everyone was ribbing me about it. Especially Brent. Telling me, I should have been able to tell the two apart, even in my drunken stupor." He continued to drum the steering wheel, the pattern slowing. "The next day, I was still feeling a bit embarrassed, but Janie and Danie seemed fine, so I decided not to worry about it. Then I noticed Danie was eating watermelon for a late breakfast. Even offered me some!" Lucas chuckled. "She hated watermelon." He stopped drumming his fingers and gripped the steering wheel tightly. "And in my fuzzy hungover brain, I started to wonder. Maybe the two girls were pretending to be each other, playing a practical joke on all of us for the night before?" Lucas cracked a crooked smile. "Thought I was being clever, asking Janie to help me put up my tent."

"You believed you were really asking Danie," Philip said slowly, following along with Lucas's logic. Lucas nodded sheepishly. "I thought I was pulling one over them by knowing they'd traded places." He sighed heavily. "I'd been all wrong."

"Janie was too good of a swimmer." Philip nodded his agreeance, knowing they were thinking the same thing. "She never would have gone to Shallow

Point to go swimming. She knew the risks too well."

Lucas forcefully hit the steering wheel with the heel of his hand.

"I don't know why Danie did what she did. She should have known better. If I'd been with her, I would have stopped her. I've even sometimes wondered if she knew what she was doing... she wasn't acting normal that day. Maybe she jumped... on purpose?"

"Lucas, ready to go?" Both heads turned at the sound of Gabe's greeting. He was walking out of the medical clinic, still dressed in work scrubs with a climbing backpack slung over his shoulder.

"I'm sure he is," Philip said good-heartedly when Gabe spotted him. "I've been keeping him company till you got off work."

"Did Lucas tell you what we're up to?" Gabe shot Philip a mischievous smile, yanking off his scrub shirt and stripping down to the white t-shirt underneath. "Pretty cool, huh?" He stuffed the discarded clothes into his backpack and tossed it into the truck bed.

"Actually, I was just advising him against it. I don't think it sounds like a very good idea. You guys got your bear spray with you, just in case?" Philip watched Gabe climb into the passenger side, moving a bouquet of flowers from the seat and placing them onto the center console.

"In my pack!"

"Never climb without it!" Lucas chimed in.

"Good. Who are the flowers for?" Philip smiled, eyeing both carefully.

"Oh, um." Lucas's face turned red. "I thought we could lay them where we found Janie. Pay our respects while we're out there."

"That's a nice gesture." Philip's smile faded. "You guys holding up all right?" He'd asked both, directing the question mainly to Gabe.

Gabe nodded his head but didn't say anything.

"Gabe blames himself," Lucas said, in a half-whisper to Philip. "He was the one who told Brent the brownies didn't have any nuts." Lucas started the truck, the engine roaring to life and drowning out anything else Lucas or Philip may have had to say.

Philip pounded on the hood and gave a good-bye wave as Lucas pulled out onto the street and steered towards the docks. Driving by Sheriff Lane, who was coming the opposite direction, Lucas gave her a light honk of a greeting as they passed.

Philip quickly jogged back over to the sheriff's office as Lane pulled into her parking spot, her tires screeching to a halt. He grabbed her door handle and pulled the door open, a concerned look on his face.

"Was that Lucas and Gabe?" Lane asked, squinting through her passenger window and then down at her wristwatch.

"Yup. And Lucas just said something interesting. Said Gabe told Brent there were no nuts in the brown—"

"Hmmm, Lucas is back early. I need to have a talk with him." Lane hopped out of the truck, too excited to realize Philip had been speaking. "By the way, I'm glad we bumped into each other! I was hoping I wouldn't have to track you down in the park." Lane stepped onto the sidewalk, watching Lucas's truck turn off the main street. She looked back at Philip with a distracted air. "What are you doing here, anyway?"

Philip dug a white envelope from his shirt pocket and held it up, shaking it lightly.

"Got the memory cards from the trail cameras. There were two I thought likely to catch sight of someone. One pointing up Indian Flat trail, the other at the base of Shale Rock. Either might have caught someone heading for the body to retrieve her camera."

"Excellent!" Lane hurried to the front door, sans 'Out to lunch' sign, and yanked it open as she gestured for Philip to hurry and walk through. "Come on! You're gonna want to be sitting down when I tell you what I found out."

CHAPTER 38

"Are you sure?" Philip asked incredulously, leaning his elbows on his knees, giving Lane a hard look.

"It was verified by an ID tech." Lane looked from a dumfounded Philip over to a flabbergasted Deputy Pickens. Both were in her office. Philip sitting in the chair by her desk, and Caleb, leaning up against the door. "Janie drowned last summer, and Danie has been pretending to be her ever since. It's my belief when the girls traded places, Janie was murdered mistakenly, and Danie was forced to live her life as her sister, to stay in hiding."

"But..." Caleb's forehead scrunched up in confusion. "Why stay around in Washington state? Why not go straight to Pennsylvania and hide there?"

"Because Janie wouldn't have done that. I think

Danie decided to act as Janie would for a year or so, to not raise suspicions. Then after some time had gone by and the relationship with Brent was obviously over to everyone, including Brent, she'd move back east. Back home to Pennsylvania." Lane ripped open the small envelope Philip had given her and took out one of the memory cards. "Do you know which card went to which camera?" she asked him, comparing the two memory cards.

"You're gonna have to give me a minute, Lane," Philip said, shaking his head. "I'm still trying to wrap my head around this."

"Why didn't Danie go to the police?" Caleb crossed his arms over his chest, leaning hard against the door jamb. "Why not tell them who she was and her suspicions?"

"She didn't know which one of them did it," Philip said slowly. He was starting to come out of his daze. "She couldn't point the finger because she didn't know who to point it to." Philip turned to Lane. "That explains why she avoided the island and ended the relationship with Brent. Poor kid. Loses her sister, her friends, and her family... all in one day."

"Wait! Why come back to the island now? I mean, she was loaded, right? She didn't need the job or the money. Why didn't she turn down this job like she did the others? It doesn't make sense." Caleb started to rub his back against the jamb of the door, scratching an itch between his shoulder blades.

"Yeah, that's a good question." Philip's brow creased, mimicking Caleb's mystified grimace. "Oh, and the memory cards are initialed."

Lane looked at the cards and then put the one initialed I.F. into her computer.

"Well, I don't obviously have all the answers. My best guess is there was a part of her which wanted to come back. Maybe she felt safe enough? Confident everyone had been fooled sufficiently that she could come back? She was still precautious. Didn't tell anyone she was coming. Didn't meet up with her friends. Maybe this trip to the island was a trial run? A way to see if she had indeed fooled them all?"

"She hadn't..." Philip stood, motioning for Lane to vacate the seat in front of her computer. "Scoot, I'm driving."

She begrudgingly stood up, handing Caleb the second trail memory card. Caleb took it with a curt nod and headed back to his desk up front.

"So, how do these trail cameras work?" Lane moved to the extra chair, placing it slightly behind Philip to his left so she wouldn't crowd him but could still see the monitor.

"These are motion activated. Anytime some-thing walks within a certain range of the camera, it takes a picture every five seconds until whatever has walked by is then out of range." Philip moved

347

the mouse, double-clicking on a file, opening an additional screen where several thumbnail-sized black and white photos popped up. He clicked on the first photo, a deer nibbling on a sapling, and enlarged it to normal size.

"Is this going to take forever?" Lane's tone was clearly impatient. She inched her chair a hair closer.

"Shouldn't think so. There's only twelve hundred pictures." Philip smirked, hitting the arrow key, moving to the next frame.

From the front, Caleb gave a groan of protest, "Fifteen hundred photos!"

"Stop your complaining, Deputy!" Lane hollered, then settled her eyes back onto the screen. She leaned forward up against Philip's shoulder. "Please tell me these are timestamped."

"Time and date. All nice and tidy. Won't take me long."

"Good!" Lane sat back. "So, I was thinking. Brent must have felt Danie was a threat to his and Janie's relationship." Lane watched Philip tab to the dates they were looking for.

"You're still thinking he's the guilty party in both deaths?" Philip asked, surprised. He'd started rapidly clicking through the shots.

"I'm hoping he is," Lane said, rubbing her forehead. "If he's not, then we may still have a killer on the loose."

Philip lowered his voice, not wanting Caleb to overhear. He was doubtful Lane had gotten the chance to have a word with her deputy about his loose lips.

"You know, I keep thinking of the expired EpiPen." He looked over his shoulder at her.

"Pretty irresponsible," Lane agreed. "Thought the kid was smarter than that."

"He was." Philip faced forward again.

"You think someone switched out his EpiPen?"

"Starting to wonder. Especially after what Doctor Hadley said."

"What did Doctor Hadley have to say?" Lane asked, perplexed. "When did you talk to him about Brent's EpiPen?"

"Shoot!" Philip slammed his palm to his forehead. "I completely forgot to tell you. I talked to him last night."

"Tell me what?" Lane hit Philip's shoulder, forcing his chair to swivel towards her.

"Doctor Hadley only prescribed it eleven months ago. Which means Brent had been packing around the EpiPen for less than a year. Doctor Hadley double-checked his records. According to him, there's no way his prescribed EpiPen should have been two years expired."

"Might have been a mistake made by the pharmacy?" Lane offered her voice sounding unconvinced.

"Doctor Hadley said it was highly unlikely."

"So, someone swapped out his good pen for a bad one? Why? Killing Brent... what would it achieve?" Lane leaned her elbow onto the back of Philip's seat, placing her chin in the cup of her hand. "I guess if maybe he knew something? Dead men tell no tales, that sort of thing."

"Possible revenge?" Philip threw another theory into the mix.

"Are you thinking someone figured out he'd killed Janie and didn't want to wait on the justice system?" Lane looked at Philip, her eyebrow arched.

"He was the only suspect, and his granddad is a lawyer. May have been worried he was going to get off scot-free?"

Lane fretted her bottom lip, thinking. "Or maybe someone was trying to set him up as a scapegoat?"

"It would be a bold move."

"And it sure would confuse everything."

Philip grunted his agreement, turning back to the computer. He clicked on the next frame.

"Lane! Look, it's Janie... err... Danie. It's the girl!" Philip held his hands away from the keyboard, keeping them clear of hitting a button by accident. "She's heading up trail."

"Okay, let's see how soon someone we know comes along."

Philip hit the arrow key a few times and stopped on a picture of Gabe.

"He must be heading up to go huckleberry picking." Lane nodded, having flipped back to the interview with Brent on her notepad. "Keep going."

Philip tabbed through shots of rabbits hopping across the trail and came to a frame of Gabe coming back down.

"Okay, that fits as well. Keep on going," Lane prodded him again to continue. "We should see Brent next."

Brent's image flashed onto the monitor. His head was held high as if looking further up trail, his face anxious and eager. The timestamp matched roughly the time he'd given Lane during the interview.

"So far, so good. Let's see what time he came down. If he really did come back this way or—"

Philip hit the arrow key and another picture popped onto the screen. It took both of them a second to realize what they were looking at.

"Son of a bitch!" Philip's chair fell over as he rocketed out of the seat, charging out of Lane's office for his truck. Lane, following a hairsbreadth behind, barked for Caleb to follow, tossing him her patrol keys.

"Radio Kody. Let him know we're coming!" she yelled as Philip hit the front door. "If he sees Lucas and Gabe, tell him to stop them!"

CHAPTER 39

"I should have figured it out!" Lane slapped her notepad hard against the dash of the truck in frustration. "I can't believe I didn't see it!"

"Don't be so..." Philip jostled against the truck door as they maneuvered over a large hump in the old jeep road. "...hard on yourself. He fooled us all."

"Can't you drive faster?" Lane yelled over the rumbling tires, failing to keep the impatient irritation out of her voice. "They could already be halfway up The Mole Hill by now!"

"Lane, these jeep roads are not made for speed!" Philip suddenly lurched to the opposite side of his seat. "I'm going as fast as I can without tearing out the motor." Philip gritted his teeth, swerving hard to avoid a major rut. "I'm doing my..." The truck bounced hard as it hit a dip in the road, cannoning its way back out. "My best. We'll lose the axel if I'm not careful."

Lane braced herself with one arm on the dash, the other gripping the handle above the passenger window, and decided to hold her tongue. She knew Philip was pushing the vehicle as hard as he could. It wouldn't do them any good if they had to find the two men on foot.

"Besides, Lucas said they were heading up to Cougar's Cap. It's just a few miles up ahea—" Philip slammed on the brakes, bringing the truck to a skidded stop, dust billowing up from behind.

"That's Lucas's truck, isn't it?" Lane asked, waving the flying dust away, coughing. She recognized the bumper sticker "I stop for hot chicks and Big Foot" stuck to the back window on the driver's side.

"Yup, and this isn't Cougar's Cap." Philip snatched his two-way off the cradle radioing into Kody.

Lane anxiously listened as Philip informed him they'd found the truck, guessing the two men were heading up a different route than originally reported. He gave Kody some brief and hurried instructions before hanging up the radio, grabbing his shotgun out of the middle console, and jumping out of the truck.

"Listen, Lane. There are two ways they could have gone." Philip waited until she had climbed out and walked around to the front. He pointed to a marked trail on their right, a weather-worn wooden park sign at its head. The sign stood adorned with paper plates stapled to it, the names "Pilgrim" and "Tripp" scrawled in black marker. "That way or..." He looked behind. "This way." He pointed to the dense woods facing Lane with no clear trail she could see. "This leads to the waterfall at the beginning of the creek and the other way..." He nodded his head towards the wooden park sign again. "Heads to a small camping ground. There's an abandoned logging mill way back there."

"Which way do you think they went?" Lane asked, pondering their choices, her impatience rising.

"I don't know. It's a toss-up. Both would be great places to plan an accident or hide a body. I think maybe..."

"Time is of the essence here, Ranger. He's not safe. We're going to need to split up." Lane started to make her way past him, walking towards the unmarked trail. "You know where the logging mill is, and you've got longer legs than me. You'll make better time. If you find them, let off a shot, and I'll head back your way. If I find them, I'll do the same."

Philip debated on arguing with her. He didn't like the idea of splitting up, but she was right. They had to find them before another convenient accident happened. With a determined look, Philip shook his head, stalking over to where she stood. Towering over her tiny frame, he suddenly cupped her face. Bowing his head down to her eye level, he made sure he had her full attention.

"You be careful, Lois," he said firmly, his eyes riveted to hers. "I mean it." He then let go and headed towards the marked trail in a steady jog.

Lane turned and watched him till he was out of sight, her heart racing. Taking a deep breath, she faced forward, unsnapping the button on her holster. She then made her way to what she thought looked like a trail and stepped upon it.

Unsure if she was indeed heading in the right direction, Lane's eyes scanned the forest ahead as much as the light would allow, the woods being dense and dark. Trying to use what little tracking knowledge she possessed, she was fairly certain someone had recently been through there. Though she wouldn't have put money on it. The path, if she could have called it that, was barely visible. Several fallen trees lining the path blocked her way, causing her to climb either over or through them. A few times, her duty belt caught, and she had to reverse direction so as to unhitch herself from whatever she snagged. At her current rate of speed, if Philip didn't find anything, he might actually make it back to the truck and follow in behind her. But then, that was most likely wishful thinking on her part. She knew she was walking into a potentially dangerous situation to confront a conniving murderer.

Not everything was clear, but pieces were starting to come together. Who had been following Janie... The manner in which the missing photo had been discovered... Everyone's recollections of who first discovered the floating body. Even the EpiPen made perfect sense.

Lane was forced to slow her pace even more, pushing back on the low-hanging boughs of pine as she started to make out the sound of running water. Looking up, she could see the small waterfall, white water cascading down over dark stone, running into the small creek etching its way through the island. She continued forward, now having a point of reference.

As she grew closer, the sound of the waterfall became louder, and the trees started to thin out replaced by large bushes and brambles surrounding a small clearing. She pulled her gun from its holster, gripping it in both hands. She then pushed through the bushes, using her shoulder to bulldoze her way through. The waterfall mist brushed against her face, the cold air a mixture of fresh pine, and the peppery smell of bear spray. She paused for a second and listened for voices. There was only the loud rush of water crashing over the rocks below. Her eyes drew to the top of the waterfall, coming completely into view, and then panned down to its base.

There, lying halfway in the running water, was a pair of sprawled legs, a can of bear spray floating beside them, and a water bottle on the opposite side. Lane's eyes roamed up to the face of the young man and then quickly moved to who was standing over him. She half-lurched, half-stepped into the small clearing, leveling her gun.

"Gabe! Stop!"

At Lane's shouted command, Gabe's head snapped up, his eyes red and swollen, large streaks of tears coming down his cheeks. His arms were raised high in the air, still hefting a large rock over Lucas's head, his muscles rigid, veins bulging. She'd caught him seconds before crashing the rock down onto Lucas's skull.

"Gabe, I want you to slowly toss the rock to the side," Lane said firmly, taking a small step towards him, her gun aimed. Lane watched him hesitate, the large stone dangerously hovering above his unconscious friend.

"Sheriff, you don't understand. He's suffering." Gabe's arms wavered, his voice sounding harsh and strained. "I'm... I'm just putting him out of his misery. He... he fell. Trying to climb the waterfall...and..."

"Gabe, I'm not going to ask again. Put the rock down."

"Sheriff, please." Gabe chucked the large rock to the ground, the stone sounding a heavy thump as it hit the wet soil. He took a step back from Lucas and wiped his eyes. "Look at him! He's suffering."

Lucas's face was a mask of blood, red liquid running freely from a large gash on his forehead.

"Gabe, you need to step back further." Lane's blue eyes were cold, her face blank. "I can guess what happened here. Now, hands up!"

"NO... that's not... this isn't... He actually attacked me! It was self-defense. He... he just went nuts. He told me he killed Janie." Gabe started to walk towards Lane, his hands out in a beseeching manner.

"Stay there!" she warned, her eyes darting between Gabe and the sight of Lucas's chest, watching for the tell-tale signs of breathing.

"He lured me out here... and... I'm so glad you're here." Gabe tried to take another step forward.

Lane, using her gun, motioned for him to move back. Not seeing the rise and fall of Lucas's chest, she started walking towards the two, her gun still tracking on Gabe.

"Not a step closer, Gabe," she said firmly, bending down over Lucas.

"Listen, I'm just trying to explain!" Gabe took a halting step back, his voice pleading.

Grabbing Lucas's limp wrist, Lane felt for a pulse. After a few seconds, she switched to his neck, her face pensive. She looked up at Gabe, her eyes watering.

"Thank God, there's a pulse," she said quietly to herself and then stood up. Louder, she said, "Gabe, up against the rock wall. I want you to slowly put your hands behind your head."

Gabe didn't budge, his face etched with complete and utter shock.

"Sheriff, please. I'm not the bad guy here." Gabe pointed over to the prostrated Lucas. "He attacked me! With bear spray! I need medical attention. It's in my eyes... my throat."

Lane shook her head, reading the scene. To her, it looked as if Lucas, in an effort to protect himself, had used the bear spray to ward off Gabe's attack.

"Lucas attacked you? I don't think so. That's not what happened here."

"I told you it was self-defense. We need to get him help." He edged forward. "If you let me, I can leave and go get someone. You were right. I wasn't thinking clearly. I panicked. He needs a doctor."

Lane aimed her gun a few feet above Gabe's head and let out a single shot.

"Help is already on the way," Lane said coolly, knowing Philip would be making his way to her. "Now, turn around slowly and put your hands behind your head!"

Gabe shook his head, putting his hands up in the air but not behind his head. He continued to face her, his eyes intent on her gun.

"I'll comply, but I just don't think you're understanding what happened here. And... Lucas needs my help. You know... I... I can help him medically. I was in medical school! I work at Doctor Hadley's office! You know that, right? If you'll—"

Lane cut him off. "You're right, I do. I imagine with working at Doctor Hadley's office, it wasn't hard to come across an expired or used EpiPen. Even easier to replace Brent's good EpiPen with the expired one," Lane's voice hardened. "You brought the brownies made with almond flour, convincing Brent they were safe to eat, causing him to go into an anaphylaxis shock. Forcing him to use his EpiPen, which you knew was no good." Lane shook her head, amazed at the young man's audacity. "I also know I completely misunderstood Lucas. I'd made the mistake of thinking it was Brent he was talking about when he said the picture fell out of his pocket. But he hadn't meant Brent's pocket. He'd meant yours."

Gabe's smile fell, and his stance changed, becoming guarded and ridged.

"Sheriff, you've got it all wrong," he said desperately. "Lucas did all of that. Not me."

"Lucas will make it," Lane said with more confidence than she felt. "You can't make him your scapegoat like you tried to do with Brent. He'll attest to what occured here, and he'll testify how the picture fell out of YOUR pocket. The picture which was missing from Danie's backpack the day she was pushed off the cliff."

"Danie?" Gabe shook his head, laughing. "You mean, Janie!"

"No, Gabe. Like you, I figured out the two girls had switched identities last summer." Lane smiled as Gabe blanched. "You know what else I figured out? You were the one driving Lucas's truck and stalking her in Seattle." Lane darted a quick look down at Lucas, surprised to see his eyes flutter open and then close.

"I don't know what you're talking about," Gabe said, anger in his voice.

"You also drove his truck that morning. You gave her a ride into the park, didn't you?" More pieces were starting to come together. "Came across her walking and offered to give her a ride in and then pretended to go your own way?"

Gabe licked his lips as he stared down at his friend, concern no longer lining his face. He looked back up at Lane and smirked. "I said, I don't know what you're talking about."

"How'd you find out she was on the island? Did you just to come across her? Did Brent tell you?"

Gabe's smirk widened, and he haplessly shrugged his shoulders. "I've already said, I don't know what you're talki—"

"Doctor Hadley..." Lane's head fell back in comprehension, remembering Sue had said the doctor and his wife were at the restaurant when she and her niece had dinner at The Royal Fork.

Gabe's smirk flatlined.

"You followed her up the trail, and then what? Realized Brent was behind you? So, you made your way back down? I know you followed him afterwards. We've got you on a trail camera. It shows you clearly following behind Brent back UP The Mole Hill."

"Sheriff, this is insane! I have no idea wha—"

Lucas suddenly jerked and groaned, drawing both sets of eyes. Lane bent down and said his name a few times, but all she got in response was a mute fluttering of eyelashes, his head wound still bleeding freely.

Lane frowned, frustration clearly lining her face. All this talk wasn't getting Lucas any help. The poor kid was starting to come to and would be in a world of hurt soon.

"Okay, then." She stood up. "Gabe, you're going to help me carry him out." She decided Lucas didn't have time to wait on Philip. "I'll have you sling him over your shoulder, and we'll walk out of here together. Then I'm putting you under arrest for the murder of Janie and Danie Engles and Brent Allister. If we don't hurry, I'll be adding Lucas to the list and another life sentence to your mounting tally."

"Lane!" Philip's voice boomed through the air.

"I'm at the waterfall! Lucas needs medical attention!" Lane hollered and then said to Gabe sternly, "Stay put."

Seconds later, Philip broke through into the clearing, his shotgun held against his shoulder.

"What happened here?" Philip asked, panting out of breath.

Lane stood two feet away, looming protectively over Lucas. She nodded towards Gabe.

"He tried finishing Lucas off by crushing in his head with a rock. Lucas is barely holding on. He needs medical attention." Lane stepped up next to Philip. "You want to help me out here, Ranger?"

"Happily," Philip growled, laying his shotgun down on the ground and stalking over to Gabe, who withered at the sight of Philip's expression.

Quicker than Lane would have imagined, Philip manhandled Gabe onto his stomach, allowing Lane to put a knee into his back. She did just that and grabbed his wrist, pulling it tight and high behind his waist, slapping on the cuffs while reciting his Miranda rights.

Seizing the closed cuffs behind Gabe's back, Philip pulled him to his feet then pushed down hard on his shoulder, causing the young man to flop down onto the ground in a sitting position.

"Philip, this is just one huge misunderstanding," Gabe said, nodding towards Lane. "She's got it all wrong! She's convinced I—"

"You stay there and shut up," Philip ordered firmly, turning his back on Gabe's words and walking

THE PUSH · A ROCKFISH ISLAND MYSTERY : II

over to Lane, who was tending Lucas's head wound. She had wrapped his t-shirt around his head, applying pressure to the gash.

"Let me have your pocketknife." Lane stuck her hand out while looking down at Lucas, her eyes worried.

Philip, curious as to why she needed it, pulled the small knife from his pocket and placed it in her hand.

"He's starting to come through." Lane curled her hand over the pocketknife then looked up at the tree line. "This clearing isn't big enough to get a Coast Guard chopper in here, let alone the stretcher. We're going have to take him out of here ourselves."

"I've got him." Philip carefully hoisted Lucas into a sitting position. Then gripping under Lucas's armpits, he brought him to his feet, a weak groan escaping the injured young man's lips.

"You sure you got him?" Lane looked skeptical, watching as Lucas wobbled on his feet, his muscles weak. Philip simply grunted, steadying the young man.

Bending over, Philip put his arm through Lucas's legs and pulled him down tight over his back. With a weight lifters jerk, Philip stood up, hefting him onto his shoulders. Grabbing Lucas's limp arm with his one hand to stabilize him, he then walked over and retrieved his shotgun, still lying on the ground.

"See, no sweat." Philip gave her a cocky smile.

Lane looked unimpressed. "Head out, Ranger.

365

We'll follow behind." She nodded towards the trail while starting to unbutton the bottom of her uniform shirt, quickly working her way up to her breasts.

Philip raised a questioning eyebrow as Lane flicked open the pocketknife, giving her tank top a quick sideways slice.

"What are you doing?" Philip asked seriously, giving her a hard look as she handed back the pocketknife.

Lane yanked down on her white tank top, ripping the fabric into a long strip, leaving her midsection bare. "Don't wait on us," she said sternly. Ripping the strip into two, she made her way over to the creek.

Philip glowered at Gabe, a silent warning to behave himself, and then started his way back to the truck with Lucas slung over his shoulders in a fireman's carry. "On my way."

"Right behind you," Lane said over her shoulder, giving him a quick smile before dunking the strips of fabric into the water.

CHAPTER 40

Wringing out the torn strips, Lane picked up Lucas's left behind water bottle, clipping it onto her duty belt.

"Looks as if Lucas managed to get at least one good shot in with the bear spray," she said, approaching Gabe. "Your eyes are all bloodshot."

"They really burn." Gabe squinted up at her, his eyes red and puffy.

"Oh, I don't doubt it." Lane tilted her head, a small smirk on her face.

"It's not funny." Gabe scrunched up his eyes, blinking hard. "And I can barely see!"

"Here." She bent over him, tilting his head back. "Your sweat is causing the pepper residue to run into your eyes."

"Well, if you'd uncuff me, I could do something

about it," Gabe said miserably, shaking his head free of her hand, trying to shimmy the drops of sweat from his brow. "Hold still!" Lane gently grabbed his chin, tilting his head up. "I agree. You need to be able to see where you're going."

Taking the wet fabric, she carefully wiped his face clean, focusing around his eyes and forehead.

"See, that should help." Lane said brightly, taking the second strip and tying it around his head in a makeshift headband. "Hopefully this should keep the sweat from getting into your eyes."

Stepping back, she took a look at her handiwork and stuffed the excess fabric behind his ears so the headband wouldn't slide down. "Okay, now let's get you up."

Circling behind, Lane grabbed Gabe by the handcuffs and helped hoist him onto his feet.

"My mouth and throat feel like they're on fire," Gabe complained, starting to walk forward.

"That's the bear spray," Lane acknowledged, knowing how he felt. She'd never been bear sprayed, but she had been pepper-sprayed before, which was more intense. He would have had her sympathies if he hadn't been a killer. "I'll get you some medical attention when we get to the truck."

Moving to the edge of the clearing, Sheriff Lane with her prisoner in tow, entered the dense woods. She pushed back the long brambles, determined to leave the waterfall behind, and started looking for the path.

Spotting a gnarled tree she thought looked vaguely familiar, she headed in its direction. It didn't take long to realize the hike out wasn't going to go as quickly as she had hoped. The forest floor, itself an obstacle course, was heavily covered with ferns, large tree roots, discarded pine cones, twigs, and broken limbs. All things one could easily trip over or roll an ankle on. Even the trees themselves were of no assistance, crowded together, blocking much of the view forward as behind.

Several times she had to patiently hold back branches or indicate where Gabe should step as he stumbled along half-blind and handcuffed. At times, she even managed to get a few steps ahead, only to have to return and help him untangle from a bush or a broken tree limb a few minutes later. As if that hadn't been frustrating enough, he was also persistent in constantly and annoyingly declaring his innocence.

"I'm telling you, Sheriff. You've got the wro—"

"Watch your step," Lane instructed as they approached one of the many fallen logs littering the forest floor. "And your head," she added, turning around and putting her hand protectively over his.

"Why are you being so nice to me?" Gabe asked, eyeing her suspiciously. "You think I'm a killer."

"I KNOW you're a killer." Lane gave him a withering look.

"Sheriff, I know how all of this looks, even the trail camera. But I can explain all of it. You've got to hear me out. Lucas is the one..."

"Give it a rest, Gabe," Lane said, annoyance heavy in her tone. "Watch it." Lane stepped over another log and scooted around a rotten stump. Suddenly, she held up her hand in a fist, cautioning Gabe to stop, and started to say, "Hold up."

Gabe didn't and managed to trip over the stump, crashing into her.

"What's wrong?" Gabe blinked heavily, his eyes still bloodshot and puffy.

Shoving Gabe back to his feet, she focused her eyes ahead, peering further down the way. A knot of doubt had edged its way into her thoughts. She didn't think this was the way she had come. In fact, none of this was looking familiar. They'd either veered off course or missed the path completely. Heaven knows she didn't think to leave behind a trail of bread crumbs on her way in.

"Sheriff, these cuffs are too tight. Any chance of..."

"Gabe, just be quiet." Lane took a deep breath, taking in their immediate surroundings, trying to find her bearings again.

A large number of splintered stumps and fallen logs led her to wonder if there had been one heck of a wind storm a few years back. The logs abandoned where they fell to decompose back into the ground they'd sprouted from. Also, the bushes were thicker here, continually snagging at their clothing and her duty belt. No, this was not the way she had come.

For a brief second, she thought of retracing their steps to the waterfall. But she was anxious for Lucas, curious to know if Philip had been able to get him help in time. She was also eager to be rid of Gabe as well.

Lane dropped her fist and started forward, looping to the left. There were more fallen trees but less bush to contend with. She crawled over a large log, bits of bark and dried moss clinging to her pants. She reached behind and grabbed Gabe's elbow helping to balance him as he attempted to swing his leg over.

"Here. Lift up your right leg a little higher. Higher!"

"I am!" Gabe grumbled, falling into her and losing his balance, his dead weight almost knocking her down to the ground.

"Gabe, let me get your arm."

"You know, this would be A LOT EASIER if you'd at least let me have my arms upfront! I can barely keep my balance this way," Gabe complained, having slid over the log face first.

With Lane's help, he slowly lumbered back to his knees and then his feet. Mud and pine needles still covering one side of his face.

Lane sighed, realizing he had a point. "Okay, just... here. Sit on the log." Lane patted the large log he'd just climbed or rather, slid over face first.

"Thanks." Gabe blinked his eyes again and then tried to swallow. He grimaced and stuck out his tongue, sliding it over the bottom of his front teeth. "Mind if I have a little bit of water?" Gabe nodded towards Lucas's water bottle dangling from her duty belt. "I really need to wash my mouth out."

Lane nodded, unclipping the water bottle and unscrewing the top for him. She then walked over and tilted the bottle over his mouth, letting a small stream flow before tilting it back. Gabe nodded his thanks as he swished the water around his mouth, then spat it to the side.

"Thanks. That's better."

Exhausted herself, Lane plopped down on the log beside him, looking up at the woods around them. Absently she took her shirttail and wiped the sweat off her forehead. It was a warm day. Even though they weren't directly in the sun, the air was humid and hot, the trees trapping the heat in their denseness.

"Sheriff, why exactly do you think I killed Danie?" Gabe suddenly asked, spitting once again into the bushes. Lane started to bring the water bottle up to her mouth, craving a cool drink herself. "Didn't anyone tell you I was the one who performed CPR?"

Lane sighed, bringing the bottle back down without taking a drink.

"Rejection." Lane watched him closely, seeing his slight flinch. "I think you knew she preferred Lucas over you. But even worse, she preferred to be alone than be with you. She wasn't planning on getting serious with anyone. She was going to head back east, and when you suggested you should go with her... I think you saw she didn't care either way."

"That's not true. She said she thought it was a great idea," Gabe said, a touch of indignation in his tone.

"I'm sure she was just being polite," Lane countered, her mouth quirking up, seeing his anger start to bloom. "But you were too dense to know it."

Lane brought the water bottle back up to her lips and took a long pull from it before screwing the top back on and returning it to her duty belt.

"I'm far from dense, Sheriff," Gabe said, a slow smile spreading across his mouth. "You gonna let me have my hands upfront or not?"

"Yeah, just a second." Lane pushed off from the log and worked her way behind him, grabbing the cuff key from her pocket and inserting it into the right cuff.

Twisting the little key, she started to pull his hand out, keeping the wrist bent. If he tried to pull away, she could yank up, causing a high amount of pain to keep him immobile.

"You hear that?" Gabe asked, turning his head. "Sounds like a helicopter."

"Means Lucas and Philip made it back to the..." Lane suddenly swayed on her feet, hit by a wave of lightheadedness. "...the truck." She blinked her eyes and shook her head trying to shake the feeling.

"That's not good," Gabe said quietly.

"Why... why is that not good?" Lane swallowed, now feeling extremely nauseous. She tried to put the key back into the cuff but missed, her hands unsteady.

"What's taking so long? You feeling okay, Sheriff?" Gabe suddenly stood up from the log, causing Lane to lose her grip on his wrist. "You need help?" he asked a cold smile upon his lips.

Lane stumbled back, almost losing her balance.

"Sit back down," she slurred, taking a faulting step forward, trying to grab at his wrist.

"I think you need to be the one to sit down," Gabe said, his smile widening. He took a step forward, swinging both hands upfront, the left cuff still hanging from his wrist.

"The water bottle..." Lane's head whirled. "You spiked Lucas's water bottle," she slurred. "That's how you knocked him out."

"Don't you have all the answers today?" Gabe lightly pushed Lane down onto the stump. "Though you're wrong about one thing. Danie never rejected me." Gabe peered into her eyes, pulling down on the skin above Lane's cheek, checking her pupils for dilation. "She was going to pick me."

Lane shook her head away from his touch but found she couldn't do much more, her eyes already drooping closed.

"Want to know how I know?" Gabe grabbed Lane's chin, shaking her awake. "Because she held my hand that day." He let go of her, pushing hard as he did. "She was super shy, you know. I would put my arm around her, and she'd shrug out of it. Or I'd hold her hand, and she'd take it away. But on that day, she grabbed MY hand. It took her all summer, but she'd finally decided on me."

Gabe stood up as Lane toppled to the side. He grabbed her, steadying her on the log.

"In retrospect, when I went to take a nap in my tent, the two girls must have swapped places. I should have known right away, especially when she said she was going to go swimming. But I wasn't thinking clearly and thought it the perfect opportunity to steal a kiss." He took a tentative step back, eyeing Lane to make sure she'd stay put.

Satisfied, he started to grab at her closed fist, looking for the cuff key, and continued to talk, knowing she could still hear him.

"It took me a little bit to find her. I had thought she'd gone to the low beach to wade in the water up to her ankles... Danie not being a swimmer per se." He grabbed Lane's other hand finding it empty. "But she was up on the point, on the very cusp, looking down at the water. I snuck up behind her and put my arms around her."

He leaned back, a deep frown on his face. "Did you drop the key?" He got up and started to walk around the log.

In response, Lane blinked her eyes a few times, her head falling back against her shoulder blades, fighting to stay conscious. She tried to tell him to stop, her words coming out as a croak.

"What did you do with it?" Gabe shoved her off the log, pushing her to the ground, checking to see if the small silver key had maybe fallen into a crevice. "Not there," Gabe said to himself and then to Lane, "I'd startled her, of course. Felt her reach behind and grab me, pulling me close against her body. Then she suddenly whispered... Brent."

Gabe worked his way over to Lane, sticking his hands in her pockets, and ruffling through her duty belt. "She said it in such a sultry way as if she relished the very sound of his name on her lips." Gabe stopped, shaking his head as he stood stooped over Lane. "I was completely shocked. The betrayal Danie had shown. Not only to me and Lucas but to Janie! To lure Brent out there... and Brent! He was no better! Janie loved him, and he obviously had meant to meet Danie there. Which made his sudden desire to go looking for firewood on his own so devious."

Gabe stood up, breathing hard.

"Before I knew it, I'd grabbed her by the shoulders and whipped her around to face me. To see MY face and know I knew her betrayal! Then... then it was a gut reaction to shove her. I wanted her as far away from me as possible, and I just..." Gabe shrugged his shoulders. "I just pushed her as hard as I could, and down she tumbled, right off the side of the point."

Gabe suddenly frowned and squinted at Lane, looking her over. "Hold up. There it is!" He bent down, spotting something silver. "When I heard the splash, I realized what I had done." Gabe sighed in relief. He had found the cuff key in the folds of Lane's pants.

Lane thought about reaching for it but couldn't make her arms move.

"I want you to know, Sheriff. I tried to do the right thing." Gabe sat down heavily on the log. "I tore off my shirt and dove in after her. When I reached her, she was semi-conscious, having split her head open on a rock. I started to drag her back when I realized she'd tell." He worked the small key into the lock of the cuff, giving it a twist. "And if she told, I'd lose everything. My scholarships, my friends, my career, my freedom... my life would stop. I loved Danie... but no woman is worth all that."

Gabe tossed the handcuffs down on top of Lane, standing up to straddle her waist, reaching for her gun holster.

377

"So, I used my forearm and held her down until she stopped thrashing. Then I quickly made my way to land, put my shirt back on, screamed for help, and waited till I heard people coming."

He unsnapped the gun from the holster. "I had started to wade myself back out to save her when Brent went all superhero and got to her first. Between the two of us, we managed to get her back to dry land, and Kevin started CPR. I was worried he'd actually be successful, so I told him to go for help. Then it was just a matter of pretending. When the ranger showed up... Well... then I gave it my honest-to-goodness try. But by then, she was long gone."

Gabe held Lane's gun in his hand, looking for the safety. Finding it, he flipped it off and placed the gun on top of the log.

"At the funeral though, I started to suspect something wasn't right. Janie... Or rather, who I thought to be Janie, was looking at everyone like they were the boogieman. Wouldn't let any of us come anywhere near her. A few months later, I happened to see her on a street in Seattle. She was wearing this pretty yellow dress with a large yellow hat. I have to tell you the sight made my heart stop. She looked just like Danie would..." Gabe grunted as he flipped Lane onto her stomach, pulling her arm behind her back. "That's when I guessed they'd switched places. I wasn't a hundred percent sure, so I followed her a few times, borrowing Lucas's truck. Always careful to be sure she never saw it was me."

Gabe felt Lane resist and yanked hard on her arm, causing a yelp of pain.

"You can imagine the panic I felt... and the joy. Danie was alive! Yet, she could destroy everything if she realized it was me." He tightened his grip. "With her coming back to the island, I was worried she might talk to the others and piece together where everyone was at. I couldn't risk that, emotions being so high since it was the anniversary."

Gabe tightened his hold and bent over her, his spittle hitting her face. "You'd guessed right, though. Doctor Hadley had told me he'd seen Janie at The Royal Fork having dinner with her aunt. Even told me how Sue mentioned Janie would be taking the next couple of days to hike up The Mole Hill." Gabe patted her cheek, drawing her eye. "I wondered what she was really up to, so I waited a day or so to see if she'd contact me or the rest of the gang. Strangely, no one seemed to know she was even on the island."

Lane tried to turn her head away, but he shoved her face down into the ground, pressing her cheek hard against the small pebbles and pine needles.

"Stop squirming. I can tell it's already starting to wear off." Gabe reached over and started to yank on the water bottle, trying to wrench it from her duty belt.

Lane, buying for time, did as she was told. She'd

heard the helicopter land and leave, hoping beyond hope, help was soon on its way.

"She didn't... know?" Lane managed to ask, dirt and dried pine needles sticking to her lips and chin. She was starting to feel better, her thoughts slowly losing their haze.

"That I killed her sister?" Gabe unscrewed the water bottle lid. "No, not for sure. I don't think she ever figured out which one of us really did it until it was too late."

He brought the opened bottle up to her mouth, pressing it hard against her lips and teeth. Lane wriggled her shoulders, jostling the bottle.

"Damnit, stay still!" With his other hand, Gabe squeezed her cheeks hard, forcing her to open her mouth, and poured the remaining water in.

"SO, you see, Sheriff. Danie never rejected me because it was Janie who thought I was Brent. Not so smart, are you?" He stood up, kicking her hard in the ribs before stepping over her and chucking the water bottle as hard as he could into the woods. As he did, Lane let the liquid dribble down her chin, having managed not to swallow. Gabe walked back over, looming over her.

"To answer your earlier question by the waterfall, I'd seen her walking into the park." Gabe suddenly chuckled. "You should have seen the look on her face when she first saw Lucas's truck. All nervous and scared. That is, until I pulled up in the driver's seat, giving her the explanation I had borrowed his truck. Even fed her a little white lie, saying Lucas had let me take it, so I could be a good grandson and pick some berries for my grandma's preserves. Believe me, she was instantly at ease. I then drove her into the park and dropped her off at the base of Indian Flat trail with a friendly good-bye.

"You followed her... up the mole hill... she didn't see you?" Lane said the words slowly, trying to keep him talking and distracted, buying for time.

Gabe shook his head. "I don't think so. Though I spooked her a couple of times, so I know she was on edge. When I heard someone behind us, I quickly made my way down and ran into Brent," Gabe grunted, the handcuff slipping out of his sweaty hand as he tried to snap it around Lane's wrist. "I was actually worried she might confide in him, Brent being Mr. Perfect and all. But she gave him the brush off, and once he was gone, I walked up on her and pushed her off. Another terrible accident."

Gabe grabbed Lane's free arm intent on getting her completely handcuffed.

"Of course, originally, that's what I hoped everyone would think. But when I saw Brent was intent on telling his story, how he was the last person to see her alive... another possibility came to mind. I wouldn't have to spend the rest of my life looking over my shoulder if Brent was blamed for her murder. Then good ol' Philly boy starts coming around. Acting like everyone's big brother and asking about Danie's drowning. That brought up a whole new set of problems. Starting with Lucas unknowingly pointing the finger at me and then picking up the photo I had planned on planting on Brent in the ambulance. So, sadly, Lucas had to..."

"LANE!" Philip's voice resounded through the woods, and Gabe's head tilted up, his eyes searching. He let go of her arm and reached for the gun sitting on the log, clumsily gripping it in his hand.

"LANE? You out there?" Philip's voice boomed again, slightly closer.

Gabe shakily pointed the gun towards the trail, then suddenly changed his mind, putting it against the back of Lane's head.

"Gabe, don't do anything stupid," Lane mumbled, quickly putting herself in his shoes.

He was in a quandary. If he killed her using the gun, Philip would be upon him in no time. Standing his ground wasn't a great idea either. He needed to sneak back through the woods, hike himself out, and get on the ferry or steal a boat... if he had any chance of an escape.

"Gabe... don't be dum—"

"Shut up!" Gabe said harshly, pointing the gun towards the trail again, having spotted motion.

Philip was getting closer and making good time.

Desperate, Lane wiggled against Gabe's leg, trying to make noise, kicking with her feet.

"Stop that!" He put a heavy boot down on her back, pinning her to the ground.

"Maybe they're still at the waterfall?" Philip's voice projected as he grew closer. "You see anything?" He apparently wasn't alone. He had help.

Gabe hunkered down as Philip came into view, and Lane's thoughts crystallized.

In these dense woods, if Gabe made a run for it now, he most likely wouldn't get far. He also knew the ranger was armed and dangerous and no longer on his own. It was now or never. She had to do something.

Gabe took aim, grounding in his heel, feeling the sheriff move underfoot.

.

CHAPTER 41

L ane let out a gasp, the boot heel digging into her spine, her face mashed into the ground. She couldn't see Philip coming, but she could hear him. She could also sense Gabe's desperation, convinced he was going to do something rash if she didn't act.

Pinned to the ground, with her left arm still bent behind her and the other lying limp by her side, Lane started to feel around with her lose arm. Gabe, his full attention on the forward trail wasn't paying her any attention as she frantically groped the dark foliage.

With fingers splayed, her palms brushed against crushed pine cones and broken twigs as she pawed at the forest floor. Anguished, she dug her fingers into the soft dirt and pulled herself to the right, stretching for a thick broken limb.

Feeling her move, Gabe dug in his heel, applying pressure. Lane grimaced, her chest crushed against the ground, her breath cut short. She continued to stretch, her fingers weakly brushing against the broken limb.

It was no use. She couldn't reach it.

Craning her neck as much as she could, her watery eyes scanned the ground, desperate for anything. She couldn't see much, and her chest was on fire. She stretched again, this time above her head. Her fingers suddenly fumbled against a rock, and she gripped it, pulling it into her palm and down to her side.

"Lane?" The sound of Philip's voice caused her stomach to drop. "I think I see them!" Philip pushed back branches, his pace speeding up. "Everybody okay up there?" he called again.

"No! Lane is hurt!" Gabe yelled, squinting with one eye, trying to line up his target. "I can't help her! I'm still handcuffed! She's hurt bad!"

"We're coming!" Philip plowed through the tree limbs and fallen logs as if they were wind. "Tell her help is on the way!"

Gabe changed his stance, and Lane felt the pressure lessen. She was finally able to take a deep breath.

"You... were... wrong...," she croaked through gulps of air. "It was Janie... the whole time. She... played you... the fool."

Gabe lurched back as if physically punched, his eyes glued to Lane. "You're wrong." he sneered, his face full of anger and disbelief, the gun still pointed down trail.

"She... used you... to make Brent jealous. They switched the night before... Janie was Danie ALL DAY. It was NEVER Danie."

"Liar," Gabe yelled, stepping completely back, straddling her. "It had to be Danie. She held my hand!"

Steeling herself, Lane heaved onto her knees and quickly rolled to her side, bumping up against Gabe's leg. Catching him by surprise, she swiftly brought the rock up in a back-handed motion, slamming it as hard as she could into his left knee.

A loud crack sounded as rock hit bone, shattering his knee cap. Crashing down into the thicket, Gabe fell on top of her, sending a loud howl up into the air. The gun going off as he collapsed in pain. Numerous shots, flying wayward down trail.

Taking advantage of Gabe's stunned reaction, she reached up, her fingernails digging against the side of his face leaving long red rows of scratches. She then snatched at the tank top headband, yanking it down and encircling his neck, twisting it around her hand as hard as she could, doing her best to cut off his air supply.

Gabe panicked, the gun still in his right hand. He reached up with his left, grabbing at Lane's fingers, scrambling to loosen her grip on the fabric. Failing to do so, he pointed the gun at her, his face red, eyes bulging.

Waiting for this moment, Lane abruptly let go of the bandana and watched as he sprung back. Using her training, she immediately jerked her head to the side and out of the gun's line of sight. She then slammed the side of her hand against Gabe's wrist, breaking his hold and ripping the gun out of his hand.

Rolling out from underneath him, she kicked his injured knee as hard as she could. He let out a scream of pain, clutching at his leg. Lane staggered to her feet, the handcuff still dangling from her wrist, and pointed the gun at his head.

"Don't!" she panted, planting her foot on his chest. "Move a muscle."

"Sherriff?" Deputy Pickens came bursting upon them, his eyes wide. "Are you okay?"

He found Lane standing over Gabe, her foot planted firmly on his chest and her gun pointed at his head.

"I need your cuffs, Deputy." She ignored his question and then looked behind him. "Where's Ranger Russell?"

Caleb grabbed at his own duty belt, pulling out his handcuffs, taking a wide berth around Gabe as he rushed to make his way over.

"He's been shot," Caleb reported, nodding for Lane to go. "He insisted I come looking for you."

"Careful, pretty sure I shattered his knee cap."

Lane nodded towards Gabe before holstering her gun and taking off at a dead run.

Thrashing her way through the woods, she spotted the trail she'd followed in. Turns out, she hadn't been as far off course as she'd imagined. Doing her best to keep up pace, she followed the path, her eyes searching for Philip. She still wasn't feeling quite herself, but the adrenaline rush had cleared a good portion of her head. Panic was doing the rest.

"PHIL!" Lane's chest about collapsed, spotting his prone body lying on the ground, his leg propped up on a fallen tree limb. She skidded to a stop, quickly giving him a once over.

A stray bullet had pierced his inner thigh, blood rapidly pouring out. Philip had managed to get his belt off and around his thigh but had passed out before being able to cinch it.

"Oh, please. Not an artery," Lane prayed, clambering over Phil's unconscious body and roughly sticking her finger in the wound itself to apply pressure.

With her cuffed hand, she grabbed the belt strap and brought it up to her mouth, biting down on the belt with her teeth. Placing her hand back onto his thigh, she held the belt in place. Then pulling her head back, she yanked as hard as she could to cinch it up.

Getting the belt to tighten, she took her finger out of the wound and gave the belt another hard cinch, jerking Philip's leg up with it. She then ran like hell heading back to the ranger's forest truck, branches and limbs slashing and clawing at her face.

Crashing through the woods, the dangling cuff caught on a broken branch and about pulled her off her feet. She desperately untangled herself and got back up, clutching the loose cuff in her hand, stumbling over the trail as fast as she could.

Finally spotting the forest truck, she sprinted over, jerking open the door and plucking the two-way radio off its cradle.

"KODY! Can you hear me?" Lane yelled into the two-way.

"Sheriff Lane, that you? Over," Kody asked, surprised.

"Yes, Kody. Listen very carefully. Philip's been hurt... shot. I need you to get help to us right away!" Lane impatiently waited for Kody to respond and then added, "Over damnit, Over!"

"Sheriff, Ethan is already on his way. ETA fifteen minutes." The two-way radio squawked, and Lane cut in.

"No good, Kody. I've got two injured. The ambulance isn't going to make it through this jeep road. We need a chopper!" Lane was already straining to hear sirens. Maybe if she could get Philip to them... but she was scared to jostle him.

"But the Coast Guard hasn't reached the mainland yet with Lucas!"

"I don't care! Tell them to come back! Have them send out another chopper! Call Search and Rescue! Get their team over here. Just get me a chopper now, Kody! Over and out!"

Dropping the handset, the coiled cord bounced against the dash, swishing back and forth. Lane brushed it aside, grabbing the small medical kit and snatching the blanket Philip kept behind the driver's seat. She hesitated, wondering if she should try the Coast Guard herself, but dismissed it. She had to help Philip now and trust that Kody would do all that he could.

Jetting back into the woods, Lane started talking to God. Begging for Philip's life to be spared and promising anything he required of her. Philip just needed to stay alive.

CHAPTER 42

Ethan Richardson gave out a low moan as the jostled ambulance rumbled to a stop. Leaning against the steering wheel, he peered out from the bug-smeared windshield, eyeing the jeep road ahead warily.

Directly in front of him was a giant dip in the road. He could see where large, knobby jeep tires had gouged a rut in the old trail and where the road ascended before dipping down into a larger groove. The old jeep road itself, lined with evergreens on each side, made it impossible for him to circumvent the man-made crater.

Easing the ambulance forward slowly and then thinking twice about it, Ethan stopped with a hard jerk before picking up the CB radio. "Kody, I can't go any further. If I try, I'm going to end up high-centering the ambulance. This rut is way too high in the middle, and there's no way to drive around. They're going to have to get Phil to me. Over."

"Ethan, the chopper is still twenty minutes out. You've got to figure something out. Over," Kody's voice was tense and forceful.

Ethan took a deep breath. Kody was right. Twisting in his seat, Ethan looked into the back of the ambulance, taking a mental inventory. He nodded to himself and swung back around, speaking into the radio.

"Kody, I'm going to grab my kit and head out on foot. I don't know how long—"

A horn sounded, and Ethan quickly looked at the side mirror. In the reflection, he could see Jerry Holmes's truck coming up behind him, bouncing up and down the jeep trail, a cloud of dust in its wake.

"Hold tight, Kody. I think the cavalry just arrived. Over." Ethan quickly hung up the handset as Jerry's truck skidded to a stop behind him. Clambering out of the ambulance, Ethan ran to the driver's side, motioning for Jerry to roll down his window.

"Get that meat-wagon out of our way!" Dr. Hadley snapped. He was sitting next to Jerry. His face as white as his hair, glasses askew on the bridge of his nose. Despite having a white-knuckle grip on the handle attached to the glove box, the old doctor had been tumbled and tossed along the jeep trail.

Jerry, leaning out his window and blocking Dr. Hadley's view, motioned towards the ambulance. "Ethan! I need you to back up. There's a turn-off about a half-mile back." Jerry rolled his window up, not waiting for Ethan's response, and reversed his truck down the road.

Giving a thumbs up, Ethan ran back to the ambulance and snatched up the handset. "Kody, catching a ride up with Jerry and Doctor Hadley. Keep pressure on the chopper. Over and out!" Ethan hung up the radio and started carefully guiding the boxed vehicle backwards down the jeep road.

Seeing a spot where he could pull over to the side, giving Jerry's rig enough room to push through, Ethan made a hard-left, narrowly missing the pine trees. He then quickly hopped out, bowing his head to miss the overhanging limbs, and ran to the back of the ambulance.

Pulling up beside him, Jerry rolled down his window again, signaling he was going forward up the road.

"Hold on! I'm coming with you!" Ethan yelled, reaching the back of the ambulance, the double doors coated thick with road dust, pulling them open. "Come on, Jerry! Need your help!"

Jerry hopped out and grabbed the end of the portable backboard stretcher, which was being pushed through the ambulance doors. Pulling it the rest of the way out, he placed it in the back of his pickup truck. He then took Ethan's large ambulance medical kit and placed it next to Doctor Hadley's black bag.

"Need anything else?" Jerry snatched the blankets folded on the gurney, tucking them under his arm.

"Do we know anything more about what kind of injuries we're dealing with besides a gunshot wound?" Ethan asked Jerry, his eyes falling on the tank of oxygen.

Jerry hurriedly shook his head no. "Kody called Hadley. Said there were two injured people by the waterfall. I think we should try to bring whatever we can."

Ethan hopped out of the ambulance and unhooked the oxygen tank. Cradling it in his arms, he quickly headed towards Jerry's truck.

Jerry ran ahead of him, opening the backseat door, doing his best to help Ethan crawl in with the tank still clasped to his chest.

"Ethan." Doctor Hadley turned in his seat to face the young EMT fireman.

"Doc." Ethan moved the tank to the seat next to him, belting it in and then himself.

Jerry hopped in, slamming his door roughly, and put the truck into drive. "Hold on, it's gonna get a little bumpy," Jerry warned, rolling up his window.

Doctor Hadley, facing forward again, braced himself against the door.

"How much farther up do you think?" Ethan

asked, being jostled side to side, Jerry doing his best to maneuver the large rut.

"Little over a mile. You almost made it to 'em." Jerry shot him a quick smile in the rear-view mirror.

"How'd you two end up here?" Ethan returned the grin.

"I noticed Calvin had taken the ferry with the fire department's pickup. Figured you were heading up here with the ambulance."

"Yeah, originally thought I was only coming out for support. In this type of location, usually, people are airlifted out. But with more than one person injured..." Ethan grabbed the tossed blankets off of Jerry's middle console, tucking them around the oxygen, doing his best to cushion the tank so it didn't bang up against the inside of Jerry's truck or come dislodge in all the swaying back and forth.

"Same thought as we had," Doctor Hadley said, giving Ethan a quick fleeting glance before looking up front again.

"Any word on the first person they pulled out?" Ethan, swaying and bobbing with the truck, took hold of the headrest in front of him, watching the road through the large windshield.

"Coast Guard got'em. Taking them to Swedish H. They've got a capsized boat out on the sound, so their other helicopter is working that scene. Plus, a pile-up on I-5 has the hospital helicopter running back and forth. We're on our own until one of those free up or search and rescue can get here."

"This must be it," Doctor Hadley said, spying the forest ranger's truck and the sheriff's rig parked behind it. "Stop here, Jerry." Doctor Hadley unclipped his seat belt, giving Jerry a hard look before pulling on the door handle. "And bring your shotgun."

CHAPTER 43

Running back to Philip, Lane skidded to a stop, dust and grit landing on his legs as she quickly unfurled the blanket, hastily throwing it over his mid-section. He looked far worse than when she had left him, his face startlingly pale, lips slightly tinged blue.

Dropping to her knees, she took a deep breath before willing herself to take Philip's wrist, her trembling fingers resting against his skin. Head bowed, she let out a sob of relief.

There was a pulse.

As weak as it was, there wasn't much time. He needed help... if only help was on the way. She scooted closer and laid her hand across his forehead. It felt cold and clammy despite the sweat beading on his skin.

"Phil? Help is on the way. Can you hear me, Ranger? You with me?" Her voice sounded steady and reassuring to her own ears, though her hand shook as she reached for his. "You better be! Because I'll drag you out of here by your hair if I have to. You hear me?" She nervously chuckled, hoping he'd open his eyes with a smart mouth comeback. Philip lay still and unresponsive. "Don't worry, Phil. I'll get you out of here."

Leaning back on her heels, Lane quickly scanned the ground around him. She was looking for anything she might be able to make a stretcher out of with the blanket. Maybe between her and Caleb? Caleb!

"I'll be right back, okay?" She didn't know if he could hear her, but it was said more for her than it was for him. She gave his hand a quick squeeze before standing up and carefully stepping over him, heading back for her deputy.

Knowing the way much better, she swiftly headed into the thicker woods, clasping the handcuff in her hand to prevent it from snagging on anything.

"Deputy Pickens?" Lane called out, stepping over a large fallen log and bending low to avoid bumping her head on the tree, which was crisscrossed over it. "Deputy? Are you alri—"

Caleb suddenly stepped into view with Gabe's arm draped over his shoulder, the latter holding his weight off his bad leg as best as he could.

"Right here, Sheriff." Caleb waved. "We were making our way to you."

Lane noticed the arm dangling by Gabe's side had been handcuffed to his jeans. Caleb's way of making sure Gabe didn't use his free arm for any mischief.

"Here." Lane stepped around them, looping her arm through Gabe's and helping pull him through the fallen logs.

"How's Ranger Russell?" Caleb asked, trying to heft Gabe alongside him.

"Not good, but still with us." Lane gritted her teeth, scraping her back against the log, trying to keep Gabe's shoulders level with Caleb. "Kody is trying to get us a chopper, but looks like we're going to have to drag him out on our own."

"I can help him if you let me out of these cuf—"

"Shut up!" Lane and Caleb said at the same time as they hefted Gabe over the last log.

"But if he needs..."

"I'm not letting you anywhere near him." Lane's cold blue eyes burned. "Here, Caleb. Put him down."

Together, they eased Gabe to the ground, handcuffing his hands behind his back and securing him to the log.

"I don't think he's going anywhere," Caleb said, trying to catch up to Lane, who was already heading back to Philip. "Unless he takes the whole log with him." Lane stopped short at Philip's feet.

"Gabe is the least of my worries right now."

"Do you think it's such a good idea to move him?" Caleb wiped the sweat from his brow with the back of his hand and looked down trail.

It was fairly open compared to what they'd just walked through, but they would still be jostling him around quite a bit.

"I don't think we have a choice." Lane took a step back, her eyes still lingering on Philip's face. She was concerned his color wasn't returning and wondered if he might already be in shock.

"Okay, and what about this guy?" Caleb jerked his head back towards Gabe. "Do we just leave him?"

"As much as I'd love to..." Lane pursed her lips together in thought. "We can't leave him behind."

"Then what do we do? We can't carry Phil out on a stretcher and help Gabe hobble out at the same time." Caleb ran his hands through his hair, exasperated.

"Maybe if you sling Gabe over your shoulder and then we could rig a stretcher? Try to carry Philip out that way?" Lane rubbed her forehead, trying to think it through. "We just gotta get him to the tru—"

"Sheriff Lane!"

It sounded like Jerry... Lane's head snapped towards the direction of the yell, her hand falling away from her face. There was another bellow in the same voice.

"Deputy Caleb!"

"Jerry?" Lane hollered back, surprised to hear

his voice.

At a run, she headed in the direction of his call, pushing her way through bushes and tree boughs.

"Jerry!" she yelled his name again, this time her voice flooded with relief. Spotting Jerry not far from the trucks, her heart lurched in her chest to see Ethan and Doctor Hadley right behind him. The old doctor doing his best to hold a back-board brace under his arm like a surfboard, his black medicine bag gripped in his left hand.

"Oh, thank God!" Lane waved her arms, drawing Jerry's attention. Help had arrived.

CHAPTER 44

Lane stood back, doing her best not to hover. The new arrivals were carefully placing Philip on the back-board brace using it as a stretcher. Their hurried motions blocking most of her view.

Ethan, who had taken charge, hastily beckoned Caleb over and instructed him to help Doctor Hadley support Philip's head. He then quickly swabbed the inside crick of Philip's elbow before reaching back into his medical kit.

On the other side, Lane could see Jerry strapping a blood pressure cuff around the opposite arm and vigorously beginning to pump. His face stoic and pale, which Lane thought did not bode well.

Doctor Hadley, positioned at Philip's head, moved over to make room for Caleb. He then showed him how to hold the oxygen mask over Philip's mouth, mumbling something to Caleb about needing to bring Philip's saturation levels up.

"Sheriff, give me room?" Ethan asked politely, reaching past her leg, grabbing for a sterile package.

Despite her best efforts, she was hovering.

"Sorry." Lane stumbled back a few paces. Ethan glanced back, making sure she was out of his way, and jerked his head, indicating for her to move further to the right.

"I need to get fluids into his system, so the remaining blood he has can carry oxygen to his brain," Ethan explained, catching her eye.

Lane quickly nodded she understood and took another step back, watching as Ethan carefully inserted an IV needle, taping it down. He tossed the packaging to the side, it landing at her feet.

"Here, Sheriff. Take this. It's plasma," Ethan instructed sharply, handing her a clear bag attached to the IV line. "And keep it held high!" He then lurched to his feet, motioning for Caleb to take Doctor Hadley's spot. "We need to take a look at that leg."

Examining the belt tourniquet, both men voiced their concerns. Lane, hanging on their every word, realized due to the length of time the leg had been bound, nerve and soft tissue damage may have already evolved. Waiting was no longer an option.

"Go stand by Caleb, Sheriff. I need room." Doctor

Hadley grabbed the trauma shears from the medic kit and started cutting through Philip's pants, ripping the fabric away from his thigh. He then tossed the excess material and shears to the side and took a deep breath.

"Ready?"

Catching Ethan's eye, the old doctor gave a curt nod before gripping the tourniquet and wrenching the belt buckle free.

"Got it!" Ethan said through gritted teeth, pushing down hard on Philip's leg, leveraging his full weight against him.

"Don't let up!" The old doctor warned, starting to apply padding.

Wrapping the thigh with tight pressure bandages, his wrinkled hands moved with steady confidence. Lane was surprised by how little time it took him. She inched a step closer.

"How's it looking?" Ethan asked her, turning his head, trying to see the doctor's hands, then glancing up at Caleb. "He still breathing?"

Caleb jerkily nodded his head, yes. A wry smile, cracking his face.

"Alright. Think we got it!" Doctor Hadley placed a bloody hand on Ethan's shoulder, indicating he could relieve pressure. Both sat back on their haunches, breathing hard.

"Well?" Doctor Hadley asked, still sucking in air

from the exertion and adrenaline.

All eyes turned to Jerry, eager to see if their efforts had made a difference.

"His blood pressure is coming up." Jerry nodded, a small smile breaking across his somber face. "I think he's stable."

Doctor Hadley gave Ethan a hearty slap on the back then used him as leverage to pull himself up. Lane rushed over and grabbed the elderly doctor's arm, assisting him the rest of the way.

"Thank you, Sheriff." He waved her off, giving her a tired smile. "I'm good."

Gingerly, he pulled a white handkerchief out of his back pocket and patted his sweat covered face, tossing the bloodied handkerchief to the ground with a grunt.

"This is hard work for an old man. I'm all tuckered out."

Lane watched the doctor's smile falter.

"What's going on here?" Doctor Hadley pointed towards Gabe, who still sat on the ground handcuffed. He started to walk towards him and Lane put a restraining hand on the old man's arm.

"He's the one who swapped Brent's EpiPen," Lane said softly, her grip tightening as she felt the doctor stagger back, unsteady on his feet. Caleb stepped up behind the doctor and put a reassuring hand on his back.

"I'll take a look at him," Ethan said quietly and got up. Using the back of his arm, he wiped his brow before snapping off his latex gloves to grab a fresh pair. "What happened to him?"

Lane handed Caleb the plasma bag to hold and walked with Ethan over to Gabe, who was sitting flat on the ground leaned up against a tree trunk, his legs stretched out. He was looking pale and tired, though his eyes were still puffy and red. She frankly had forgotten all about him.

"I smashed his knee in with a rock," Lane said, giving Gabe a steely-eyed glare. Ethan's eyebrows shot up as he looked from Gabe back to Sheriff Lane. "Believe me," she added, "It was in self-defense."

Ethan nodded his head, not questioning the sheriff, and started to bend down to look at Gabe's knee. He suddenly stopped, tilting his ear over his shoulder. "Hear that?"

Everyone paused, holding their breath.

"It's a helicopter!" Caleb announced loudly, pointing to the sky, their eyes eagerly scanning the horizon. "There!"

A bright orange and white chopper came into view, steadily growing closer.

An unexpected moan sounded from the ground, and all eyes wandered down to Philip. He was trying to say something, his head slightly moving back and forth. Jerry put a reassuring hand on his chest, instructing him to stay still, and signaled for Lane to make her way over.

"Phil, you've been shot. We've got you hooked up to some plasma, and the helicopter just got here. They'll be taking you to the hospital. I need you to stay still," Jerry said calmly, his hand still on Philip's chest.

Philip's eyes fluttered open, focusing on Lane and then on Jerry. He moved his hand up, trying to push away the oxygen mask. Caleb and the plasma bag moved with him, fearful of him pulling out the IV.

"Ranger, keep still," Lane said sternly, utter relief causing a lump in her throat. "You're still not out of the woods yet... literally."

Philip's eyes wandered from her to Jerry, and he tried to remove the oxygen again, mumbling through the mask.

"Here. He's bound and determined." Jerry moved the mask to the side so Philip could be heard.

"Jer, I need you to... take care... of uncle chu—" Jerry replaced the mask and gave Philip an exaggerated nod of the head.

"I will. Don't worry." Philip fumbled for the mask, and Jerry huffed, "Last time. No more talking." He removed the mask, and Philip's eyes wandered to Lane.

"You... okay?" Philip's eyes ran across her face and down the front of her uniform.

Lane suddenly imagined what a sight she must look with the front of her uniform unbuttoned and covered in mud, her hair falling out of its bun, a large bruise forming across her chin and cheek, along with the deep scratches up and down her arms, already looking swollen and red. All in all, she thought she probably looked better than she felt.

"I'm a big girl," she reassured him with a nod and a smile as she self-consciously started to button up her blouse, covering her bare mid-section and the remains of her mud-stained tank top.

"Must have worn your... big girl panties toda—" Lane moved the mask back over Philip's mouth, giving him a teary-eyed smile.

"Yeah, he's going to be fine."

CHAPTER 45

L ane pulled in front of the veterinarian's clinic, taking the parking spot next to Jerry's pickup, happy she'd caught him at the office. Springing nimbly from the truck, she leaned back in, grabbing the large basket of homemade muffins sitting on the front seat. This was her last delivery, having dropped off a basket at Doctor Hadley's and another at the fire station. A small token of thanks.

It had been a month since Gabe's arrest, most of it a huge whirlwind. The first week was daunting, dealing with the media frenzy the arrest had caused, hardly being able to go anywhere on the island or the mainland without a small crowd of reporters nipping at her heels. Thankfully, Caleb, finally coming into his own, ended up being quite a big help, warding off the cameras and pushy reporters, allowing Lane to spend what little free time she had filling out copious amounts of paperwork.

The second week, just as chaotic, was spent documenting Gabe's confession and building the case after his arrest. Charged with the twins and Brent Allister's murder, Gabe was also facing three counts of Attempted Murder against Lucas, Lane, and Philip. With the new evidence Lane had managed to collect, it promised to be an open and shut case.

However, with the advice of a particularly sharp and sleazy lawyer, Gabe ended up pleading not guilty, declaring an Irresistible Impulse Insanity Defense. Meaning, he knew what he was doing was wrong but couldn't help himself.

Despite the plea, the State Prosecutor seemed confident the jury wouldn't swallow the hogwash. And hopefully, Gabe would spend the rest of his life in prison. Lane prayed he was right. Gabe was a dangerous young man who was a threat to society... not to mention, he'd been deadly to those who were his nearest and dearest friends.

When Lane hadn't been locked in her office, buried under an ever-growing mound of paperwork, she was over on the mainland bouncing back and forth between hospital rooms.

Lucas, recovering from a severe head injury, ended up making a full but slow recovery. It had taken several weeks to piece his hazy recollections together, and even then, there were still moments he couldn't quite recall. For instance, he couldn't remember why the two friends had dropped the idea of the cave hunt in favor of the waterfall hike. Or how his full water bottle had suddenly become empty, leading to Gabe's offer to refill it from the creek. It must have been then that Gabe slipped the drug into Lucas's water bottle unseen.

What he did recall was feeling nauseous and a little dizzy after drinking from it. Standing near the waterfall, he had been unable to find a good foothold. Trying to determine if it was something they should even attempt, Gabe had grown impatient and began to goad him. Calling Lucas a chicken, among other names, pushing him to hurry and begin the climb.

Succumbing to Gabe's peer pressure, Lucas made it only a few feet off the ground before losing his footing. Staggering back to his feet, he remembered his legs feeling rubbery and tried to tell Gabe he wasn't feeling good, the words heavy on his tongue. This was when Gabe attacked him from behind, wielding a rock.

The stone had glanced off his temple, crashing down onto his shoulder, having stumbled to the side at the last second. Later, he had told Lane it had been pure reflex to grab his bear spray. Said he didn't even remember pulling the trigger before passing out. It was also his good luck he had fallen backwards instead of forwards on his face, where he most likely would have drowned.

Lane theorized at this point, having been in essence pepper-sprayed, Gabe had dropped to the ground, spending several minutes in agonizing pain. Unbeknownst to anyone at the time, Lucas's actions had given Lane and Philip the advantage, allowing them a chance to catch up.

Once Gabe was able to see again, he got back onto his feet, grabbed the biggest rock he could manhandle, and stood over Lucas, intent on crushing in his head. He would have succeeded had Lane not come bursting upon the scene right at that moment.

Lane surmised Gabe most likely would have claimed another accident. A worn rope or loose rock, perhaps? Staging it to look as if Lucas had slipped and fell. Loose rocks collapsing down on him, crushing his head. People may have found it suspicious, but there would have been no way to prove it to be murder.

Gabe's attempt to make Lucas a second scapegoat and muddy the waters of Danie and Janie's death almost succeeded. After interviewing Lucas, it was clear he had never found the memory card for the camera or even approached Brent about it. Gabe had it in his possession the whole time, framing Lucas and even hinting it might have been him who damaged the memory card. Lane also came to realize there was never anything between Janie and Lucas beyond friendship. Gabe's efforts to smear his friend and create suspicion was just an attempt to send her down a false trail.

After collecting Lucas's memories of the attack, along with Philip's interviews and Lane's notes, plus handing over the trail camera pictures, it was now in the hands of the court and lawyers. All in all, they'd been lucky... without the trail camera, the pieces may never have come together.

It wasn't luck Lane attributed to Philip's recovery, though. The bullet which pierced his thigh had missed his femoral artery and all major nerves. He was lucky to be alive, with luck having nothing to do with it as far as Lane was concerned. Her daily prayers were filled with gratitude.

His hospital room was constantly filled with well-wishers and flowers, ...and Harry. Colleagues from the U.S. forest station and wildlife department came and went, along with half the island and out-of-town family. Lane would pop her head in daily, say a quick hello, and make sure he didn't need anything before heading out to let his visitors enjoy their time with him. After two weeks, he was released but stayed in Seattle with his uncle Chuck and cousin Julie while working through his physical therapy. She hadn't been able to see him since and wondered when he would be returning back home to the island.

Speaking of the island, the majority of the folks were thankful everything had come to light. However, there were a few who seemed to hold Lane to blame. Mike Allister, for one. He held her solely responsible for his grandson's death. Telling her, in no uncertain terms, if she hadn't been suspicious of Brent, Gabe might have very well let him be, pointing the finger at someone else. She alone, in his opinion, aimed Gabe straight at Brent much like a loaded gun. She knew he was speaking out of grief, and though she was sorry Brent had died, she wouldn't apologize for doing her job. She could have added, that if his grandfather lawyer had allowed the boy to speak freely, things might have worked out very differently.

The rest of the people were those who had known Gabe in a different capacity and could not be convinced of his guilt. After all, ...he was a boy who grew up on the island, a volunteer for the fire department, and a man who took down their ailments on a clipboard and calmed their fears at the doctor's office. Someone they had always found to be kind and trusting and because of it, it left them feeling all the more violated. But there was nothing she could do about that.

Gripping the basket tightly, Lane walked up to the front counter, saying a friendly hello to Alice the receptionist, a chorus of dog barks and howls greeting her at the sound of her voice.

"Hi, I just wanted to drop these off for Doctor Holmes." Lane attached a greeting card to the gingham cloth covering the muffins and placed the basket onto the counter.

"Oh, blueberry. Those are his favorite." Alice smiled, peeking under the blanket before leaning in to whisper, "Mine too."

Lane returned the smile, slipping one of the muffins out of the basket and handing it over.

"Here."

"Hey! Those for me?" Jerry had stepped out of an examination room to cross the hallway into another and spotted Lane. Quickly tossing a clipboard into a slot by the door, he made his way up front. "Oooo, blueberry!" He handed Alice a file and quickly mumbled something about room two needing a flea treatment. "I didn't know you baked?"

"A new hobby," Lane admitted. "Also, my way of saying thank you and my apologies for not being around for the last month."

"Well, I'm glad you're here." Jerry snatched up a muffin. "Can you come back and chat for a moment?" He waved, muffin in hand, beckoning Lane to follow him into his office, and then turned to Alice. "Tell George Barnes and his basset hound, I'll just be a few minutes."

Lane followed behind and took the seat offered

to her as Jerry sat on the corner of his desk. She watched as he gave his mustache a quick curl.

"How have you been?" Lane started, taking a quick glance around his office, never having seen it before.

"I've been good... really good." Jerry's smile spread wider. "How about you? Things finally settling down?"

"Getting there. Once the trial is over, I might get my life back." Lane watched as Jerry pulled at his mustache again, recognizing the nervous tick. "You okay, Jerry?" Jerry gave a jittery laugh and nodded his head.

"Yeah, I'm great!" He stood up, moving a stapler to the side before sitting back down on the corner of the desk. "I'm really great."

"What's happened?" Lane smiled at his anxiousness, curious as to what had him so giddy. Whatever it was, she couldn't help but smile along with him.

"The completely unexpected." Jerry ran a hand over his smile. "And hopefully, ...you'll understand."

"Jerry, for goodness sake, tell me already!" Lane chuckled. He was clearly trying to keep his excitement toned down.

"My ex-wife and I... we're..."

"You're going to be grandparents?" Lane's mouth split into a huge smile. "Oh, how exciting!"

"No! ...No, at least... not yet. Or... I hope not. Not for a few more years." Jerry put his hands up as if to ward off Lane's good wishes.

"Oh, I'm sorry," Lane said, mystified. "You were saying you and your ex-wife..."

"We're back together."

"Oh!" Lane sat back in her seat, not expecting that particular piece of news.

"I didn't mean for it to happen. Never dreamed it would happen!" Jerry leaned towards Lane, his tone apologetic. "With Amy living with me and doing so good, Heather and I started talking more, and then she came over, and we sat down as a family. I took her to dinner a few times after that, and next thing I knew..."

"The old flame was lit." Lane smiled slowly. "That's great, Jerry. It is really."

"You mean that?" Jerry stood up, straightening his white coat. Lane stood up with him.

"Of course! Does that mean Heather is coming back to the island?" She started to make for the door.

"It's a bit soon for that, but I'm hopeful." He quickly leaned past her, opening his office door for her. "I've told Heather what a great friend you've been. Think we could get together for dinner some night? Maybe Philip would like to tag along?"

Lane turned her head, looking back at Jerry with a wisp of a smile.

"Maybe."

CHAPTER 46

Philip pulled up to the cottage spotting Lane's patrol truck parked by the backdoor. He hadn't called ahead, being it was a Saturday morning, guessing she'd be at home. He opened his driver's door and gingerly stepped down before pulling out a cane. His thigh still pained him a great deal, his limp a constant reminder.

According to his doctor, the pain would dissipate over time, along with his minor limp. That is, as long as he continued his physical therapy. Though his thigh was healing up, his ego was a little bruised. Here he'd gone running into danger, trying to save the damsel in distress... and, she ended up saving him. With a little help, of course.

Looking back now, all things having come to light, he was grateful for Lane's insistence on inves-

tigating the twins' deaths. He'd doubted the two accidents had been anything other than coincidence, and
Lane... per usual, had proved him wrong. Though
maybe if he had paid closer attention a year ago, he
might have been able to prevent what happened.

Struggling with guilt, staring up at his hospital
room's ceiling, he had asked himself... "What could I
have done differently? What could I have paid closer
attention to? Why didn't I ask more questions? Why
didn't I notice more? What if I had..." On one of her
visits to his room, Lane had warned him of the dan-
gers of thinking in circles.

"You could bury yourself in what-ifs... and it
won't change a damn thing." She'd reached over, taking his hand, careful not to bump his IV, and continued, "The future is what matters. So, focus on that,
Phil. I need you around." That, for some reason, had
made him feel much better. And maybe, it was why
he was at her cottage now? Well, there was a second
reason he'd come to visit... one he had been putting
off. However, if things went well...

Tonight was Miss Hattie's big birthday party. The
whole of the island was gathering down at the high
school gym where there would be cake and punch,
streamers and balloons, and dancing. Thinking of
Miss Hattie reminded him, he owed her an apology. She'd practically solved the whole thing from the
very beginning. Philip could still hear her words and

see the intensity in her runny blue eyes.

"It was silly for her to put herself in that kind of danger," and "Danie... Janie... Same girl."

Philip turned his head at the sound of the cottage door opening.

"Phil?" Lane stepped out onto the small landing, a wide smile on her face.

"Hi! Hope you don't mind me just dropping by?" Philip carefully stepped back and grabbed a small carrier, along with a plastic bag from the back of the pickup. "I wanted to drop something off."

Lane, her hair pulled up in a messy bun wearing a sweater over a cotton t-shirt and jeans, took the first step to the backstairs, her arms crossed over her chest.

It being mid-October, the weather had turned chilly, especially in the early morning.

"What do you have there?" Lane squinted at the animal carrier, unable to make out what was inside. She turned her eyes back to Philip, his gait hampered by a limp, a wrinkle of pain crossing his forehead with every other step.

"I hope you got some coffee on?" Philip ignored her question, reaching the bottom of the stairs.

Lane bent over, trying to see into the carrier. Whatever was in there was furry. She smiled and held the door open, taking a step back into the cottage.

"Need help?" she asked, watching Philip take the first step.

"Nah, I got it. Do this all the time in therapy," he said confidently, managing to get up the three steps with no difficulty.

"What do you have there?" Lane asked again, taking another quick look at the pet carrier. "Did you get me a cat?" she asked eagerly, her excitement apparent.

Philip put the carrier onto the kitchen table and turned it so Lane couldn't see inside.

"Can I have a cup of coffee first?" Philip asked, pulling out a chair from the kitchen table and carefully lowering himself into it. He dropped the plastic bag onto the floor before hooking his cane to the back of the chair.

"Yes, sorry!" Lane quickly made her way over to the coffee pot, filling up a large mug. "You look good, Phil. How are you feeling?" She pulled open the cabinet door above her head, reaching for a container of powdered creamer.

"Good. Glad to be back home on the island. Planning on returning to work on Monday." Philip turned the animal carrier back towards him, sticking his fingers in through the metal grates, giving the occupant a light pet on the forehead. "Doctor finally released me to full duty."

"So, are you done with physical therapy as well?" Lane brought the steaming mug over and carefully placed it in front of him.

"No, not by a long shot. Got a standing appointment once a week for the next three months or so. Though..." Philip took a sip of coffee. "They say I'm making great progress. Gave me a gold star on my last visit."

"You hungry?" Lane asked, heading towards the fridge.

"No... uhh, I had something to eat before I headed here."

"Oh, okay." Lane sat down at the table, eagerly looking between the animal carrier and Philip. "So, what's in the carrier? What did you bring me?"

Philip took a deep breath, an apologetic smile crossing his lips.

"You know when you said you thought there was a catch to living here?" Philip began to unlock the cage door on the carrier. Lane's smile disappeared.

"Uh-huhhh." Her eyes squinted into a cautious slit.

"You weren't exactly wrong." Philip opened the small door, giving the animal inside a rub under its chin. "Uncle Chuck is needing someone to not only take care of the cottage, which I know you will do, but he also needs someone with a BIG heart and a KIND soul to take care of his little buddy. His daughter Julie isn't allowed to have pets at her condo."

"Oh! Is that all?" Lane sighed in relief, shaking her head. "What kind of cat is it?"

Philip winced as he reached in with both hands,

gently grabbing the occupant.

"It's not a cat." Philip smiled, pulling out a puffed furball.

Lane stifled a yelp and instinctively scooted her chair back across the tile, standing up in alarm.

"Careful, you're gonna scare him!" Philip held the animal across his forearm, its large tail fluffed in the air. "He can't hurt you." Philip chuckled at her reaction, scooting his chair closer to her. "Here. Just pet him."

"I don't know, Phil. I've never petted one before." Lane slowly reached out, tilting her head to catch the animal's eye before running her hand along its back. "He's so soft!" she whispered, her fingers trailing down to its fluffy hindquarters. "OH, it's rough at the tail, I see."

"Yeah, their tail is coarse compared to the rest of them."

"Phil! I can't keep a skunk!" Lane sat back in her chair, realization coming to the forefront of her thoughts. "Aren't they illegal in Washington state?"

"Well..." Philip lowered the striped skunk to the kitchen floor. It quickly pounced its way into the small dining room. He sat back up. "They are if you take them from the wild... which this one was."

Lane started to shake her head.

"If it's against the law."

"Just hear me out, please?" Philip put up a pleading hand, reaching for the coffee mug with the other. "Uncle Chuck found him when he was just a baby. His mother had been run over in the road leaving four pups behind. At first, he was going to let nature take its course. One by one, they got picked off, being too young to defend themselves. There was just this one left." Philip put both hands up, Lane starting to interrupt. "Now, Uncle Chuck decided to rescue it... which he shouldn't have done... but he did." Philip put his hands down, moving the carrier from the kitchen table and putting it on the tiled floor. "He originally had planned to return him to the wild once he was old enough. But... Well..."

"He got attached," Lane finished, hearing a loud thunk as something heavy was knocked over in the living room.

"Yeah. He then approached Jerry and had him de-scent the little guy, making him an official pet."

"Jerry should have turned your uncle in. He's supposed to report things like that."

"You're right," Philip agreed. "But you know that nice x-ray machine Jerry likes to brag about?" Philip didn't need to expound on the question.

"Phil, I don't feel good about thi—," Lane started, hearing another crash come from somewhere inside the house.

"He's super old. He's only got like a year left. I'd keep him, but Uncle Chuck is insistent he stays here in his home." Philip picked up the bag by his feet. "Here, I've already got some food for him, and this is the internet website where you can order more." Philip pulled out a small manilla folder, handing it over. "He's had all his shots, and my uncle will pay for all the vet visits."

The black and white striped puffball waddled into the kitchen, its little nose twitching. It was bigger than Lane had realized.

"Oh, by the way, he's potty trained for a litter box, and here's a book about skunks." Philip placed it on the table by her elbow. "Also, you won't want to let him outside to wander by himself. They have a tendency to get lost. Uncle Chuck use to keep him on a long tether in the front yard."

Lane shook her head, realizing why Philip mentioned people avoided the place. Seeing a skunk scampering around in someone's front yard would surely deter visitors.

"I still don't think this is a go—"

"Just... think about it..." Philip gave her a pleading smile.

Lane lifted her foot as the black and white ball of fluff skidded under her seat, smacking into the chair leg. She suddenly remembered reading somewhere about skunks having bad eyesight. She flopped the manilla folder down on the table and picked up the book by her elbow, starting to flip through it.

"Hey, I heard about Jerry and Heather getting back together," Philip deftly changed the subject, giving her a small smile as he tried to coax the skunk from under her chair. "You doing, okay?"

Lane frowned, flipping the book closed.

"Yeah, why wouldn't I be?"

"Well, you and Jerry..." Philip left the assumption linger in the room. Lane shook her head.

"I told you, Ranger. He was just a friend."

Philip nodded, a smile tweaking his lips.

"Harry tells me Hattie is going to have quite the birthday party tonight. Cake, games, ...dancing? You going?"

"Was planning on it." Lane's eyes were lingering on the walking plush toy wandering around her kitchen.

"Need a date?"

Lane looked up, her blue eyes a little wide. Philip smiled slowly, a steady red flush making its way up his neck.

"Yeah, actually... I do." Lane smiled back, her hand absently going to her lips.

"Pick you up at six?"

"I'll pick you up," Lane countered, unable to resist. Philip shook his head, ever amazed.

"Okay, but I'm driving," Philip conceded, lowering his arm to the floor, trying to garner the skunk's attention.

"Phil, you sure it'll only be for a year?" Lane sighed, still unsure.

"Might not even be that long." Philip carefully bent over and scooped the skunk up into his arms, giving it a rub under the chin before snatching his hand back. "Oh, and he bites... so, don't get your fingers close to his mouth."

"Great." Lane frowned, slouching in her chair.

She'd fallen in love with the cottage and couldn't imagine moving back to the tiny upstairs apartment above Hattie's. She was stuck and, technically, she owed Philip. She was in no position to decline.

"Here. Try holding him. He's a little grouchy in the mornings if he hasn't eaten, but other than that, he's just fine." Philip leaned forward, handing Lane the fluffball.

Lane looked down into its beady little black eyes and smiled. He was awfully cute... for a skunk. How much trouble could the little critter be?

"What's his name?" She lightly ran her hand down its back, stopping short of its tail.

"Stinker."

Lane sighed. Of course, it was.

"You know..." She suddenly swiped the small animal up from her lap, lifting him high in the air, carefully twirling him around so they were face to face. She spoke directly to it, "You know I should be mad about this, don't you?" She shot Philip a playful smile before facing the skunk again, it's little nose twitching in her direction. "But I just can't be. He's so dang cute!"

At her smile, Philip's heart skipped, and he suddenly wondered... Was she speaking of the skunk or talking about him?

A playful smile of his own twitched his lips.

Probably both.

The story isn't over!

Don't miss the next exciting and intriguing adventure with Lane and Philip in **BOOK III:** *False Findings*.

FALSE FINDINGS

CHAPTER ONE

A full moon, unveiled from its dark castings, shimmered down upon the salted waters and the old dock jetting from the island's shore. The dock itself, beaten and worn, bore the white peaking waves of a riled ocean, its encrusted pilings standing firm against the tumultuous tide. Beside it, held captive by a rusty cleat, was its lone companion, a rowboat, the wooden counterpart, pulling and surging against the old dock, much like an undecided lover.

Hollow and thudding footsteps, sudden upon the pier, resonated, the hour past midnight, pounding heavily upon the wooden slats, the dock no longer abandoned. The white rowboat at once sinking further into the water under the unexpected weight of a passenger.

Quick, deft hands, unburdened from their heavy load, untied the small skiff from its slip, hastily throwing into the bow its weather-worn line, the rope, landing haphazardly against the cargo lying limp on the timber floor.

Pushed away from the dock's fender, the rowboat, oars dipping in and out of the sea-foamed waves, slipped silently away while grunts of exertion, marking time with the oars rattling inside their rings, sounded above the splash of the blades being driven into the dark.

The rower, eyeing the distance from the pier, abruptly lifted the poles from the ocean, the waves crashing against the small boat, bitter cold water slopping over the side.

Was this far enough out? Or rather, deep enough?

The oars were pulled in.

Time was a factor.

Visible from the secluded pier under the moon's spotlight, the rowboat now buoyed over the tempestuous water, swaying precariously, side to side, struggling to carry the load. At its stern was a large man, whose dark outline stood stark against the lit horizon, hesitation clearly visible in his stance, a wooden oar held high above his head.

As if sensing the delay, impatient waves splashed against the gunwales sloshing up and over the side, daring him to continue. The moment of indecision passed and the oar came crashing down, the blade cutting into flesh and bone.

Overhead, reaching and stretching, grasping sky in mass momentum, dark clouds moved steadily with the wind, touching the moon and overcoming its brilliance, its glorious radiance engulfed and swallowed whole. The absence leaving the dark deeds upon the water hidden from view.

The crunch of bone was sickening.

The man tugged on the oar, the wooden blade causing an unpleasant sound as he wrenched it free from the corpse at his feet. With a deep breath, he brandished the oar into the air once more, bringing it down hard, a loud THACK sounding across the water.

The oar was brought down again.

With more effort on each descent, he wielded the weapon into the air, a cascading spray of red following the arch of the upward blade before the downward fall, each sinking hit sounding denser and wetter than the prior.

He was going to be sick.

With a final pitch, the oar broke in his hand, the blade fastening tight into the bloody mass. It was more than he could take. He lurched to the edge of the boat and fell hard on his knees, heaving over the side.

His stomach emptied.

Pushing back, his labored breaths visible vapor on the winter air, he sagged down onto the wooden seat, exhausted, the small rowboat, in return, rocking dangerously, threatening to topple him over.

Instinctively, he grabbed the sides to steady his balance, leaving bloody hand prints on the gunnels, stark against the aged whiteboards.

The exertion of driving the oar down with all his force and trying to keep his balance in the small boat had worn him out, not to mention the deed of killing itself.

There was still so much more to do.

Wearily climbing to his feet, he worked the oar free, tossing the cracked pole to the floor. He then reached down and began to undress the body, his hands untying the worn winter boots, wrenching them off, thick woolen socks with them, shakily dropping the pair to the floor. He then lumbered to the waist, undoing the button and zipper, tiredly tugging and pulling each leg free. He moved up to the chest, lucky the shirt was a button-down, a heavy flannel, and paused at the last item, deciding to leave the underwear on.

There had to be some decency in death.

He laboriously sat the body up, hefting it onto the bow seat and clumsily tied the small boat anchor around the waist. Then cinching the ratty rope tight, he said a short prayer, an apology of sorts, and pushed the body over the starboard side, the splash much louder than he had anticipated.

As if coming out of himself, he glanced up and nervously surveyed the nearby waters, shooting an anxious look towards the old wooden dock.

All was still and silent.

He needed to hurry.

Grabbing the rope tied to the bow of the boat, he jerked it free of its rusted ring, casting it down onto the floor. He then knotted the laces of the heavy disregarded boots together, hastily stuffing the socks into the toe, dropping the boots down onto the bow seat. He then snatched the rope from the floor, his heart pounding in his ears.

Had he gotten everything?

Staggering a step back, he took inventory, his eyes wide.

There was so much blood.

Panicked, he grabbed the flannel shirt and sloshed it into the cold water. Pulling the sopping mass out, he used it to smear his bloody prints off the gunnels and wipe the oar handles clean. He then tied the shirt arms to the old rope and snatched up the jeans legs to do the same.

Picking up the bundle of clothes, he threaded the corded rope through the tied laces of the heavy boots, knotting them together, a makeshift anchor of sorts.

About to toss the mass over the side, he suddenly realized he had forgotten something, and hurled everything down, quickly rummaging the jeans pockets.

He'd almost made a terrible mistake.

With trembling hands, he pulled a leather wallet free. Correcting his error, he stuffed the wallet back before hunting through the remaining pockets, finding them empty.

Satisfied, he then took the boots, carefully dunking them into the freezing water, letting the ocean fill the space, and pull the bloody bundle under.

That deed done, he stood up, his knees feeling weak, and tiredly reached behind his neck, grasping his own bloody t-shirt, pulling it over his head before grabbing the handgun stuffed in his waistband, yanking it free. He swayed with the little boat, his stomach churning and his skin goose-pimpled, waiting to see if anything would resurface.

The waters stayed dark.

Good.

Taking a deep breath, he wrapped the t-shirt around the muzzle of the handgun, doing his best to muffle the sound, then pulled the trigger, sending four bullets into the bottom of the wooden vessel, seawater beginning to seep in. He pulled the trigger again, hearing a hollow click.

That was it. It was empty.

Tossing the .22 into the water, a splash announcing its descent, he gauged the distance to the awaiting dock, a regret coming to mind.

If he was a stronger swimmer, he could have rowed further out.

It probably would have been wiser.

Well, there was nothing for it now.

His heart pounding in his ears, he plunged himself over the side and into the dark waves, desperately clawing for the surface, an irrational fear taking hold as an imagined hand, reaching from the depths, stretched out to touch him, the fingertips of revenge a hairsbreadth away.

Bobbing up like a cork, he gasped for air, his arms slapping down upon the rough waves.

He was safe.

Nothing could touch him now. He only needed to make it to shore.

The hard part was over.

Thank You!

Thank you for reading the second book of the Rockfish Island Mysteries series, The Push, A Rockfish Island Mystery:II. False Findings:III is now out and available on Amazon. The soon to be released fourth book in the series, Within the Pines, will be available summer of 2023.

If you enjoyed The Push: II, would you be so kind as to put a review on Amazon, Goodreads, and Bookbub? Thank you for your support!

ALSO BY J.C. FULLER

A ROCKFISH ISLAND MYSTERY SERIES

Black Bear Alibi

The Push

False Findings

Within the Pines - Available Summer 2023

Made in the USA
Middletown, DE
26 October 2023

41441883R00250